CHUCKWALLA

CHUCKWALLA

GUY RICHIE

authorHOUSE®

AuthorHouse™
1663 Liberty Drive
Bloomington, IN 47403
www.authorhouse.com
Phone: 1-800-839-8640

First published by AuthorHouse   08/03/2011

ISBN: 978-1-4567-7897-2 (sc)
ISBN: 978-1-4567-7915-3 (ebk)

Printed in the United States of America

Chapter One

I had not long been issued fatigues. I was sat on one of the drill tables, which had been placed to left of the main office, having over-heard a conversation, involving camp security. "Hmm, a brand-new SLR with a full magazine, missing." I wondered where it could be. The office door came open, as the lieutenant stepped out. The sergeant ordered us to fall in. Lieutenant Pinner addressed the cadet's. "We are on the training area this morning, map reading and field craft." It was Sunday and freezing cold. "Bombardier Roberts, I want you to organize volunteers', for next Saturday's charity collection detail, for the town centre."

I was at weekend camp; having been there a few occasions before. Billets made of wood, all painted green, with solid fuel burners in the middle. Fourteen to sixteen beds in each building complete with steel lockers. A large assault course was over to the left, and a water silo painted in green stood next to it, followed by the shower block and toilets. My billet was situated not far from the bedding stores and the armoury. There was even a picture hall on the other side of camp. It was the Christmas camp, and this was the twenty-third day of December. I was on for my one star. We arrived at the bedding store, were issued with bedding, and were settling in to our allocated billets. After a few failed attempts, a joint effort was made to get the stove in the middle of the room lit.

I had camp security on the brain and was talking to one or two of the other privates whom I knew where common blaggers. I explained about the missing rifle and what I'd overheard. "Let's find out who is who in the camp. Right, we need a plan." I and three cadets conferred. "Boot polishing and tooth-pasting details during the course of the night. I will cause a distraction, and you search their lockers to see what we can find it."

After the fifth attack on other billets, some resulting in pillow fights, I noticed we were running a bit low on boot polish, although we soon had a collection of names and their detachments—and even a selection of pilfered chocolate and sweets—as we sat and scoffed at most of the evidence.

I had been out to one billet in particular, cadets from Sherwood had caught me up at the door. I had gone in low and sneaked under the beds. The whole dorm was asleep judging by the grunts and snores, I could see the target. I quietly opened the tin, digging through it as much as I could. Then I noticed the man's eyes flickering. I raised my voice. "And who do we have here, then?" I let him have it—I'm talking up his cheek and forehead and down his left ear. One of my crew slipped his hand in the door and did the light trick, flashing it on and off, and then the whole group ran in. Well this particular cadet rose up and started wiping his face with his nice white sheets. I sized up how big he was and made a break for it, grabbing one of his boots and making for the door. He realized what had just happened and went for his other boot, slipping it on.

"Crikey he's coming," I said as I threw his boot on his billet roof on the way out. "I'd better not lead him to our billet," I thought, and so I ran the other way, getting near the picture hall before I turned around. I heard someone running my way and stepped up a gear, speeding past the guard house until no one was around.

Then I heard, "Oy, Cadet, come here." I stopped and turned. Oh no—it was the duty sergeant coming back from his rounds. I marched over and came to attention in my pyjamas, a brush in one hand and a tin of kiwi in the other. "Name, Private?"

"Max Rocks, Sergeant," I told him.

"Detachment?" the duty sergeant snapped.

"Chuckwalla."

"Right, Cadet Rocks. What are you doing out this time of night?" The sergeant looked at his watch.

I could see my assailant in his under pants and one boot on, black polish face and all, giving it the escapee routine as though he had been caught under a spotlight. He moved like some sort of commando, trying to backtrack without the duty sergeant seeing him. I tried to keep a straight face between breaths. "Been to borrow a brush and polish, Sergeant."

The sergeant sighed. "Get back to your billet now, Private."

I made my way back to the billet, walked in the door, and headed over to my locker. Some of the protagonists who had assisted in boot polish detail sat huddled in the middle of the billet playing three-card brag around the pot-bellied boiler, which was by now glowing red.

The door came flying open, and the CSM was now in the billet with two other sergeants, one of them in a red sash. The duty sergeant, with whom I had just had a close encounter, screamed, "By your beds." Everyone found their beds and stood.

The head NCO of Chuckwalla, Robinson, brought us up to attention. "At ease," the CSM said. Everyone relaxed as the CSM and his staff addressed the room. "Right, I have complaints from several detachments in this camp that certain misdemeanours have taken place, and I think that this detachment is responsible."

Every one stood quiet except one individual who couldn't stop sniggering. The CSM walked over to him and held the shinny end of his staff up to the man's nose. "Down and give me ten. Now!" The private got up after he flopped the last three press-ups. "That will do. Right, on your feet and stand to attention. Know anything about this?"

I prayed, Keep your mouth shut. Keep it shut.

"No, sir," the private answered. I was relieved.

"You don't sir me! Another ten, get down!" The private got up after he flopped the last two and stood to attention. "That will do." The CSM could see he just didn't have the strength. "You see this crown?" The CSM was tapping at his wrist with the shinny end of his staff, drawing attention to the gold crown emblem inside a laurel reef that was held in place on a leather strap. "It makes me a sergeant major. What does that make me, Private?"

"Sergeant Major!" the cadet said.

"I can't here you, Private."

The cadet raised his voice and screamed, "It makes you a sergeant major, Sergeant Major!"

The CSM nodded "That's better. Right, stand at ease, stand easy." The CSM walked down the room before stopping at me. "Private?"

I came up to attention. "Yes, Sergeant Major."

He looked at my hands. "You have boot polish all over your hands." The CSM again raised his voice. "You are half dressed, and it is two in the morning. I want an explanation right now, Cadet."

I searched my brain for a reasonable explanation. "Erm. I've been bulling my boots and cleaning my webbing belt. I was just going to wash up, Sergeant Major, before I hit the sack." He looked at my boots and belt and the brand of polish "Kiwi, eh? Take a note of that, Duty Sergeant. See who's got Kiwi on their faces in some of the other billets. Although I must admit, these boots are immaculate," he commented. He could find no fault with my polish job.

The CSM turned to address the room in a calmer tone. "Right, as soon as this light is out, what we want you to do is sleep. Chuckwalla detachment, attention . . . Fall out!" The cadets turned to the right and fell out. The staff switched out the light and left the room and made their way to the billet adjacent, occupied by Risley Hall.

A few minutes later one of the cadets looked out the window near his bunk and said, "Right, they've gone from the Risley Billet." We all snuck out of bed and gathered around the heat, which was by now glowing a brighter red.

"Okay, who haven't we hit?" I said. "Two more detachments are on the list. Time to switch to toothpaste." I made for my locker.

My accomplices rushed in the door of the next billet, and the men were all sound asleep. "Let's do it, lads." Three of us grabbed one of them in his bed, holding him whilst the remaining cadet pulled down his jams, poured toothpaste and Fiery Jack muscle rub over his genitals, and then we let him go. The more he rubbed, the louder he screamed, and the others in the billet all jumped up out of their beds. In the confusion the other two privates would see what they could get out of people's lockers. We ran around their billet shouting, "Who's next!" as the cadets from the defending billet made a sharp exit for the door. We flicked the light on and off like a strobe in a disco extravaganza.

"Bunch of puffs, them lot," I said as we left laughing at the cadets who stood shivering on the edge of the assault course waiting for us to leave their billet. "Won't even stand up for their billet." We returned to our bunks and divided the sweetie money that their mothers had given them. It was real skulduggery, and we were liking it!

Next morning the whole group stood on parade at 0800 on the drill square outside the tank hangers. I was looking down the ranks at who we boot polished earlier that morning. We had been marched down to the tank hangers before breakfast, which was usual camp procedure. We had a head count and inspection as we stood in the freezing cold. It was a day of basic map reading skills and weapons and field craft, with exams in progress; it was the one-star test that I knew I'd walk through.

That evening we watched a film at the cinema for R and R. After it was over, we sat in the billet. "Come on, let's do it again—they've all had canteen," I said in a fit of boredom. Later that night we hid all the goodies in the low gutters on the billet roofs and covered them with dead leaves. We sat playing cards for candy bars.

One of the other privates had been put on jankers that morning for missing his one-star test, and for throwing sausages around in the mess hall whilst we sat having breakfast, which resulted in a food fight. Later that night the reprimanded cadet who caused the food fight sat fidgeting with what looked to be a credit card. I made a grab for it, catching it on the first swipe. I looked at the name, which was familiar. "How did you get this?" I snapped.

The cadet replied, "Well, they had me mopping the officers' mess out today, so I grabbed it."

"Hang on, you took this from the officers' mess?" I held up the card and then slipped it into my pocket. "Ouch, now we are for it."

Later that evening I found the CSM and returned the card. He asked me how I came by it. "I promised not to say, Sergeant Major. Let's just say it's been found."

The sergeant major nodded and then said, "At this moment in time, Private, we have a suspect, and your face does not fit that name. I think you know who that person is. He's got to have it. Do you understand?." The CSM was showing me his fist.

"Yes, Sergeant Major."

"Good. Right, dismissed."

I was not in agreement with stealing from the officer's mess, which is why I returned the card. I knew the name on it. I walked back into the billet, and two NCOs tried to stop me as I went straight for the cadet, striking him with a left jab to the mouth and knocking him into his locker, where he hit his head. I stopped him with my left palm on his chest and swung a right hook that connected with his jaw line and took him clean over his bed. He scrambled on all fours, got to his feet, and made a beeline for the door, leaving drops of blood on the floor on the way out.

I stood and cracked my knuckles, rubbing my right hand as the two NCOs came from behind and wrestled me to the floor. They finished pinning me to the bed, and their weight was too much as I lay breathless. "They knew it was him," I blurted out. "It had to be done." With a sudden burst of strength, I moved them off me and was ready to take them on again.

"Calm down, Max. Calm down," they said as they backed off. I returned to my locker. Ten minutes later two red caps entered the room as the billet was brought to attention. I had been singled out, formally charged with assault, and quickly marched to the guard house. Searched and Quick marched in. The C.SM sat with a deck of cards. "Sit down, Private."

I could hear the private I'd rumbled within one of the cells as the medic left his cell and closed the door. "Slight Dislocation in the lower jaw and a busted nose, but he'll live." The CSM nodded, and I lowered my head.

As I sat facing the CSM, he shuffled the cards, laughing. "Do you play Pontoon?" he asked as he dealt the cards. I could hear the other private in the cell cursing and threatening he'd sic his older brothers on me. "Shut it!" The CSM bellowed, and the cadet eventually piped down. I won the first two games after I laid in the ace of spades on a queen of the same suit.

The CSM got up after I told him what we'd been up to. "An SLR and a mag full of rounds gone from this camps armoury? So that's what this is all about." The sergeant major scratched his head. "You've been conducting an upheaval to find a lost rifle. Right, I'm having a word with your CO about this." A warm smile came on his face. "You'll both stay here until the morning before I decide what to do." I asked if I'd done the right thing telling the CSM about how we were testing camp security and finding out who is who whilst we searched their lockers. "You don't frighten the living daylights out of them to do it, especially in camp," he said calmly. He pointed to a bed at the side. "Get yer head down on there till they wake you for breakfast."

"Yes, Sergeant Major."

He accompanied two redcaps from the guard house. They'd left all the boxes of canteen out, and I passed chocolate into the cell of the private I'd rumbled with earlier. "Call it compensation," I said, knowing full well he'd be eating it with a saw jaw as I snuck back into bed.

Later I was woken again by the CSM. "Private." I rubbed my eyes and checked the clock:0615. "Right, I've had a word with your CO. He's verified that such a conversation took place, although it was in private." His finger was right up to my nose. "However, I'm going to let this matter rest." He stepped back. "The other private will be held until dinner. You are free to go back to your billet. Dismissed, Private."

7

"Yes, Sergeant Major." I gathered myself up as they led me to the guard room main door, where I slipped on my berry and made my way back to my billet.

I had had a pretty rough night of it and expected more to come as we stood on the drill square at the hangers at 0800. I watched the breath expiring from each of the cadets as I looked down the massive ranks. I was trying not to chitter my teeth. It must have been minus three, looking at the frozen ground; even the old World War Two tank was white with a light coating of frost.

The relentless task of prize giving and other certification was being handed out by the major. I hadn't heard my name in the star ratings and was beginning to think I had failed. Then they came to the last. "And the award for most outstanding cadet in all fields is Max Rocks." Eh? That was my name! "Would that private like to come forward, please."

My friends whispered, "Max, that's you."

I stepped out two paces and came to attention, and then made a right turn and marched my way out of the ranks, pacing my distance as "check one two." I came to attention again and saluted the major. I had received a stripe and one star in my hand with all relevant certification. I stepped back and saluted again, thanked the major with a right turn, and marched back into the ranks, standing at attention and then standing at ease.

The major announced, "I would like to add that this is the youngest and shortest serving time for a cadet to achieve the status of NCO." The whole of Three Company gave a round of applause, which brought me back from my tired thoughts and the shock of the award; when they said no sleep till Brooklyn, they meant it.

I was relieved to find the cadet I'd rumbled with still opening and shutting his mouth and still rubbing the side of his face each time he turned around. He'd just been released from the guard house and put onto the coach back home. I held up the stripe and he nodded. He had came back to the bus with a bag full of chocolate; we were all pals again as he divided it out, complements of the CSM.

AUGUST 1979

Two men from the section had gone. I was in my second day of the rout march and had covered fifteen miles in ten hours after a late start from the base. I was suffering from both pure exhaustion and blisters as I studied the map. We were at checkpoint five. "You made good time, lad," the medic said as he checked our feet. At 1600hours as I took the cover from my watch. "Take ten minutes here, Lance Bombardier, and I'll tape that up fer you." The blister had burst on my left big toe.

A sergeant, a regular soldier from the Royal Green Jackets, was sorting the next map reference for checkpoint six. "Don't drink too much water," he warned as we made for our water bottles. I was still breathless and started to remove the shoulder strap of my webbing back pack. "No, do not undo yer kit," he warned. "Just sit and rest. Come on, deep breaths. Lance Bombardier, what should you be doing?" Our bombardier had gone back to base due to exhaustion on check point four, and all was up to me.

I got up to address the sergeant. "Check the condition of the men and all-around defensive position, Sergeant."

"Good, Lance Bombardier. Right, get it organized."

I placed each of the privates left in the section into cover, ordering weapons to cover all flanks, especially the open and vulnerable. "Good, Lance Bombardier," the sergeant said as he entered it into his book. "In the future, position of covering fire is the very first thing you do in most field situations."

We'd been hearing the constant thud of helicopters and that unmistakable beat, spotting two Westland Wessex coming in from the east and flying over low as we hit the next brow. We saw them go down into cover, and then all was silent. We also heard jets earlier, although we couldn't see them through the clouds.

I rechecked my bearing; finding a small copse, I ordered the privates to get off the road and take cover. Two Land Rovers passed, noting the time and what was seen on this particular part of the road. "They haven't seen us," I whispered, laughing.

I found the next map reference pinned on a lone oak tree marked with a big white cross. I looked at the map, ordering the group to gather around, and I checked and rechecked it, picking out landmarks to check exactly where we are. "Right, we are here and still heading southwest. This is the next point." I put a black line through the small copse on the map, drawing it onto the transparent cover and marking out the checkpoint. "Who thinks they'll not make the last checkpoint?" No one answered. The remaining men of the section started to gather their wits, especially when they'd found comfort in the map. They all agreed where we were. "Right, here comes the tricky bit: we gotta get to there without being spotted by regular army."

After we had gone down a hedge side, we could see a tank out in the distance; I found the position on the map and entered data onto the plastic sheet. "We can't follow that line," I said, pointing on the map to the open terrain after the copse we sat in, and the men agreed. I was getting concerned regarding those big hunks of metal machines, I was also concerned for our safety. Spotting others on the same field. Everyone was involved in how to get to the next checkpoint. I was looking around with my berry tilted back, putting it straight again after I cleared the sweat. "Right, it's getting near dark. We gotta move out now." The section stood arguing after a squabble over the rationed chocolate and oat cakes. "That's enough," I barked, getting between them and pushing the protagonists apart. "Field signals only from now on."

We came out of the copse, taking a slight detour from the main bearing. "It's straight down that road," I whispered, comparing the map and the compass. It was a road through heavy wooded pine trees.

"Looks a bit dodgy," one of the section remarked."

"Right, well go in staggered file and concentrating cover to alternate and immediate flanks. Move slowly and keep 'em peeled. Again, field signals only." I ordered the section to a halt, turning and putting up an open hand and then pointing into the thicket as they all dived in to it. I crawled out a little to look up the road. I could see a clearing to the right and the sound of voices. Again I checked the map. It must be two mile or so, I estimated. I pointed to two members of our group and placed my hand on top of my head. The bushes and gorse rustled as they crawled towards me, and I held a finger up to my mouth and then putt a cupped hand to my ear. We sat in a small group listening. Again I crawled out away from the side clearing and pointed to the other three with one hand up, moving it down slowly. Crawling back to the other two, I tapped their shoulder and beckoned them to follow as we made our way, one moving and one covering the other. At the edge of clearing we laid in the thicket and looked on.

The two Westland Wessex we had seen earlier were sitting on the ground with a lot of activity. I would estimate two sections were armed to the teeth with SLR fitted with flash eliminators, and they had taken up a defensive position around the helicopters. The rest of the troops where unloading some mighty fine gadgets—night intensifier goggles and anti-tank M72 light disposable rocket launchers. The helicopters where just sounding up as we hid and watched. Dusk settled in.

The thud was deafening as the Westlands started to rise. Right now was our chance, and we retreated back to the rest of the section. I laid my hand on my head, and the men rallied around. My section was watching the sky for more activity as I tried to regain their attention. "Well, go that side of the road about twenty or thirty meters in and walk between the tree lines. They may have spotted us. I'm taking precautions. Single file and again cover alternate and immediate flanks."

As we moved off, crossing the road one by one, I noticed the trees had been planted the same direction as the road, and I checked again on the compass bearing and the map, noting the sighting and the time and what was spotted. I moved the section off with a hand to the sky, chopping it forward and then turning to each alternate private to remember to cover the flanks. I did not know exactly what kind of tank sat on the hill, and there was more than one in the clearing on the way in to the copse earlier. "It's okay, where doing fine," I whispered as the section gathered around. We moved out, back onto the road again in staggered file.

There it was—the last check point. The last mile was like rising the last meter after a decompression stop: very slow. A second lieutenant and a sergeant were beckoning us over as they stood near an open-top Land Rover. We ran over to the sergeant, standing at ease in two breathless lines before him. The sergeant brought us up to attention and checked our cap badges. "Under combat conditions, Lance Bombardier, this should be blacked out," the sergeant said, indicating the badge and admiring the Acorn. "What's this badge then?"

"Artillery, sir."

"Right. Medic's gonna check you all in a few minutes But overall, excellent job, Lance Bombardier. At ease, stand easy." The sergeant brought the remainder of the section to attention.

"I want weapons ready for inspection," the sergeant said, and he handed over to the lieutenant.

"Weapon ready for inspection. Present arms." We came from the shouldered position, bringing the 303 Lee Enfield across to the left hand and pulling back the bolt, with the right opening the breach and showing the weapon was clear. The lieutenant stepping forward, placed his little finger in the breach, and pressed on the spring in the magazine housing, checking the weapon was clear before taking it from me. He cocked it, took off the safety, pulled it to his shoulder, and fired an aimed closed shot into the air before putting back on the safety and handing the weapon back. "The weapon is clear, Lance Bombardier. That's an old, short Lee Enfield 303 mark three. Some of these weapons have seen real life action and are still in very good working condition. Respect it, Bombardier, and it will respect you." I nodded at the officer's remarks, and then each private's weapon was checked systematically before we were ordered to shoulder arms and fall out.

I remembered and ordered the section to take up an all-around defensive position as the men's feet and general condition were again checked. The two green jackets came over and chatted a little while as the medic pronounced us all fit to carry on. I told the sergeant what I had seen a mile or so back. He was down in on us and talking quietly.

The officer came over. "It's okay, Sergeant," he said as he took his berry off and sat in. "Right, shortly you will be issued with a quantity of five blank firing rounds each. Another section knows roughly of your position and will be looking to seek and destroy your camp. I'm going to circle on the map their general position. You will be required to make camp. You have twelve hours to defend it, starting at 2200." I checked my watch—2033. That gave us an hour or so to make the camp. I selected a suitable site. It was good to let the fifty-eight webbing and backpack drop from my shoulders, and I felt I could float when the full weight hit the deck. I took from it a small trenching tool to dig out a foxhole and ordered the others to do the same. I considered a possible mortar attack and made sure we were well spaced out. We were in a large woods with small trees mainly, silver birch, but there were plenty of other cover such as ferns and shrubbery. I laced up a frame of thin logs and covered it with bracken before putting it over the foxhole. I lined it with my waterproof poncho and rolled out the sleeping bag.

One or two of the section had been out deeper into the wood, and instead of using the wood they brought back to make a bivvy, they were pilling it up. I rushed over and stopped them. "Don't think you're lighting that! Hey, what if you'd tripped a wire. That's all we need, a flare marking our position."

"Sorry, Lance Bombardier."

I saw them grinning. "Cold are you, lads? Right, down and gimme twenty press-ups. Tell you what. I'll do them with you." After they complained. I noticed a soldier laying down in the thicket and putting a finger to his lips. "Shh, don't say what you seen over there," I whispered. The three of us got up; it did warm us up as the glow came back between breaths.

The sergeant and the lieutenant were marking down things here and there on their clipboards while handing out the blank rounds. I had what was left of the section crouch in conference, checking the map. "I've found a patch of contours near the area of the enemy camp's location." I drew a line to it, setting the map to north on the compass and then taking a bearing on the line. "Two of us will go up and spot, leaving the rest to guard camp."

We had put down tripwires around a ten—to fifteen-metre perimeter of our camp; the sergeant armed the tripwires with Para illuminators. "Remember those when you come back to camp," the sergeant whispered. I nodded and moved out with another soldier, marching on the bearing up to the hill.

It was dark, but I could still make out the outline of woods. "There, look there." I checked the map, taking the compass and rechecking for north. "Can you see, in that tree line? Regular army would never do that—torches are flicking." Light was coming out from the trees. I soon had my map set to north and drew another line to the point of activity before checking the bearing on the map; the line finished just over to the left of the circled area of the attacking group. I jotted down the new reference and the time, and I set another bearing for camp, marching back down on a reversed bearing and taking us an hour and a half up and an hour back down over some pretty tough terrain. The lads had rustled up a bit of grub and boiled up some water when we returned, which was welcome. The officer and sergeant had been briefing the remainder of the section about the dos and don'ts around camp, keeping them occupied. They had all the twenty-four-hour ration packs laid out, picking out easy cooking food that was most nutritious and explaining that this was the point where it would be most needed. A selection of condensed cheese and apricot jam on dog biscuits and powdered potato, creamed with sun oil spread and chicken curry, tasted just right somehow while sitting in the fresh air. We left a bit of space for oat bud cuties and chocolate. I saw how the regulars had been taught to do their cooking on the Hexamine stoves in holes dug out, to hide the flame at eye level, and I was impressed.

I sat in with the sergeant and the lieutenant after cleaning my mess tins. "Right, Lance Bombardier, what have we got?" the sergeant asked.

"I have a fix on them, sir."

The officer took the map. "Are you sure, Lance Bombardier? We're talking a spread of five miles here."

"Yes, I am certain, sir." I sat clutching my rifle while he looked at where we had been.

"Ah, up there. Well done, Lance Bombardier. What is your plan?"

"We have four privates and myself. I propose this." I marked and pointed out a route to the enemy base. "Here we split, two over there and two here. I will come up in the middle sounding the attack with a single shot and overrun their camp."

The officer handed back the map, nodding. "But who will look after camp here?" he asked.

I commented, "It is well hidden, and I need all hands."

The officer nodded again. "I want to extract information, so I'm looking for prisoners. Don't overdo it, though. I don't want any injuries." He smiled. "What else are we looking for?"

I stopped and thought. "Their provisions, weapons, and ammunition, sir. Totally disable them."

"Good, Lance Bombardier, carry on.

"Know how to snap one at them?" the sergeant asked, handing me three smoke grenades.

"Oh, now yer talking, Sergeant." I stripped out the weight from my webbing, leaving the ammo and kidney first aid pouch on the webbing before freshening up with cam cream, remembering to black out my cap badge. I put a dab on each finger and then dragged my fingers from left to right diagonally over my face.

"Put those in as well," the sergeant said with a wink as he laid down two Para illuminated flares. "Issue one each to the pincer movement."

We were at the edge of the wood about twenty or so metres away from the enemy camp, and we could see their torches moving about. I could hear them cracking branches as their lights flicked off and on. I gave one flare each to the two teams and ordered them up to the top two corners of the small wood. "Fix them to the fence posts; don't pull them until I fire the shot, and then run in sounding off a few rounds on the way. Make sure you pick up the empty cases."

I could see the enemies' silhouettes in place as I released the safety on the trusty Enfield, crawling closer in. Then I shouldered up in next to a thick pine tree, levering back the safety and squeezing the trigger. Bang! The scene was lit up for a split second as I extracted the round and fidgeted in the bracken for the spent case. I was buzzing as my ears rang, and the smell of black powder mixed with a subtle hint of burnt cardboard as my vision came back. They were running around and banging into one another—must have been five or six of them. Then I heard a fizzed crackle as the Para illuminated flares shot up two glowing balls of pink and florescent blue, hovering over the wood. I was up and running and stopped at a tree. I got down on one knee as I cracked the smoke grenade, throwing it into the camp while noticing the weapons all stacked up in groups of three like something out of Zulu. I looked at the shack's they'd erected. The third was a dud as the bushes all of sudden were filled with bodies running about and falling over small shrubs and thicket. The enemy screamed and shouted amidst the crack and flash of gunfire. The word "Surrender" echoed around the wood. I'd taken my rifle and ran into the smoke and over to one of the tents, where I had seen one of them run. I stuck the butt of the Lee Enfield around the tent a few times thumping it in. Two bereted heads where soon hanging out as the magnesium lit their faces in soft smoke. I turned my weapon to cover them, explaining, "Safety is off." Then I aimed the weapon above the two of them, sounding off a shot and reloading, kneeling to recover the spent case. I kept my rifle on them, and they froze. "Do not move. you're my prisoners," I said as I stood between them and their rifles. My section had rounded up another two, and the whole place was covered in red smoke. I could hear the enemy running away into the distance as they headed up the far end of the woods. The flares went out, leaving us in the darkness. The enemies' weapons were still stood up in groups of three and four.

"That's four captured," I said as we sat them down in front of the tent. One of them was from my own detachment, and I stood laughing. "Right, we're having all your rations and ammunition and taking your weapons." The rest of my section was buzzing, checking how many rifles we'd captured and kicking in the bivvies at the same time. We got everything that had been issued to them except the smoke and Para illuminators. "I make that seven Enfield's captured." We laid them all laid out, extracted the magazines, and removed the bolts. I sat flicking the rounds out of a mag and ordered the lads to bury the canisters and retrieve the flare tubes and throw those in too.

The next thing I knew an officer appeared wearing a blue sash. "Right, who's in charge here?" As I was taking out the last round and laying down the bolt and mag with its weapon. The men all pointed in my direction as they came to attention. The sergeant major and the safety officer appeared, bending down to clutch at a piece of kite string.

"The other team tied it around the muzzle end of the weapons whilst they were stood in threes," I explained as I stood to attention whilst the lads fell in and saluted the officer.

"Right Lance Bombardier, at ease, "he said as he entered data into his book. "Take your section and fall in over there." We all sat sniggering about the events as a three-toner arrived, and we were ordered to load up an easy night's pickings onto it. The officer came over as I jumped down and came to attention, ordering the lads to fall in again. He made a weapons check to verify all rounds were extracted from the weapons collected. The safety officer observed our procedure and debriefed us. "At ease, Lance Bombardier. Here's the situation: the other team has been ordered back to the base; the ones missing have been found. Your section is to go back to where your kit is and await orders."

"On this, sir?" I didn't really want to walk back.

"Why, yes, Lance Bombardier, you've earned it. Carry on."

"Yes, sir." I came to attention and saluted him, and he turned away smiling. "Lads, you heard him—on you get."

With the weapons reassembled, it was a bumpy ride, and eventually we pulled up as I hung out the back and checked the map to see where we were. The driver, a regular RCT, got out of the cab and dropped the tailgate as we jumped off, swinging down from the rope. "Good thing it has a bench down the middle," I said as we rubbed at our asses.

"But definitely not built for comfort," one of the men commented.

The sergeant had just pulled up in the land rover. As I got the lads fell in, and he ordered us at ease. He looked in the three-toner and seen all the rifles and rations. "Ah, that's what I like to see. Take the rations off and leave the rifles on, and then split what you can between you. I want all the ammunition collected and handed in to me. Right, Lance Bombardier, fall them out and get yourselves bedded down until I come over."

"Yes, Sergeant." We made our way over to our camp with the extra privileges. "Who goes there?" I asked, seeing movement of a silhouette approaching.

"It's okay, it's Sergeant Smith," came the reply.

"Advance and be recognised," I said as we all jumped to attention and the sergeant entered our gathering. I had in my hand my beret full of empties and live blank rounds.

"At ease, lads, at ease."

"That's the lot, Sergeant." I handed the ammo to him—forty-eight live and twelve spent." Sergeant Smith walked over to hole we had dug for the rubbish, throwing in the spent 303 cases.

The next thing I knew, four flares lit the sky illuminating the outskirts of the wood, and bushes started moving as the whole place came to life. I could see the looks on my men's faces. I spotted at least five broken silhouettes moving out of the edge of the wood and down. The section leader gave hand signals as they fanned out, arranging and adjusting their weapons. To my right there was a shuffled movement as another body of troops appeared lit by Para illuminated flares as they moved forward to the woodland perimeter. The broken outline of the section leader arranged his men to the right of him. I was stunned.

"Watch and learn," the sergeant said quietly. "Right, he's waved us over. Go one by one over to him; you first, Lance Bombardier."

I rushed over as he directed me down onto the perimeter's edge. He was well camouflaged and scrim netted. He looked straight at me, with his two fingers up to his eyes, and pointed out to one o'clock. Soon all five of us were positioned against the woodland edge.

There was movement to the left as a regular soldier appeared at my side well camouflaged, making his weapon safe as the SLR was laid down. He took a long green tube from his shoulder taking off the cover from one end; a high-pitched ping rang constant as it was switch on. Soon the flares cooled and all was dark again. He passed the device to me, pointing again at one o clock.

I looked into it—all was green but like daylight. I froze at what I saw—the Chieftain Tank was well camouflaged, and there was another one. I counted four in all, putting up four fingers to the section leader. He nodded. Again a signal was made over to his right, and the right hand flank opened up with intermittent flashes that sounded like a tin tube being thumped after each flash of light. I handed the scope over and pointed out to one o'clock to the next cadet in line. The regular soldier gave encouragement, pointing out at one o'clock to him as he rearranged his position, taking his rifle with him.

The area exploded around them, lighting up their profiles as the Chieftain Tanks roared up to retreat as the horizon was lit again with flares. They were traversing at high speed, firing the odd volley of machine gun through the smoke that had just landed on and around them. I could hear over to the left a fierce firefight and estimated it was at least a quarter of a mile from where we'd just been. It was similar action to what had taken place here, but with more constant small arms fire. Then as I looked through the trees and up, there must have been fifteen flares up along a line over an estimated five-mile stretch. Firefights continued as more flares went up, with small arms fire closer in, around 250-300 meters away.

Sergeant Smith appeared with a hand on his head. We gave the scope back to the soldier and left the perimeter to run over to the sergeant.

"At ease, lads. Go down to that side of the wood and don't move."

We regrouped where the sergeant sent us, amazed at the sight. The crackle of gunfire ringing out seemed endless, although some of it was close by. I could clearly see a jet moving quickly along the horizon as blinding flashes lit up areas where it had been. The jet seemed to be slowing and going down low as it returned again. Then I saw it descend straight down. "It must be a Harrier," I said. We leaned on the fence watching the jet, and I checked my bearings and marked it down on the map. "Fall in," I mumbled as I spotted the sergeant, who wandered over to where we all stood with our rifles. I was trying to gulp down a mouth full of chocolate as I brought the section to attention.

"They've agreed to let us stay out," the sergeant said as he handed me a berry. "Don't put it on," he warned as I looked at it. "You have to give yours in exchange. Hide it in yer kit and keep your mouth shut." A Brand-new, light brown beret was handed to me as I studied the cap badge. A sword with wings and the words "Who Dares Wins." "At least you'll have an excuse not to remove your berry when you see them in camp tomorrow, Lance Bombardier—because yours will already be removed," he joked. "Right, fall them out and get your section on the truck."

I had a pocket of boiled sweets and was still plotting things down on my map. I could see the picture forming: three in the morning and I'm buzzing, pressing the cover back over my watch. It was just a question of working it out as I put the map on my lap.

The sergeant had jumped in with us as we pulled away, and he took the map from me. "What do they call you, Lance Bombardier?"

"Max, Sergeant."

The sergeant nodded "What's all this dribble then?"

"It's a Harrier jump jet; I plotted where I saw it, and that's where it went down. And these are firefights—that's the one over to left—and these are the tanks I saw through the scope. This was to the rear with sporadic incidents along here."

"Yes, Max, it was a Harrier, one of ours; you'll see why we used it in a short while." The sergeant moved on down the wagon, talking to the rest of the section.

We came to a wooded area. The sergeant ordered us out, and we fell in at the rear of the truck. A section of regular soldiers came out of the tree line. I could see another section coming out of the woods farther down. The sergeant gave back the map. "Right, Lance Bombardier, move at the rear of those lot around fifteen meters behind them; they'll take you in."

The first section moved on in staggered file along each side of the road as their section leader waved us on up. We were dismissed by Sergeant Smith and followed in the same staggered file. I was sure that these guys looked familiar as we came to a familiar setting. It was the woods where we had previously taken out the enemy camp. The section leader had pulled his section onto the road's side and was making his way down to us. It was the second lieutenant that briefed us earlier the night before. "Two of you with me, and then two, and then you." I sat and watched where they went, coming to where he directed us. "Right, single file down that hedge side. Wait at the end and group." A regular NCO took over organizing cover while they each ran down, and then it was our turn. There was a clearing that had a part of another tank column sitting on it, but they were a different breed—Scorpions. I looked at my map, jotting the tanks down as small boxes and marking "h" on two of them and "d" on the other two. Then I checked the bearing. They where motionless with a lot of activity around them as we got closer in. The fizz and the crackle of more flares hit the sky. The glowing balls of light complemented the scene as twilight was breaking with the odd blackbird snaking in.

"This is as far as we go; watch and observe," the lieutenant said. As we sat looking, one of the tanks—the closest to me—had big white chalky powder bursts in the track and around the rear. I would say this was a simulated anti-tank hit to knock out the drive, because the monster sat motionless. I could hear troops laughing and joking at the tank to the left. The third tank had what looked to be bodies laid out at the front corners; all were just asleep, motionless. I could hear voices getting raised and questions being fired at an individual also next to the third tank. The fourth tank lay to the back of the first with similar powder bursts on it.

I could see on the second tank a silhouetted man with a small arm or automatic revolver, probably a Browning 9mm sidearm, being pointed at one of the tank crew as it was placed down on the tank out of reach "You want to bring these here," he said. The lieutenant returned as I came to attention.

Another silhouette came out the turret clutching something in his hand. "At ease, Lance Bombardier." He asked me for my map. "Explain what we have here?" I started showing him the little entries and pictures drawn on to the map cover. "These are a little out but excellent. Yes, I like what is here. And what's this?"

"I spotted a jet; I'm certain it was a Harrier."

"Hence the airplane shape. Yes, I see.

"And this is where it went down."

He looked again. "Hmm, not quite there, but close enough. Here." He circled a spot near where I sighted it. "This was the target." Again he marked an area not far from where I had marked the large explosions. "Yes, this is close enough. We feel it is safe to reveal this was an enemy artillery battery being taken out using magnesium and phosphorous flares dropped inside their zone. The Harrier was scrambled to rough it up and mark the drop zone. In real live battle circumstances it would have left pure devastation. Ten para were then scrambled, and I believe the mopping up is still in progress. This is where we got the information. "He pointed to the bodies at the third tank." I gulped. "Yes, we would interrogate in real life," he said coldly. "The other team caught them as sitting ducks, knocking out two tanks and overpowering their crews, who were outside napping. The other part of the column was the one you saw and helped engage earlier. We now know where they are. The officer you saw on the tank speaks different languages; I think you know him, Lance Bombardier. Does anyone have any questions?"

"Yes," I said, bringing the map to his attention. "Then this here must have been artillery support." I put my finger on the map. "This must be their infantry here, and this is their tank column split into two. We must be somewhere here at the head of the two columns and behind their infantry. Here we have the other half of the column, gone that way south. I have the incident and the time."

The officer laughed. "And this is . . . ?"

"They're infantry," I replied.

"No, more than that—double the number. the time is about right." I amended the detail. "You have it more accurate now. Yes, this was their infantry. Royal green jackets took them out along here." The officer widened the line. "In a four-pronged, double-pincer movement—this was over very quickly." He looked at the map, amazed. "Can I keep this, Lance Bombardier? You'll be back on the base for the morning."

"Yes, sir, of course, my pleasure." He took the plastic cover from the map, folding it and sliding it in his map pocket. "Sir, why did you not hit the column we saw like this?" I asked, pointing at the white powder."

"Better ask yer safety officer, son. I'll see you get a good breakfast when you get back to the base. You'll be allowed in early; we have still got some cleaning up to do." He withdrew back over to his section, laughing.

Back at base, the rest of the dorm was still sleeping as I grabbed my wash kit and made for the shower, returning for room inspection and laying out my kit and remaking a bed pack as I stood by my bed. The medic declared my feet fine. "Lance Bombardier, get your breakfast."

I walked across the drill square and made for the canteen. "Better get sixteen big bad breakies on, chef, and put them to the side—they'll be late in."

"Whose that then, kid?" the chef said, looking at my brassard and spotting the tape, laughing.

"Lance Bombardier to you, Private. We're talking blockbuster crew," I said with dignity.

"And where might you be from, Lance Corporal?" He leaned in, studying the cap badge. "Hey, don't touch what you can't afford," I barked as his fingers started to probe at my new beret; it was a spare from my kit. I swept it of my head, remembering not to wear it in the canteen. "Look, get them breakies ordered, chef, all sixteen of them. An order from Robin Hood Country."

The chef laughed as I took a plate and helped myself to one of the best breakfasts I'd had in a long time: pancakes and stovies and battered spud brownies. He loaded up my tray for me as I poured on the tomatoes next to the spicy sausage and bacon and mushrooms. He slid more eggs on my plate and asked, "Yogurt or cereal, Lance Bombardier? Or perhaps even a selection of fresh fruit?"

I was in the middle of my massive breakfast when the group walked in. Yes, I was right—sixteen of them, two sections. I recognised their CO as I slid my plate onto the table. I could eat no more. They were washed and showered and looked human again—A big difference from the scrim net and camo cream and combat fatigues. I spied the chef pointing in my direction and the second lieutenant looked my way. I sat embarrassed as they all came and sat at the tables around me. "Thanks for that, Lance Bombardier. Oh, what is your name, by the way?"

"Max, sir."

He was nodding at his breakfast as he laid out the plastic sheet on the table; it was the one from my map. "Some rout march, that," I said and laughed as they joined in with the lively atmosphere, and the banter and chatter of the night's events filled the room.

"Look at this, do you remember the jet?" the lieutenant asked.

"The harrier," I confirmed.

The lieutenant pointed on the map cover. "Look here, four hits placed on the retreating tanks. The jet later found them and marked them up, giving us a map reference, and the information was conveyed to your command post at 307 battery, which delivered an artillery barrage with their 105mm Howitzers, wiping them out with simulated armour-piercing rounds after they fell into range. Can I still keep this, Lance Bombardier—err, Max?"

"Yes, sir," I said as I drank my tea.

Amana Teeters wore no knickers—it was written in the bandstand "Hey, I wanna meet her. Put the word out." We were standing in the park, larking around and chatting with our skateboards and trying various different flicks and turns trying out three-sixties as we compared our krypton wheels and axle mounts and laminated boards, scooting in and out the pedestrians.

Two cadets from the same detachment had been using their newfound army skills and had been busting into ice cream vans. I received a tip-off I'd that they were doing it again tonight, and so we were on patrol, looking for them near the bottom end of the park. "There they are," I said, and we rushed over on the skateboards, snatching the boxes from them.

It was Monday night Disco at the Welfare. "These give me an idea." We had parked the boxes of chock ices and flakes up on the fire escape whilst we paid entry into the Welfare. The security made us leave our boards with the cloak room attendant, and we brought in the boxes through the fire door. We certainly had the bouncers confused. We were doing a good trade, selling the ice cream. The three of us had pockets full of loose change and were standing in the bogs, counting up the money.

A youth I knew from school came in. "Who's looking for Teeters?"

"Hey I wanna meet her," I said. "Who is she?"

My pals were laughing. "She's bad news, mate, goes to the other school." Then he mentioned a name. "She goes with him? Yeah, come to think of it, I have seen her with him."

As the Four Tops blared out the disco, the youth said, "She's in here, up the top corner." We snuck our way up through the busy hall.

I made popped up in front of her with a half-melted chock ice as I caught her eye and slid in next to her. "I saved you one," I said as she took it. "They don't sell these here." She started to giggle. I told her about the rhyme in the bandstand, and she claimed she hadn't seen it. "Tell you what," I said. "Let me walk you home tonight, and I'll show it to you." Her mousey ponytail flicked as she told me to meet her outside at ten. She took her hand bag to the dance floor and joined her friends whilst sucking on her chock ice.

By ten o'clock I'd split from the crew after I retrieved my skateboard and hung around near the doors. I met her coming out as she wished her friends goodnight. "What accent's that, then? It's not from here, that's for sure," I said.

Later at the park, her head was back and she was going crazy: "Oh, yes, oh, crikey!" She released her grip on my shoulder and arched her back; she'd dragged her nails deep across my shoulder, and it was beginning to sting.

"It's not true, then," I thought as I struggled for air buttoned up my jeans. She pulled up her knickers and lowered her skirt as I tried to regain my balance. Another couple walked into view, across from the swings further up the path.

"I know who wrote that," she said as she pulled me in closer. We sat on the edge of the bandstand. "Hang on." She took a marker from my pocket. I drew in a light bulb and a pull cord under the word "knickers" as she giggled. Then I wrote "Max." French kissing was still new as we clicked and banged teeth. It started to rain, and both of us made for the cover of the gate house. She sat with her legs straddled around me and her heels. She mentioned a name. I looked out from the Elizabethan shelter behind the bandstand and across the park. "Oh, God, that was the whole lot without protection," I thought, flashing back and then remembering the name. "But I thought you went out with him for a long time," I said.

She showed me a ring she had taken from her pocket. "This much," she said, throwing it into the bushes. I looked at her big green eyes in the moonlight, stunned and looking at where she threw it. "Spoiled rich kid," she said.

"Hey wanna steal a car? I know where. Come on." I grabbed her hand and the tail of my skate board. I had a spare key for the Ford Escort Mk 1, belonging to my pal's sister; I borrowed that car for the evening.

"You keep watch," I said as I slipped into the car, started it, and took it off the drive. We got onto the motorway, she had the window down, and I was cruising around ninety—yeah! The sharp stereo was a treat, with all the mod rock tunes we found in the glove box, putting on David Bowie's *Ashes to Ashes* and *Ultravox*, and Meatloaf's *Bat Out of Hell*.

We sat at a Mecca service station. I was listening to a couple of bikers who were at the fruit machines. They were from my home town. She was checking her watch whilst I was on the pinball machine. "I haven't been out this late ever," she said. The proceeds from chock ices kept us going till late, though I saved a bit of cash for some petrol to get home. Eventually finding the seat adjuster, we sat near the old monk priory to the side of the old abbey. After walking around the Chinese gardens, it was 4.00AM in the morning, and we ended up parked at the bottom of her street. "How did you learn to drive, Max?" She was curious.

"I just sorta learned how. Why, doll?" She was still so playful as I looked at the size of the houses. "You live here?"

"Max. I have a busy week, but Saturday is okay." She was jotting down her phone number and tilting her head to snog me as she left the car.

I sneaked the car back, hoping my mate's sister wouldn't find out. I checked the petrol—yep that was about where I'd found it; I also checked the car's location on the drive. Luckily no one was around, and the owner was away working the summer abroad. I took my skateboard from the back seat and quietly slipped away into the morning. When I arrived home I snuck in and stripped, throwing my underpants in the sink and washing them. In the bathroom I slid in the bath. I looked at the deep claw marks on my back as I turned in the mirror, and I ignored the pain as I slid deeper into the bath. Her wild vision came back amidst the flares in the night skies and the heat of battle. They told us not to look at the glowing balls of light, and I could still see them. When I woke up, Mum had a cooked breakfast and was trying to get me up.

Thursday came, and we were scheduled at HQ for Bren weapons training. The lesson was taught by the CSM himself, accompanied by the BSM who we never saw very often except when the guns were here, although he was always happy to help with the younger cadets if he was around. We were in training for the annual shoot, and I'd been selected for 303 marksmen, taking place at Bisley in two weeks. I'd already had some fun with one in the Scottish borders—that was, until theyphoned the butts; nine mags and three barrel changes later and ordered to cease fire. I'd found delight watching the tracers hit the target.

The lesson had started, and we are assembled around the Bren. It was my turn to take up the firing position. After a few failed attempts, I complained, "I can't lay on it, Sergeant Major."

"Right, Lance Bombardier, back on yer feet. We'd better take a look."

So I did. "Aw, ah, bloody hell," the other NCO gasped. "Looks soar, that does." "Did you trap it in your zip in the dark? It must a been a bit a shrapnel on that last exercise."

You should have heard them. It was so bad they were turning away doubled up, cringing. "I've seen enough," said the sergeant major, placing his hand over his eyes. "Who, how . . . Where in the entire nation did you put that to get it like that?"

"On manoeuvres, Sergeant Major," I said as I zipped myself up.

"Better get nurse to, erm . . . You know, that might need to be amputated," he said, and I gulped. "Right, Lance Bombardier, follow me."

I could hear the clattering of utensils and a brief discussion as I sat outside, waiting for the sergeant major to get the nurse to take a look. I know there was a lot of laughing and joking, and a female's voice said, "You are kidding me." The sergeant came out and nodded at me. "She'll see you shortly."

The nurse was very sympathetic as she gave me a course of penicillin and antibiotics. She also felt the need to fetch the doctor to me as well. The doctor wasn't long in arriving examining me. She was sort of admiring the swelling around the wound, looking all around it with the odd "Hmm." Finally she explained, "Yes, you've torn the joining skin." She soon had it cleaned up, recommending another treatment later that day.

I walked out smiling again. They were all still covering their eyes as I walked back across the drill square like John Wayne. "Permission to re-join the lesson, Sergeant Major?"

"Permission granted; sit in just there, Lance Bombardier." Somehow he managed to keep a straight face throughout the rest of the day with the odd "Ooh" as he still covered his eyes every time he looked at me in a type of condolence.

Then came the end of the lesson. "Right, fall out. Not you, Lance Bombardier, after your treatment. NCOs room. I'll be in there."

I came out smiling again as I walked through into the NCOs mess. There was still a buzz throughout the bar, and the sergeant major sat at a table near the window looking out to the square. "Sit down, Max. Skip the formalities." I sat in the chair opposite him. "Who is she?"

"I, erm, sorta just met her, Sarge."

"Dump it. That's fer you." A bottle of coke was set on the table, and I took it with thanks. I looked out across the drill square as preparations were being made, and the battery of guns sat coupled to their tractor units, ready for pulling them out. "Howitzers 105mm—you never spotted those on yer map," the sergeant major said, smiling. "But they where there. You've been spotted."

I stayed quiet.

"Now then what we gonna do?"

"But Sergeant—"

"Shh, let me think." I could see what was running through his mind. He was bound to have spoken to the other cadets from my detachment.

I sat looking out at the guns. "Spotted, Sergeant?" I said, still looking out at the guns.

"Classy Chicas out at the local disco, ring any bells? La Doras Costa del park. Do you want more?"

"Jealousy gets ya you know where, Sergeant."

"Pipe down, I'm thinking. Well, leave this with me, Max." I finished my coke. He stopped me as I got up to leave, and I sat back at the table. "It is true. Outstanding, Cadet."

"Yes, that was said, Sergeant."

"You're still young, Max. I wish I had the chance you have. I joined at twenty-two. You're fifteen when?"

"Next year, Sarge."

"And you've been here how long?"

"Two year, sergeant."

"You can be entered as junior leader at fifteen; the ACF is a good route in. I've made inquiries. That it, if you would like a career full time."

"I've never thought on it yet, sergeant."

The sergeant major raised his voice. "Well, start thinking, Lance Bombardier." The noise went down in the rest of the room. "You shoulda put a suit on it."

"Erm, Sergeant?"

"You know. Bio spermicidal. Nuclear and live rounds, Max."

"Well, er, well . . . ."

"I'll take that as contaminated then, judging by the wound."

"I suppose."

"Ahha, I bloody knew it! Do you know whose daughter that is?" I scratched my head. "Keep scratching, Max. What am I gonna do to keep you out of it?" The sarge looked dismayed as he scratched his own head. "I don't know what else to tell ya. That's for you pointing to the guns. This is your home. Wanna another coke?" Some of the other NCOs, though a lot older, had filtered through, and I could hear the sarge growling at them on the way up to the bar. I liked it here in HQ; it was cool from the sun, and I marvelled at the pictures and trophies as if it were a museum.

"I've got a job fer you, Max," the sergeant said when he returned. "You know those privates you've been running with?" He gave me the names of two men from my detachment. "One's been in the guard house, last Christmas camp. I want them watched. You remember the names."

"Yep, I know who."

"Right. Where is the free ice cream coming from?"

"The vans at the bottom of the Chuckwalla park," I replied.

"Hmm." The sergeant looked out the window. "Have you been going in?"

I looked him in the eyes. "No, Sergeant Major. But we did rob it off the ones you told me to keep an eye on."

The sergeant major laughed. "And I know what you did with it: you've been giving it her." He looked down at the wounded area briefly. "Did you rob it off them before or after ya did that? No, don't answer that—spare me the details."

I started to smile because I could see what he was driving at: he thought I needed something cold for the wound. The sarge looked again over to the square. "You see, when they do it again, rumble it."

"Say again, Sergeant?"

"Drop a coin in the box. I can't discharge them until they've been caught."

"Oh, I see, Sergeant Major."

"You'll be given a bligh, of course. Right, Lance Bombardier, you'll be back to your detachment, so see you in a few weeks for the shootout at Bisley." He got up, leaving me to finish my bottle of coke.

I'd made a few calls to Amana's house Friday. Eventually her ma answered, as she scolded me, told me Amana was grounded, and asked me not to call again.

I was confused as we skimmed our boards of the wall in the bandstand Sunday evening. How come those two pulled her friends, and they're out at the park with their newfound passion. All I could see was visions of her and the flares. I knew I shouldn't have looked. I kept saying it to myself whilst on the skateboard as I bounced the board off the wall and back onto the wheels. The other two cadets had suffered the same as me. Flare blindness—we had diagnosed a name for it.

Then I overheard the problem. "Her ma found her knickers in the wash basket," one of the two females in clinch with one of my pals said.

I froze. "What was that?" I stepped off the board and sat down on the edge.

She went quiet, looking at the floor. "She's not been allowed out all week; we ain't seen her except talking on the phone."

"Silly sod should have washed them herself," I thought. "No wonder."

"Hey, can you get a message to her?"

"Sure, Max, I can ring her tonight."

"Tell her to tell you a time and a place, and I'll be there." I knew it was down to her.

"Cheer up, Max, more fish in the sea."

I laughed. "I caught one, but it's a bit slippery, and I gotta get it back."

I went down to the park every evening and asked for news of her from her pals. No, don't go to the house, they kept saying. A mob walked into the park and headed in our direction. "Hey, this looks dodgy," I said as I knelt beside the other two.

"Right we're just nipping to the corner shop." The two lasses with my pals made a sharp exit.

"All new faces," I noted, "from the other school."

The group stopped at the swings and gathered. They started hurling abuse at us, and we tried to ignore them. One in particular was swinging a golf club around. "Right, I'll deal with this," I said as I jumped from the bandstand and walked straight over to them. "ACF what? What are you calling us?"

The youth started to back away into his pals. I snatched at the golf club, pulling it from his grip. "The golf course is over there," I said, looking at him. I started pressing on the shaft, bending it and letting it spring back.

My two pals walked over and stood on either side of me. "What's all this, then?" one said as the pair stood eyeing up who was going to be first.

A selection of six youths stood around us, and at least one I knew to be older. "I've gotta bone to pick with Max," one said.

I moved right up to his nose and stared. "What's your problem?" It was the youth I'd taken the club from.

"You're in for a tanking; wait till my dad gets you."

"Big words from a little fella."

"I know your face from the swimming baths. And all the time you where eying her up," he blurted out.

"So that's what it's all about? You must be Teeter's brother." I did get the hots when I saw her in her swim suit and had to make it down to the deep end, where the water was cold. I thought back as her vision and the flares came back. "What you planning on doing with this, then?" I asked, waving the golf club at him. His mates were very quiet while we did the talking, and they melted away one by one. "We'd better walk up the road with you. Your crew's missed out and all that." I handed him back the club. "You never know who you might meet around here."

We walked off the park, trying to recruit him "It's just a question of a haircut. And hey, we might be able to do something with him. At least he stood his ground," I said, nudging my two pals.

The kid was telling us about his hobbies and pastimes as the two lasses came out the corner shop. At least his music taste was good; some of the bands he mentioned were awesome.

"You've gotta turn up at ten o'clock Sunday, kid. You know where the Detachment is? Then you can come on Wednesday." He was just thirteen—eager beaver, we thought. Just wait till he was in. We were sniggering at each other, covering our eyes as we turned to one another and left him safe at the corner of his estate.

I'd looked over the fence, having just heard that the two cadets who Sergeant Major Smith had told me to keep an eye on were robbing the ice cream vans again. We'd gone down to the park inquiring where they were. The info was gathered by the regular crew that hung around in the bandstand. They explained that there had just been a chock ice fight and that the two had gone back for more. Bits of evidence were splattered all over the walls, with gold and silver wrappers blowing about in the breeze.

I got another cadet to couple his hands with his back to the fence whilst I gained the height to look over. I had my full weight on one foot, and I could hear the cadet who had hold of my foot puffing and panting whilst I looked. I could see one of the cadets making his way out the van via the sliding glass at the side, and boxes were stacked at the bottom of the fence on the other side as I looked down.

"The other cadet must be in the factory," I said to him as I jumped back down. "Come on, we need a phone box." We made our way back over the garden and the chain link fence. "We can't use that box—they'll see us." We made our way up to the park where I knew of another phone box.

We were just about to turn on to the park when the other cadet ran like the clappers all of a sudden. A panda car pulled up alongside me. An officer had jumped from the passenger side and confronted me. "Right, stay where you are, son. Can you tell me where you have just came from?" The panda sped away, leaving the officer standing in front of me. I started to stutter and went quiet. The officer then said. "Why has your friend run away?" I still remained quiet. "I think you and your friend have been robbing them ice cream vans, right?" The officer took a breath. "Right, I am arresting you on the suspicion of theft. Anything you say will be used in evidence in court." He put the huckles on my wrists.

My attention turned to the panda, who had returned with the other cadet in the back seat. The boy was crying, claiming he hadn't done anything. I was bundled in the back of the car with him. I sat all the way to the station with my head down. The situation wasn't looking good. In the station we were all interviewed under caution when our parents arrived. Then we were released under bail conditions. We weren't allowed to go to the park, which was one of the conditions. After the police had finished their inquires, a further five were arrested and charged. I knew two names but didn't know they'd been involved. The police managed to obtain statements from two of the individuals that put me in the frame. I was charged with handling stolen goods. Mum had grounded me for three months until the day in court, along with the rest of the boys involved.

A fight had broken out in the toilets within the juvenile court over the fact that at least two of the boys had been fingered due to information given—or grassing, as it was put. I found it amusing. Let's just say there was a chain reaction. Well, for my part in it I received twelve hours in the attendance centre at a school in the city, to be attended every second Saturday afternoon for a two-hour session of parade and PT. Mum lifted the grounding embargo and reckoned I got off with a slap on the wrists.

Those that went into the vans and the factory custodial sentences where imposed, and sent to a YO prison on the east coast. The headlines in the local paper read, "Local Ice Cream Gang Whipped by Police." For the next few weeks this became a topic that became more a comedy than a crime committed. At school I'd get the odd torment—lines of conversation: "How did they extract the information? Was it the softly approach?" "You'd better get your home work done, or I'll have you whipped."

Chapter Two

Harrogate was cold and damp. Sergeant Major had suggested I go to recruit selection weekend. I'd done most of the tests, mostly written and physical; medical abilities were also assessed, and then I'd return to school the following Monday, having to wait on the results. I'd put down royal artillery as my first choice. I waited for that letter to arrive.

School was okay having opted for the favourable science and physics, enjoying art and technical drawing. My exam results had been passes, and I felt I could do better having re-joined the sixth form in September to take O and A levels.

A week later Wof met me at the corner as we walked to school, He asked if I'd heard anything yet from the selection board. I'd had the letter in my pocket and had already read the bad news. I drew it from my pocket and gave it to him. "Oh, shit. Failed the medical? How come?"

"I have only one kidney," I explained.

"Well, I've known you all that time, and you never told me that before."

I frowned. "I found out when I was in the hospital to have my appendix removed."

Wof took two cigarettes from his pocket and offered one. I didn't smoke, but I took it any way. I coughed and spluttered all the way to school, though

36

it made me feel even worse, and Ispewedon a wall just before crossing the road to access the school field.

"I think you'd better turn back and go home," Wof said, looking concerned.

"No, I'll be fine."

We made our way in to the school. Green block was full of students as Wof gave me a Wrigley—to hide the smell of tobacco, he joked. He left me at green block as he went to his own form, red block. Wof was taking his exams next year.

It was bang on 9.00AM as the bell sounded, and the students took to their chairs. Mr Beaton started to take the register over the moderate din. I sat with my usual crew, checking my time table. Assembly this morning for the rest of the school; I got free time. I rustled in my bag for my notes on physics, trying to take my mind of the bad news.

Mr Beaton called me over to his desk. "We are a man short this Sunday. Five aside football—are you interested?"

"Well, yes, sir."

"I'll tell Mr Hope and let him know we now have a side to play." Mr Hope was the PE teacher. "Turn up at the gym with yer kit, 10AM."

"Who we are playing, sir?"

"Arnold High," he said as he closed the register.

At break time Wof stood at the corner of the Barn, which was basically a five-a-side pitch volleyball and basketball court, all under a modern corrugated roof structure with flood lights so it could be used at night. "What's cheered you up?" he asked as lit his cigarette, offering me one again, which I refused.

"I have a match Sunday."

"Hey, what you mean, a match?"

"A match with Arnold High Sunday, five a side."

"Arnold High beat the third year," he choked out as Paula and Deb turned up with their dolled-up, school tart image. The stereotyped dumb blonde fit the criteria of Paula, and the secretary brunette profile fit Deb.

"Hey we are looking for cheer girls Sunday," I remarked as they rustled in their pockets for cigarettes.

"What, them two, cheer girls?" Wof chipped in. "You need yer eyes testing."

Deb responded by putting her hand to her hip and giving that sexy stance.

"Yeah, man, that's it," I said. "A couple of coloured poms, and you're good. A coupla more moves choreographed like that one, and presto—cheer girls."

We all burst out laughing.

Deb was very well developed for a girl of her age, and her intelligence was starting to show. "What are you needing cheer girls for, Max?" she asked.

"We have a five-a-side football game Sunday."

"Shall we go give em some support?" Deb asked Paula.

Paula laughed. "What time on Sunday?"

"Ten o'clock. We are playing Arnold High in here."

Wof took a drag on his cig and blurted out, "They'll get hammered. He's a cripple for a start. Army turned him down 'cause someone nicked his kidney."

Deb and Paula looked at me as if to say, "Is that true?" I pulled out the letter and gave it to Deb. She read it. "Oh, Max, I'm so sorry. Yes, we will be there and will give you some support."

Wof piped down, knowing full well he was out of order. The bell sounded, and we made our way back to classes.

Ebo turned up after school at my home, and I invited him in. "Me Dad wants a hand loading out the scaffold—a tenner each if you're interested. He wants us on Saturday morning." Ebo wasn't interested in my activities in the cadets, although I did try to get him to join when I did. "Are you doing anything on Saturday?"

"Well, no," I replied.

"Right. Be at mine at 7.00AMbecause Dad wants an early start."

I reassured him I'd be there. Ebo was roughly the same height and same age as me and had taken on an apprenticeship with his dad's business, which was a small building firm, when he left school. I'd often help out through the summer holidays, and his dad offered me the same apprenticeship. Tez, who always kept a close eye on our activities when we were growing up as kids, said he'd leave the position open if I wanted it, explaining he had plenty of work. Ebo's other two brothers were also employed with the firm; it was very much a family business.

"Come on, let's go down to Babs and have an hour around the track."

We made our way through the RAF camp on our skateboards, which was a shortcut. Babs was in his back garden with his KX 80 crosser engine; it was half stripped, having seized up the previous Sunday. His brother Gee was already out on the track on his Honda c70; mine was hid in the shed. Babs's dad had told me to keep it there after I was chased across the common and over the RAF camp by the cops, for wearing no helmet. I had a narrow escape, losing them at the tunnel. Ebo happened to be riding pillion and also had no helmet on when the patrol car gave chase.

We crouched down at the side of Babs, who was tending his KX 80. Ebo looked at the damaged piston and rings. "Whoops, you made a good job of that."

"Farron engineering rebored the barrel and skimmed out the head. I've had to have a new piston and rings installed—oversized of course, to match the new bore."

"Expensive, was it?" I remarked. Babs smiled. "I thought so—yer dad paid for it, I take it. Come on, Babs, leave that; you can get a shot on my c70."

Babs dropped his spanner and opened the shed door, undoing the padlock. My c70 leaned against the shed wall. "Nah I'm going to finish this; you two go and race Gee."

Babs walked to the back gate and opened it; the path led straight out to the track. We stood at the gate. I opened the seat and checked it for petrol.

"Some in the can in the shed, if you need it," Babs said before returning to his task.

It had been raining slightly and was dark. The floodlights from the airfield were enough to see what we were doing. The track had been made by us scrambling about and had got worn in to a marked-out circuit. I could see Gee in the distance as Ebo kept hold of the moped whilst I kicked her over. She fired up on the third kick as usual. Over the course of owning the Honda c70, we'd removed everything down to its bare essentials, and it looked mean. Babs, who was only nine years old, had his dad weld up a modified exhaust system for it after I snapped the original one in two doing jumps over the stream. We'd taken it in turns to go around, and the thrill of it was worth getting covered in mud.

After our petrol got low, We decided to call it a night. I left Ebo at the corner and said I'd see him up the school club tonight, at 8.00PM. We needed to change out of our track duds and get something to eat. All the excitement down at the track had made me hungry, and I could smell fresh cooked milk bread as I stood my skateboard at the back door. My brother Pat was soon at the freshly cooked loaf with the bread knife; he liked the butter to melt into it whilst it was still warm. I stripped of my duds at the back door.

His pal Spaniel had turned up and was sitting in the back room with Mum as I walked through stripped down to my pants and vest. "Hi, Spaniel, going up to the club tonight?"

"Well yeah, we might just go up there," Spaniel replied.

"Is there hot water, Mum? I could use a bath."

Mum said, "There should be plenty."

Pad was in the kitchen asking if we'd make a foursome on the table football, a newly installed machine inside the school club. "Yeah sure, no probs. I'll take some two pence for the slot."

Spaniel went through his pockets. "I have some; I'll save 'em for the game, then."

The club was busy. Daz and Alex were on the pool table as usual. Ann, the club leader, had collared me at the door asking for money for the

Motorhead gig, of which I'd already paid half; she reminded me the gig was next week. "I need the money in as soon as possible."

"Erm, what day is it on again?" I asked while I scratched down my name to sign in.

"Next Tuesday. I want the money by Monday. Today is Thursday, which gives you all weekend."

Daz's drew on to what was being said. "Are you definitely going, Max?" He walked over to the desk. "I'll pay it for him; he can owe me the money."

"Hey, nice one, Daz, thanks."

He paid the outstanding balance to Ann, who retired to the office to sort out her paperwork, beckoning another member of the staff, Jill, to take over at the door. Daz and I followed her into the office. "Tickets will be issued on the way to Demont Ford Hall on the bus; be here six thirty. Any questions?" She took Daz's money.

"Can't think of any. Can you, Daz?"

By this time Alex was poking his head into the office, trying to get Daz to take his shot on the pool table.

"You paid up then, Max?"

"Looks like it, mate."

"Hey, well get the back seat and have a laugh on the way there."

"Where have you been getting yer wedge?" I asked Daz.

"Started at the colliery, worked a week in hand; that's me first week's wages."

"Hey, I want the cash back as well," Alex chirped.

"You'll be waiting till next Christmas to get it back off him."

Alex was laughing whilst he followed Daz back out the office, walking to the pool table where Daz took his shot.

"Don't give it to him, Max," Alex shouted.

Daz miss cued and said to Alex, "Oy, never mind."

Alex rushed to take his two shots. "Just take yer bleeding shot. Always flaming stirring it." Daz soon had the game back underway as I slipped ten pence on the table. "What's wages like at the colliery then, Daz?"

"First week's wage is £120.00, and you take home more next week. I get area bonus whilst training. He's started," he said, pointing to Alex.

"You're at the colliery too?" I asked, and Alex nodded.

Ebo was at the table football. "Coupla warm-ups, Max?"

I took up stance at the opposite side to him, the TV blaring away in the background while other club members sat in front of it. The table tennis setup was out. A couple of new faces were there; two new chicks were attempting to play—well sorta; they spent more time retrieving the ball because every time they missed it.

I stopped the ping pong by my foot, and the young female came over. "Thanks," she said as I bent down to pick it.

"No problem. Who are you two delightfuls, then ?"

"Shan and Susan. I am Shan and that's Susan."

"Pleased to meet you," I said as I handed back the ball. "This is Ebo, and these two on the pool table are Daz and Alex. Are you going to become members? You know, regulars."

"Yes, we just did." She giggled and went back to her game.

Alex was soon over at the football table sniffing for info. "Do you know her, Max ?"

"I do now," I laughed as Spaniel and my brother came through the door after signing in. They dropped loads of two pence on the table. I said to them, "Ann wants the Motorhead gig paid up."

"I've paid mine," Spaniel replied.

"I ain't going; I got something else to do," my brother said.

"You'll lose your deposit," I warned. "Right, best of three, and then we swap around. Let's get started."

We had been playing for nigh on an hour, and I was beginning to learn the technique of passing the ball when I heard, "Max, yer wanted on the phone." Ann was hanging out the office.

"Who is it? I'm busy."

"Its yer mum; she's tripped over the Hoover," Alex blurted out, trying to be funny. The ball got sunk by a crack shot from Ebo as I left the table.

I walked into the office, and Ann handed me the phone. "Hello?" The line was silent as Ann walked out and closed the door to give me a little privacy.

"It's me, Amana."

"Hey, I ain't seen you for time. How are you?"

"I need to see you, Max—urgent."

"What you mean, urgent, doll ?"

"I'm in a phone box, and my money's running out, so I'll be quick. Can you meet me down at the park, the top pavilion? I'll make an excuse to take the dog fer a walk 9.30."

"Well, sure, doll." Just then the line went brrrr.

I shot out the office. "Erm, Ebo, Pat, Daz—I got to miss. Might get back for last ten minutes," I joked as I looked at my watch; it was 8.50, so if I set off now I'd just make it.

"Oy, you got ten pence on table you ain't played yet." Daz handed me the money as I passed him.

"See y'all later."

The park was quiet when I arrived with five minutes to spare. I could see Amana walking into the park through the main gate with her dog, a little Jack Russell she called Rusty. I watched her as she made her way up to the pavilion, and I waited for her to get a little closer. She had on a long black leather coat and a white fluffed-up scarf and hat to match.

As I sneaked around the other side of the pavilion, she went in to the front, and then I jumped out. "Hey, doll, remember me?"

"Max!" she said as she grabbed at me and pulled me in close. I hugged at her warm, scented body, loving every second of it. She was silent as I stared at her face.

"How did you know where to find me?" I asked.

"Shh," she said as she kissed me and then broke away, looking for her little dog.

"It's okay, he's just by the tennis court, see?" I pointed him out.

She called to him and the little dog came to her. She placed him back on the lead as she sat down, and Rusty jumped on her lap. I sat next to her. "Come on, Max, I'm starved. Let's go to a chip shop."

We walked off the park and made our way down to the bottom end of town. "My treat tonight," she said as we walked.

"I've tried to get hold of you, doll, honest."

She stopped me. "Yes, I know—you phoned every week for three months."

"Yer ma, doll, she wouldn't let me talk to you."

"I know that too. She just wanted what she thought was for the best."

"And what do you want?"

"It's not for me to say—yet. You see, I'm going away."

I was shocked. "What do you mean? Yer frightening me."

"My father's work," she explained. "He's being relocated."

"What, another town, city—where ?"

"Saudi Arabia," she said sadly.

"Saudi Arabia?" I choked. "How, what, who, where . . . What do you mean? I ain't never going to see you again!"

"Shh, it's not till next month."

"Huh. I'd better make the most of you tonight, then. Come here; I want double rations."

The glow from the chip shop sign seemed even more inviting as the brightness of the shop front got closer and the smell of fish and chips made me slaver on the approach. "Get the little dog a battered sausage," I remarked.

She giggled in my ear and whispered, "Hey, I heard that. Took awhile to recover; does it want to see action again?" I nudged her. "What you having to eat?" she asked with a smile.

"Get me a chip cob and a carton of curry sauce and a can of Diet Coke. Plenty of salt and vinegar."

I held Rusty for her as she stood in the queue. We walked up the high street eating our chips, and Amana was breaking off bits of battered sausage and letting them cool before dropping it down to Rusty. We came to a bench in the middle of town and sat down. The air was still but cold.

"What happened to yer brother? I ain't seen him for a few weeks," I said.

"Our Kevin's down in Devon at his granddad's. He made a fine cadet."

"He hasn't left us, has he?"

"No he's not left the cadets; he's just indisposed." She giggled.

"He'll be staying then ?" I asked.

"He wasn't pleased at getting his head shaved," she remarked. "Says he wants his long hair back."

"So he's gone AWOL then."

"Not quite," she replied. "He will be looking after the house under supervision of my older sister. That reminds me—my folks are away to some pre-move meeting this weekend. My big sister will be around, though, checking up."

I butted in. "Erm, are you inviting me?"

"We will see how things pan out," she replied.

It didn't take long to reach the edge of the estate where she lived. "Do you still have the number I gave you?" she asked.

"Well yes, of course I do. I have it at home, although I did memorize it."

"You memorized my number?" She pulled me in close. I whispered it in her ear. "Let it Ring the phone three times, then hang up, then ring again. Then I'll know it's you and I'll pick up. Saturday evening around seven o'clock." She gave me a right smacker and then broke the embrace. She and Rusty made her way to towards her house.

Friday morning was my day for window cleaning. I'd woke, looked out the window, and was instantly blinded by the sunshine. "Ace," I thought. "Can get some dollars today. Sod school." I ran downstairs, made a quick instant coffee, and took it back upstairs to get ready and change into work clothes, complete with body warmer. At 8.30 I was out the door, grabbing my ladders and bucket and chamois.

I had a few tricks up my sleeve to make the glass sparkle. A quick drop of vinegar in the water and a squirt of Jif lemon does the trick. I also found if I finished them off with old army scrim net after a good chamois, they gleamed streak free even in blazing hot sunshine. Now, usually when dinnertime came, I would go back to school, but on this occasion I thought I'd work on. I'd planned out my free lessons on the time table so I could work Friday mornings, with social studies in that particular after noon. I loved the subject, but I needed the extra money. I was gaining new customers at the same time; the round was getting bigger, and the decision had been made.

The first was a new customer, and I marvelled at what was lined up on the dressing table when I went up the ladder. Three different dildos, all different colours; one of them must have been twelve inches and as fat as my wrist. I was taken aback and nearly fell off the ladder. Obviously she had been late for work and forgot to put them away. I got back down the ladder and thought, "Well, if I do the windows, she'll know I seen 'em." I gave that house a miss. Or did she want me to see them? Either way I got a fright and wasn't taking any chances. I made for the next house, on the next street. Let's just say if you'd seen the woman who lived there, I think most would have done the same. Talk about frying burgers under yer armpits. She could do a double cheese melt, no problem.

I'd been out collecting money owed from the folks that were out working during the day. I'd cleared thirty-three pounds sterling. A shit, shave, and shampoo later I made my way up to the school club. It was always disco night on Fridays. I had been asked to DJ, and I helped set the equipment up and got the turntables pumping. Wayne, who usually did it, never turned up on time. I'd more or less rely on records people brought to the club on the night. Daz and Alex always brought their new albums to the club, having been given Tokyo tapes—the new album by Scorpions and a selection of Kiss albums, which were very popular. The club had its own selection of music, most of it old classics like Led Zeppelin and Deep Purple. Also punk rock was on the scene, although The Sex Pistols where old hat by now, and Public Image Ltd was formed by Johnny Rotten. The club had its own collection of punk, so it was half an hour rock music, half an hour punk, and half an hour charts and soul music. I was a rocker and liked the punk scene.

Daz and Alex stood at the turntables and helped pick out the favourite tracks. Ever heard that saying "Hang the DJ"? Let's just say up there at the club house, it could easily happen. I paid a lot of attention to what people asked to be put on. I handed Daz the money I owed him for the Motorhead gig.

"Been out doing the rounds, have we, Max?" he asked.

"Yep," I said with a smile. As Daz added to his wedge I added, "I bet you two are loaded again."

"Hey, who wants to go to the Welfare later?"

"They won't let you in." Daz replied.

"Why?" I asked, just curious.

"You ain't old enough."

"Well, they let two broads from our school in; they go every week. My next door neighbour asked earlier. I said I'd give it a try."

"What time you meeting him?" Daz asked.

"After I do the last rock set—leave here around 9.30, get there before ten. Said he'd be in there and would sign me in."

"We'll walk down with you, but I ain't going in."

The club house was packed when We left. Ann commented on my instant success as a DJ and said I could do it again if I liked, just so long as I turned up early enough to set the rig up. Daz and Alex were shouting, "Hurry, Max, come on" at the main door.

"Yes, Ann, I would like that."

Ann told me not to worry about putting the rig away this week, but I would be required to do so in the future. I left the club house buzzing.

Alex and Daz were probing on how I managed to achieve DJ status. "I don't know, really; Ann just asked me to do it," I said.

I stood at the side entrance of the Welfare, having left Daz and Alex at the bridge. The disco I was interested in was downstairs in the Welbeck suit. I'd caught sight of Paula, one of the girls from school; she was walking up to the main doors saw me hanging around the side door. As I made my way over to her, she was producing a card to show the door men. "Hey, Paula, you look fab," I said. "God, I mean stunning."

She lent in to me and said, "Why thanks, Max." She had on a black evening dress that could have fooled anyone that didn't know her, and a white leather jacket padded on the shoulders and snug on the waist, with a handbag to match. I wasn't used to talking to her at eye level; she was in her high heels. Her hair was tied up and trusses of curls dropped down the side of her face.

"Hey, what's with the card?

she laughed, "It's my older sister's—shh," she whispered.

"Erm, can you sign me in with that?"

"Why sure, come on."

I walked in with Paula, and the place was swinging as coloured lights flashed all around. Older men stood in groups with their pints and chasers, talking to their wives and girlfriends and other men's wives. Some of the men were still black around the eyes, from the mines; you could tell who had just come off the afternoon shift.

I looked around for my next door neighbour, but she wasn't anywhere to be seen. "That's not like Lisa to do that," I thought. Next thing my hand was taken, and I was being pulled onto the already packed dance floor. "Hey, Paula, I can't dance."

"Just follow what I do," she said. So I did. "Hey, you can dance. Looking fer someone?" She'd noticed as I still looked around for Lisa. Paula picked up her handbag from the floor and whispered out loud, "Come to the bar with me."

We struggled to get served; "It's like climbing through Zulus at Rourk's Drift: you need a drink by the time you get to the waterhole," I noted. "I'll get this, Paula—save yer cash." Paula was still laughing. "What you having?"

"A dry martini and lemonade, please, Max." I ordered a pint of lager and then her drink.

Then the lady who served me said, "Why haven't you cleaned my windows today? Sorry, I didn't catch yer name."

"Strewth—it was the woman with the dildos on her dressing table," I thought whilst she took my order. A vision of the three dildos came to mind, and the words "Hear none, speak none, and see none." I didn't know she worked here; she must have had two jobs.

"Erm, I'll call and do them soon, honest. And my name's Max."

Paula was listening in. "Hmm, you're popular," she said as she squeezed into me.

I could hear the miners around us laughing and saying, "Did you heard him? It's like trying to get through a pack of Zulus. Ha!"

We retired to a table where there wasn't so many bodies, and I sat talking to Paula. She was discussing her career prospects and I mine. She retired to the ladies room to powder her nose and was away for ten minutes. "That big hunk of a half brother of yours is on the bowling green arguing with Senny," she said.

Now my ears pricked up as she pulled at my arm. "This I got to see." The pair of us made a beeline for the side door. "Well, I don't see him in here. He musta been upstairs in the grab a granny night disco," I said.

We came to the side doors after running up the corridor. Paula stopping to take off her high heels on the way. I could see through the large glass panels onto the bowling green, where there were two groups of males. I could pick out Big Tony with his creases sown into his denims. Senny, whom I spied wearing a white Fred Perry and jeans, was pointing at him as he lunged forward from the two that stood on either side of him, and Rubble moved forward. Big Tony leapt at Senny and delivered a big right to Senny's fizz. I could hear the punch connect. Rubble moved forward with his dukes up to take on the other two, who were backing away with their hands up, claiming they didn't want trouble. The blow had knocked Senny backwards as he went over and didn't move, knocked clean out. Rubble saw what just happened and was pushing Tony away, leaving Senny's pals to try and bring him back to life. Rubble and Tony like just disappeared.

I could hear Big Tony's new girl friend screaming and shouting as she ran after him along with my half sister, our Stella, who was going out with Rubble. "Oh my gosh," she said as Paula had her hand up to her mouth.

"Wow, man, that was awesome—did you see that punch?" I was buzzing.

Paula was still in shock. I knew what that was about as I grabbed at her waist. She didn't seem to mind. "Is she going with Big Tony now?" she asked, taking her hand from her mouth.

"You know what it's about," I said as I put my finger on her lip. "He's poached her off him."

"Gosh," she said. She was still in shock as we walked back in. She stopped to slip her high heels back on. "Max, I'm going to order a taxi; come with me." I stood with her at the phone under the smoky bubble. "Ten minutes, outside the main entrance? Okay." She put the phone down. "Come on, Max, let's wait outside.

We stood and waited arm in arm as she chittered from the cold. I took off my jacket and placed it around her shoulders. I was still sweating from the heat of the action and all the excitement. We watched as people, mainly couples, filtered out with buzz of the scene that had just taken place as our taxi arrived. She gave her address and gave back my jacket as we jumped in.

Paula stayed on the edge of town. I'd been to her house before, attending a New Year's party a few years ago. "Oh, yer coming in with me," she said as she pulled at my arm to get me to get out of the taxi. I paid the fair and walked arm in arm to her door. She produced her keys from her handbag, which had been slung neatly over her shoulder. "Shh," she said as we entered the house. Her ma and pa where still watching TV as we walked into the lounge. Paula kicked of her high heels.

Her father sat on a big lush white leather sofa watching an old movie, and my attention was drawn to the VCR. Her Father had remembered me from the party. "Max, come and sit down. I hear your retaking your exams."

"Yes, I thought it best to," I replied as I sat beside them. Paula had grabbed her shoes and disappeared as I heard her footsteps running up the stairs.

"I'm glad my daughter decided to retake hers," her ma said, getting up from the sofa. "Would you like a tea or coffee, Max?"

"Erm, yes, a coffee would be nice; milk and sugar."

She made her way into the kitchen, and I heard the kettle getting filled and the clatter of crockery. I could hear footsteps thumping back downstairs, and Paula came through and sat where her ma had been.

"Want a drink, love?" her ma shouted.

"Hot chocolate, Mum."

"How long is the recording time on these VCRs?" I asked.

"It depends on the tape. You can buy an hour or even three hours. The Betamax is better quality, although more limited on buying films for it."

Her mum arrived back with drinks. Her dad had out on the coffee table a decanter of expensive whisky and a tumbler a quarter full. I could smell the aroma as he reached for it. "It's only on the weekends, Max, don't worry," he said as he smiled and took a drink. I laughed at the look on his face—one of pure satisfaction as he swilled the whiskey around in the tumbler.

"That's yours, Max," her mum said as she put down a mug. She sat over in a chair with her drink, her hands cupped around her mug. She looked deep in thought. I could see which side of the family Paula had taken her looks. Her mum was still a very attractive woman and was very well spoken, even though she had in her rollers and hair net and was dressed in her house coat.

"Mum, can Max stay tonight?" Paula asked.

"Well, I can't see why not," she replied as she rose from the chair. "I'll make up the spare room."

I grabbed at Paula's hand and said, "I need to be up at six in the morning; I have some work to do tomorrow."

In the middle of the night, I heard the door scrape over the carpet as Paula sneaked into my room and slipped in beside me. It was 2.30 AM. "Shh, go back to sleep, Max," she said as she pulled the duvet back over us. "I do worry about you sometimes," she whispered as her head hit the pillow.

Paula shook me and woke me up. I looked at my watch: 5.30. "I'll run the shower for you and wait downstairs," she said. I laughed, slapping her backside as she ran over to the door in her white bra and knickers. She switched on the light and disappeared to the bathroom, where I could hear the shower being switched on.

I got to Ebo's house in good spirits. I couldn't wait to tell him about the incident on the bowling green but thought it wise not to tell him about Paula. His mum answered the door and invited me in. "Pour yourself a coffee."

Tez, Ebo's father, was just taking a slice of toast out the toaster. "Forgotten yer snap, Max?"

"I'll call in the shop on the way there and get some," I said as I got myself a mug. Ebo ran downstairs and came through carrying his work boots. "I'll need to call in at home and get changed," I said, filling the mug with coffee from the percolator.

Tez laughed. "Been out on the tiles, Max ?"

"You could say that," I acknowledged with a smile.

Ebo had the fridge open and brought over the milk. "Have you been a dirty stop out?"

"Yep," I replied, taking the milk bottle. Ebo reached for his mug." Just a friend," I added.

"It'll be female, knowing him—he can't keep away from 'em," Ebo's mum said, joining the conversation. I just went bright red. "Ah, his colour's up. I told ya!"

"I bet that was her I seen you eating chips with the other night in the town," Tez butted in.

"No, that wasn't her."

"Bloody hell, how many women you got, then?" Tez said, picking up his morning paper. I decided to stay silent. Right. Ebo, the Blocks are on the job. You and Max should have it all loaded out by high noon."

"No problem, Dad."

Teg walked through carrying his boots. Teg was Ebo's eldest brother. "Come on, Ebo, I want that mixer started by eight, and it's already seven fifteen."

"It will take twenty minutes to get there. Max has to get changed first," Ebo replied.

Teg looked me up and down. "Right, I'll take you over to yer house now in the truck, he said, putting on his boots and reaching for the keys on the table. "Come on, you two."

On the way out I bumped into Poke, the second oldest brother. He was also carrying his work boots. "Hey, Max, I thought I heard your voice."

"All right, Poke. Hangover?" I noticed he looked a bit on the rough side.

"Six pints and a curry, and out like light," Poked laughed. "Won 'em all at darts again, so I celebrated."

Mum wasn't too pleased at me staying out all night when I came home and ran through to get changed. "Sorry, Ma, won't do it again," I said, just to get the flea out of my ear.

We arrived at the job. "Here you'll need these," Teg said, throwing me a pair of gloves as he took his tool bucket from the truck. "Right, Ebo, load the corners out first. You know the crack. I'll set up the mixer for the first mix."

At high noon we were back at Ebo's. Tez handed me a tenner, and I thanked him as I took it. "Nah, don't need to thank me; you did a good job fer me today," Tez replied.

"This gives me a good start fer Monday."

"What you doing this afternoon?" Tez inquired.

"I have to go in to town to by new jeans—I have a date," I said as I snapped the tenner.

Ebo's father replied, "Give me that tenner back. There's a shop near the train station that sells good jeans. Always a discount on all our work clothes—Levis, Lee Cooper, Brutus. I get them fer all our lot. Do you want me to ring 'em?"

"Why yes," I said as I handed the money back.

"I'll tell 'em to throw in a new shirt as well, and pick yourself some new boots."

Poke came in from the garage. Going in to town fer new clobber, Max?"

"Yes, yer dad's just making a call to the shop."

"Come on, I'll take you down in the truck. I'll leave our Bess here." Bess was Poke's pet springer spaniel.

The shop in town had a good selection, all the latest fashions and top brands. "I need a new shirt," Poke said as we looked through the racks. We spent a good hour trying out jeans and boots until I was happy with what I was buying—or should I say, put on Tez's account. My bill alone came to sixty sovereigns. Poke had picked out three new shirts, and I had new Levis 501, a Levis shirt to match, and a new pair of black Doc Martens. They even threw in a leather Levi belt.

Poke dropped me off at home. "Can we book you fer next weekend, Max?"

"Yeah, sure," I replied.

"Here, me dad asked me to give you this back." Poke handed me a tenner. I was shocked. "Poke put up his hand to stop me from talking. "Mate, you earned that. Dad reckons you've got expensive habits." He laughed.

I'd been arguing with my brother because he'd used all the hot water without switching the immersion heater back on. I'd usually make a coal fire in the back room, which heated the back boiler, but I had not been in all day to light it, so I had to wait. Sod it. I ran out the house and down to the phone box. I'd remembered to let the phone ring three times before ringing again.

"Hello, Max," Amana said when she picked up.

"Hi, doll, are we on fer tonight?"

Amanas said, "Hang on," and left the line. A brief discussion took place with another female in the background. "Come to the house at eight; my sister will be out then," she whispered.

"Sure thing, doll. See you then."

I'd gotten bathed and changed into my new clothes and overdid it a bit with the Brute. Mum reckoned I'd used the whole bottle. "But you do look smart," she commented.

I went over to the school field, remembering to take an apple out of the fruit bowl in the kitchen. I stood at the edge of the paddock whistling. The dapple grey bay and the chestnut mare stood over at the far corner. I made click-click noises with the back of my throat and my tongue. "Come on, then," I shouted. They trotted over, the dapple grey leading and being followed by the chestnut. I held the apple out in my hand. "First one gets it," I bellowed. The dapple grey was first over but wasn't interested; he was just happy to see me, nodding his head as I stroked him between the ears. The chestnut wasn't fussy and seemed to be thankful for the treat. My mind flashed back to the summer of '76—and one crazy day in particular.

Ebo, Wof, Carl and I had been in the valley playing tag. Carl later moved to America with his family. It was just a game we played on the way to the swimming baths, where we'd spend our Saturday afternoons. We had came out the valley and gone the back way, passing the senior school and exploring the old orchard. We'd been there throwing sticks to knock the pairs from the branches the previous September. I'd seen the horses in the paddock and was fascinated. Then the idea came to play the three musketeers, all four of us choosing names. I was D'artagnan. "I need a horse, dear fellows," I said, and I called one over. We all had our swords—long sticks we'd snapped from the elder berry—and we found they snapped when we fenced with them.

"Go on, then, I dare you," said Carl. Wof chimed in too.

Before you know it I was up on the fence and jumped on the dapple grey's back kicking into its side. The horse just bolted, and I was trying to get hold of her mane. I'd managed to stay on when the horse just stopped. I was propelled through the air and landed in the thicket. The horse walked over and stood leering at me whilst I untangled myself from the bush. My T-shirt was ripped, and I was scratched all over from the nettle stings. I looked over at the other three musketeers, who fell about laughing. I got on that horse another two times, and more or less the same thing happened. Mum wasn't pleased when she found out I'd cracked a rib.

I wished the horses good health and peeled myself away from them. ain't I came to the top of Amanas street. I must have left the smell of Brute all the way from my house. I thought it would wear off a bit by the time I got there, but it didn't. I checked my watch: ten past eight. I knew I shouldn't have stopped at the horses, and I increased my pace.

I rang the door bell and heard music playing. Amana came to the door; I could see her outline through the glass. The house seemed quiet as I walked in the front door. Amana closed the door behind me and locked it, leaving the key in. "Max, you're late."

"I know, doll, I've been running around like a blue-arsed fly." Then I noticed her: She was just wearing a T-shirt, and I mean just a T-shirt, with Judas priest on the front.

"Come on through," she said as she led the way, walking me through into the lounge. Talk about spacious. "I can offer you a beer if you'd like one."

"Yeah, sure, doll."

"I'm going to order something to eat; would you like something?"

Too late—I'd got her in an embrace and had my tongue straight down her throat.

"Phew, Max," she said, the next thing we knew, our hands started wandering. It was a big lounge, and we ended up all over it. She swiped the lamp of the table and knocked over a vase. Magazines got knocked from the dining table. We ended up on the sofa for the grand finale. The scratches on my back were deeper than the first time with her, not to mention the bites on my neck.

"Huh, Max," she said as she put her T-shirt back on. "My sister will be back at eleven."

I was pulling on my jeans and looking at my watch: 10.50. The place was in a mess. "Christ, have we been at it all that time?"

"Hmm, superman," she said as she straightened up.

I slipped the Doc Martens on just in case I needed to make a quick exit. I helped her put the cushions back on the couch; I'd pulled them down to avoid getting carpet burn. Both of us were grinning. "Now about that beer," I prompted.

"You can take one with you. Come on, Max, my sister will be here in a minute." She ran into the kitchen and returned with a bottle. "Here, now go." I pecked her on the lips. "Ring me Wednesday night, eight o'clock," she whispered.

I left the house and walked up the street, spotting a taxi turning into the estate. I hid behind a parked car whilst it passed.

On Sunday morning I'd missed cadets again and had gone for the match instead. I'd not been to cadets since I'd had the news about my rejection and was deciding whether to hand in my uniform. I arrived at the Barn. Mr Hope stood outside the changing rooms with a match ball under his arms, in his black track complete with whistle around his neck. "Good of you to turn out, Max. You're playing forward first half. Get changed and into the barn fer warm-up. Take a shirt from the bench; you'll see them on the way in."

I'd noticed some of the lads were already here because clothes hung on the pegs. I changed into the school colours, the legendary gold and white stripes, and headed out into the Barn.

"Hey, Max, you made it," the captain said, trapping the ball and turning his attention towards me. "Try a few passing techniques and shots on goal." I looked around to see who was here. "Team up with Gee. We are still waiting on one player to arrive.

When everyone was there, the game got under way. Paula had turned up with Deb and a few others, cheering us on.

"Yes, good, Max." Mr Hope was watching from the side line as a cheer went up; I'd struck a cracker from the halfway line, curling it with just enough rise and placing it top right corner of the net. The players of Arnold High held their hands to their faces in disbelief.

The captain called us together. "Right, we are up one goal, and it's five minutes before half-time. Keep the red shirts marked down, lads." We played a tactical defence, intercepting the ball midfield with a few failed shots on goal as the whistle blew for half time.

Mr Hope was ecstatic. "Good show, you guys. Good close marking and good passing. Take a breather for ten minutes."

Paula and Deb shouted me over. They were still jumping up and down, trying to keep warm. The two of them were made up in their usual tarty image—war paint, pencil skirts, high heels, and all.

Deb was first to speak. "Good goal, Max."

"Good? That was a classic," Paula corrected her.

I stood sweating me cobs off, still trying to gain my breath. "Did you like that one?" I said between breaths. "Was it as good as Archie Gemmil's goal in the World Cup?"

"Brilliant, Max, from where I stood," Deb said, moving closer and batting her false eyelashes at me. She had her hand on her hip again.

"I'm nipping out fer a cigarette," Paula said quickly. "Are you coming, Deb?" I could sense a hint of jealousy rearing its ugly head.

As Paula and Deb retreated from the Barn, the team captain called us over again. "Right, Max and Gee, I'll keep you two up front. Keep up the pressure and take the chances. Goalie, you were fantastic, keep that up. You did some splendid saves and were quick at putting the ball back into play—caught them of guard a few times. Right, the defence could be better. Tighten it up, lads, keep them red shirts pinned down."

The whistle blew to start the second half. Fifteen minutes into it we were still one goal up. Again I'd retrieved the ball from midfield and saw Gee make his run. Out of the corner of my eye I could see him unmarked as I chipped the ball over to him. Yes, what a goal! Gee had lunged forward and headed it into the bottom left hand corner. The girls were screaming, "Max, Gee, Max, Gee! Two to none, two to none!"

Eventually the whistle blew. A clean game well played, with no injury time. We shook hands with the opposition. Mr Hope came into the shower room as we were getting changed. "That score just placed fourth from the top of the league! Well done, lads. The next match is away."

"Who are we playing, sir?"

"Bass Ford High. I'll post all the details up on the notice board."

The following Thursday came. I'd made the decision to hand in my uniform and had gone to the detachment; I sat on the table in civvies, waiting to see Captain Pinner. Some of the cadets made comments that they were gutted over me leaving the ACF.

Captain Pinner tried to talk me out of it. "You do know you are up for promotion end of this month."

"This is news to me, Captain, I said bluntly in an effort to make things less painless for us both.

"I have the relevant paper work here sent from HQ. I've made arrangements for you to go down see Sergeant Major Smith tonight. I've just gotten off the phone; you are to see him at 9.00PM in the NCOs mess. You are to leave your uniform here; you won't be needing that."

After he'd finished reading the paperwork, placing it back in an envelope marked confidential, I got myself down to HQ and caught the bus. The BSM acknowledged my presence and showed me through to where Sergeant Major Smith sat.

I'd seen that look on his face before and knew it was serious. "You wanted to see me, Sergeant Major?"

"Skip the formalities, Max, sit down." I sat in at the front of him. "Do you want to work for the MOD?"

"Erm, come again, Sergeant Major?"

"This dossier is top secret. I want you to sign this and then read it."

"Sign what, Sergeant Major?" I was curious.

"Let's just say it's an official secrets act, and you ain't reading that without signing this."

"I'm not sure, sergeant."

"Max, you can never speak of what is in that dossier."

Before I knew it I'd signed it. "I haven't just signed my life away, have I, Sergeant Major?" I joked.

He handed me the large brown envelope. I opened it and read the contents. I slammed it down. "A tracker? You put that in my watch?"

"Shh, shut up," the sergeant said with his finger up to my mouth. The BSM wandered over and was laughing. "You see, Max, that's how we know you always tell the truth. Now keep that zipped."

I went quiet and read the rest of it and began to smile. I'd had the watch since my twelfth birthday. I started to laugh. It was an experiment that proved to be a success.

The BSM chipped in. "We also wanted to see what type of character you where. You fit the bill, Max. Wanna carry on with it? It's your decision. For Queen and country, right, Sergeant Major?"

I handed the dossier back. "Yes, I'll carry on with it." The BSM and sergeant major looked relieved. I looked again at the digital Casio on my wrist. "My mum got this for my birthday. How did you do it? Are you suggesting my mum's involved?"

The BSM stopped me, putting up his hand. "We swapped it when you where in the guard house; we had a key to your locker." My mind went back to Christmas camp and the incident regarding the stolen credit card. Yes, my watch was in my locker. The BSM continued. "It's linked to a satellite and surveillance aircraft. The aircraft is called TR1A. This aircraft can stay in flight for twelve hours and can pinpoint targets from eighty thousand feet. Your watch omits an hourly signal; we can scramble it and pinpoint you wherever you are; so long as you wear the watch, we can find you. You'll get a new watch every two years."

The sergeant major smiled and said, "You are to send the old one back here to me at the battery; you know the address." I nodded. "Just let us know where you want the new watch sent."

1983, LINTON COLLIERY

Mr Flint, the personnel training officer, had scored me another line on the blackboard. I'd been laid off, cutting my building apprenticeship short by a year. "What's all this, then?" asked a helmeted miner, black faced and all.

"It's how many times I've come looking fer work," I said.

The man looked at all the lines made on the board. Mr Rocks . . . I know that name. Are you Evelyn's lad?"

"Why yes, how do you know her?"

"She goes to same club as me and the missus. Tell you what—you don't need to call again." The man's eyes seemed to smile. "I'll send fer you for interview. Put him down." He signalled to Mr Flint and walked out the door.

"Well, it looks like you landed a job, everything being well at interview." Mr Flint looked confident.

"I was still trying to come to grips with what the man had just said. "Who was that?" I asked.

"That's only the pit manager, Mr Heartson. I need your full address and post code."

I was out with Gee and Beno with the dogs. The two little Jack Russells, Lulu and Sue, were checking a few rabbit warrens near Beeley Village. I had the letter in my pocket unopened. "Fresh droppings here," I said as I cleared the bolt-hole and staked out the net. Gee and Beno snooped around and found the other holes. Beno proclaiming we'd got it all covered and took Sheba the Ferret from his shoulder bag. She was soon on the case as he offered her to the hole, her nose twitching faster. He covered the hole with a net after she'd gone down. She had on her beeper collar so we didn't lose her. Each of us sat quietly around our selected bolt-hole.

I could hear thumping in the ground. "Coming your way, Max," Gee shouted out. Bam! A large buck hit the net as I made a grab for it. Lulu and Sue got there first, nipping it dead.

"There's another," I said as the ground started to thump. "Your way, Beno." Bam! Another big buck hit the net as the ground rumbled again. They were shooting out everywhere, at least two getting out of the nets and escaping, far too quick for the dogs.

"I think we cleared that one," I said when all went quiet.

Beno agreed, taking his black box from his bag. The red light started to flash. "Let's see where she is," he said as he scanned the box over the mound. The red light would stay on constantly when she was located. Thumping started again as Beno had his ear to the ground. "That's where she is. She's got hold of one." Gee took the spade and started to dig. "Careful she's close." Beno scanned the ground again, and soon the back of the rabbit was exposed as I made a grab for the dogs. I didn't want them frightening Sheba back into the warren.

Gee and Beno soon had both the ferret and the young rabbit out of the hole. Gee let the young rabbit go free after he examined it. Sheba had had hold of the rabbit's ear. He carefully placed Sheba back in her bag and put the magic box in there too. We gutted what we considered edible and threw away one rabbit after spotting white spots on the kidneys. We had three rabbits each. "Good day," I said. "Time to open this." I sat and opened the letter and read. "Yahoo, my interview's on Friday."

"What's all that in aid of?" Gee asked as he stood leaning on the spade.

"An interview at Linston Colliery."

"Why, you jammy sod," Beno chirped up. "You've got an interview at the colliery?"

"Yeah, man, it's there in black and white," I said, showing them the letter.

That night. I stood at the local bar and ordered a pint of lager. "Got ya a dinner if ya want it. Cost ya a coupla pints, though," I said to Toff as he stood at the pool table setting up the balls. I opened my combat jacket.

"Yeah, deal," he said when he saw the dangling rabbit. Toff walked over to have a better look.

"Big doe, fresh today," I remarked as I took it from my jacket and handed it to him. The landlady turned a blind eye as she slid a nice cool pint onto the bar, and as I took a long drink. "He's paying," I said, licking the foam from my top lip and winking at her.

Toff took the rabbit and placed it near his table before returning to pay for the drink. "Game of pool, Max?"

"Go on, then." I made for a cue.

"Best get a few games before fat-bellygut-bucket arrives." I knew what Toff meant. He usually ended up playing all night. "Winner stays on rules."

A few locals filtered through, and soon the board had names on it. Toff left me with two stripes on the table before slamming home the black. "Another pint, Max? Hey, ask if they'll play doubles," Toff said as grabbed my empty glass.

One of the locals got up from his table and looked at the board. "You Jeff"? I asked.

"Yes, I'm Jeff."

"Friggin' hell, it's Max. can't you remember me?"

"Why yeah, from the track, down the side of a Rolls Royce years back. Good old days, them."

"That old scooter with the union jacks on the panels?" Jeff said and smiled.

"Ha, yeah I remember it. Musta been six of us on it, chased by the Rozers over the common. Ha ha! Ebo with the clothespin hooked on to the throttle cable 'cause we fell off it and snapped the handle bars. Yeah, I remember!"

Toff came back from the bar. I asked, "Do you remember him?"

"Yeah, Babs and Alex's mate. Why?" Toff said, handing me a fresh pint.

"Tell Toff about that scooter. Wanna game of doubles?" I asked as a 5'11" female came over.

"Remember her, Max?" Jeff asked. She had bleached blonde hair and a freckled face, with an a hourglass figure, and she stood smiling at me.

"Now then, let me see," I said as I looked her in the eyes.

In the background I could hear Toff laughing as Jeff told him the scooter story and how the police gave up the chase after they'd driven into the woods and hid the scooter and they all ran off. "He was changing gear on one side, and Ebo had the clothespin, pulling the throttle, and God knows how many other bodies hanging off it."

My attentions was drawn back to the girl. "It's, erm, what's her face. No, hang on, I'll get it. Bonus's sister. Tracy! That's right, isn't it?"

"Yeah, you remembered." She smiled even more.

"Can you play pool?" I asked. "Game of doubles, perhaps?"

Jeff was still buzzing on to Toff. "What do you think Jeff?" Tracy asked. "Doubles?"

"Yeah, sure, Trace, we'll sticks you and Toff.

"Agreed. Set 'em up, Max," Tracy said as she put in the money. "Hey whose bunny?"

"Mine," Toff said.

"How much?" Tracy asked him.

"Ask Max."

She looked at me after she broke, sending two spots down.

"Coupla pints, and you can have one, but you'll need to stop by."

"Okay, Max, yer on. Do you still live over at the estate?"

"Yep."

Tracy smiled and said, "I'll find ya," before sinking another spot. "What you having, Max?"

"Same again—fresh glass, babe."

If it weren't for Toff fluking his two shots, we'd been in serious trouble as I approached the table. Having seen a plant in the top right corner, I took aim. Smack. "Oh, what a player," Toff roared after the table came to rest. One in the corner bag planned, another dropped, and then another—all stripes. That equalled the odds. They had one spot on the table, leaving three stripes. as I studied the table, chalking up.

Tracy returned from the bar and arranged the drinks. "There you go, Max. Jeff, that's yours." I took my second shot, selecting a stripe sitting on the middle pocket and hitting the white with a little left hand top, sinking the spot and coming off the cushion to set myself up just right for the next.

"Oh, look at that semi-stun-swerve-screw back," Toff joked as I sunk the next. I snookered myself behind the black as I paused. Toff was over trying to work out the next shot with me. "Middle of the back cush," he suggested.

"I'll try it." I couldn't see any other option and took the shot. The white came to rest behind the last remaining stripe.

Tracy and I had our heads in close. "Yep that's touching," Tracy agreed. "Look at that, out of a snooker, and he snookered us."

Toff burst out laughing. "Get outta that then," he said, nodding to Jeff.

Fat-bellygut-bucket walked in the main entrance with his trusty cue and headed over to the bar. "Put me name down, Toff," he bellowed.

"Ain't enough room on the board," I said under my breath, and Jeff squared up to line his shot up, laughing. Toff was still sniggering too.

"Ha ha, missed two shots."

"That's you two barracking," Tracy remarked, starting to laugh as well.

Toff then missed the black and sunk the white ball. I stood with my hand over my eyes. "How did you manage that?" I asked, and then I could see why: Tracy was leaning over, going through her handbag with all her cleavage hanging out. "Hey, that's barracking," I laughed as Tracy straightened herself up and took the first of her shot on black, retrieving the sunk white. "Never mind, Toff." I patted him on the back. "You coulda parked the front wheel of a Harley Davidson in those." Toff cracked out laughing again.

"What you two on about?" Jeff asked, looking over at us.

Tracy sunk the black. "Another pint, Max?" she said with a smile.

"Put the names up again, Toff; Tracy's buying."

The night progressed quickly, and the shout for last orders came. I was well slewed, swaying about as I ordered a few rounds of crisps, putting the selection of flavours on the table. "Help yourselves."

"I'll pop 'round tomorrow fer the bunny, around five," Tracy said as Jeff and Tracy put on their jackets to leave.

"No problem, doll. If I ain't around, just ask me ma, and she'll sort you out. Ask her nice, and she might throw in a frozen pheasant. Payment in beer, of course."

"Sure, Max—might see ya tomorrow, then. Bye folks," she said, and the two of them left.

Toff and I walked back along the track, cutting through a small group of trees. "I fancy doing some fishing tomorrow. Interested?" I said.

"Where are you thinking of going?" Toff asked.

"I've seen some good places up the Lean, where it's faster running water. Free line a lob worm downstream, and who knows what we might land."

"Small rods, then," Toff said, stopping at his gate. "We'll need to dig fer some bait first thing tomorrow, say around 5.30."

Next morning I rose and looked out my bedroom window. A golden sheen spread across the horizon. "Going to be a grand day," I thought as I made for the bathroom.

Toff was in his backdoor with the spade and a bait box at his side. "Plenty off big fresh lob worms in it," he said. There was still a ground mist lingering about when we got down to the river. We set up our tackle and started to fish. Toff stood about fifteen metres from me as we slowly walked downstream, free lining the lob worm.

Suddenly the rod jerked, causing me to strike. "Hey, I hooked one!" I shouted down to Toff, who reeled in and came to my aid.

"Easy does it," he said as he got hold of the line to bring the fish in to the bank. "Hey, that must be at least a two-pound rainbow."

I was buzzing with excitement as it lay flipping around on the bank whilst Toff set up a keep net and placed it in. We must have caught another three each during the course of the morning, all roughly the same size. I left Toff at the end of the street. See you in the pub tonight then, at 7.30."

I stood in the kitchen gutting the fish and preparing two of them for the freezer. Mum looked pleased at the catch. "That's fer our tea tonight," I said as I washed up and went out into the garden, picking a few fresh herbs Ma had planted out from a packet of mixed seeds. I crushed a few leaves of parsley and mint and sniffed at them in my hand. "That will go with the salad," I thought. "The fish can go in newspaper and then be soaked in water with a knob of butter and some fresh garlic enclosed—a little trick I learned that removes the scales when cooked." Mum had made fresh milk bread, and it was on a cake stand, still cooling. I couldn't resist a slice of that with butter.

Tracy arrived at the front door. I opened it to find her smiling away. "Go round to the back door, Tray," I said, and I made my way back through the house. She stood out back looking anxious. "Right, Tray, I got pheasant, venison, rainbow trout, and skinned pheasant, as well as rabbit." I soon had Tracy sorted with an array of fresh and frozen game. "You pay fer all my beer tonight—as much as I can drink."

She knew I'd be hammered after four or five pints and agreed. "See you tonight, Max."

I sat twiddling my thumbs when Mr Heartson's secretary called me in. I was asked a selection of questions—hobbies, interests, where I'd gone. Finally he said, "Why do you want to work here?"

"I need work," I replied.

Mr Heartson just roared with laughter. "You'd best try elsewhere, 'cause they don't do much work here." I became a little disgruntled and agitated by his outburst, and apparently he could see it. "You're hired, kid. I will set up a time fer your medical. You'll get that in the post."

"Thanks, Mr Heartson, will that be all?"

"Yes, Max. Close the door on the way out."

A month later, I'd passed the medical with flying colours and had a date set for mines fire and rescue training. The class was held at a colliery, set up with all facilities necessary. I'd just gotten through the first week, mostly classroom and simulated firefighting techniques—use of extinguishers, powder foam and water, and which type of fire it applied to, electrical or oil or wood. I was also taught how to use a high pressure fire hose.

The instructor commented, "From now you'll be getting paid at the end of the week. You'll need these to draw yer wages." He gave us colliery motes. "Brass. These are temporary. You'll be given a new one when you get to your assigned colliery."

The ride down in the cage was the first time I'd gone underground. I stood in my yellow helmet, of the type given to trainees, with a self-rescuer and a battery pack. I moved them around to find the most comfortable position. It seemed to take a while before we came to rest, and all six of us switched on our cap lamps. The air was cold, and a constant breeze blew in our faces.

The instructor moved us in to an old substation room made into an underground classroom, near the pit bottom. "Right, this is still a working colliery; they're working in a seam further down known as black shale. This is an old seam known as Tupton. Now it's used just fer training purposes. Further down the drift we have haulage and locomotive facilities; most of you will be asked to work on ganging teams to supply the colliery with materials—chock nogs, boards, tins, rings, plates, panzer chain chocks, Dowty, and Gullick—which we will do during the course of the week. I'll split you into pairs so you can learn light signals with the cap lamp. You'll also be put through all the safety features.

On my first day at Linston Colliery, Daz and Alex stood in the foyer when I walked in. "Max, over here," Alex said. I walked over to them. "What you doing here?"

"I work here," I said.

"What, you started here at this pit?"

"Yep," I said with a smile.

Daz said, "Hey, that's a team. Have they given you a locker yet?"

"No, I have to see . . . Erm . . ." I fidgeted with a letter. "Mr Whirl."

"That's development, you jammy swine," Alex butted in. "Old Terry will put you right; he's the overman. That's all the best jobs. We are on seventeen's ganging."

"Yep, I did some of that already."

Daz stopped me. "You've seen nothing, mate. Wait till you see where we are working—the roof's buckled right in."

"What you got fer yer snap?" Alex inquired.

"Nothing yet."

"Canteens through there; pasties are brill." Daz pointed out the way. I could smell the bacon sammies being cooked as men walked through and joined the queue.

"Hey, forget that fer a minute; go and see Terry. He's in deployment." Daz pointed the other way. "Through there. Third blackboard down."

I walked in, looking at the boards that stood on a waist-high bench. Groups of men stood around, some in work clothes. sampling each other's snuff. The smell of chewing tobacco and fags lingered, and the whole place seemed to have this blue haze.

I walked down to third board. "Look, he ain't even changed yet," said the man I believed I was looking. "Name?" he asked.

"Max Rocks," I chirped.

"Ah, new face. Let me see. Right, you need that." He handed me a new motley with my pit number on it. "And sign here fer that. Take that to the shower attendant, and he'll issue you with a locker and key. Where's your work clothes?"

"I ain't had any yet," I replied.

"Take this line down to the stores."

"Erm, where's the stores?" I asked as I took the piece of paper.

"Out the main exit and over to your right." He pointed out the window and over the pit yard to a hanger marked "Stores" over the door.

I got vest and pants in green, orange trousers and jacket, and no socks. My helmet was bright yellow, and I had a self-rescuer belt, steelies, and a donkey jacket. I walked through to the shower reception and also the medical area. An older man in round rimmed glasses gave me a locker key. "Clean clothes this side. Dirty clothes that side." I got changed at one locker, walking through the showers to the change at the next set. "Sign here." I was soon changed and stood back in deployment.

Daz and Alex stood both in their work clothes eating hot pasties at the second board, which was marked "17ns coalface." They were talking to the deputy on the other side of the desk.

Terry called me over. "Right, yer on track laying with Simpson." The name sounded familiar. He took two more motes from the board, wrote in my name on the board, and placed the motes in my hand. "Give one to the onsetter when you go down and one to come back up."

I turned around and saw someone I knew from school. "Hey, Sinbad."

"First day, Max?" he said.

"I didn't know you worked here."

"Since I left school. Got plenty off snap with ya."

"I'd forgotten about it, Sinbad."

"Have you clocked on yet?" he asked.

"Erm no."

"Well, you'd best do that first. I'll take you over. Come on." We walked across the yard and into the lamp cabin. I found a card with my name on it as I looked in the rack. "Just look fer yer number. It's on your mote," Sinbad said.

I clocked on and took a battery, light pack, and a self-rescuer, slipping them on my belt. "Have I time to get some grub from canteen?"

"If ya hurry. Hey, you haven't kept yer locker key, have you?"

"Why yes, I have it here."

"You'll need to put that back on the wall in the attendants room; you can't take that down with you—you might lose it."

"Oh, okay. I just need to get some dollars for the canteen."

"And that's another thing—don't leave cash and valuables in yer locker." I frowned, and Sinbad added, "Give anything of value to the shower attendant; he'll keep it for you till you come back up from the mine."

I came back out the shower room and put the key back on the wall, finding the hook with its number.

"The only way to get the key is to show your mote to the attendant. You'll also need to show that to the cashier on Thursday or Friday, when you draw yer wages."

"Erm, yeah, I'm familiar with that part of it," I said.

"You've got five minutes till we go over to the headstocks. Go get yer canteen. I'll wait in deployment and find out where we are."

I could hear the familiar chuff of the engine, powered by steam, as we stood ready to go down. "Hey it's warm as toast. Why is that?" We were in the pit bottom, just stepping out of the cage.

"This is the return side of the pit; all the air in the mine comes back this way."

We walked past some sidings and through to a track where a diesel locomotive sat complete with riding carriages. The whole place was whited out on the brick reinforcing. "That's the old stables down there, where they used to keep the ponies. It's now a loco garage." Sinbad pointed out the direction.

"Hey, can we go see? I wanna take a look," I said, curious.

"We'll need to come down earlier next time. This way." We walked alongside the carriages. Sinbad looked in each one. "In here, Max."

Daz and Alex sat playing cards. Hey, Max, you made it down then," Daz said as we entered the carriage. "Mars bars, Max. You playing?"

"Yeah, man, deal me in. Sinbad, are you in?"

"Yeah, sure."

We sat playing three-card brag. "Highest hand takes a Mars bar, to be paid on Friday," Daz remarked. "I'll keep note of it here in me book." He beamed after he let out a loud long fart. "Phew, that's humming." We all had our heads out the carriage. Soon we were playing cards as the carriages pulled away.

The ride was like that of a ghost train in a fairground, except here you got your money's worth. We clipped our cap lamps into the steel works above our heads on side light, which provided enough light for the dealing of the cards. I was up three hands by the time we got to the top of the drift, where we stopped.

"Right, all change, Houston station," Alex joked as we stepped out.

"Now what?" I asked Daz.

"Another train to catch, Max. A haulage man rider."

"Crikey, how far in do we go?"

"Another fifteen minutes yet. Then we're only at the bottom of the drift. We have to walk from there."

I tried to watch where I was going. "We are on track, move up, on twenty-fours." Sinbad looked pleased. "Told ya, didn't I, Daz? Jammy swine's got the best job. The lye be going out the pit at 12.30." Alex sounded off.

"Jammy, git licking Terry's ass already. Look, all brown around his nose. All I got was a button job when I first started." Daz had his light up to my face.

"Button job? What's that?" I inquired.

"Sat on a road end watching a conveyer belt all the time during the shift. You haven't seen that yet, Max—it's on the intake side."

"Where's twenty-fours?" I asked.

"Turn left, bottom of the drift. It's top end of the loco track. We are going that way, seventeen's is just out by from twenty four's," Alex replied.

We stepped onto the man rider; this was an open-top version of what we'd already been on, but cable driven. I looked down the drift at all the twisted and buckled rings and broken boards and bent tins. "Well, at least the track looks straight," I thought. "Is it a coal face?" I asked, and they all burst out laughing. "Well, I don't know, do I?"

"Yeah, Max, they're all numbered," Alex butted in, snapping back.

Daz put his hand on my shoulder. "You'll soon see patience; calm down. Cards, lads." Daz was already shuffling them.

Sinbad had his tin out. "Pinch, anyone?"

I took one and then another, placing it on my wrist in neat piles. Then the breeze sort of scattered it before I got it to my nostrils. Daz, who sat opposite of me, cracked up with laughter. "Give us a pinch, Sinbad. Like this, look, Max." Daz took it straight from the tin and held the pinch to his nostril. "Try again," he said as Sinbad held the tin out.

I took the pinch as I was shown. I couldn't stop sneezing all the way to the bottom of the drift. "Was that yer first pinch of snuff, Max?"

"Yeah—achoo!" I was still at it as we came to a halt. Daz put away the cards, and Alex tallied the score in his book. "Right, Max, we owe you five bars each."

"Hey, how do they work that out?" I asked. "And what am I going to do with twenty bars?" I was puzzled.

"Keep playing." Sinbad seemed confident. "We've got all week." The end of the week, came, and I owed sixteen Mars bars to Daz.

Six months later, I was put with a team on what they call development. The team had not long completed twenty-fours and was placed on the development of a new face, on threes at the other side of the pit. Little Fred asked me what I had on my snap, and I told him it was hare. Fred had this knack; it was snap time, and I knew the next question. "I haven't tried hare; can I get a bit?" Fred replied. I offered him a sandwich of which he took gladly. "Hey, that's nice. I like hare; can you get any more?"

"Sure, Fred."

"What's that I've tried?"

"Duck, pheasant, and venison. You're getting to be a connoisseur."

Lou had a quiet word with me—"'Cause you come down here and help out with materials, look after him, and you'll always get yer 65 per cent bonus. Upset him and it could be 50 per cent, if you know what I mean." Somehow they'd wangled it with the overman that I should get 65 per cent of the development bonus, which was different from the 100 per cent on a coal cutting contract. When worked out, 100 per cent of coal cutting was often around the same as 65 per cent of development bonus, which boosted my wages considerably. "You're all heart, Max."

Little Fred enjoyed his sandwich as Big Lou started the Dosco, and the whole place filled with dust. I stood and watched the big white monster's rotating boom tear away at the rock. The spotlights followed wherever the boom and cutter went. I was stood up on the Dosco next to Lou, who was driving it. Phil and Charlie smashed the lumps at the front end. The tins above clattered and cracked as the weight came on to them. I somehow got used to hearing the groans and the creeks. That Dosco was pure heavy industrial violence as its tracks cracked and creaked backwards and forwards. Then all was silent and dark except for the cap lamps that showed the dust for its real thickness. And that was with the built-in water sprays. The team kept on cutting.

When the dust settled, everyone took down their masks to speak. "Max, help Phil with the rings and then go down and start the chain."

"Right, Lou," I said as I jumped to it. These rings were sixteen by twelve—we were talking heavy shit. The Dosco did the rest with ease after the ring had been assembled and the struts were put on loosely, using the lifting chains and the boom. In an exposed environment, there was no cover in the freshly cut rock. The Dosco had two umbilical arms at the front of it to sweep the rock onto its roller system feed that dropped onto a conveyer.

I often watched for the oversized rocks and broke them with a sledgehammer. I could start the belt at the panels and move it along and then latch it out from the development end. Once the belt was full, all I had to do was walk down and start the chain and clear the back log onto the mainstream belts. From the chain I would watch for the stakers—usually big lumps that had got through and blocked the chute to the mainstream. I'd had that before, and it was a nightmare. The operator on the previous shift had left me all his spillage, and I'd spent the whole shift clearing it up—resulting in a tenner each from the guys on the previous shift, to make amends after I complained about it. Terry fined them for leaving the job in such a state after he himself had seen me clearing it up. That's what happened when they cut from the bottom up.

"Too much to handle," Lou commented when he handed me the shovel. "All four of 'em Muckin' in fer the first hour of the shift." I'd noticed Lou would always cut from the top and work down, taking out the centre. "The way they've been doing it is tough on the picks. I'm sick of leaving messages fer 'em." I also knew what Lou meant by that. We'd been stopped a few times while fitters replaced new picks to the cutting barrel at the end of the boom; the gangers had to bring fresh timber after the previous shift used it all, timbering up the big holes that dropped out the freshly cut works. Picks are the teeth on the Dosco's rotating cutting boom.

Lou had worked the headings for ten years; Terry had pulled him off the coal face. So Lou knew the score. Harry the deputy would often jot down the cutting times before assembly. I used to sit with him on occasion. He'd say Lou always beat the other shifts on the cutting and seventeen by twelve ring assembly. I questioned old Harry's activities because he was the one with the Davey lamp. Each shift would confer come the end of the week, he said, just to see who cut it. That's where old Harry got the name Big Hitter.

Now the whole deployment was filled with laughter. Butsey had just put down the phone after he checked out my story. Butsey was the deputy on the other shift that followed in the same heading I worked. I'd slept in and phoned to ask to go on afternoons, which was granted. Butsey had phoned the local rozzers and found out who had got cleared out the Lido the night before after I explained I was steaming drunk. The Lido was an open-air swimming pool at the edge of town. My fizz fitted one of the names that had been taken as details by one of the officers, who had been caught on the high diving board after the police besieged it. We had refused to come down. They noticed we stood chattering, and the two officers, one male and one female, got wise and told us, "It's okay, we're not letting you down. If you do, we're arresting you, and you'll be in the cells for the rest of the night. So you can stay up there for one hour, and then we might consider letting you go." Well, after the novelty had worn off and we had stuck it for an hour, we cracked. Man, I was getting blue in the lips. Even iron man Burt had goosebumps that looked like golf balls.

The conversation with Winnie went on. "Ha ha, I seen him bomb drop you," Winnie remarked.

"Yeah, straight after I dived off and performed a mistimed roll and spin that ended up in a belly flop. Then whilst I was under, Burt held me under, so I made a grab for his knackers. He soon let go." We roared with laughter.

Winnie, who also happened to be there at the Lido party, said, "Well, he was pissed as a newt." I rambled on. "Winnie had been sober and stood talking to me outside the Welfare and had agreed it had been a hot, steamy sort of a day. It seemed like a good idea to go and cool down, so where better to do it—except the Lido shut at 8.00PM, and we happened to have scaled the fence at 12.30pm. Winnie drove us down in his Capri with myself and two broads; Paula and Leann, who overheard us talking, wanted to accompany us. We took a ghetto blaster and a selection of tapes from the boot of Winnie's car, and twelve cans of beer. I got out of the Welfare at last orders." Butsey was crying with laughter, urging me to go on, whilst Winnie stood like a nodding donkey smiling at the story.

"As we stood on the top diving board, besieged by the local police, Burt got impatient. 'I don't know about you, but I'm going down,' he remarked, and we all followed and descended one by one. The officers were waiting at the bottom and took our details, and they also wanted to know who the instigators of the Lido party were. Winnie was one of those who had, and hoofed it with the broads when the police first showed up, leaving me there on the high board, stranded. Burt was the first down and the first questioned. 'Well, it started out with just us,' he told them. 'Ain-'t that right, Max?' I nodded and Burt sounded convincing. Then he told them, 'A few more as passers-by came in. Well, the next thing I know there's around twenty of us swimming about. Ain-'t that right, Max?'

'Well, yeah,' I muttered whilst I stood freezing to death.

Winnie had left behind his ghetto blaster, whilst Wham's song 'Club Tropicana' boomed out in the background." All three of us were crying with laughter. I took a breath. "The female officer had seen the funny side and ordered us on our way. I put on my clothes and gathered up Winnie's and the two broads' clothes, placed them in my shoulder bag, took hold of the boom box, and was shown out through the main gate by the police and a key-holder. Bert was still laughing as he phoned a taxi from the phone box just across the road. We shared the fare, and it dropped me at Market Place. I made my way to Winnie's, who lived just a couple of blocks away and had come to the door and burst out laughing. He took me down to Paula's, where I produced her clothes and some un-drunk cans of lager. Her folks were away on a weekend break. I was invited in, and we partied, I stayed the night on the sofa. Leann had the spare room."

Butsey was still laughing at the story and put me on locos for the shift.

The next morning I walked into the usual gathering, straight away. Lou said, "I see you recovered from Lido fever, then." It started the whole deployment laughing, but on my own shift this time. I sort of laughed with them, but the jokes wore thin. I was just about to venture on what they call a doubler—coming off afternoons and going back on day shift. Lou had said I looked whacked and ordered me to stay out and work the chain. "Don't fall asleep," he warned as they went on up the heading. Well, the chain had been running constant with no dirt falling onto it, so I'd stopped the chain.

The next thing I know Big Phil had me under the armpits, pulling me free from all the debris. "Fer fuck's sake, Max. It's a good job I came to check on you. Just as I woke, you nearly got buried alive." He laid me back in the middle of the track and latched out the belt, pulling at the green cable after he dug for it. "Didn't you hear us buzz ya at snap time?"

"Erm . . ." I was still in a daze.

Phil had had to clear his way through from the roof. They'd started the belt from the panels, thinking I'd gone on walkabout creek and left the chain running. After I'd stopped the chain, the belt feed from the heading had been running with dirt coming of it. You can work out the rest. The whole of the two headings had to bail me out. That was nine of us plus two deputies cursing me blind whilst we shovelled the huge mound back onto the chain. I had to buy them all a mixture of bacon sammies and pasties when we got showered, to keep their gobs shut in case Terry found out.

Chapter Three

APPROXIMATELY A YEAR LATER.

It was a Friday. I had been put on locos for a few weeks whilst Flinty, a dev loco ganger, was off work after he had trapped his foot under a ring whilst he lost his grip unloading seventeen by twelves. I'd been talking to Lou and Phil. Terry walked over and stood at the development board. "What's this I hear—you can use a trowel?" Terry was waiting for an explanation.

"Well, yes, I can," I replied.

"Right, I'm putting you in with Duffy and never sweat, building substations and air doors days regular. You will be on the half twelve-man rider, out the pit to order materials to be taken into your district, starting on Monday—you don't clock of till time, though." Terry put up his finger to warn me and make the point. "Wait for Duffy at the bottom of the drift. Abe will point him out." Abe was the head loco driver and knew most folks. Terry went on to say, "Your last shift on loco's today."

By now I was getting quite a stock of Mars bars at home, having had a good few runs with Daz and the crew.

"Changed job, lads," I said as I settled in to the man rider, playing with my frozen orange.

"What's that, then, road end?" Aleck butted in.

"Nah, development still. Building substations and air doors."

Their faces dropped. "You mean you're out on the half twelve?" Daz asked. I nodded. Daz had meant the half-twelve man-rider that took the pit bosses out of the mine first. "Why, you . . . Look, clag nuts round his nostrils—he's been that far up." Daz shined his light on my nose.

"I ain't never been on a road end. Don't insult me." I shone my light into Alex's eyes, and then I stuck my nose in the air. "Cards." I pointed to Daz's top pocket.

"Oh, yes, your royal highness." Daz liked to be cheeky.

"Friggin' best job again—I don't know how he does it," Alex moaned.

"Stop whinin', Alex," Daz said whilst shuffling the cards. "We all know he's the man for the job." Daz started to deal the cards. as the man-rider pulled away.

At the bottom of the drift, I found Abe and sat while he looked at the materials in-by movement tasks. Abe also knew why I got kicked off locos a few months ago: after I worked the summer holidays, Terry knew I wouldn't be paid holiday money until the second year of employment, so I'd been asked to work the holiday.

Chalky, whom I was teamed up with at the time, had put about the pit that I had his sticky seconds and wouldn't work with me over nicking his girlfriend, Meg, then had told the rest of the gangers that I'd been with her the same night as him, calling me a low-down, dirty snake in the grass. We'd just unloaded in the heading and I had jumped in the 1st tub and circled my lamp to reverse out by.

I'd signalled side to side to stop whilst I jumped down and opened the safety gate. Abe nodded as I circled my lamp, moving the locos out through the opened safety gate. I stopped as I signalled my lamp side to side and slid the safety bar back through the stays on the safety gate, before I jumped back on the loco's rear. After we passed through, Abe moved the unloaded train on out.

Snap time had come, and the conveyers had drawn to a halt. "Right, Max, what's eating Chalky?" Abe asked as he reached in the parked loco that was sat in the sidings for our snap bags.

"Well it was like this," I started as we walked down the gate away from the chug and the fumes of the loco, which was left running. We found a good quiet spot and then arranged some stone dust bags to sit on and propped up some boards for back rests. "Well then, I'd traded my own road dirt bike, a TS 185, for an off-roader, a KE 175, with Raggy, one of the bikers I used to hang around with from the school club. He recently bought a Colt Celeste 1600cc in sporty red for 750 sovs. Poor man's Ferrari, I called it."

"Yeah, go on," Abe prompted.

"I'd sat in the bar with Pellet and Raggy, having just done the deal with the bike, when Meg walked in and asked if I'd go over the road and see Jill. Sure, I'd said as I finished my Diet Coke and walked over the road with her. When we walked in the house, Jill asked if she could get a small loan until she got paid, and I gladly handed over the money.

"'Is that yours?" Meg asked as she marvelled the Colt and its alloy, sixteen-inch wheels. I'd knew she'd seen me park it up before going into the bar. Now, Jill had been one of the better youth leaders at the school club in the early years and had taken Meg in as a lodger.

"'Come on, I'll take ya for a spin,' I said, and she grabbed her pink denim with sequins around the shoulders in lace. We'd been to the Harvest bar outta town and had gone from there to Mecca Village on the motorway and passed the time eating fries and taking turns on the pinball. Meg wasn't too hot at playing it but was learning. We pulled in at the abbey on the way back and . . . well, one thing led to another."

Abe nodded as he checked his watch. "Yeah, but you knew Chalky was going with her," he said.

I stopped him. "He's been putting his hand down his trousers and saying, 'Smell my cheese,' after stuffing his fingers up my nose when we are man-riding the cage. So I told Meg." Abe couldn't stop laughing. "It was her who said that's a dirty trick and then asked me to give her a good seeing to. I never told anyone about it—until Chalky told everyone, and you're the first I've opened me mush to."

Abe stopped laughing. "It'll blow over, Max," he said as he got up to take a leak.

"He's never done it since," I commented.

Abe burst out laughing again. He drew back up his fly and said, "Do you know him and little Andy went to Palace Night Spot in the city and scored a couple women? Andy walked his home, along with Chalky and the bit he pulled. Andy reckoned previously he'd been snoggin' with her half the night whilst in there and even took a smoochie last dance of the night, claiming Chalky was all over it."

"Does Meg know?"

"I wouldn't have thought he'd have told her." I sighed quietly as Abe carried on. "Do you know Chalky got her into her flat, halfway up Victoria Centre?" Well, he's got her in the bedroom. He pulled her skirt up and got a shock." Abe looked serious.

"What you mean, got a shock?" I asked.

Abe pointed to a set of lifting chains that sat next to a block and tackle set. "Well, it had a set of them in its tights." I put my hand over me eyes in sympathy. "Andy claims he came running out the bedroom white as a sheet and told Andy to get running. 'It's a bloke, it's a bloke!' he kept shouting as they stepped in the elevator. Little Andy claimed it was a blonde bombshell, though he thought her voice was a bit deep at the time."

After we'd stopped roaring with laughing, I assured Abe, "That will be one of little Andy's likely stories. I've known him years—he tells 'em, ya know."

"I think it's true," Abe said. "There's some dodgy people living in those flats in the city. TVs an all that." Abe got up and threw his left-over snap on the conveyer belt.

"I ain't seen Meg around for a while since," I said to Abe. "I've been told by Jill she joined the police force. She was going on about it at Mecca." Abe went silent. Soon the hour dinner was over as the alarm signalled to restart the belts.

Monday came, and I sat at the bottom of the drift. "Here he comes now, Max. Duffy, over here." Abe directed him over as he separated from the rest of the men who had just stepped off the man rider and were walking in to their allocated jobs.

"Ah, you must be Max. We're over on threes." Duffy was looking at a row of tubs in the sidings and spotted the building blocks in three of them, with threes chalked on the side. "Hey that's same new face heading as Lou and crew. It was them who told Terry you are a builder."

Oh, now the penny dropped. "What about tools?" I asked.

"Don't worry about that; here's the worry." An older, grey-haired fellow walked up towards us, helmet tilted back.

"Who's that?" I asked.

"Never sweat," Duffy replied. "We'll be down to our vests, and He'll still have his donkey jacket on. He likes to go for walks—especially when you want him."

"Walkabout Creek," I corrected him.

Never Sweat joined us and looked me up and down. He looked like he was handy with a hod.

"Oy, less of the hod. I'm the mechanic, not the oil rag," I said. Duffy started to laugh at my outburst.

Abe stopped and joined the conversation. "Well, I wanted him back on here. Max had the locos off to a T." Abe was biggin' me up. "I kept asking Terry for Max."

"I've got a good one at last, then?" Duffy inquired.

"Yeah, grafter," Abe said.

I'd been on locos a few times when they were short on staff since the summer holidays. Time in the mine seemed to fly by on that job because I was always on the move. The locos that worked the face gates were smaller in size, although all the track was same gauge as the locos that brought us into the mine. The loco gangers took materials to the end of the gates, where it was then taken in by different set of tailgate gangers. That was where materials were moved in by haulage down to the coal face. Loader gate was the opposite end of the coal face that housed the conveyer belt system; also the air was pulled into the face via the loader gate and exited at the tailgate. The gangers would often have to rearrange and unload onto the haulage system due to floor lift and weight on the rings. The coal face was kept in constant supply of timber, nogs, boards, rings, struts, chocks, plates, and boxes of nuts and bolts to hold the lot together. Daz and Alex did this job on seventeen's with Ralph the mouth, who drove the haulage whilst Daz and Alex took the run.

Right here I marked it in the track. "Look," I said as I shone my light on the chalk mark Duffy had made. He went to a steel lock-up and undid the padlock.

"Well, at least Abe got that bit right." Duffy meant he got the location of the tool box right as he squeaked open the lid, pulling out a trowel and a brick hammer and throwing them at my feet; he also handed me a spirit level and measuring tape. "Abe will have our blocks here soon, so don't you walk off."

Never Sweat had his hands up and changed the subject. "Right who's got a nice warm pasty for me, then?"

"Don't give him nothing, Max, that's what he does—goes on the scrounge. That's another reason he goes walkabout."

I started to laugh. "So you go by Never Sweat?"

Never sweat chirped up. "Hey that's a truly well-earned name, and I like to live up to it, thank you very much." Never Sweat was serious.

Duffy broke out his flask. "Tea, lads, or coffee; I got both. Might as well have a minute."

"Yeah, sure, Duffy. Coffee please, mate, milk and one sugar." A white, badly chipped steel enamelled mug of hot coffee duly arrived in my hands. I noticed we were out by the bottom of threes. The air was a lot colder. "I think I'll keep me donkey on," I said as I laid the mug where I could find it and hitched up my collar. I set out a couple of stone dust bags and laid a few loose boards against the side for a back rest, picking up my mug and sitting down, warming my hands. Never Sweat and Duffy did the same.

"Inside the hour, Abe said." Duffy took his time piece from his tin and looked at it. "I told Terry we'd have this up and working within the week."

I spat out a large mouthful a hot coffee. "What's up? Too hot fer ya?" Never Sweat joked.

I knew in normal circumstances that the job would have been three days, max. But this was a mine, and conditions changed. "Easy pay," I thought. "Easy."

Abe and the blocks arrived, and we unloaded the tubs and placed everything where we wanted it, the sand and cement and the blocks all stacked neatly. Abe even remembered to throw in the spots for the cement mix. Never Sweat knocked up a mix and got us going, and then he did his disappearing act. "He'll be down at the gate bothering the headers," Duffy said.

"He'll have a job getting anything outta little Fred," I said as I picked up the trowel. I set a block level to the chalk mark and lined it through to Duffy, who then measured out the door opening.

Snap time came. "That's okay on the surface," Duffy said, "but it won't stand up to the weight down here. You need to change the bond around like this."

I shone my light on his side to see. "Yep, got ya." I made note of it and eventually did mine the same before we got to halfway up to door height. Now every time the loco passed us, we had to take down the string line, which made it a bind. Abe's gangers would toot as they came to the corner of the junction end to warn us.

Terry made a comment on the work, explaining, "Don't worry, Max. It's up and started, that's the main thing, and you don't have to point it up, either, although I do like to know you can do it."

"Yes, Boss," I said as I took a pinch a snuff and offered some to Terry, who had fingers like sausages and half emptied my tin.

Duffy laughed, and Terry said, "Right, lads, carry on," as he made his way out.

"We'll be off soon," Duffy said, and he started to clean his trowel. "Down tools, Max. That's us laid the last blocks of the shift." He looked at his time piece. "It's 11.40. A coffee first, and we'll make our way out." Duffy reached for his flask.

"What, you mean we really do catch the half-twelve manrider?" I stopped what I was doing.

"Yep."

"Oh, I thought they were kidding."

"Nope. Days regular and the first manrider out. And you still get 65 per cent dev bonus. Mint, man."

"I like this job," I decided.

Six months later I stood at the bar in the Welfare. "Here, that's from me dad," Lorrain said as she pushed a twenty-sovereign note into my hand. I'd been out on strike for just over a month and was beginning to feel the pinch. She knew I needed the cash. Her dad was my deputy in the headings.

I thought on old Harry, Fred, and Lou and hugged her waist. "Tell old Harry thank you."

"Now, what you having to drink, Max??"

"Lager, doll."

A lager and a Jack Daniels and coke arrived in front of me. "It'll be cold when you go picketing," she said. I looked at my watch. "I'm coming with ya," she said, grabbing at my arm.

Plute and a few others off different shifts stood around a brazier near the main gate. "It'll be area ballot," they were saying as we walked up to them. Loz was warming her hands.

"What do you mean, area ballot?" I asked Plute.

"There's a ruling in the NUM rules that states a national ballot cannot be held over redundancy. I just came from the meeting at Berry Hill, so it will be judged by area ballot. McGreggor is out to wheel his axe."

A few miners passed in their cars as the night shift started to arrive. Some Rozzers stood at the brazier, keeping quiet as Plute jumped out into the road, flagging down the faces he knew and pleading with them. "Come on, man, it's your jobs we're fighting for," he urged them to vote in favour.

The two officers stepped over to him on his return. "Sir I must ask you to reframe from standing in the road to the main gate; you must keep to the grass verges." Plute knew not to argue with them and took heed.

Then we started to see the bulk of the shift come in. "Man that must have been fourteen or so cars that reversed and turned back," I noted as we cheered. Some even parked outside the main gates and joined us.

"Yes!" Plute said. "Now they've got a fight on their hands."

Loz put her arms around my waist. "Come on, Max, walk me home. I'll buy you fish and chips." I wished the pickets good night as we left.

We sat in the gate house on the park, just chatting. Loz had remembered the old days, although I only remembered her face as it all came flashing back.

"And ya never saved me a chock ice," she mumbled as she crumpled up her chip paper and threw it at me.

"Oy! Bins over there!" I pointed towards the swings. I still had a big lump of cod in batter and was enjoying it as Loz picked up her wrapper and waited for me to finish. "Remember how we used to skateboard everywhere?" I asked, and Loz smiled. "I wish I had it tonight." I screwed up the rest of the cold chips and wrappings and swilled down the last of the Cod with my coke. I took the wrapper from her hands and ran over to the bin and back. "Now, tonight was a result," I said upon returning. "I think our pit will vote in favour to strike."

Loz had her fingers crossed. "Me dad's backing you." I smiled; although I knew deputies were another union, he'd still have to give cover to any NUM members still working. "Time I was in," Loz said, pulling at me to walk her home.

A week passed. Linston voted in favour by 80 per cent to strike, and most stood out on the picket lines around the colliery; there were also pickets from Yorkshire who welcomed our stand. I recognized one of the lads from Markham Main and stood chatting with him. They'd been out weeks before me. I'd agreed not to cross when I first met the fella. The police were increasing their numbers and had been using closing-in techniques, forcing the pickets over on to the grass verge. They started pulling out the Yorkshire pickets, arresting them and then taking them away. I could not believe what I was seeing: grown, working men battling with the law. This was getting out of hand as police started pulling out Linston miners and beating them with their truncations on attempts to resist arrest. This started as peaceful and was being aggravated. Miners started lashing out into the blue line, which struggled to hold them back. Police helmets where getting knocked off and pinched; uniforms were tugged and pulled at. Then later twelve white meat wagons pulled up. The doors flew open, and riot police ran to the line and lined up as the original line fell back behind the new row of shields. I could see more scuffles right in front of me, resulting in more arrests. The shields pushed me back as officers reached out, taking the Yorkshire picket.

Later I stood talking to a few who had fallen over. Man, this was a war, Spartacus style, as the police battered their shields, which caused a lull. I saw grown men crying over the new events. This was serious stuff; I only wish I'd taken a camera because the press where forced away by the police during hostilities.

Then the afternoon shift started to arrive. Shouts of "Scab" hurled out from the crowd as the 20 per cent crawled past the gates. The pickets broke through the shields into their path under chants of "Get a wedge on, lads." the police counteracted by letting them gain ground before forcing back the intrusion. Police fell out from the ends of the line and grouped up in the middle, striking everything in their path that was breaking through. I had seen blood pouring from head wounds as picketers pulled other men back from the clutches of the shields and the onslaught.

Later that evening it was broadcasted on the main news that any picketers flying pickets would be arrested if they were found to come from another area.

Four months into the strike. Sam the music man and I stood in the queue for a food parcel. We called Sam the music man because he'd often make up good tapes of not so well-known bands, like The The, Section Twenty-Five, Devoto, The Three Johns, Stockholm Monsters, And The Wake. I would often listen to them on my Walkman whilst standing on the picket line.

Sam smoked cannabis and took speed, and he often would offer it to me. I would just be sociable and join in, getting absolutely off my face on occasion. I started to meet people within the drug circle—mostly miners from other pits. Sam worked at Chuckwalla and had been on strike the same amount of time as myself. He had seen what had been happening on picket lines.

"Well, I don't know about you, but I'm outta here next week," I said.

"Got a ticket, then?" he replied.

"Yep, Lorret de Mar, here we come. Sold me video and hi-fi and me car. Here's the ticket; sixty-eight sovs open return, six sovs to get to London, and the rest spending money." I opened the roll of cash.

"Traveller's cheques," Sam intervened. "You need to change that fer them. Get 'em at the travel agents. It's harder fer anyone to steal."

"Can you make some tapes up fer me an Eric?" I asked.

"Is he going again?"

"Yeah. Talked me into going. Different woman every night, he reckons." Sam laughed. He too had sat and listened to Eric's escapades in Spain last year. "I got to see fer myself." Sam nodded.

It was April during the year-long strike, and we'd just come out of the underpass as the lights came bright. We were moving through Paris when I woke; I'd gotten drunk on the ferry and had been sleeping it off. It was 12.00 PM, and Eric was laughing and joking with a few cockneys that sat towards the rear of the bus. A friend who he'd shared a room with last year hadn't turned up at the bus station, but *his* friends did, and Eric had already met two of them before. "We'll get the same hostel," one of them commented, "Hostel Palu."

We arrived at the Lorret bus station at around 6.15PM. The air was warm, evidence of a hot and sunny day. "This way," Eric remarked as we walked the narrow back streets. A club, Dirty 30, was on the corner of the street that led to Hostel Palu. All the small, rendered, white-washed buildings were mostly souvenir outlets, and restaurants seemed to be onwards from there as I looked down the street, noticing it was packed with holiday makers, with mainly German, Spanish, and some English being spoken. I took it that was the way down to the promenade. "Donde este la Playa," Eric corrected me in Spanish just as I looked left and saw the route up to the bigger hotels.

An old Spanish woman sat in her living room when we entered the Hotel Palu, which doubled as reception. She asked for our passports and explained it was 250 pesetas per night each for the two-bedroom. I took the bulk of my changed Spanish money, leaving me with around 1000 pesetas and 200 sovs in cheques. We paid three weeks in advance as she gave each of us a key. "You can get this back when you change traveller's cheques, or if you decided to leave," she said in half English and half Spanish. She got up and placed our passports and the money into a safe.

The room was quite large with built-in wardrobes, which locked with a key. We opened a door that stood between them to find a shower room and wash basin and toilet. To left in the main room was a pair of French doors with the shutters closed. I beelined to open them to let in the light, selecting the bed nearest the window, which was single and neatly made up. Eric set up his stereo using matches to plug the wires into the two-phase sockets (he forgot his adapter) and started the music going.

I looked out the window, which looked over the back of Dirty 30. The sea lay beyond the pan-tiled roofs, the sky was a light cobalt blue. "Hey, a room with a view. Is that where you've been poaching the women from?" I asked as I looked at the club.

"Nah, they won't let anyone not a resident in," Eric said as he started to unpack his belongings.

There was a knock at the door. One of the cockneys we'd left at the station came in. "We've took another hostel closer the beach," he said after he sat on Eric's bed. "Got a pen?" I undid my case and found him one and a notepad, and he wrote down the hotel name. "Sancose at 7.30; we'll all meet there."

"Sancose, what's that?" I asked Eric after the cockney left.

"Bar Sancose—you get a big bowl of soup of the day, an evening dinner, and apple pie an ice cream fer 150 pesetas; a pint of beer is included."

I was gob smacked. "How much?" I rubbed my hands. "What do you get fer dinner?"

"We don't," Eric said. "Go all day and then just get that at night, at Sancose. It gets too hot to eat during the day."

"But it's only April."

"You'll see tomorrow," he joked. "Right, I'm off in the shower."

Sancose was starting to get busy. The two cockneys had already ordered and had picked a table near the window. "Over here, guys," they said as we stood at the bar as we studied the set meal and ordered. We went and sat down. The boys said their room had cost them 300 per night, each. It wasn't long before the grub arrived with ice cold beer.

"Hey what's that? That's not a pint," I said. The glass was long and tall, with Damn written on it.

"It's a litre," Eric said.

I studied my plate: a steaming hot bowl of spicy minestrone soup and bread rolls served in a basket with small portions of butter. We slurped and conversed. "Which part of the Old Smoke are you from, then?" I asked the cockneys.

"I'm from Battersea and he's from Bognor."

"What is it you do?"

One of them told of how he went door to door with kitchen accessories and acted deaf and dumb, and how he showed a card that introduced himself. The other was a carpet dealer. I placed my hand over my eyes in response to the con man.

"Why, what do you do?" he asked.

"He works at a colliery, and he's on strike, and you know what I do—or did," Eric remarked. He'd just given up his job at meat processing factory.

"You're a striking miner?" one of them asked, and then he went serious. I wondered if Eric had said the right thing. "Ah, brilliant, mate!" He reached out to take my hand. The other guy was an obviously a Tory as he made comments of how we should go back to work.

The main meal arrived: half a well-roasted chicken, roasted spuds, mashed spuds, peas, carrots, a big slice of stuffing, and Yorkshire pudding, all topped out with gravy. The food turned a three-on-one heated debate about the strike into silence as we all got stuck in our food. We'd opted for an early night as Eric showed the way along the prom (playa), passing the viewpoint on the rocks and turning left up the main drag, calling in at a few bodega bars on the way, where live Spanish music in a Gypsy style was being performed.

I enquired about the bar's origins, and a well-spoken Spanish bartender gave me the scoop: it was a seventeenth-century piece. I looked up at all the meat hanging above my head. "Cured ham," he commented. "You try some maybe, with olives in oil." I was still stuffed from Sancose and declined as I took my half of lager and sat down, listening to the music. Eric retired to the hostel after he drunk his.

Two local girls dressed in traditional style were Spanish dancing in the middle of the small dance floor. Then two female's came and sat down. After a brief conversation I found out they where Dutch and had been here for nearly two weeks—and this was there last night. They spoke surprisingly good English. "We have plenty of sangria and tequila, if you want to come and party."

"Yep." I'd drunk my drink and was up like a greyhound at the offer. I walked arm and arm between them along the prom and to a posh hotel.

The view was stunning as I walked out onto the veranda. This was the ninth floor, and I looked at the sea as flecks of light played on its surface. The music soon was up and pumping in the main room, and I was offered a drink by one of the two blondes when I walked back through. We sat on the veranda, but it was not all that wide, and we shuffled about. The girls had told me their names were Hanna and Ulna, and that they worked in a large jewellery store in the city. They were very well tanned.

There was a knock at the door, and more people arrived from next door—a German family that spoke good English. The male introduced himself, his wife, his daughter, and his son. The kids were in their early teens and were now dancing with Ulna in the main room. I thought about Eric getting his early night.

"Yes, we are in favour of your cause," the father, Jan, said when I told him of my situation. We sat chatting about the strike until the small hours, and the family left, wishing me luck.

I woke with Ulna around 9.15AM. "Phew, Max, what a party," she said as she rose out of bed. "We need to pack—do you mind?" I took the hint and left them to it. I got dressed, pecking them both on the cheek and wishing a safe flight.

The late morning sun was loud and vicious as I found my way back along the cobbles. My head was still hungover as I put the key in the lock. It didn't fit, and I fidgeted around, getting on my knees and looking in the key hole. The door unlocked and swung open to reveal Eric standing there. "Bloody hell, Max, there's no need to get down and beg to get in." "You left the key in the lock, you dafty."

"Who ya got in here, then?" I looked at my bed, still made up.

Eric laughed. "Accident, mate. I forgot to take it out the door." He took his own key out. I made my way in and grabbed my shower bag, walking through to turn on the shower and setting it on cold.

Eric rolled a couple Spanish cones from the camel's eye he sneakily produced. "You didn't bring that on the ferry, did ya?" I said as I came out from the shower room. "You sneaky sod."

"Customs never checks going out," he remarked.

"Yeah, but surely you can buy that here. And fer a lot less than what you paid fer that." After a cold shower I was feeling better. "Beach, then," I said as I grabbed at my shorts, slipping them over my swimming trunks. I grabbed a large bath towel and flip-flops I'd bought before I'd come out.

The beach was packed when we arrived, and it smelled of coconut oil. It seemed to even seep from the sand as I looked down the beach at all the mixed variety of bathers; the view was distorted by heat waves coming off the hot sand. We found a spot and laid out our towels. As I sat I rubbed on my sun tan cream, factor seven. Eric lit a bifter, and we sat smoking it as a Rasta walked over, smelling the joint. Eric offered it to him.

"Nah, I'll light this one." He pulled a monster of a bifter from behind his ear, lit it and smoked it through his thumbs with his hands clasped. He offered it to me. The Rasta had explained he'd flown out from Leicestershire and had a job as bar man. He pointed out the bar along the Playa. "Call in," he said. "It's okay—keep that. I got to work." He got up and made his way in the direction of the bar he pointed out.

"Man, that was good weed," I said as I chuffed away on the spliff. The next thing I knew, I woke to find a half deserted beach. I looked at my watch—5.30 in the evening. My head was throbbing and I felt sick. I looked around for Eric, whose towel had gone.

I walked back through the crowded streets and back up to the room. Eric was sitting with the two cockneys smoking dope. I walked in as they all burst out laughing.

"Man, you're a rock lobster. I mean well cooked, man. Look at the colour of him!"

I was starting to sting all over. Get a cold shower and then go and buy some after sun," one of the cockneys advised.

"Where the fuck did you mizz to?" I asked Eric, who was still laughing.

"We couldn't wake ya, Max, you was out cold."

I went down to one of the shops and bought a bottle of after sun and covered myself in it. It brought a lot off relief. After getting dressed, I made my way down the packed streets and walked down to Bar Sanco, where I opted for a light salad. I just wasn't hungry and still had a splitting headache, although it passed after I'd drunk a few beers.

The lads had already eaten and sat doing their usual—talking the piss out of people passing the window. "Come on, Max, drink up; it's party time."

"Yep, be right with ya," I said, and they left Sancose.

I was thanking the owner, who had come over for a chat. He also agreed with the strike. "Never cross a picket line," he commented. "Stick it out, mate." I asked him for work. "I'm not in need of anyone yet, but who knows, maybe."

"We'd been here a week, and I hadn't seen Eric pull a woman yet. I was beginning to get a bit suspicious of his sexuality, even though I'd known him for years. I'd been introduced to Danny, whom Eric had met last year and who was working as a DJ. Danny was Dutch and gave us a handful of free passes; he also dealt some good cannabis—250 pesetas for a good stick of the stuff, which happened to be Moroccan knockout. Man, this place was just buzzing as I stood up in the DJ cab, set high in the tubed-out terracing. Lasses were coming up and heading back down the steps and asking for their favourite tracks—mostly Dutch and German songs, with the odd English one when I would help Danny out by looking through his albums and finding what they wanted.

A lassie from Glasgow appeared as I picked up the accent. Danny couldn't understand her, so I stepped in. "What does she want me to play?" Danny asked.

"'Blue Monday' by New Order," I replied.

Danny was soon sifting through his albums. "I have the twelve-inch version."

I went down the fire escape—styled stairwell and on to the dance floor. I walked over to the lassie from Glasgow and danced with her. Eric and the other two cockneys had moved on to another club, although I knew where to find him. I stayed on, talking down in the chill out room to the Glasgow lass. I soon found out she was from the same town as where my mum was born and raised, and I got on fine with her.

"I need you to do me a favour," I said. I gave the name of the club and Eric's description. "I want you to go pull him." She was sitting with her sister and two friends from her hotel, one of them from Devon. "Hey, you're gorgeous," I said to the girl as I leant into her ear. She giggled.

The Scottish lass said," I'll see what I can do," and the four of them got up and left.

Danny stood with his newfound love as I climbed back up the stairs to the decks, waiting there as she squeezed my arm on the way down. She returned with her friend whilst I was browsing Danny's albums—a lot of bands I'd heard of but had never seen or heard before.

"Good dance material?" I questioned.

"Yes," he replied. "I will play it." Danny took the album from me. I'd seen the band's review in a magazine.

"Where you from?" I asked the stranger who was stood looking down at all the revellers.

She turned as if she did not understand. She was dressed gothic and was same height as Danny's bird, who came over and translated for me. "She's from Hamburg," came her reply.

"Ask her if she'll come with me to the beach tomorrow."

A brief discussion took place between them, resulting in something being written in eyebrow pencil on one of Danny's flyers. She handed it to me as they walked down to the dance floor, beckoning me to come down as the album I'd picked out came on. It was followed by The Cure's twelve-inch version of "Caterpillar". The dance floor just filled with people.

"She likes how you dance," Danny's girl said to me after the track finished. I was sweating, hot and bothered, and I opted for the fresh air near the air duct. The two of them stood next to me, enjoying the cool air-conditioning. "We are going back to the hotel; she'll see you tomorrow." The girl from Hamburg leaned over and pecked me on the cheek as the two of them left to tell Danny of her intentions.

I climbed the stairs and thanked Danny for his hospitality and made my way over to the next night spot, The Slipper. It was a large bar that turned nightclub after 12.00PM. It was two thirty in the morning, and nowhere could I see Eric's posse when I walked in. I ordered a drink and introduced myself to a blonde from Manchester, who bought me a round after she spotted the NUM badge on my shirt. I sat talking to her and her fella until three o'clock, when he talked about having to get up early and work on the trains for British Rail. I wished them good night and left.

I got to the hostel steaming drunk. Next door had just been taken by the two cockneys who had moved in that day, and music seemed to be coming from their room. I heard men's and women's voiced and tried the door, but it was locked. I bent down to look in the keyhole. Damn, the key was in the lock.

The door across the hall came open; a couple of hitchers had taken up residence there. "Max, come on in." They sat building reefers and told of their travels, claiming they walked from Bradford. I'd heard our room's door open as I opened the lads' door to see who was there. The lass from Scotland stood there as she went and chapped next door. I entered in to the corridor.

The next door came open as the girl from Devon appeared, and the lass from Scotland beckoned to her to come out. "Oh, hi, you made it back home then," she said as she spotted me. Eric was just slipping on his T-shirt and was smiling.

"You dirty whore!" I shouted in.

Eric laughed. "Hey, you're back."

The girl from Devon ran down the corridor and took my arm. "Have they been humping you?" I said to her.

She cracked up laughing. "No, just partying. Let me see your room." She walked in, still latched on my arm. "Hey, this is a better room," she noted as she looked out the window.

I could hear arguing in the corridor between the Scottish sisters. "You're not stopping here with this lot; you're coming back with me and Eric."

The lass from Devon started nudging me. "I'm staying with you," she said.

"Oh, right."

Eric had walked out and tried to calm things. "See you later, Max. I'm going."

"Shush," I said, pointing at her. "Lock the door." Eric nodded on the way out, and the lock clicked after he closed it.

We could hear them all in the corridor as the cockneys accused Eric of stealing his women at the final chucker. The other cockneys shouted out for the girl from Devon. "She's gone back to her hotel," said Eric. "Left two minutes ago." I could hear them clambering about as they all chased after her, and I heard them go quiet and lock their door.

The pair of us sat quiet till they'd gone. "Right, take me somewhere quiet," she said, "before they realise and come back."

"I know just the place." We sneaked out and slipped away down the street. I found the bodega bar where I'd heard the live Spanish music. All was silent, but at least it was open as I looked at my watch: nearly 4.00AM. I ordered a Diet Coke with ice, because I had had enough to drink, and got her a white wine. As we sat down, she snuggled in close.

"Tell me about yourself then, doll. Sorry, I didn't ask your name."

"My name's Brenda, and I'm a registered nurse."

"Cool." I explained my predicament as a few locals sat enjoying the space. "I love how they speak. I'd like to learn when I have more time," I said. She could already speak it, which turned me on.

We left and went back to the hostel. "Ace—Eric's still out," I said as we walked in the room relocking the door. Soon we were ripping each other's clothes off and were at it. "Speak Spanish again," I kept saying to her.

We joined the two beds together. and went at it till we heard a bang on the door. "Oy! That better not be that broad from Devon, Max. You cheapskate!"

We burst out laughing. "That was your groaning that woke 'em up," I whispered. She slapped me straight across the back side, and it started me off again.

Ten minutes later there was another thump at the door. "Max, you low-down dirty snake in the grass! That better not be her. Do you know how much I spent on her tonight? A fucking fortune, mate." I put one of Sam's tapes on to cover the noise.

Later we sneaked back out again when all was quiet, passing Eric on the main drag as we went down to the beach. "I'm going to get me head down, mate." He said.

"Sure, Eric, see ya later." We reached the beach at 6.30 in the morning.

"I'm outta here on the midday flight tomorrow," Brenda said.

"What is it with me?" I mumbled. "I can't get one just arrived."

"What was that?"

"Oh, nothing."

"Take me back to the hotel, Max. I've had a fantastic time, a night to remember."

I took her arm. "Hey, doll, I ain't much good at good-byes considering the practice I've had." She smiled. We left a glorious sunrise, turning our back on the sea. We walked on and bought breakfast further on from a side stall, a hot Tortilla and coffee.

I got back to the hostel and collapsed on my bed, waking around 12.30PM. Eric was still sound asleep as I rose out of bed and switched on the shower. I left the shutters closed but opened the windows; the room reeked of last night's events. I stepped out fully refreshed, and shortly after that the cleaning lady came in, shaking at Eric to get up and showing him the brush end of the broom. "I think she means it," I said, and Eric rose grumbling, making for the shower. I stepped over, opened the shutters, and looked up. "Damn, it's overcast; no sunbathing today."

"Oh hoohoo! Max, ya left it on cold again! What were you saying?"

"It's overcast," I yelled as the cleaning lady set about the room. "I'm nipping fer a bottle of water."

"Yeah, sure," came his reply.

I considered buying wash powder to wash a few clothes as I went through my trousers and found the flyer. I only had ten minutes after I looked at the address. "That's the same hotel as them Dutch birds," I thought as I remembered Ulna. She would be back at work, and I tried to think what she looked like in her uniform. "Right, forget the wash powder and the water." I raced off to the hotel.

The lass from Hamburg sat just inside the main doors with her beach bag to match her black gothic style. She looked as sexy as a slick black alley cat in heat. I studied the more refined bodylines in her cut-off jeans and black bikini top. She got up to greet me just as Danny appeared from the bar with his woman. The sun looked like it was about to break through as we looked up through the doors, feeling the warmth as it brightened.

"Good to see you again, Max," Danny said as he guided us through the lounge and asked what we would like to drink.

"Just a Diet Coke for me, Danny." We sat chatting at the bar.

"Looks like it's going to be fine after all," Danny commented. "I was getting worried. Hey, I have these fer you and your friends." He handed me more free tickets. "Weekend passes. Like gold dust. They will only accept tickets after midnight—no cash payment."

"Thanks, Danny." I was flattered.

"Where is Eric?"

"He was in the shower last I seen. Expect he'll be on the beach later."

Danny nodded. "Is he still smoking that crap he brought with him?" I nodded and Danny laughed. "Hey, I may let you DJ if you decide to come. I also have good weed." He took a small sample from his pocket.

"You're a star," I said as I smelled at the contents. "Give me two bags."

"Five hundred pesetas."

"Done," I said, and we shook hands. I counted out the cash and handed it over to him. The girl from Hamburg smiled as I put the weed away. "Do you smoke?" I asked her.

"Ja, ja," she said, nodding.

"Are we ready to hit the beach?" Danny said, and we made our way into the hot sunshine and down the main drag. Danny treated us to an iced lolly each from a Gypsy woman. The sun melting them between licks as we sucked on them.

"Phew, it must be in its eighties. Come for a swim," I prompted the Hamburg girl. She accepted after a translation, taking off her cut-offs.

Even Danny's eyes bulged at her figure. "Man, now that is hourglass," he said as he spied me looking at her behind, smiling and nodding.

We walked down to the sea, minding not step on anyone. She was letting me pick her up and throw her as Danny and his girl joined us. All of us swam to the deep where we paddled water as waves passed through us. The water was lukewarm, getting colder around the waist down.

"I'm getting out," Danny finally said. "You can stay." He made for the shore. We stayed in the water another five minutes and followed suit. The girl from Hamburg held out her sun oil when we got back, and we dried each other with the towels.

Danny smiled as I took the bottle, poured some oil into my hand, and smeared it all over her gently. She seemed to enjoy it rubbed onto her back. "You're a hit with her," he whispered. I smiled like I knew it already. "Offer her out," he said under his breath. "You ask, I'll translate."

I asked her after I did her front, and she laidback on her towel. She spoke, but I never caught what was said. Danny nodded. "She will think about it," he replied. Then he explained, "She'll say yes—I gave you the last tickets fer Saturday and Sunday night." The penny dropped. "Gold dust," Danny said again.

Later that day, after a siesta I jumped back in the cold shower. "I think I overdid again in the sun," I complained to myself.

Eric was out buying provisions from the market, and he came back with a load of goodies—French sticks, wash powder, tins of pâté and sunflower spread, an array of fresh tomatoes and salad, a mixture of peppers, and a large bottle of ice cold Lilt. We sat munching.

I pulled out the tickets from my back pocket and tossed two to Eric.

"Hey, Max, cheers," he said as he looked at them.

"That leaves me two tickets; that's fair."

"Yeah, man, you're a star." Eric put them away in his wardrobe.

"Danny asked where you were," I mentioned.

"I'll go. Saturday night, is it? Tell him I'll see him then."

I stopped him. "I won't see him till then, either. I have to meet a bit of floss just before, at 8.30."

"Bit of floss, Max? Who's that, then?"

"Ah, just wait and see."

We sat stuffing our fizz. I knew Eric had been sniffing around a lass from one of the clubs that worked the door.

"You have a couple of days to find her and ask her. The tickets will speak fer themselves, mate."

"Oh, I don't know," he replied. "I've only just met her."

"Well, that's your chance."

"Right, we'll find her tonight and I'll ask." Eric went to his room and closed the door.

"Tonight," I prompted. "We are talking the most exclusive night club in all Loretta de Mar. She's bound to say yes."

Saturday night came. I'd put down my paint brush like an impressionist scene of the viewpoint on the beach and let it dry as I rooted about for the primary colours of gooash, looking in my case. A big roll a Coal Not Dole stickers came undone and rolled to the corner. Eric was writing out his postcards as I produced them. "Hey," Eric said, looking at them. "You ain't going to stick them about, are ya?"

"Yep." Eric laughed as I moved on to set up the ironing board and press a clean shirt and trousers. I plugged in the iron and finished by polishing up my shoes. I even broke out my last pair of brand-new socks. I'd kept a pile of pesetas to phone home in my wardrobe and gathered them, ready to take with me. "I've seen a few from my colliery," I said as I stood ready.

Eric replied, "You wouldn't," putting down his pen. I nodded. "Give some." I reached in my case and threw him a roll. He started rubbing his hands, and I smiled at what I knew was running through his mind.

I'm not kidding, we stuck them everywhere—on shop windows, notice boards, all up and down the promenade.

I left Eric to go meet the cockneys, who had gone out much earlier to Sancose. I'd split to go meet up with the lass from Hamburg. I even stuck one on her; she didn't mind as she took my arm in reception and pouted sticking them on the revolving doors on the way out.

We stopped at an art shop with a local working artist selling his and others' works, and I marvelled at the paintings. The lass spoke, but I couldn't understand her; I just agreed, "Ja," sneaking a Coal Not Dole on one of the paintings when no one was looking.

It made her chuckle and put a hand to her mouth. "Ja, lakopled off, mizz." I moved us towards the shop doorway. The pair of us fell about laughing as we walked out the door. She said loads, and I just kept saying yes and nodding. She could have been calling me all the names under the sun for all I knew—I still agreed with her.

She tugged at my shirt, pulling me around the corner of a narrow street. "Light me, please," she said in English.

"Hey, you can speak my lingo."

"Yes," she said. Very well, do you think?"

"What's with the put-on, doll?" I asked as I scratched my head.

"I'm toying with you," she said with a chuckle.

Danny was up in his nest and waved us on up. "What is this?" he said as he looked at the stickers. He put two on his decks, and I watched them turning on the decks between discs.

I nodded, laughing. "Another one in favour," I thought.

Hamburg whispered, "Find me some good tunes," as she took what was left of the roll and went down and headed towards the ladies room.

I'd picked out Corgi's master mix and found some New Order mixes, The Beach, and a version of "Brick in the Wall". "Man, that dance floor's going to be steaming," Danny said when he saw what I was picking. "Yes, later," he added as he showed me his list. "We've got till 10.00AM tomorrow."

Hamburg was back, and she gave me back the roll smiling. "You haven't," I said as I looked in her eyes. She nodded.

Danny's girl walked on up. "She's put a big heart on the mirror in them."

I looked at Hamburg. "Did ya?" She nodded. Well, I had to give her a hug. "I got to make a call home; fancy a walk to the phone box?" She nodded again. "I'd better get through this time; here, you listen, I'll dial the number." The two of us stood over the phone. She had a better clue on the procedures.

My bro answered. "Yeah, Max, how's the weather?"

"Hot and steamy and brown as a berry. Quick more money in." I handed Hamburg more change, and she stood smiling while she dropped in the coins. "Where's Ma?"

"She's here, hang on."

She'd asked if I was getting fed and was worried, because I hadn't phoned for a few days—a week, to be precise. "I popped a card in the post. You should get it soon," I told her as the money ran out. "Right, let's go eat," I said to Hamburg as I put down the phone. "Ma's orders."

Hamburg showed the way up a few back streets to a place at the top end of town, a restaurant on the side of a high stone wall. I'd been past it and never knew it was there. We walked on up the winding steps. "Let's try veggie," she said as she put down the menu.

"I'll pick the wine, then," I said, trying to look professional. I hadn't a clue about the wine, so I just pointed at an expensive one that was kind of least expensive, if you know what I mean. The waiter recommended one further down the list but the same price. "Yes, that will be fine," I said, trying to keep a straight face.

Hamburg took care of the nosh—small plates of dips and blended seaweed, she explained—as a form of quiche arrived. "Real tortilla," she explained.

"Mmm, nice," I said as I got stuck in. "You read Spanish as well, then." Man, that tortilla was hot as I rolled it around my mouth. I sampled the wine. "That's a nice fruity body." I looked at her, spluttering and coughing as I regained my posture and cleared my throat, placing a sticker on the bottle. A German couple on the other table cracked up laughing when they saw what I'd done. I put the stickers all over it. "Do you think they followed the trail?" I joked.

Hamburg was in hysterics. "Well, they did arrive after us."

"Shh, they will hear you," I said. Then I stood up and asked loudly, "Did you follow the trail?"

"Vere are you from?" A female blonde-haired six footer boomed out in broken English.

"Chuckwalla," I replied as I sat down.

Hamburg stood up and said something I didn't understand, but she got them talking to us. They conversed in German, pointing, and then she pointed the finger as I'm nodding. I watched the volleyball match of German conversation, throwing a roll at the waiter to get his attention.

He came over frowning, after he'd retrieved the half-battered roll and bringing it back to the table and talking in Spanish. Then he looked at the bottle and smiled again. Hamburg translated, "What's the matter? You don't like those rolls?"

"Nah, I was trying to call him over and didn't know what to say. I want a plate of chips."

"Chips?" The waiter looked at me, still smiling.

"Well, you said vegetarian." I looked at Hamburg, who was struggling not to laugh.

The night ended with the two of us going up to her hotel and getting blitzed. Her apartment was even higher up then the Dutch birds. I left her steaming as I walked out the hotel. "Phew, I can think again," I thought as I made for the night spot.

It was 5.30 in the morning when I walked in. Danny was still hammering out the tunes, and the place was still busy as I perked up a bit. Danny was nodding and chuffing on a bifter as "Another Brick in the Wall" boomed out. "I saved ya that one," he said as the dance floor filled out. I just had to dance, thanking Danny and making my way down to find a space. Danny pointed out a tall blonde on the dance floor, and I made my way over to her. The DJ gave me the thumbs up message. Her eyes connected with mine as she started to move with me. She wore leather tan hot pants and a waist coat and cowboy boots to match a tan that would show up Raja.

I whispered to her, "Want to go up the crow's nest?" She bent down and nodded, nearly giving me the Chuckwalla welcoming kiss. "I'll take that as yes then." I took her hand and led her through and on up. "Okay if she looks through the tunes?" I asked Danny. He signalled to go ahead, handing me an unlit bifter. I turned it down, but the tall blonde took it and lit it. I started to laugh as she pulled out all the charts. "Madonna?" I said out loud.

"I'm trying to force the album back on; it's been on twice when I was in earlier." I still had "Like a virgin," in my head when I hit the restaurant. "Bloody hell, enough, come on. "Too late—she's got the album *Undone*. Danny's taking it. It sort of went from there to a relaxed Frankie Goes to Hollywood song as I took the spliff. I grabbed at the tall blonde's waist, and before I knew it we were banging hips at the top of the stairs.

There seemed to be more and more people on the dance floor as I looked around. The tall blonde had out her compact, chopping out a couple of lines, pretending to look through the albums, and rolling out a mil note. She offered me a line, and I snorted it. Danny offered the spliff. I gave her note back as the back of my nose tingled. My heart starting to race as the lights got brighter.

"No, you keep that," she said.

"Hey, thanks." I put the mil in my pocket.

Danny was nudging me as I turned around. "She runs the place." A big smile came on my face as I nodded.

She grabbed me around the waist, and I looked down at the sea of young people on the dance floor. She pulled at my arm and led me downstairs. "This way," she said. Before I knew it I was out a side door and into the morning sun. She was putting the key into a white ragtop Mercedes sport. "Jump in." I walked around the other side. It was 7.30AM as she pulled up at a lay-by further on up near the beach and dropped her seat back slightly. She wasn't saying much and just stared out to sea.

I had to break the ice. "What's your name?" I asked her politely.

"Anna." She turned to face me, flicking her long blonde hair over her shoulder.

"Oh, I thought you where the blonde from ABBA." She smiled. "Well, you never can tell in these places," I added.

"What would you have said if I'd said I was?" she asked.

"I would a probably asked her if she was that blonde who runs that exclusive night club in Loretta de Mar."

Her hand slapped on the dash as she freaked out with laughter. "Come on, Max, let's go fer a walk." I figured Danny must have told her my name, and I stepped out the car and walked arm in arm with her in the surf, stopping to roll up my trousers and take off my shoes and socks.

We found an inlet. "It's more private here," she said as she led me over to some smoothed out rock. Her finger slipped through the loops of her boots, which she slung over her shoulder. We sat down together and looked out to sea, but then she got up and took off her leather waist jacket and slipped off her hot pants. She stood leaning over me in her white bikini, pulling at my arm. "Strip. Come on, strip, Max."

"I've no swim wear on," I said as I leered at her firm physique.

"What does it matter?" Next I knew, she'd taken off her bikini top. "Come on, Max, let's swim."

Well, when in Rome . . . I stripped, laying out my clothes and neatly folding them. She looked at my privates, just staring. "Well, I said I've no swim wear."

"Last one in gets the first round," she yelled as she made a dash for the sea, getting a head start. The sea was cold as I chased her into the waves and she swam deeper out. Then she was circling her bikini bottoms above her head. "Now we are equal." She smiled. "Well, come and get it then!" I was over to her quicker than a great white. Now I had never done it in water before, and the coke had taken effect. She was very professional about it and seemed to know how to get things moving. She disappeared under the water—and oh my God.

We'd just about completely dried out by the time we got back to the car. "Max, you do know I'm a kept women."

"I know," I said, turning to her.

"My husband owns a string of clubs all over Loretta." I noticed no rings on her left hand, and she caught my look. "I wear them when he's around, which ain't been too often lately."

"It's okay, doll, you don't need to tell me all this." I thought about the life she'd been leading. "You certainly know how to pack the dance floor."

She smiled again. "It takes years of practice." She switched on the ignition, putting back the ragtop. The heat was beginning to build. My watch had steamed up, and I looked at the dash. The time was 9.45. "I need to get back to cash up and lock up," she said, and we pulled away.

I was still high as a kite when I walked back in the room. Eric was still in his bed. I pulled out the note and rolled it out. Anna's number was written across it. I copied it down and then changed what numbers I could on the note. "I'd better watch where I cash that—bank, I suppose," I thought, pushing the note into my pocket. that was another three weeks' rent. I sighed in relief. Sixty sovereigns in traveller's cheques left. I closed the cupboard, locking it.

"Hey." I stopped and looked where the voice came from. It was a big fellow with dark hair. "Your friend tells me you paint. Can I see your work?"

"I have one not finished; I just started it," I explained.

"Show me when it's finished." He turned to go back in the shop. I carried on down towards the beach. I could feel myself being taken down from one level to another very gently as I sat at a café ordering a coffee. The tiredness was creeping in, though it was 10.30AM. I went back to the hostel and changed to go find Danny. Eric was still sound asleep.

I found Danny at his perch in the hotel. "Ah, Max," Danny said with a laugh. "Still up and about, I see."

"I need some more of that Charlie she had last night."

Danny nodded. "I'll see what I can do. Oh, that ticket I gave you—what did you do with it?"

"I still have it in my cupboard. I kept it fer a memory."

Danny burst out laughing. "It's valid for tonight also."

"Yeah. Will this take care of the Charlie?" I handed him the note.

"More than enough. I need to give you half that back." He counted out five thousand pesetas, handing it to me.

"Right, I need that fer me rent."

"Yes get that sorted." Danny said.

"You know whose numbers on that?"

"Sure, Max, why? Have you phoned her yet?"

"No, why?"

"If I were you, I would," he warned. He could see I changed the numbers as he put the note away.

"I didn't know where to cash it." He nodded. "Is, erm, Hamburg around?"

Danny frowned. "You just missed her. She left in a taxi and will be at the airport by now."

"I never got chance to say good-bye to her." I slammed my fist down, annoyed.

"It's how she wanted it," Danny said before calling over the barman and ordering two tequila sunrises. "You'll need to phone her whilst she's still there." Danny slid over one of the drinks and a card. "That's the office number to the club," he said as he laid out the change. 'She'll be there till 1.00AM, waiting fer the cleaners to finish. Take the change and phone her." He nodded towards the phone in reception.

At first she spoke in Spanish as I'd recognized her voice. "It's me, Max."

"Oh, Max!" She changed to English. "I will be in the club after midnight." She explained about some running around she had to do, and then she had to go to bed. I could tell she was still high as a kite.

"See you after midnight then, doll." I came back to the bar smiling. Danny had disappeared leaving half his drink. I sat back up on the stool and waited. I tried to work out the deal I'd just made. Then as I felt at the roll of money in my pocket Danny had given me back.

Danny came back. "I'll pass it you under the bar." He showed me a wrap and a bag of weed.

I nodded and felt under the bar for it. Then I drank my drink and thanked Danny. "'Nuff respect, as they say in Chuckwalla." Danny sat repeating it as I left.

The two hostellers had the door wide open as I went to open mine. "How's the holiday?" I remarked.

They'd been down to the hyper-mart and bought bottles—a chilled beer. The contents of their rucksacks were strewn around, and the place smelled of smelly socks and BO. "Come in," they shouted as I moved aside the maps and loose bits of other camping accessories.

"Hey, anyone want weed?" I asked as I sat down. I'd seen the rizzla on the table.

"I might be if it's any good," came the reply.

"I'll build a sample." I reached for the weed. One duly arrived on the table. They even had roach cards, throwing down the one pack. They reached for the bag and smelled its contents.

"How much?" one of the males broke open a beer and offered it to me, which I gladly took.

"Cheers." I smiled whilst building a bifter and lighting it.

"Yeah, man, that's genie tackle," one of the males said as he offered it to his roommate. "How much?"

"Well, let me see. Ten sovs fer the bag."

"Deal." They reached in their bags, going half each.

I could hear our door come open. Eric stood there in his denim shorts. "Max, I thought I could hear your voice," he said as he walked in.

"What's on the agenda today then, Eric?"

"Never mind that—where you been all night?"

"All night?" I jested. "And that's coming from the man who had two tickets fer a good night out."

"Nah, went up the Slipper."

"Hey, what's that?" one of the males chirped up.

"They're still valid fer tonight," I told Eric.

He still didn't seem interested. "Let these two have 'em. Don't waste 'em." He retired to the room.

"What kind of music are you into?" I asked the pair.

"Club dance," one of them said as Eric returned with the tickets. "What's it worth?"

The other took hold of the tickets and looked. "Tenner each." Both rummaged in their rucksacks again.

"Oy, don't you think you're best leaving that with the old lady downstairs?" Eric asked. "She's got a safe, you know."

"Yes, our passports are in it. That's only small change," I thought to myself, "Mind yer own business."

"Right. Who takes Charlie?" one of the men closed the door as Eric moved out of the way.

"You can get Charlie?" Eric asked. I nodded and Eric grinned.

"Fifty sovs gets a good deal," I explained as I showed them the wrap minus one line. The two men were rummaging back in their rucksacks again, counting out the cash.

Danny was still sat at the bar when I walked in. He spotted me an ordered me a tequila sunrise. As I sat down I said under my breath, "Need more Charlie."

Danny nodded. "What, you sold two grams already?" he asked.

"There was two grams?" I scratched my head. "You didn't say there was two grams—I just sold the lot fer fifty sovs." I could see I'd made a mistake. man by time I walked up the hill I was proper spaced as the bar kind of looked bigger.

"Well at least you got yer money back fer the sake of a walk down the street and back," Danny said, chuckling. "Paid yer rent yet?"

"Oh, I forgot."

"Right. Wait here, gimme the fifty." I handed over the dollar, he disappeared into the lift in the reception. That was all the Spanish money gone, and the exchange wouldn't be open till after siesta. Danny returned, giving me the wrap. "Remember, it's two grams," he whispered.

"Right. Where can I get this change at this time a day?"

"Here at the hotel they are open," he said as he looked at his watch and pointed out the Beuro de Exchange. "In reception."

"Right, I'll be back," I said, changing up the dollar. I'd walked in and sorted things up front with the old woman. "That's three weeks up front."

I left the room and went on up to our landing. Eric was out, and I took to the paint pallet. I kept looking out the window to try and match the sea colours and the sky, rearranging and toning in places. I'd been down to the beach and had sketched an outline of the scene, trying to imagine the rest when I got back to paint it. There were a couple of slappers from Cardiff; I could hear them next door as the two cockneys followed them in.

I laid down my brush. "That's it, finished."

One of the females from next door had entered my room and sat on the bed and looked. "Hey, don't think you're getting up to yer tricks with her," one of the cockneys sounded off. I laughed.

"Hey, that really is good, I like that," the woman said, all her cleavage hanging out of her beach dress. "Can I have it?" She studied it closer.

I laughed again. Someone needs to see it first," I replied.

"Right, we're out on the town. Coming, Max?" one of the cockneys asked, changing the subject. They left the room.

I took the finished piece down to the art shop, and the man there examined it. This needs to be bigger."

"Which bit?" I asked as I looked closer.

"All of it."

"Oh." I saw what he meant.

"You have an eye for the colours. You need to work bigger, and then I would be interested in finding space for your work. You'd also be better working in oils. Take a course on it when you get back home." He handed the painting back. I nodded as the man went back into his shop.

I walked back up to the hostel and put away the painting and set out the ironing board. I pressed out my slacks and a clean shirt. I was smiling as I'd noticed some of the Coal Not Dole stickers had been defaced. "I'll only put one over it," I thought as I stood ironing away. "Plenty rolls of stickers left in the suitcase." I laid out the clothes on the bed and got in the shower—cold, of course.

The two from the room opposite came back. I could hear them talking fast Bradford, and then there was a knock at the door. "Come in," I said, and the pair entered with eyes like golf balls.

"Sheesh, man, where did ya get that?" one asked. "I've been smashed all day."

"Haven't you had any since dinner?" I inquired.

"No, man, I'm still out me face."

I thought, "That means they ain't checked it yet." Then I said to them, "Is it all right if I get a wee pick-me-up?" They gave me the wrap. "I'll just nip in the shower room, in case anyone walks in." I checked the wrapper—same as when I gave it to them, I'd noticed. I swiped nearly half back, adding into a rizzla and folding it away. I made out I'd took a line as I walked back out and gave the wrapper back, snorting one of my nostrils. The guy just slipped it back in his pocket. "Cheers," I said. "Bit of a lift."

"Right, we're off to get changed," they said and left the room.

Eric walked in with scuff marks all over him. My jaw dropped. "I've just been mugged by a bunch a wops," he blurted out. "Look at the state of me, man." He was in bits and plopped down on his bed. "Had big knifes to me, they did."

"What did they take?" I was trying to sound sympathetic.

"All me cash, me watch, and me resin."

"They nicked that camel's eye you've been carting about the last three weeks?"

"Yeah, man, God damn took it."

"Right. What you been getting up to, broad wise?"

"Nothing, man, I ain't done nothing," he replied.

I scratched at my head. I'd just changed a cheque this morning and had the biggest bulk of it on me. Eric was devastated. "I can give you a small loan."

"Nah, I'll get me sister to send me some cash out. I'll change another one tomorrow."

"Need a snifter?"

Eric brightened a bit. "Cheers, Max." I took down the mirror and chopped out two fat lines. "Woo, man," he said as he handed the note back.

"Do you need money to go out tonight?" I asked.

"Nah, I'll stay in tonight."

"What? You just took a line of Charlie and are staying in? That's a waste, man." Eric sat back on his bed and took off his ripped T-shirt. I saw the bruises starting to appear. "Oh, man," I groaned as I looked closer. "Right, get yerself cleaned up, and we'll take a look around fer 'em."

Eric wasn't interested. "Nah, I'll get something to eat and settle in fer the night."

I shot across the landing and chapped the door, which came open. "Go and look at the state of him," I said as I pointed back into the room. The pair came out, towels wrapped around them. We all stood around Eric. "Tell 'em what's happened." Eric started to tell the story.

"Who are they?" the pair asked after they listened.

"That's just it. He says they're locals, but he won't say who," I butted in.

"Just point 'em out," the two warned. I could see they were upset by Eric's condition as they retired to get changed.

I was sure they cracked his ribs as I watched him struggle on the way into the shower. "Ooo! Max, you've left on cold again," I could hear him yell as I changed into clean clobber. Eric came out the shower.

"I'm telling ya, get changed and we'll go find 'em. I'll iron yer stuff; give it here."

Later we walked around Loretta—the two cockneys from next door, the slappers from Cardiff and the two from Bradford—checking all the local haunts. "Well, at least they saw a mob with him," I thought. They must have gone to ground after we checked the top end of the old town.

We ended up in the Slipper. Eric decided to stay with the two cockneys and the lasses from Cardiff. "We'll look after him," they said.

I handed one of the lasses a few notes and said, "Get him pissed. And a few fer yourself."

Just before midnight I'd gone to the club with the lads from Bradford. I thought I'd better not take them up to the crow's nest because Danny had one or two standing up there already, although Danny had acknowledged I was in. I spent most of the night talking to Anna, who was working the bar. "I'm just going fer a snifter," I said, and I went through to the toilets, stepping into the cubicle.

As I walked back to the bar, my heart was racing again. Anna had on a cheeky white two-piece and boots to match. I noticed no rings. "That's on the house, Max," she said, sliding me a cool drink over. Her tan just glowed.

"Where are you from, Anna?" I asked.

"Kensington. My parents still live there."

"What made you come out here?" I asked as I tried to fathom what was in the cocktail.

"I got married."

"Arranged Marriage?"

"Convenience." She smiled.

I played with the stirrer. "It wasn't love, then."

"Kind of," she said before breaking away to serve a customer. She came back. "I'll get another member of staff to cover, and then I'll sit this side." She pointed to the stool at the side of me. She disappeared into the back whilst I looked around. The two from Bradford looked like they scored with a couple of brunettes.

Anna returned and laid down her handbag on the bar and slid onto the stool. "Well look at you," I said. "You look a million dollars." She flicked her hair. "Hang on, I'll be back in two minutes."

I walked up the steps to the DJ booth. "Put some ABBA on." Danny nodded, returning to the bar.

Anna asked, "What you got planned later on, Max?"

"Not really sure," I replied as I took hold of the stirrer in my drink.

"Party my place?"

"Okay, yeah. What, everyone invited?"

"No, just some close friends," she warned. Just then Danny kicked off the intro to "Dancing Queen". Anna smiled. "You never asked for this, did you Max?"

"Yep." I took her hand and pulled her to her feet, leading her onto the mobbed dance floor.

Later I met Anna at the side door and stepped out to her car as she leant over to let me in the passenger side. She drove out the narrow side street and up towards the new end of Loretta. "Hey, this is the same hotel as Danny," I noted as we pulled in the car park.

"He'll be along later."

We walked through the reception and into the lift. I saw her press the top floor as the doors closed. I just couldn't keep my hands to myself after she gave me the sexy stare. The doors came open as we carried on. "I'll keep my finger on this," she said cheekily and kept her finger on the door button. "Max, you're a real live stud."

"I'll take that as a compliment." I was still out of breath as I did myself up, and we stepped out the lift and went to her room.

"I'm just going to run a shower—want to join me?" she asked when we walked into the en suite.

I'd been here before and remembered Hamburg. "Erm, is this your pad?" I inquired, surprised.

"It's on lease from the hotel. I use it when I'm working the club."

"Oh." I started to strip, and I could hear the water running; she was already in the shower as I studied her outline through the glass.

I opened the door. "Mmm, come here," she said.

Danny stood out on the veranda with his chick when I walked out to them. "I seen something on the TV earlier, I meant to say," he said.

I leant on the rail. "What is it you seen, Danny?"

"Oh, bad scenes in your country. Mass fighting with the law," Danny's woman said. "Org something. Orgee. Hey, orgy. Mass orgy."

"No, that's the name of the place," Danny replied.

Anna came out to join us. "Danny was just saying how he seen something on TV about the miners' strike."

Anna chipped in, "Yes, Orgreave—a coking plant." I still wasn't sure what they meant. "Mass picket at Orgreave," she explained.

"Oh. Why, what's happened?"

"A lot of arrests and injuries. I seen the picture on the news. Police on horseback lashing out at people with their long batons—it was horrible. I thought you'd seen it."

"No, there's no TV in the room."

Anna looked at her watch. "There may be something on." She walked through to the lounge and switched on the TV.

"What, at 5.30 in the morning?" I said as I walked through.

"Watch," Anna commanded, and she searched the channels. She stopped on the news, although it was in Spanish.

I sat down and studied the screen. "Oh, man, that's the worst I've seen up to yet." I remembered some of the scenes I'd seen at my own colliery as the horror unfolded.

"This was a few days ago," Anna remarked.

I went quiet, looking at the floor as I turned away. "Turn it off; I've seen enough."

Anna clicked the remote, put it down on the coffee table, and took my hand. 'Some of your friends there?" she asked. I nodded. She pulled me to my feet. "Right. No more coke, okay? Bed." She led me through.

"Anna, I have trouble at the hostel. My roommate came home badly beaten up. Some locals mugged him fer his watch and some cash."

Anna dropped her evening dress and pulled back the satin sheets. "Come here," she said. "Shh, just be quiet and listen."

All I could here was Danny and his chick in the lounge. "I'm worried about him," I said as I turned to her.

"He's just a room pal."

"No he isn't; I've known since we were kids and cadets."

Anna laughed. "What cadets?"

"Army cadets."

Anna reached over and sat upright and lit a pre-rolled bifter. She thought for a minute. "So you came here together?"

"Yes," I replied.

"And what's happened?" She handed me the spliff and the ashtray.

I told her the story. "It was him who introduced me to Danny."

"Oh, now I see." She took back the spliff and the ashtray.

"He won't tell me who the locals are that set about him."

"When you find out, let me know. I guarantee something will be done about it," she reassured me. I lay back, still worried for him, as she cuddled into my chest.

Next dinner time I walked back to the hostel. Eric was still lying on his bed, and I could see the bruises had gone a mouldy colour of brown and blue, and the scuff marks had scabbed over. His eyes came open as I jumped on my bed and lay back. "What's on the agenda then, Eric?"

"I might take a walk up the Buccaneer, see if I could get me old job back." He seemed confident. "That's the place I worked last year."

"Yeah, I remember you telling me. Come up if you fancy a walk later, say around three."

"Yep, fine."

"How's the wounds?"

"Oh, I try not to think about it."

"Still suffering memory loss?" I joked as I prodded for names.

"Look, Max, there's not a lot we can do about it now—just let it go."

I heard the door opposite open with a knock. The two from Bradford came in. The pair stood looking pleased with themselves. "Hey, you can see the sea from your side," one said as they looked out.

"How did you get on with those chicks?" I asked.

"Okay, fine. We're going Wednesday."

I knew the club wouldn't reopen till then because I'd been fully briefed by Anna. "How was the Charlie?"

"Space magic fly." The pair smiled. I couldn't stop laughing. Eric was holding his ribs trying not to laugh. "We've bought more beers if anyone would like some."

I could see Eric was still in pain. "Yep, better crack out some anaesthetic. Want a line, Eric?" I took down the mirror. A smile came on his face as I poured out the last of what I swiped yesterday. Bradford arrived with the beers as I chopped out four fat lines.

"Hey, I came back here steaming. Thanks fer that, Max."

"The two lassies from Cardiff must have told him," I thought.

"Proper slewed, mate." Eric was nodding.

"Did they play nurse to ya?" I asked.

"Ooo, nurse nursey!" I felt his forehead.

"Right, that's enough," Eric stopped me. I could see he didn't want to laugh.

I relented.

"Hey, put one of Sam's eighties tapes on." I pointed at the stereo.

"Cool tunes," the Bradford lads said as they settled down and started to build reefers.

I got up and checked my wardrobe, looking for my stash. Two bags a weed and a bit of resin I hadn't touched since I bought it, and two grams a coke. I took the cash from my pocket and threw that in. I still had sixty sovereigns in traveller's cheques and about thirty in Spanish notes. I set the loose change on top, saying, "And that's the call home tonight." I locked up the wardrobe and sat down.

"So are we humping them two chicks, then, or are they just ornaments?" I asked.

"Ha ha—ow!" Eric cringed with laughter.

The two from Bradford looked at each other, going bright red. 'We're still working on it."

"Bring 'em here; we'll show how to go on," Eric piped up, which started me off laughing when I saw the colour on the two.

"Hey, that blonde looked cool—the one you were dancing with to ABBA," the taller of the two said, trying to change the subject.

"Oh yeah," Eric piped up. "Ya kept that quiet, Max. Tell, tell."

"It was just a dance," I played it down.

"Well, you never came back here till dinner."

"I just went fer a walk," I said, smiling.

"It was that coke." Anna had told me to zip it on the way out and to ring her Wednesday. I changed the subject.

"What's this job entail, then?"

"Oh, the Buccaneer." Eric was looking confident.

"Well, it's handing leaflets out and collecting glasses next morning. It pays the rent."

"Well, I'm squared up fer the next three weeks with the rent." Eric looked surprised. "How you manage that?" he asked.

"I wangled it."

"What, selling Charlie?"

"Yep," I said bluntly.

Eric smiled. "They'll deport ya if they catch you."

"You mean jail," I jested.

"No, they'll deport ya."

The two from Bradford butted in, "Oh best be careful, then."

"So this job, Eric—what you mean handing out leaflets?"

"They call it propaganda in the corners. You stand and get folks to go to the pub."

Again the taller of the two from Bradford butted in. "Oh, now I see. That seems straightforward, and then you go collect the pots and bottles next morning."

"Well, it's half two," I said, checking my watch.

"I'd better get a move on," Eric said. We left the hostel and walked to the Buccaneer, which was just a stone's throw from Hostel Palu. I ordered two bottled beers and saw the pool table was open, so I fumbled for change. Eric had placed a coin alongside mine as I pushed the slider home. The balls dropped, and I could hear what was being said at the bar, between who I presumed to be the landlord and Eric.

"Look, I can't take you on this year, Eric. You need a work licence, a permit. I've been threatened with a large fine if I do." Eric pleaded with him, but he was firm. "Nope, I can't do it. I'm sorry you came all this way. Yes, I do need staff, but with no work permit, I can't help ya."

Eric knew he'd fucked up; he also knew it was the start of the season. I felt sorry for him as I called him over. "Want to crack 'em?" I took the triangle away from the balls as Eric took the cue. "Well, can't you go back home and get a permit?" I asked.

"It's not as easy as that." Eric looked at the table thinking up his shot. "It takes three months to process."

"So you knew about it then?" I asked as Eric sunk a stripe.

"He took us on last year without one, so I assumed."

"I see." Eric missed his next shot, and I came to the table. "And you've been here three weeks to find that out."

Chapter Four

I'd decided to rejoin 307 battery. Griffon, a contact from the SAS under whom I trained since 1990, had given me reason to. Most of the training was field and close quarter combat, along with survival techniques, often finding myself in situations of interrogation and security. In the 307 battery I was installed as a recruit.

We sat at a bar in a small village just outside Chuckwalla. Griffon was telling me of his adventures in Aden for the tenth time and how they'd trained the natives to rise up and fight for themselves. He also talked of mad Mitch and his Sutherland Argyles, who ordered the search of every home in Aden, explaining that every door was kicked in and property was searched, and how terrorist activity fell to zilch. After that they had retrieved a mountain of weapons, most of them handmade and vintage, along with an array of AK 47s and RPGs.

After a few pints of lager, Griffon looked around to see if anyone was earwigging the conversation. "Orders from HQ are that I want you to find out everything about the setup there at 307." I want names, firepower capabilities, what's housed there—and I want you to look for laps in security. I in turn will make a full report and forward it to the correct dept within the MOD. This is to be done at the top level; a captain there has asked for this to be done. Does this name look familiar?" He showed me government documentation, all earmarked confidential.

"Yes, I know who that is," I replied.

"He will be keeping a close eye on you. Don't worry, he won't let on."

I rubbed my hands. At last, a mission. We ordered another round.

Griffon made it clear reports were to be kept verbal and that I was to report to no one but him. "You'd be doing it of course to improve security and the safety of the personnel that operate within 307's structure." On that note all was agreed.

Griffon ran an unarmed combat class on the first floor in a public house within the village, and he would have me and a few other selected individuals assist in the running of the class, which was my cover for meeting up with Griffon and relaying info to him in the bar downstairs over a quiet pint. The class mainly consisted of police women and men plus women from other professions keen to develop their personal protection skills. We were used as fall guys. I didn't mind the bumps and bruises; I was just happy to know they could get themselves out of a sticky situation should the event arise.

Six months later I was through the recruit process, finding most things easy and a recap on things I'd done before. Most of the drills I'd learned as a child; the rest of it was common sense.

I'd been back to Griffon explaining I'd scaled the fence and caught the night guard sound asleep in the back of a three-toner, having taken in a raiding party of two women and two males—all recruits whom I'd talked into doing it after a few pints. I Explained that we'd had free run of the place and access to the store's hangers, even the NCOs and Officers mess. Griffon just could not believe what he was listening to. "And to top it all they'd let the recruits know that the 105 Howitzers where being replaced by the larger 155s."

Griffon slammed his fist on the bar. "Is this true?"

"As true as the day is long."

"You mean you got in outside normal duty hours and could have blown the place to pieces?"

"It's worse than that—I could have set hidden charges to coincide with personnel arriving." I showed him a diagram of where they could have been placed.

He swiped at the paper and looked. "I thought I told you to keep it verbal." He took his cigarette lighter to it. "You know what would happen if they found you with this?" Griffon shook his head. "Do you know how many balls I'd have had to kick to get you out the slammer?" He slapped me straight across the forehead. "Right, I'm recommending a full security review in light of what you just told me."

JUNE 1994

I'd been invited along on a gunnery weekend to Sunnybrook, which was one of many sites used for artillery work. I'd been out to the ops bunker overlooking the impact area, staying out all night. The bombardier had OTHSE set up along with Star-bright light intensifier, and observations were kept on infantry movements. During the course of the night, every troop movement was carefully marked on the map, and radio contact was made back to the battery, giving six-figure map references that in turn would confirm friendly or hostile during the course of the day; this could be denoted by the sash colours worn by opposing sides. Everything was put through the hands of the safety officer to verify correct procedures had been undertaken; references radioed in were checked and double checked, to make sure no one was hurt.

"Right. We are sending up the next two recruits," a voice said over the airwaves. I'd seen a salvo of shells drop after the L/F Howitzers 105s opened up from eight miles away at precisely 9.30AM just to range them in; the impact area was clear of all personnel, and all personnel commanders had been informed that rounds were in the air, which also went out to any movement by air in the designated zone.

The Land Rover pulled in with the fresh recruits, who jumped out. I threw my webbing on and climbed aboard. I arrived back at a clearing, the 105s all at the ready just as another mission fire came in. Immediately I was given ear defenders and ordered on to charge filling detail setup away from the rear of the weapon. This involved the placement of colour-coded cordite in bags loaded in to the charge, which was then rammed home into the breach after the warhead. This information was given along with elevation and horizontal in degrees by a built-in computerized system, which relayed to the weapon from the command post housed in a purpose-designed vehicle parked near the guns, who were in contact with the ops. All of it worked on the theory of Pythagoras, or trigonometry. In a nutshell the ops spotted the target, and coordinates were radioed back to the command post along with ops' position; these were entered into the computer, which plotted the positions. From there it worked out the distance to the target area and any other relevant info needed to deliver the warhead to the target area. The guns must have pounded for half an hour as each mission fire came in.

At that point the blue sash, the safety officer, stepped down from the command post. "Number two gun knocked out; cease firing. Number three gun knocked out; cease firing." We had been spotted and had taken hits from hostile aircraft, and we were ordered to fall in away from the weapons. "In roughly ten minutes a three-toner will arrive to take you all to a field hospital, where you will be designated an injury. At ease, lads; take five minutes and chill out—but no smoking," he warned the recruits.

God damn if I banged my hip again. I'm going to jump out and walk. We'd been on the three-toner for over half an hour and were thrown about like laundry in a tumble dryer. I was beginning to feel sick and I made my way to the rear of the vehicle, grasping the rope and looking out. I could see over to the left a large red cross in a white circle on a large green marquee system, pegged out in a clearing and set deep in the forest. "Thank God fer that. we are here, lads." A cheer went up along with sighs of relief. I stood at ease in our designated squads outside, waiting to get called in. It wasn't long before we were inside.

The doctors had the relentless task of form filling—which drugs to prescribe, and even amputations were discussed alongside the nurses, a lot of them male, which sort of surprised me. It brought down the reality of war. In my case it was first degree burns, or flash burns, and I'd had my clothes cut away from my legs and chest—well, simulated; I took them off myself, really. I received a simulated drip and a morphine injection. My eyes were all bandaged up. The nurses explained injuries such as mine were usually fatal and would be given preference. We spent most of the afternoon at the field hospital. From there we were moved to a stockade shelter to bed down for the night, and we were ordered off duty and given free time.

We spent most of the night laughing and joking and each of us using the remainder of our rations. One of the recruits was trying to use his karate skills on one of the younger recruits. I had noticed the kid being picked on during other occasions. I reached into my back pack and pulled out a utility knife and stepped over to the pair, unlocking the knife and holding the blade. I asked the karate expert if he would like to choose me as his new sparring partner. "Tell you what—try and attack me with this." I offered the handle to him. "Come on, I'm more your size. Take the blade."

The others went silent, and he eventually took it. I waited for his attack, and he did just as I thought he'd do: he came at me with a thrust to the stomach. Well that was easy; I stepped to the left of him, parrying his thrust with the palm of my right hand and taking hold of his arm with my left, forcing his arm behind his back with the aid of my right. I kept him moving in the same direction he was going, bumping him off to the side of the night shelter.

He was raging; I could sense it. "Want to try again?" I teased. This time he came with an overhead, downward thrust. I stepped into it, blocking with my left arm and sneaking my right arm under his arm locking my hand into my left arm and stepping through again. I kicked into his calf with a back heel, which landed him straight on his arse. I then locked out his wrist and took the knife from him, holding it to his throat and making sure he could feel the cold steel dig into him. Then I let him up.

He backed away, shaking his head. I folded the knife and placed it back into the webbing. The rest of the recruits were still silent. I looked at the kid who'd been picked on, and he smiled, nodding. I rolled out my mat and sleeping bag and broke out the rest of my coffee, heating the last of my water from my canteen. The kid came over and sat down. "How old are you, son?"

"Nineteen," he said. "I thought I'd try this first to see if it suited to me. You know, try it out a bit before I join the regs."

"Yes, this will give you a good insight." I was eager to keep the kid interested. I'd noticed he was quiet and did as he was told. "What do you think of the army life ?"

"Erm, mixed feelings," he replied. "It's not how I expected it to be."

"And what did you expect?"

"Well, I didn't know what to expect, to tell you the truth."

I laughed and said, "Life ain't easy, mate. The secret is to make it bearable and to listen in and do exactly what they tell you. Then you won't go far wrong. What do they call you, son?"

"My name is Simon."

"I'm Max." I put out my hand, and he shook it. I noticed he had a good grip. That was a good sign, at least. "Get yourself a mug; you can have half of this."

I knew I caused bad feeling with karate kid and went over to him after I finished my coffee. "No hard feelings, eh?" I said as I stood over him.

"Where did you learn that?" he asked.

"I just learned it. You see, I was like our friend Simon over there. At the moment he is deciding his future."

"Who the fuck are you?" he asked.

"They call me Max." I grinned. "No hard feelings, man."

The next morning I rose, and it was just daylight. I made my way out to take a leak. I looked at my watch: 6.30. They'd be here at seven to take us back out the guns. I rushed back into the night shelter to repack my kit. The rest of the gang was just stirring. Simon and I were the first out and watched for the three-toner to arrive as we sat on our webbing. The grass was covered with dew, and a low mist was still present in the lower parts, covering the woods and fields; the green of the trees broke through higher up. The sun was just rising out of the low grey cloud cover. I enjoyed the warmth.

"It's here; I just seen it on the rise," Simon said as he rushed into the shelter to tell the others. Two of them were still in bed, and he came out laughing. I rushed in the door, picking up their kits and throwing them on the two corpses. "I ain't waiting around here all morning for you two—get that packed, and let's move out." I could hear them groaning as they stirred.

We arrived at the guns and jumped down from the three-toner. The chef had been up early and prepared breakfast; the smell of its delights made my stomach rumble. The BSM was having a shave and was grinning at me as he sharpened his cutthroat on the belt. "Good night's sleep, Max?"

"Why no, Sergeant Major, bloody freezing in that night shelter."

"Who ordered that?" he inquired.

"I don't know, sir. They took us there after being discharged from the hospital."

"Those stockades are like bloody fridges," he commented. "Ready for some breakfast?"

"Sure am, Sergeant Major."

Sergeant Major Smith appeared. "Friggin' hell, it's the lance bombardier. How have you been keeping, Max?"

"Fine, Sergeant Major. Hungry, though."

"Right, break out yer mess tins and go see chef, chop chop." I grinned, pleased to see him out in the field.

We road shotgun in the tractor units on the way back to base. The battery had decided to wrap up early before the burning of the cordite ceremony, which once taken was not allowed back. We arrived back at roughly 5.00PM,and the BSM ordered the bar open, where a few pints were made welcome after helping put the equipment away.

Sergeant Smith came and sat down at the table. 'Does it feel good to be back home, Max?"

"It sure does, Sergeant Major."

The next thing I knew it was party time. The rest of the battery walked in, and soon the bar was filled with bodies of all ranks, with individuals taking turns to entertain the rest of the troops. Then it was my turn. I was pissed as a rat crawling out of a cider barrel, so I gave them the old "Allowetta, shontie Allowetta" song, and every one joining in. Then I went and forgot the next bit, so I started to make it up. The BSM stopped it when I said, "How I love her collie flower tab?"

"Collie flower tab?" he shouted. "We ain't having that one. Come on, Max, you got to draw the line somewhere."

I had to go sit back down, and the whole place was in hysterics. I said, "Well, with this amount of alcohol in me, I ain't fussed."

The BSM just wanted to do his Lancaster bomber bit—it was top secret, and you have to have signed the official secrets to see it.

Then the final act—Sergeant Major Smith. This one involved dropping your khakis and shaking your wily in a circle at the end of the song. The funny thing was, only me and Sergeant Smith did it. Everyone else bottled out. Then I saw the flash on the camera. Sergeant Major Smith rushed straight over to the person that took it. "Give me that bleeding camera." I was soon over, backing him up. I'd seen situations like this get out of hand. Sergeant Major Smith took the spool from it. "What happens in here stays in here," he commented. I agreed whilst I was swaying about like reeds in the wind.

THE MARKETPLACE, JULY 1994

I'd just come back from personal protection classes; it was Griffon's last session before he went abroad; he wouldn't say where he was going, leaving my half-brother Big Tony and Lee to run the class. I'd seen a brown Renault GT 5 turbo being thrashed around the marketplace. Then it was parked, with two males running away. I knew who they were. They came to the block I was staying at to see another resident there, whom I also knew. Noggin was his street name, a white guy around 5'10", medium build with short cropped hair. He wore Nike gear with a baseball cap.

Having seen them and knowing full well that wasn't their car, I thought I'd do a bit of poking about. I knocked on my wall that divided my flat from Noggin's and went to the window. His top vent came open. "Coming round, Max?" he shouted. "I've just put on a video."

"Yep, two seconds." I laced up my boots and shot downstairs and turned the corner to his door. Noggin opened it and invited me up. He sat with two other friends, Anton and Butley. Anton was white and had a stocky build; he around 5'10" and wore all Adidas stuff, and he always wore a cap to cover his brown hair. Butley was white, 5'7",and medium build. He had ginger hair and wore VSL and polo shirts with Armani jeans. I knew them both—dodgy characters who smoked weed with Noggin.

"I've just seen a GT5 getting tanned, and guess who I seen get out of it?" I said as I sat down.

The pair started laughing. "It was took last night from the airport. The owner of it works there," Anton said.

"Yeah, and he's been seeing this schoolie. We ain't mentioning names, but she's thirteen," Butley added.

"And how old's the owner?"

"Twenty-six."

"And you know this fer sure, do you?"

The pair of them nodded, and Anton said, "That's his passport," throwing it to me. I took a look, noticing the name; he was Muslim. "He's been giving her ecstasy."

"Has he now? Any proof of this?"

Anton shook a box. "Pills retrieved from the car."

He threw the box, and I caught it and looked in. They had smiley faces on them—must have been twenty pills in it. I wiped my prints from it and threw the box back. "Get rid of them."

Noggin lit a bifter, and the air soon filled with the smell of skunk. It kind of hit me straight in the nostrils.

"We also found kinky underwear under the seat; the kid claims he forced her to put it on. And these." I looked at some artwork done on an audiotape box. It was not unlike IRA or UDA promo paintings, but this had an Arabic or Eastern writing alongside the logo, and it said "Al Qaeda" with an AK 47 through the middle of it.

"Right, I need to take a look in the car."

"We ain't driving that car anywhere." Anton and Butley started to panic.

"It's okay, I just want to look around it inside."

Noggin reached for his jacket. "I'll come down with you, Max."

We walked across the market. It was a Wednesday night, and not many people were about. I pulled my sleeves over my hands and opened the door; they'd left it unlocked. I fidgeted in the glove box and found a set of plans. I opened them out. It looked like two large buildings. I couldn't understand the writing, but the design was similar to the artwork seen earlier. I looked under the driver's seat. There were samples of kinky underwear, all different types, including a leotard in black. "Right, Nogg, I've seen enough. Lock it and lets mizz."

I spent most of the night pondering over what I'd seen, and I decided to go and see my commander the next morning. I passed through security at the main gate.

The captain's secretary invited me through. "He won't be long, Max, he'll see you shortly."

When I was allowed in, the captain sat at his desk and addressed me by my second name. "What can I do for you Rocks?"

"I'm not sure, sir. I have come across this on my travels." I handed him the passport and explained the whole story of how I came by it and what I'd seen.

The captain made a note of the name in the passport and then handed it to me. "Put it back where you found it, or hand it in to the police," he said sternly. "And if you want to remain a part of this battery, then you've got to keep out of stolen cars."

"But sir, I haven't stolen it."

"Dismissed, soldier. About turn."

I left the office disgruntled. I could tell the secretary had been earwigging at the door as I walked back through, she'd just got back to her desk as I opened the door. She was smiling. "Tough morning, Max," she remarked.

"You could say that, Miss Money Penny," I joked.

I walked downstairs and headed out to the main gate. To the left I heard, "Oy, Max." I turned. Sergeant Major Smith stood with his hand on his head. I ran over to him. "In my office," he said, pointing. "What brings you here?"

When we reached his office, I threw him the passport. He looked at it quickly. "Well, he looks dodgy, fer a start. I can't even pronounce the name on it. Mohamed what? How did you come by it? I ended up telling him about the GT5 and its contents. "You did right, Max, yes you did. This is what you are trained to do. The Captain told you to put this back, you say? Better do that, then." He handed it back after copying the name and number from it. "Can you get those plans?"

"I'll see if the car's still about, Sergeant Major."

"Good work, Max. Dismissed."

I spent most of the evening searching for the car. It was Thursday evening, and the stalls for the flea market had been erected; the whole place buzzing with traders. I eventually caught up with Anton and Butley, who stood over at the far end of the market place near the toilets. "Where's the Renault?" I asked the two quietly. They gave me two names, claiming they took it and fired it. "Did they save those plans?"

"I don't know. I shouldn't imagine so," Anton answered.

"Yeah, but they would have seen them, wouldn't they?"

"Well, yeah, they'd have seen 'em. Why, Max?"

"It's just suspicious, that's all." I couldn't work out what an airport worker would be doing with them.

I handed in the passport to the police station that same evening anonymously. A few months passed, and I went up to Mum's. She'd sold the house an got herself a flat in the middle of the same estate. "There's been two officers looking fer you."

"What, police?"

"No, two MPs." I went white. "Just kidding!" Mum was laughing. "No, two army officers; they said you're to go in Wednesday evening, down to HQ. They left in an army Land Rover. Dirty thing it was, all camouflaged. Something about your address."

Wednesday came, and we were doing aerobics when I was called out the main hall. "The Captain wants to see you," Sergeant Major Smith said.

Miss Money Penny showed me through in to the captain's office. "Ah, skip the drill. Sit down, Max." He pointed to the chair at the window. "I'm suspending you on medical grounds." My jaw dropped, and he quickly explained. "I'm placing you undercover." My ears pricked up. "I want you in a civilian capacity. I don't want you seen coming here."

"You mean I might be on to something, sir?"

"I think you might. Some inquiries have been made regarding information you've given." The captain looked at official documents. "Sergeant Major Smith will give you a debriefing on the way out. That will be all, Max. Good luck." The captain put out his hand and I shook it.

Sergeant Major Smith was waiting in the secretary's office. They were laughing and joking. "What does he call you?"

"Miss Money Penny," she replied. The two of them broke out in laughter.

"Come on, Max, downstairs—follow me. Here's the situation: I want you to keep an eye on these." He gave me two names and addresses. "That's the local Al Qaeda."

"Who is Al Qaeda, Sergeant Major?"

"Not much we know about them; they're a Muslim terrorist faction—a very dangerous organization. We've had reports about known individuals who are in this country. I am activating the tracker as of midnight tonight."

He nodded at my watch. "Spend ten minutes and read that." It was details of the tracking device and those who had access to it. I placed the info back in the envelope and gave it back to the sergeant major.

"You'll need to set up as a local gangster, get a name fer yourself. The police are working to try and get these people behind bars. Until that happens, I want these two kept an eye on. You won't even get close to them if they think you're clean or working undercover, so do what you can to access their facility. Any questions?"

"That's no holds barred then, Sergeant Major?" I remarked.

"Correct."

I ran straight into PC Hardy coming out the entry, and he startled me. "I want a word up here, out the way." he walked up the entry. "You handed in a passport?"

"Erm, yeah. What about it?"

"We've been looking at some CCTV footage." PC Hardy looked at his notebook. I went quiet. "I'm not here to run you in."

My mind flashed back to when I was I kid. PC Hardy had caught us scrimping in the old orchard. He was younger and fitter then. He had just given us a good ticking off and sent us on our way.

He finally found what he was looking for and gave me a name. "Jemma." I looked at him and nodded, and he put his notebook away. "That's another one," he said. I could see what he was driving at. I knew the family. I'd also heard about Jemma's escapades with her ex boyfriend, Beeston. She was thirteen and he was nineteen.

I went back to the crew in the block. I brought the subject up after sitting in with Nogg, Anton, and Butley; Nogg already knew about it. "Hey, Beeston, he owes me a dollar," Anton chirped up. Then he said, "What's he done, and how do you know her?" Anton was paying attention.

"I know her sister and her boyfriend. Her ma works in the booth around the corner." Nogg told him the rest.

A week or so passed. I heard Beeston had been kidnapped after his house was robbed with him in it. They blindfolded him, stashed all the goods in a safe house, and drove him to a remote spot, with all the handles stripped out the back doors of the car so there was no escape. He was then given a good roughing up and his trainers set on fire with lighter fuel. He was last seen running across the field trying to douse the flames.

I had my hands across my eyes. "He'll grass," I said. "You'll bring it all on top."

"Who was involved in that?" Anton asked

"Houlahan, myself, and another—you don't know him."

Anton was fidgeting with his spliff. Your suppose to . . . Oh, it doesn't matter. I knew it was a waste of time saying anything; they'd done it and that was that. What was you going to say, Max?"

Becky, Anton's girlfriend, sat in with us. I said, "Well, I'd have put a ski mask on, fer a start." Becky and the rest of crew roared with laughter. "Hey, shh!" I could hear whistling outside and knocking on the wall. Dean in the lower right flat had his head out the window. "What's up?" I shouted.

"Can I come up?"

"Go down, then I'll let you in."

Dean came up. "Friggin' heck, it smells like an allotment in here. Who's burning garden rubbish?" Everyone burst out laughing again as Nogg handed him the spliff. "I was wondering whether to call the fire brigade," he continued, and everyone split their sides. "Hey, good shit, this." He took a few large puffs on it. "Who's coming to the pub?"

"Nah, watching a vid tonight," Nogg said.

"Well, I'm off over the road," Dean said, and he disappeared.

Nogg had gone to his girlfriend's, and I'd returned to my flat. I just happen to look out down towards the market place around 11.30. Dean came out of the pub as I spied him kick the bottom door panel through at the electrical supply's trade centre, across the street. "Strewth, the alarm hasn't gone off," I thought. A long, slim box appeared through the hole, and then another one. Dean appeared a few minutes later and went back out the door with his balding head shining in the street light. He'd stacked them up and carried them across the street, put them in the entry, and ran back. His fat arse vanished as he entered back in through the hole in the door.

I fidgeted in the drawer for my ski mask and rushed out the flat, slipping it on along with a pair of gloves. I looked at the boxes. "Showers? He's nicking showers? Right." I rushed across the street and in through the hole. I just caught him walking back from behind the rack with a pile of boxes, and he dropped them. He let out a scream. "Shh, it's me, Max. Shut up."

"Friggin' hell, Max." He held at his chest whilst he got his breath back. "I thought it was the grim reaper."

"Shh. I want to take a look around," I said, spotting a torch on the desk.

"There's more upstairs," he said, and I switched the torch on and shined it up the door well to the stairs. We got up there, and Dean had already pushed the door back. The windows were boarded up, and the place was pitch black as I shone the torch in.

"Hey, we could use these." I had hold of miniature CCTV kits, complete with monitors, and some colour CCTV cameras and sensors.

Dean had a large cardboard box open. "Shine the torch in here, Max?" They where burglar alarms. We started laughing. "I'm emptying the place," he adamantly declared. We spent the rest of the night ferrying items back to the flat. "I can shift the lot," he said, counting up the goods.

"I'm keeping one CCTV box set."

"You can't set that up here, Max—he'll look out and see it."

"Nah, it's to trade with someone." I placed the box into the cupboard.

"Trade fer what?"

"Transport," I said calmly. Dean nodded.

The next morning, one of Dean's friends took the lot, handing over eight hundred sovereigns in cash. Dean split the cash with me. "That's a good start," I thought. Next evening Big T had a recessed personal protection class, and I sat downstairs with a pint. I explained I had something to trade and that I had a transport problem, explaining the task of keeping an eye on two individuals that stayed in the city. Big T gave me a time to go over to his house.

A few days later I had a meeting with two of T's associates. I took possession of a brand-new Suzuki 500 sling shot and a Freddie Spencer race replica helmet—both nicked, of course. Having got the bike home with still a small outstanding debt. I stripped it down to its bare essentials to lose extra weight. I needed to be slick and fast. I pushed the bike into the entrance and covered it with a bed sheet.

On Friday evening Nogg had came up to the flat and spotted the bike on the way in, lifting the cover. "Hey Max, that's a cool looking bike. Is that yours?"

"I borrowed it," I replied as we walked upstairs and I loaded infrared film into my new camera.

"That's a smart piece of kit," he said as he noticed the brand.

"I got it fer next to nothing from the flea market—sixty sovs. I went into the city today and fetched this fer eighty sovs, complete." I snapped the zoom lenses onto the camera. Nogg tried it out the window. "I also got this fer twenty-five sovs." I showed him the new flash gun as I stuck a piece of written film over it. Nogg looked interested. "If anything happens to me, Nogg, retrieve this camera." I was serious. "You'll do that fer me, won't you?"

"Well sure, Max," Nogg said, confused.

I put the camera away in its bag. "Come downstairs; you can help me put this plate on." I'd had a plate made for bike, and it read "ROX 69". Nogg laughed as he held the new plate straight whilst I screwed it home.

Later that evening I took the camera, jumped on the bike, and took the back roads into the city. I parked the bike around the corner from one of the addresses given by Sergeant Smith. I walked along a bit, setting the zoom lenses on the property in question and placing the camera through the opening in my helmet. I had the lens looking through the opening with the smoked visor covering so it couldn't be seen. All I had to do was slide the visor open and take my gloves away from the flash unit.

Two young broads came out of the entry where I stood. "Like your sexy black leathers, mister."

"Get out of it. What do you think I am, a cradle snatcher?" The pair giggled and walked down the street. I looked at my watch: 9.50.

Then the door came open. I aimed in the right direction just as a car passed. It was a city cab. Using it as a cover for the flash, I let go a volley of snaps as I watched the pair of Asians dressed in black climb into the back of a black series 5 BMW, which had pulled outside as the pair got to the gate. I noticed one using a mobile phone. "They haven't noticed me," I thought. I returned to the bike and moved to the next address, again leaving the bike around the corner. The Black BMW was parked outside as I took a note of the number. Again I did the same set up in the helmet, but this time I waited further up the road. A 6'2" Caribbean Rasta man came out the side entry, and I snapped away at him. He'd gotten into the BMW, started it as his Rasta music boomed out, and sped away, smoking the tyres. Right, that explained the mass of colour I'd seen on the driver's side when the car pulled up at the first address—it was his hat. I laughed as I retired from the scene.

It wasn't long before I was back home. I whacked the rest of the twenty-four exposures and removed the film from the camera, placing the spool in the cupboard; the unused films were kept in the fridge. Nogg had heard me come in, and he banged the wall for me to go around to his place. "I'll take the film in and express it," I thought. "But what if . . . Nah, can't express it. I'll save it fer now." I had the number of the BMW

I d spotted a course at the local college in the paper: "GNVQ, all courses." I thought I might inquire about that, taking a note of the enrolment date, which was in a few days. I wondered if they did photography?

Things were very much the same the next few days. I went to the marketplace and talked to the known local car thieves; they hung around the graveyard.

"Yep, we can take it," a guy named Thrower said confidently. I handed him the number and the address, as well as the plate numbers of the BMW.

"I need to look in the car," I said as I handed the piece of paper over.

"We will give you a shout. Hang on, Max, I want a favour."

"What's that?"

"I'm after taking a car out the leisure centre."

At that point Tubby and Chad walked over. "Which car's that, then? It wouldn't be that RS turbo, would it?" Chad said loudly. "We warned him to keep away from her."

Tubby turned to me and nodded toward Thrower. "He's got woman trouble, she's been going with the life guard."

"Oy, I was inside, remember?" Thrower said, defending his integrity.

"So what's the favour?" I waited for his answer.

"I want you knock out the freaking security camera in the car park."

"Oh, okay. Leave it with me." I left the scene.

That same night Nogg and I took a walk and just happened to be in the leisure centre car park. Do you think you could sell them?" I asked as I looked up at the cameras.

Next thing I knew he was shimmying up the pole and back down again. "I need some tools. Come on, easy job." We hitched up our collars and pulled our hats down as far as they'd stretch. We soon returned, tooled up. Nogg shimmied up again. "Here, catch." One of the cameras came down, catching it I placed it on the deck.

The following Friday the local rag read, "Cheeky thieves stole CCTV cameras," and there was a fuzzy picture of Nogg's face. We couldn't stop laughing—it was the main topic all night. We sat in the flat that evening with Nogg and his girlfriend, Fat Becky, and Anton and Kelly. I sat with Kelly—we were just friends Because she was only nineteen.

We heard a whistle outside. "Max, come down, I want you." Dean stood out on the pavement. "Nick and Thrower told me to say, 'Bingo,' and it's in there." He pointed to the carpet shop car park. They'd already taken the BMW. I was buzzing.

They sat in the car with ski masks on as I looked outside. I grabbed my own mask and gloves out of a drawer and left Nogg and the rest of the crew to look after the flat.

"Jump in, Max." I got in the back, and the BMW sped away before I'd even got the door shut. From the thud of the bass, I knew Thrower had slammed one of his own Dreamscape tapes in the cassette.

"Good pickings so far, Max. Where did you get the information on this? Look, a rolled, fat joint in the glove box." Nick lit it.

"What's in the boot?" I asked.

"We don't know yet; can't get it open." Thrower turned the music down slightly so we could hear each other. I arranged the eye sockets in my ski mask so I could see the pair of them. We came to an address I knew up on the other estate and pulled down the drive and around the back of the house. Another car thief came out—Snotty; I might have known.

"What's up?" he asked.

I shouted out, "I thought you gave all this up."

He looked surprised. "I know that voice. Max, what you doing in with these two crooks?"

"Slide hammer, I think," I said as I got out, looking at the boot. "Got one?"

Snotty went back into the house.

"That's why we came here, Max," Thrower said, laughing.

Snotty returned with the right tool for the job. A couple off whacks on it, and the boot sprung open. In the boot lay a briefcase over to one side, and also a holdall. I grabbed at the briefcase. "Who's got a fat screwdriver on him?" Thrower produced one, and we stood popping the locks as the lid flipped open. "Strewth." There were two bags, a white powder, and a stack of cash. "That's got to be coke." I poked at it and looked at Thrower, whose eyes seemed to bulge at the sight of the cash.

Nick made a grab for the holdall. "Hey, there must be at six ounces of weed in here, man." He tipped it out in to the boot along with a pair of smelly trainers. "Right, two bags of weed and some of the cash. All right, Max?" Nick offered.

"Well, yeah."

Thrower counted out the cash. Four grand, clean," he said. He counted out one grand and handed it over. "I ain't interested in the rest of the haul.

The other bags caught my eye. "Hey, what's that crystal stuff alongside the coke?"

Snotty opened one of three bags. "Looks like vanilla ice, man." He smelled at it. "Ha ha ha, we struck rocks!" Snotty started to work out its street value. I'll see you get a cut, Max."

We dropped Nick at his flat and put the car back where they had found it. We stripped out the stereo and stabbed the tyres and whipped out the distributor, throwing it over a fence further down the road.

"This way, Max," Snotty said as he led me and Thrower down a side street. The stolen RS Turbo sat in the side street. "Jump in; I'll take you back." I jumped in, and he reversed at a thousand miles an hour into a handbrake spin as he smoked it down the boulevard, soon reaching top speed. I never got back from the city that fast on my bike. When we pulled outside my flat, the effects of the g-forces were still present.

"I can afford to retire," Snotty joked. "But if there's more like that one, don't hesitate, Max." He smoked it, leaving me in a cloud of burnt rubber at the side of the road.

I arrived back in the flat. The crew was all monged out; bodies lay over each other, with a smell crossed between a skunk and poison perfume. Becky came to first. "Hey, Max, want to date with slab cracker?"

"Who's slab cracker?" I asked, laughing.

Noggin came to. "Ooh, wide load, mate—she hangs about near the bench on the market."

My attention turned. I could see where Dean had his hand right on Kelly's. "Oy, off her. You're too old fer her." I turned to Nogg. "Has he gone out with her since I've been out?"

"Nah, Max, he's just winding you up."

The commotion woke up Kelly. "Mmm, Max. Come here." She held out her arms as I dived on her for a cuddle.

Dean moved off the bed. "I know when I'm not wanted." He headed for the door.

"Where do you think you're going?" I snapped. Dean stopped. I threw him an ounce bag of weed. "Skin up," I demanded.

"Hey Max, where did you get—"

Just before Anton had finished, I threw Nogg the other one. "Skin up."

"God, Max." Kelly had her arse right on my crotch. "Oh, yes, *yes!*" she shouted louder and loader as she waggled around on me. Then she forced her hand into my pocket and pulled out the wedge. "You don't look the type to carry this amount about," she said as she spread the cash on the bed.

"Here, get your hair done," I said, peeling a couple of notes from the spread handing her the cash. I pointed to the bag I tossed to Noggin. Take half of that, Nogg; sell it if you like. Give the other half to Anton. Let's just say easy pickings, eh, lads?"

We spent the rest of the night getting battered. I'd had the VCR rigged to the stereo whilst we watched *Wyatt Earp* and *Forrest Gump*. Whilst I was out, Nogg had fetched a box of twenty-four brews and stocked my fridge. I snuggled down with Kelly, and everyone was happy.

SEPTEMBER

I went to enrolment night at the local college and asked about the art and design course, specifically about developing photographs. The professor said, "Yes we do a unit within the QNVQ structure, which covers processing methods."

"A dark room, you mean?" I said as I struggled to take in what the teacher was saying.

"Yes, exactly that. Can I sign you up?"

"Well, it's all new to me, so I suppose so."

"It's a full-time course, and there are grants available for materials and books. You will also still get benefits. Are you unemployed?" he asked.

"Yes, I'm on jobseekers allowance."

I started the course the following Monday at 9.00PM. I sussed out the setup and found my way around the facilities until it became second nature. The group consisted of a variety of people from old to young. Most of the afternoon was spent in a tutorial whilst the head teacher explained the units that were to be taken over the next two years—all sixteen of them—and the session ended with forms to be filled in for materials and brushes. He said fifty sovereigns would be paid by the college. "Yep, I'll have some of that," I thought. Next day I sneaked into the dark room in my dinner hour. All the trays were already set out as I extracted the spool that had been sitting in my cupboard the past few weeks.

"Hey, these at least turned out," I said to myself, looking at the close-ups. I took down the odd picture and examined it. Others were just a blur. I realized I'd not set the shutter speed, or I must have moved it somehow whilst it was in the helmet. Either way the shutter speed needed to be increased. I let the photos dry, relocking the door. I took the keys back out of the office, spotting that the teacher had nipped out near home time. I took down the fresh pictures, placed them in my bag, and replaced the keys.

Snenton was busy with traffic. I'd tailed two suspects I'd recognized from the photos on the bike, keeping back to avoid being noticed. They were travelling in a black H Reg Mercedes. I sat for awhile at the top of the street as they pulled in at an address in a row of terrace houses.

I spotted the Raster, who answered the door. He was arguing with them, and tempers flared and then calmed. "I just don't know, man," he said as questions were fired at him, some in a Middle Eastern language. The two went into the house and came out half an hour later. I'd circled the block a few times, trying not to look suspicious and choosing different places to park. They got in the car and drove, and I followed them along the boulevard, where they turned left. I thought I knew where they were going as I followed.

They turned into a busy car park, and I held back. Yes, the Black Orchid. It was the largest night club in the city. I positioned the bike in another car park opposite, removing my helmet and breaking out the zoom from my camera bag. I watched them leave the car and go in. I waited another five minutes and mizzed, getting back to the marketplace. I pulled a wheelie straight across it as I gave the handle bars a tug in second gear and powered her up at the 3500 revs, right past the car thieves who were cheering and waving from the confines of the graveyard. I timed it just right to drop the front end and make the turn right to the main drag that led to my flat and in through the gate leading around to the building. I Dismounted and turned off the bike using a small, five-millimetre screwdriver, before pushing the bike back in its hiding place.

I changed back into my casuals as Nogg banged the wall. I went to the window. "Coming round?" he asked.

"Yeah, sure, give me two minutes." I put the camera away. I hadn't taken any shots, just used the zoom for a closer look—a dry run.

Noggin's girlfriend opened the door for me. Woda sat with his latest girlfriend, Venables, as I walked in. Kelly was patting the bed, and I sat beside her. "Give us a hug then," she demanded, so I squeezed her tight.

"Mmm, that smells nice," I said as I took a sniff at her.

"It's Dupe." She giggled.

I peeled myself away from her embrace for a sec. "Right, Nogg, before I forget. Down to business. Fancy a walk?"

"Where?" he asked.

"The Market," I replied.

Woda butted in. "I'll walk on with you, Max. Hang on, let me just get this skillet together," he said as Nogg finished installing the roach to his joint.

"We'll take it with us. Only take two ticks; then we can come back and get battered." I reminded him about the brews still in my fridge. "Must be ten bottles left."

Woda soon looked anxious. "I'm up fer that." The three girls where yapping on about some record that just came out by the Fujis as we left the flat.

The air had took a turn cooler for the autumn as leaves started to fall and blow about the market place. The car thieves always stood where they stood because they knew they could make a sharp exit should the situation arise. I found Thrower in a dodgy Escort van, posing as a builder chilled out in the back with his power pipe and his little round spectacles on. Dreamscape was blaring in the back ground, and the back of the van reeked of skunk.

"Have they found that RS yet"? I inquired.

Nogg came to my side. "You mean he's had an RS Turbo away?"

"Ask him," I said.

Thrower was nodding as he laid in the back of the van. "That's what smoked past your flat a week ago, Nogg. I thought I'd better bring the crew up to date." He laughed.

I handed him the number of the Mercedes and where it could be found. "It's a rag top in black," I added.

Thrower looked at the number again and then at me. Then he broke away from the subject. "Hey, I just seen some Evil Knievel go past here on the back wheel—like just a blue flash. He was damn lucky, whoever it was. The last person to try that smashed his bike at the wall over there."

Nogg nodded in my direction. "That was Max. He just came back on a mean-looking blue street fighter bike." I scowled at Nogg for telling him.

Thrower muttered, "Rox 69," just as he took the ear piece from his ear; he'd been listening in to a portable scanner. "Oy they're looking fer that bike." He showed me the portable unit. "They'll have a chopper unit up, Max, if they see you on it again." He grinned as he got back to the car. "Black Orchid?"

"The car should still be there," I said.

"Right, leave it with me."

Nogg was fishing for the info on the piece of paper I'd just given Thrower as we walked away. "Hey, what's all that about?" he asked as we walked back into the entry.

"Just a bit of business, lads," I said as we went through the door.

"You has been up to no good—I can tell, you know."

Kelly also fished for answers as we walked back in. "Three wise monkeys."

"Them three," Nogg chirped.

"Right, I'll nip and fetch those brews." I changed the subject. "Here, you three go get a pizza—get two or three, even. I'm starving. Make sure one of them is four seasons, doll."

"Why are you paying, Max?" Kelly asked, flashing her eyelashes.

I peeled off two twenty notes and gave them to her. "Get the biggest, fattest pizzas they've got, doll." The three of them put on their kickers and new Nikes. "Right, who's fer a brew?" I said after they'd mizzed out. I made for the door.

"Look in the fridge, Max," Nogg said. "No need to go next door." I walked in the kitchen, opened the well-stocked fridge, and came back with three bottles of Scorpion, offering them out. I bit the top from the bottle and spit the cap in the bin. Woda gave me his bottle, claiming he couldn't open it like that. Nogg bit his lid off no problem.

The girls came back after we'd rolled a skillet each, putting on a movie and setting it up for their return. Nogg played about with techniques, setting up the speakers as the room just filled with the aroma of fresh pizza. Everyone tucked in as the boxes lay open.

"What's the film?" Kelly asked, putting the change in my lap.

"*Mission Impossible*," I replied, giving the change back to her. "That's fer going."

"Thanks, Max." She snuggled in closer as we sat back, stuffing our faces. "Turn it on, then." Venables sat with Woda, and Nogg sat with his woman.

Halfway through the film, Kelly said, "I'm sleeping with you tonight, Max, if that's all right. Although I need to be up at seven."

"Have you got work to do, doll?" I asked, still a little surprised.

"I work at a hair dressing salon on a Saturday in the city. Ma thinks I'm staying at Venables' house tonight. You'll cover for me, won't you, babes?"

Venables sighed and said, "Don't make it too regular."

I was proper pissed when Kelly and I walked in the door—I mean I was hanging man. Kelly had to hold me up whilst I climbed the stairs. I woke at two in the morning as Kelly was shaking me. "Max, someone's shouting up, tooting their hooter with ski masks on. Hey, is that who I think it is? Tell me you don't know them." Kelly turned to face me, waiting fer an answer. I came to, rubbing my eyes and looking out the window. Kelly was furious.

"Keep it warm, doll. I won't be long." I saw the car go in the car park straight across from the block and put the lights out.

"That's if I'm still here," she grumbled as she sat on the bed, still looking out.

I went in the drawer and took my ski mask and gloves. I was rubbing my hands as we drove out the car park. Nick drove across the market and flashed his lights, and Thrower followed in the escort van. Eventually we pulled into a car park near the Blidwood Bottoms. I could hear stereos playing loudly, and there were a lot of cars there as we arrived; something was happening. Then I realized Murph and the crew and his big blue bus was there, with a generator, PA decks, and a light rig that'd blow one's mind. They were holding a free 24 hour rave as DJ SY pumped out. I'd been here a few times in the past.

"It' there, look," Nick said as he pulled the RS in beside it.

"We don't need these on, then," I said, pulling off my mask. Thrower pulled into the spot on the other side. "Right, what we got then?" We got out and started to look around the car. "Cleanly took—I'm impressed. Use the old American slide, did you?" Nick laughed. "What's in the boot ?"

"I'm trying to open it," Thrower said, arriving on the scene. "Just act natural, lads. Folks passing and all that." We turned to smile at the ravers. "Click it, it came open." We turned and looked in. The same holdall and a suitcase. We stood looking around.

"I can sell the car," Nick piped up. "At least a grand."

"Hey, we can't sell it. I want to see in that case." Thrower tipped the holdall out. "That's heroin." I could see through the cellophane. It was a brown powder in four weighed-out bags. There were more bags—crack cocaine and cocaine and another six bags of weed. "I want nothing to do with that," I said, poking at the heroin.

"Hup, don't be hasty." Thrower fiddled with the locks on the suit case.

Nick handed him a fat screwdriver. "It's all right, it's all clear—bust it." Soon the case was open.

"Somebody planning a trip," I muttered. There were even airport tickets, and I looked at them. To Egypt, return fare with a name Muslim in origin. I couldn't pronounce it. The smell of Paco Rabanne filled my nostrils as I searched through the clothes in the case. "Hey, what's this?" Foreign and British currency along with traveller's cheques, fifty-sovereign notes.

"I can get rid of the foreign currency and the cheques; you keep the cash, Max," Nick said as he made a grab for the bundle. There must have been a grand and a half in cash as I stuffed it in my pocket.

"Right, I want a bag of that Charlie," I said after I rethought my strategy. "And a bag of that smack." The haul was shared out as we locked up the boot.

Nick said, "You take the RS, Max. I'll take the Merc. You follow in the van." Thrower smiled, happy with the deal. "I'll flash the lights if I pick any thing up on the scanner."

We put the Merc back at the Black Orchid with the stereo stripped out. We also took out the distributor and downed the tyres before pulling away. I sat in with Nick in the RS 2000 when Thrower flashed his lights behind us and turned off at the last junction. We'd passed a routine patrol car on the boulevard.

"Let's see how this baby handles," Nick said, hitting the gas. He jumped two sets of lights to get off the main drag. A T 5 traffic patrol had the other side of the roundabout closed off on the approach, forcing us left.

"Don't go to the top of here—it's a dead end," I screamed as I sat with both arms locked, my hands pressing on the dash. I noticed a blue light closing in as I looked around. The next I knew, the whole world spun as Nick pulled the hand brake and turned a 540 as he gunned it after selecting first gear, swerving to miss the oncoming patrol car. We just lost them. Nick laughed, and I was just relieved I was still alive as we passed another oncoming T 5. "They hunt in pairs," I joked. "And now they're going that way." I pointed my thumb backwards. "You'd be better to head towards Sherwood." Again Nick skipped every set of traffic lights, narrowly missing an articulated lorry. "Right, now take the road to Arnold and slow down, act normal." I still had my hands over my eyes. Nick's driving seemed to be removed from the heat as we found ourselves on the back road into Chuckwalla.

"Jump out, Max. There's the key to the lock up. You open up the doors and I'll drive her in." The RS purred like a cat as it sat on tick over, filling the lock up with fumes. Then all was silent. Nick left just enough room to slide out the driver's side.

"Security at the Black Orchid must have rumbled us," I said as I locked up the doors, handing back the key.

Nick pulled out a mobile phone, switching it on. "Yeah, yeah. Lost 'em, mate. We are at the lock up. Yep, meet you there." He hung up. "Come on, Max, up here." We waited at the top of the next street, away from the lock up.

Thrower turned up. "Whooee, that was close." Nick was still buzzing. "Jump in, Max."

"I think I'll walk. Thanks, lads. I've only got to go a few blocks. I'll go up the back streets." I stashed the drugs in an out building, just outside the back door. "Right just forget about that fer now; say nothing to no one," I said to myself.

Kelly woke and turned to face me as I slid in beside her. "Don't run with them, Max, please, I'm begging you." She'd been crying, and her mascara was all over the place.

"Shh, go to sleep, Kelly." I swept the hair from her forehead and kissed it. "Go to sleep, doll."

"I fancy a spliff, Max."

"Right, I'll roll you one." I got out of bed and flicked on the light. Hopefully this would shut her up.

"Phew, I like your legs, Max—a bit on the milky side but sexy."

"Hey, naughty naughty," I said as I rolled a two skinner each. We sat on the bed looking down across the marketplace dawn just breaking; it was 5.30.

"Max, I'd ask you to shag me, but it's the wrong time of the month."

"Well, fancy waiting till I'd finished me spliff to tell me that." I frowned. "You disgust me sometimes, Kelly. You really do. Now pipe down and go to sleep."

She knew I was only kidding. "Cuddle me, Max."

When I woke I saw this blurred outline of Kelly hopping around and trying to pull on her jeans. "Max, I'm late for work!" I looked at my watch as my vision came back: 7.30. Thank God it was Saturday—no college today.

December

Butley had a habit of bringing in boxes of garments—all fake of course. Nogg, Woda, myself, and Anton rummaged through. I picked out a couple of YSL shirts and a few pairs of slacks. "These will do fer tonight," I thought, handing Butley the cash.

I'd bought a blue XR3 earlier that day after spotting it in the paper after a tip from the battery. The daughter of the captain whom I'd seen had said it was in the paper. I'd phoned from a call box and made arrangements to go out and see. It looked good and turned out to be a reliable runner. I bought it with eleven months MOT and six months Tax.

I had talked Chad and Tubby into going in to Black Orchid to gather new info on the two suspects, having tactfully pointed out the two Asians to them a week earlier. I waited outside with a camera and had taken up a good position in the car park whilst Jody fidgeted with the dash with one of the Mickey toys out of a Happy Meal. Jody was Chad's girlfriend and told us she was nineteen; afterwards I asked her auntie, who laughed and told us she was sixteen.

"Let's go to McDonald's, Max." I was left to baby sit again. I relented after she'd asked for the sixth time. Chad, who was eighteen, had pulled her a few weeks ago. Chad and Tubby insisted I'd be better off sitting with a female in the car, to give me a better cover. We returned to the Black Orchid. Jody had ordered her usual chicken nuggets and an ice cream sundae.

"Erhh, that's sickly," I said as I'm looked through the zoom to the main exit.

"How many women you slept with, Max?"

"A few. Why, Jody?"

I spotted Chad and Tubby walking out the main door and back towards the car. They had a woman with them. "Fiver to get in Max," Chad said. "Lots of E knocking about in there, and guess who's been selling it?"

Strewth, it was Etna. "Oh, hi, Max." Are you coming in, babes?"

Tubby said, "Go on, Max, it's jumping in there." He seemed to have that beam on his fizz.

Etna had my car door open and pulled at my arm. "Come on, Max."

"Okay, okay," I said, slipping the cover back over the lens and putting the camera back in its case. I got out of the car and dropped the case in the boot.

"Keys." Chad held out his hand, and I dropped them in it. Chad jumped in the driver's side, and Jody got out to let Tubby into the back seat.

Etna took my arm and walked me over to the main doors. She went to the bar whilst I looked for the two Asians. I couldn't see them anywhere in the main arena. Etna came back with the drinks; she got me my usual Diet Coke.

Then I caught sight of one of the men going into the foyer with a white, blonde-haired male in his early twenties following him. I figured they'd gone into the bogs to do a deal. I nudged Etna. "I want you to buy some pills off someone."

"I've already took one," she laughed as she started dancing to the music. She rummaged in her handbag.

I stopped her. "No, I don't want to take one—I just need to know if this particular person is selling."

"Who is it?" She started to look around.

I'd seen the Asian return, talking to one of the bouncers. "That's him, with his back to us."

Etna clocked him. "Leave it with me." I handed her twenty sovereigns from my wedge. Etna's eyes bulged as I put the wedge back in my pocket discreetly. She wandered off, leaving me at a table with her daughter, who had turned up with a friend, having caught a taxi. I'd known Michele for years and more or less watched her grow up.

"Watch our bags whilst we go and dance, Max," Michele said, and the pair disappeared into the packed arena as Etna came back. She placed four pills in my hand under the table, and I closely examined one of them. They were smiley faces.

"I've seen those before," Etna commented. "I usually get Doves." She paused. "I've heard bad reports about those, Max. I very nearly never bought them."

"Did you get these from the guy I pointed out?"

"Dirty bleeder asked me to go back to his yard with him. I told him where to get off, of course." I knew Etna had only came for a night out. I also knew her fella.

After we left the night club, we made our way to Blidwood Bottoms and spent the rest of the night at Murph's free rave.

The next morning I rose and put on the radio. Chad and Jody, who had stayed here off and on, where still asleep as the news came on. I found there had been a girl, nineteen, rushed to Queen's Medical. She had been out on the town and gone to a party, where she collapsed. She later died in the hospital after doctors battled to save her life. The cause of death was dehydration due to taking ecstasy.

I stopped and thought about what Etna had told me. I knew she was a skilled nurse, and she knew what she was talking about. I placed the pills in an envelope along with a photograph of the male that sold Etna the pills, and I handed them in to the local police, having written Black Orchid on the front.

Later that week a few arrests were made, and a person had been charged with her murder. Police also issued details of the pills in question, warning people not to take them. These had been made up of heroin, MDMA, and traces of cocaine and crack cocaine. "One down, two to go," I thought, remembering who was left. It had struck me that although previously I had my suspicions, it was a chain to a factory making the deadly pills we'd been hitting, and now we had a young girl's life taken from her—and there could be more that evening.

Anton was circling around on his mountain bike. "Oy, I told you to get rid of 'em," I yelled.

"What?"

"You know what I'm talking about. Right, who did you give them pills out to, from out of the Renault?"

"Why?" I figured Anton had seen the news. Usually he told me straight away.

"I meant you to flush 'em." Anton still evaded the issue. "You're barred from the flat until you tell me."

One of Nogg's bredgins turned up He'd been seen in Nogg's a few times and liked his mixes—a common housebreaker. "I hear you're a bit of a lad," he said as I turned to face him. I read his movement and sensed a kick rising, counteracting it with a standard foot block. I caught the top of his foot with the underside of my boot, resulting in him hopping around the marketplace. Anton burst out laughing as he rode away.

Nogg wasn't pleased at me for barring Anton. I explained about the killer pills and that they had been dished out around here a while ago. "Oh, Etna told me about those." Nogg now understood. "Yeah, I seen it on the news. Remember that Renault GT 5? That's the same pills. I know who's got them."

I stopped him. "You mean they're still in circulation?"

Nogg seemed agitated. "I'll get them tonight," he reassured me. "You'll need to watch out while I bust in."

"Hang on, let me get this straight. How many are left?" I wasn't letting it drop.

"Twelve, maybe. They never took anymore; they all had a bad time on 'em."

That night me an Nogg walked along the back streets to where the killer pills where housed. "He'll be out on the blag," Nogg said as he stopped at the rear of some terrace housing. "Shh, wait here. Whistle up if you see anyone around." He disappeared over a wall and came back ten minutes later, throwing me the pills. "They were in the corner of the window sill." I checked to see how many had gone from the original amount. "I'm taking this too." I laughed. Nogg was legging it down the street and back to his house with a stereo system—nothing suspicious about that.

I decided to walk the other way, just in case. I figured he'd probably nicked that off a person that had nicked it in the first place.

I'd just walked in the door and could hear shouting coming from next door, and that unmistakable sound of something getting the crap kicked out of it. I thought I'd nip and investigate. I thumped the wall and stood in the entry at Nogg's door when I heard a bump, bump louder and louder. I jumped back as Nogg's washer came crashing through the glass panel in the door. I looked up the stairwell and saw Woda and Nogg with his cap tilted back scratching his head. Nogg said, "I told you to wait fer Max and not to let go. Now look."

Nogg's girlfriend and Venables had come down the top flight of stairs, their hands over their mouths. Woda, a white guy who had dark hair and was around 5'10" with a thin build, stood shaking his head. I could tell who had had the heavy bit. "Are you okay, Max? Sorry about that."

I pulled the washer out from the door and moved it to one side, minding the glass. "I'll get a brush and dustpan," said Nogg's missus, and she disappeared back upstairs. I walked in through the newly made hole.

"I'll have to put a new door on that," Nogg said, still scratching under his cap.

"Before we do any more, I want you to witness this," I said as I walked into Dean's toilet, who must have been out at the pub. Woda and Nogg looked in, followed by Nogg's missus and Venables. "That's the killer pills gone." I split the bag and emptied them in to the pan, flushing the handle.

After we cleared up the mess, Nogg said, "Right, you wait here, Max, whilst me and Woda nip out." I sat in with Nogg's missus and Venables. The two arrived back twenty minutes later with a new spanking dryer. I could see them disappear up the entry with it from the window and heard the two of them puffing and panting up the stairs.

"That's a brand-new, top-of-the range dryer, you numpty,"

"Hey, I thought it was a washer. Ha ha! I thought it was lighter than the one we took out."

I came to the top of the stairs and asked, "Have you two been at the weed again?" I could see something wasn't right.

Nogg was scratching the back of his head again under his cap. "It's no good, Woda. We'll have to go back. Max you wait here."

Twenty minutes later, the pair returned empty-handed. "Max we need a hand. We got it as far the bone yard. Look at me, I'm sweating like a rapist."

I couldn't help but laugh. "What, you left a washer in the bone yard?" I asked.

"It's a bran' spanker." Nogg was still trying to get his breath. "Them car thieves will end up poaching it." Woda looked knackered, tying to straighten his back. I took pity on them and went and helped them get it home. I had visions of Thrower and his crew making off with it in his van.

"Where did you find this?"

"Outside the utility old fogies home." I groaned and put my hand over my eyes. They chose not to tell me until after I'd helped them up to the kitchen with it.

I decided to move the bike to another location, operation Al Qaeda mob, ceased to exist. I scanned the known area were they had been staying; the house was in darkness every time I went to check it out. I clocked the Rasta man at his address a few times, having found out it was just weed and small amounts of coke. He obviously sold it from his premises judging by the small amount of traffic going to his door, and although I still considered him a future target. I let the matter cool, whilst keeping a note of his car reg.

Mum had said it was okay to place the bike at the back of her flat. A friend also had offered his mum's garage, and the bike was stored away, who's father was an officer at 307 battery.

Bangers and Dean were mizzing around the market, smoking tyres in a fairly new silver XR2 Turbo. It was the first time I'd seen one up close. "Smart looking car," I commented as they pulled up. Nogg and Woda were over to the right of me laughing and joking and talking to Thrower, who was sat on his mountain bike. Tubby and Chad stood alongside them, watching the smoke rise.

Something caught my eye. A car had pulled onto the market and the door opened. It was a black XR3 with the back windows silvered out. They'd just stopped to picked up a lassie who had been standing on the corner—a young blonde aged around fifteen. One of the Asians had jumped out to let her into the car.

"Hey, ain't that the chick whose been going with Johnnsy?" Chad said, drawing attention to her.

"Who?" Tubby's face lit up. They circled by us, then I caught sight of the driver as he put up his widow. Now where had I seen him before? I scanned for a better view. The Black Orchid. I presumed he was the brother of one of my targets, judging by the photos and what I'd already seen.

"Johnnsy will have that away," Thrower shouted over.

"Black Orchid," I shouted back, and Thrower nodded in agreement.

Bangers, who happen to notice, was listening to the conversation, asked, "What's Johnnsy's girlfriend doing getting in with them?"

"She'll have met them down at the Black Orchid," Tubby and Chad noted, commenting on the Morris Minors Act.

"I know him," Bangers said as his eyes fixed on the XR3 that sat at the traffic lights.

"How do you know him?" I asked, and my ears pricked up as I waited for Bangers' reply.

"Weed smoking smack head." Bangers seemed sure. "He gets his weed same place as me."

I looked at Dean, who looked blank and said, "I don't know him—don't look at me." Dean was still looking at the black XR3. "I'm thinking that's his weed we had been smoking a couple of months back." The XR3 sped off from the traffic lights.

"Hey weed? Who's talking weed?" Nogg and Woda asked, joining in the conversation. "I'm taking orders if you want any."

I stepped closer, nearer to the driver's side, and crouched in. "He needs taught a lesson. I need to come down with you when you score."

"I'm picking up tonight, in forty-five minutes," Bangers replied.

"Hey, I want a Henry," Nogg butted in from the passenger side.

Thrower was looking over from his famous stance, all suspicious.

"Can you give ten minutes? Meet you back here," I said. Bangers agreed and mizzed.

I walked back to the yard with Nogg and Woda. They were rubbing their hands at the thought of getting stoned. "I hope it's good weed, man—I'm gagging," Nogg said. The two of them disappeared through the door.

I walked over to the out building, reached into the outhouse, and retrieved the brown packet of heroin from where I'd hidden it. I made my way up to my pad and changed out of my college clothes into my black USAF jacket and jeans. I slipped a saw blade and a fat screwdriver down my jeans.

Dean jumped out as I jumped in. "See you later, Max. How many bucks you got on you?" I reached in my pocket and drew out a wedge. "Hup, more than enough. Lend me a score." I peeled off a couple of bills and handed them over to Dean.

"Sheeks, Max, how much you looking for?" Bangers' eyes popped as he stared at the money.

"How big's the dealer?" I joked. I was all of a sudden fighting g-forces again as we sped away.

We arrived at a semi-detached house a quarter of a mile from the state pen, which looked quiet. "This looks dodgy," I thought as we pulled in. Then I said to Bangers, "The geezer in the blacked out XR3—how many times you seen him?"

"Put it this way: most times I've been down to score, he's been there."

"He's probably the man bringing the weed to your man," I commented, and Bangers nodded. I could see a set of headlights in the mirror turn the corner. "That's him; just pull in."

"What you up to, Max?" He could see I sat readjusting the saw blade to stop it digging in my skin.

"Right, you act normal and just go in." I peeled off 240 in notes. "Get me two ounces, and take that fer their trouble." I handed him another twenty. "I'll wait here."

I watched the lone driver fumble about in his glove box. Where was the lass he picked up earlier, and the other Yids that were with him?

Bangers took the dollar and left the car. The driver in the Black XR3 sat for two minutes and looked to be talking into a mobile phone. He left the car, disappearing into the same drive Bangers went down. Now was my chance, and I got out, slipping on my gloves.

I casually walked over with the fat screwdriver stuffed up my sleeve and looked around. I inserted the screwdriver and lifted the window seal on the driver's door, sliding down the saw blade and still looking around. Clunk. That was the noise I was looking for, and I pulled out the saw blade, replacing the seal. The door came open as the unmistakable smell of Paco Roban filled my nostrils. I slid the bag of heroin under his seat and relocked the door and returned to Bangers' XR2. I waited for Bangers to come back out whilst I took out a small notebook and jotted down the XR3'splate number.

Bangers ran back to the car and jumped in. "Cop that lot, Max." He threw me the two ounces of weed. We were soon back at g-forces for most of the way back.

"Just stop here; I need the phone," I said, and Bangers pulled in. I dialled 999 and gave the details of the car and driver and where it was last seen, and then I returned to the car.

Later Bangers dropped me at the entry. "Any time, Max. Later."

The *Bodyguard* with Kevin Costner was on the video when I walked into Nogg's. "Men's night tonight," Nogg said as he and Woda sat impatiently.

I threw an ounce onto Nogg's lap. "Take a Henry outta that." Soon the spliff building got under way. I was showing off with the Spanish extra-long cone.

Nogg cracked out the beers. "Scorpion, anyone?"

I counted out what cash I had left—just over a grand. I placed it back in my pocket and returned to my flat, scuffing and bumping off the walls, missing the odd step. The hustle and bustle was shut out as I closed the window.

"Max. Max. Max." I knew the voice—Kelly. I opened the window, looking at my watch: 3.00 in the morning. I reached in my jacket pocket and threw down my keys. She trundled up the stairs, and the door came open. She walked over and threw the keys on the bed.

"I hope you locked it," I said.

She smiled. "Max, I sneaked out again. Am I all right to crash here?"

"Are you at your Saturday job tomorrow?"

She looked breathless and pulled me to her. "Give us a hug, Max."

I never saw her get up the next morning, and I felt around for the warmth of her body. I'd been out like a light. I got up and made for the bathroom. Written on the mirror in cherry lipstick was a message from Kelly: "See you tonight—8.30. Luv, Kelly." My fizz was covered in lip marks all over. I laughed and switched on the radio and ran the bath.

Then came the news. "Police arrested and charged a man believed to be supplying heroin and marijuana after the police stopped the suspect last night in the Snenton area for a routine check. The latest reports was that the male, aged twenty-nine, is still being detained and held for questioning and will appear before the magistrates Monday morning." I could hear the cell doors slam from here. I slipped on my jeans.

The city was mobbed with Saturday shoppers. I bought a mobile phone, taking it on an orange network. Woda and Nogg bought one each too. We sat in McDonald's with a variety of nuggets and burgers, trying to figure out how to use the text facility.

"Yep, I got the hang of that," I said as I looked at the "message sent" on my screen.

Nogg's phone soon beeped. "Hey, Max, you did it; I got it." I'd written "Dickhead", and we laughed when he read it out loud.

I'd also bought new Levis—the full set of T-shirts, underwear, jacket, and jeans and boots to match; I even got the belt. "I'm going out in style," I thought as we walked back to my own XR3.

My phone was ringing just as I got changed into my new clobber. It was Nogg. "Come round; we got something for you. Door's open."

"Two minutes, Nogg."

I walked in, and Woda sat with a PlayStation control. "Hey, that's cool," I said as I looked at the game quality. "Brill graphics."

"Damn, your turn, Nogg," Woda said, and Nogg reached for the control. "There you go, Max, legal E." Woda handed me two pills.

"Ain't no E legal, mate." I looked at them. They were red and diamond shaped.

"Hey, I've had one, and they're all right," Nogg said, smiling his head off.

"I've had two and I'm buzzing," Woda added.

"You both do look a bit happy." I downed the pills. The pair of them burst out laughing. I reached for Nogg's beer because they nearly got stuck in my throat. "Thanks, mate." The pair were still giggling and watching the screen.

"Get a beer out the fridge, Max, and get me another one," Nogg said after he looked at how much I'd just drunk from his bottle. I returned from the kitchen carrying three bottles and set them on the coffee table, removing the lids with my teeth.

"They ain't sleeping pills, are they?" I looked at my watch: 7.30PM. I took a good swig of beer.

"Nah, we wouldn't do that to you," the pair said, still giggling. "They're Viagra." The next thing I knew, the pair were in hysterics.

I started to laugh. "Ain't that what them judges have been using to, erm, you know?"

"Yeah." The pair were rolling about, guts seizing up in a fit. Nogg took a breath and said, "You're only suppose to take one, and we haven't had any."

"Why, you low-down, dirty scum, fancy stitching me with that."

"And guess who's coming at 8.30 with my missus and Venables??"

"So that's why they . . ." I started to spin out.

"Etna got them off the Internet at work," Woda said as he regained his composure. "It's all right, they're safe—calm down, Max."

That was just it—I couldn't I was up and down like a yo-yo, looking out the window.

The door slammed downstairs, and a few seconds later Dean came barging in. "Gimme them two tabs, Woda; I can sell 'em in the pub. Here, Max, that's yours." He handed me back the dollars I had loaned him.

Nogg and Woda cracked out in laughter again. "I can't, mate—Max had 'em."

"Give 'em, Max, you don't need them."

I could feel myself heating up as Woda explained. "No, mate, he's *had* 'em."

Dean's jaw dropped. "What, both of 'em?" He looked at me, and I nodded. "You'll be up like an Italian stallion fer the next week, you mad man." Dean was serious. I could feel my heart racing as he said it. "Skin up, Nogg, before I go out on the town." Dean sat down, rubbing his head and looking at me sympathetically. He saw the game and said, "Hey, give us a go on that." Woda pressed pause and handed over the controller. Dean took it and played on.

Nogg finished rolling and handed the spliff to Dean. I was pacing about and rubbing the sweat from my hands. Now I know what they meant by the term "sweating like a rapist". All these vulgar thoughts of sexual encounters started entering my head.

Dean got up and said, "Right, lads, I'm off." He handed Woda back the controller.

"That's them shouting up," Nogg said as he turned the music down. I got up and looked out. Kelly stood with Nogg's missus and Venables. Kelly stood out with her sprayed-on black miniskirt and a shocking pink top under her white padded jacket; her top was so low cut I see her cleavage. Her hair looked more highlighted, and she had on a pair of calf-length, black leather, high-heeled boots. I was grabbing at my crotch, trying to adjust things around.

Nogg threw down the keys, and they all ran up the stairs. Kelly was first in, jumping in at my side and sliding onto my knee as the other broads strolled in, clutching Alco pops of all varieties and a video. Kelly delivered a right smacker on my cheek. Then she noticed and seemed to responded to what was happening down there. I gulped as I tried to distract myself by bringing up visions of ugly people, but it was all in vain. "God, Max," she whispered. "I'm all yours tonight."

I thought, "Fer God's sake, don't get up, don't get up . . ." Too late—she did. Luckily everyone's attention was turned to what was being put on the video, and she sat back on my knee, easing back slowly.

"Open that, Max." She handed me an Alco pop, and I gladly bit of the lid. I spied Woda messing with his phone. *Beep beep.* "Hey, Max, that came from you," Kelly said as she started looking around in my pockets, finding it in my jacket. "Is that yours?" She pulled it out.

"Let me see what it says." I was trying to grab for it.

"It says, 'Who's the dickhead now?'"

Woda roared with laughter. "Just a private joke."

"Hey, I want one. That's cool."

"Here, have it; I'll get another one."

She put her arms around me, squeezing me tight. "Thanks, Max." She sat playing and fidgeting with it. Nogg had built a good supply of spliffs as we sat watching *Predator 2*.

The film finished, and Kelly whispered, "Max, that's up like a rocket," as she pulled me to my feet. "Back to yours." I'd drunk about five Scorpions and shared three spliffs during the film—I was absolutely smashed out of my skull and hadn't said a word during the film. Kelly led me up the stairs as we fell in the door, and I couldn't help but notice what she wasn't wearing under her skirt. That was it—I couldn't stand anymore. I had her skirt up quicker than you could blink. She had undone me jeans, and whoa, I couldn't get in it as I wrestled with fasteners; she still had her tights on.

"Like this," she said as she did the difficult task for me. I lay back on the bed as she stripped off the rest of her underwear. I was ripping off my T-shirt, and then she said, "Max, I ain't never done it," as she stood up on to the bed.

"Get down, doll; someone might see."

"I don't care." She straddled across me. Ten minutes later she was shouting at the top of her voice.

There was a slam. "Hey, what's that. Oh! We didn't lock the door," Kelly said, bucking me off her as the footsteps got louder and faster.

"I grabbed a T-shirt and slipped it on as I got one leg into me jeans.

The door flew open. "God, what on earth?" It was Kelly's mum, and she froze.

"Erm, how, who, what . . ." I stammered.

"Max, you of all people!" Kelly's ma rushed over to her. "And you, young lady. You little slapper!" She screamed it.

"Hey, don't call her that," I said as I struggled to put my other leg in my jeans.

Downstairs was still stood out proud as I tried to do myself up. "How long's this been going on, then?" Kelly's ma asked.

"It only just happened, and then you come flying in." I was starting to rage. Kelly's ma's eyes keep looking at my crotch, which made it even worse. I could see which side of the family Kelly was from.

Her ma sat down on the bed. "First me fella plays around, now I find out me daughter's humping a guy that's old enough to be her dad."

"Hey, less of the dad." I could hear Dean and Woda next door, crying with laughter, and I could hear faintly, "Is that Kelly's mum?"

I was trying to think about ugly people again and visions of the Predator, but all was in vain. It just wasn't going down. "And you weren't wearing protection," her ma said, and then she got up and started slapping me hard. I had to grab her arms and turn her around, clamping her down. "Right I'll calm down." I sat her on to the bed.

"What do you mean, your fella's playing away?"

"That swine Arnie's been seeing his ex," Kelly butted in.

"I just want to catch him at it," her ma said. "Kelly, lend me your jacket. I'm going to see if he meets her on the market." Kelly threw her ma her jacket as she rearranged her hair. She stormed out quicker than she came in.

Kelly had just finished doing up her bask. "Oh, Arnie will think it's me," she giggled. Her ma made for the street adjacent to the market.

Kelly opened the window to shout something, but I hushed her. "Let her go. Shh."

Downstairs it still hadn't budged, as I looked in her eyes. "Max, give it me out the window," Kelly said. I started to laugh, but she was serious. "Screw the living daylights outta me." She started undoing her bask.

Well, that was it. Her tights were down again, whilst people were coming from the pubs looking up. Kelly was screaming, "Yes, Max, Max! Oohh!" Half an hour later we were still at it. Kelly's voice was sort of getting hoarse as she clutched the window ledge. She turned it into a constant moan.

I could hear them next door: "Go on, Max, give it her. Go on, lad!" I thought my heart was going to explode as I worked myself up into a wild frenzy. Then oh my God, it happened. The pair of us fell on the bed, exhausted. I was just going to ask her if she wanted a shot on the swings again when *slam*. Footsteps up the stairs.

"I bet that's me ma come back," Kelly said as she pulled her tights back up.

The door flew open again. Kelly's ma stood there, mouth gaping open. "You dirty pair of . . . You could hear that across the market!"

"I was showing her me paintings," I said as I pointed to the portfolio.

"Yeah, and I bet she modelled fer you."

"I was winding you up, Mum," Kelly said.

We were now downstairs, and it was beginning to rise again as I tried to think of pictures of death and destruction. But all was in vain—even the old black and whites of the Somme didn't work. I had psychotic thoughts of me charging across a battlefield with a pork bayonet. Yep, the bloody thing was still up solid.

It was two in the morning, just as Kelly had wished me goodnight and walked on to her estate. Her ma clutched at my arm and whispered, "Walk me up to the garage, Max." It just so happened I needed cigs and rizzla, so I agreed. Downstairs I was still throbbing like mad and was starting to get uncomfortable.

All of a sudden her ma blurted, "I want to get even," slamming me into the wall and pressing into me. "Well, when in Rome," I thought, and I had a vision of myself in a toga with a wreath on my head.

Lights were coming on in the surrounding houses after she'd asked me to spank her again. Man, she was louder than Kelly.

I'd picked her ma a flower out of one of the gardens on the way. We'd no sooner walked in through the doors at the twenty-four-hour garage. Then there was a red flash and the screech of tyres, and *thump,* Arnie was out the car and running in. "And where the freaking hell have you been?" he demanded as he lunged for her.

I could see the rage in his eyes. "Hey, man, hold it right there." I stepped into him. He froze and backed off and walked the other side of the shelves.

"Max, don't leave me with him, please."

"It's okay, doll, I'll stay with you."

Now Arnie was beginning to rage, screaming and shouting, "You've been with him all night!" I lunged at him, and the cashier shouted, "Right, I'm getting the police," reaching for the phone.

"Max, please don't leave me with him, please, Max, come outside with me." She squeezed my hand pulling me back.

"Hang on; I want my cigs and rizzla." Arnie had turned and went out to the court, still screaming and shouting. "Are you going to serve us?" I asked the cashier.

"Right, what do you want?"

"Twenty Regal and a couple of packs of large skins." I paid for the goods.

"Max, I ain't ever seen him like that before. Stay at my side, won't you?" Kelly's ma asked as we walked out, crying. "I'm scared, Max."

Arnie was at his car with his head in his hands. He was in bits, leaning on the roof, and then he reared up again. I was thinking I might have to do battle. Kelly's ma was well endowed as my eyes sort of fixed on her cleavage. Arnie blurted out, "But I love her. I can't stand losing her!"

"You lying, two-faced arsehole," Kelly's mum said under her breath.

"Let me sort this out," I said. I grabbed him by the arm and turned him around. "You pick a funny way of showing it, mate," I said calmly to him.

"If you love her, then prove it to her properly and let her go. Let her make up her own mind."

Kelly's ma said, "I want to go to my mum's, Max. I ain't staying with him. I already took the kids over last night." She was crying her eyes out.

"Look, I'm sorry," Arnie said.

"Max, he'll batter me if you leave me with him. He's done it before."

"Hey what, he's done what?"

She pulled me back. "No, Max, don't give him the satisfaction."

There was ten minutes of arguing before the police turned up, pulling into the garage. "Erm, we better mizz," I commented. Arnie had calmed down and agreed to take Kelly's ma to her mum's, and we all jumped in the car.

When we arrived Arnie was still pleading with her not to leave him. She squeezed my leg as she got out. "You are history," she said, pointing to Arnie as she got out the car. "Thanks, Max, you're a babe." She made her way down the drive.

Arnie sat with his head in his hands again. "More fish in the, sea Arnie," I said. "You can't go on abusing her, you know. I ain't going to stand fer that, or if you batter any other woman. Do you hear me. Now, get this pile a junk shifted."

Arnie stopped crying. "I was drunk—I didn't know."

"Save it fer the marines, Arnie."

He was quiet when we approached the market. "Just drop me here," I said. "Remember what I told you."

When I turned to face my building, I was shocked. The front of the block, most of the windows had green slime running down them, mine included. I picked up one of the ping pong ball-sized cases that were slimy and bust open. Someone had hit the whole block with a paint-ball gun, as I looked up at the mess and then at my watch: 4.30 AM. I made my way into the flat, skinned a bifter, and fell asleep.

Chapter Five

Aztec figurines, Mayan monuments, temples, the Dresden codex, a calendar of events—all of a sudden they became clear in my mind. I'd parked opposite an open field near Bawtry South Yorkshire. I remember I needed to be at the car auction early; a cheap banger was required to get me to work. The old silver Ford Escort XR3 I sat in would have needed considerable expense to make the next MOT. I had a couple of months' tax and MOT left, so I decided it was time for a change.

I'd texted a friend with whom I shared accommodation to meet me at the auction. He was a local and knew more about the procedures of finding a reliable runner. He'd insisted on finding a diesel. He wouldn't say why, but that's what we were looking for.

My mouth was watering at the thought of eating fish and chips while looking around the car lot. When moved through the clouds, a very large, white, object reflecting light all around it. This thing was enormous, some kind of music in my mind played as it passed me. I could see the vast windows patterned into mullions and transoms with people walking moving, all set in platforms that reflected the colour of the sky like self-camouflage. I heard a constant buzz and drone, although it was a kind of a musical wind charm. I felt unusually warm and nauseated. Strange I felt drawn into the invisible axis on which the huge craft seemed to turn.

I couldn't work out, what I was doing in the field, that side of the fence; my mobile phone was ringing, I was wondering, "Did I really dream it, or did I see it?" For a minute I thought I had seen all the future disasters and superiority, the likes of which you can only see in dreams and nightmares. Yet it was still clear. Should I tell anyone these were predictions that I had recently documented?

I crossed the road, got back in the car. I took my phone from my jacket and answered. It was Paul, sounding agitated. "Are you going to get here or what? The auction starts in ten minutes."

My head was splitting, and I felt flu symptoms at work. I ached in places I never knew I had. "Give me fifteen minutes, Paul, don't mizz."

Bawtry was buzzing with activity by the time I'd followed the little country roads in. Paul was on the phone again. I saw a space in the pub car park opposite the auctions, so I grabbed it and answered the phone. Paul was excited. "Where are you, Max? I might have found something for you."

"I've just arrived," I said, and he met me at the main gate. I locked the car and dodged through the slowly moving traffic at the traffic lights. I could see Paul's black ponytail.

"Peugeot 309 1750 diesel any good to you?" he asked.

"Better let me take a look where is. Is that it, next in?"

Paul was laughing. "You'd better get in and bid; don't go more than three hundred."

I walked into the main hangar, with the smell of burnt petrol fumes and the hurried swarm of traders over every lot as each car took the stand. Paul winked, a prompt to start the bidding. The price was soon up to 240, and I clinched the deal at 245 plus 25 pounds indemnity. I'd spotted a six-month ticket on it while I was bidding, so I knew I could take it away. We spent the rest of the night moving the car I'd bought back to Sunny Donny and retrieving the XR3,with a well-earned stop for fish and chips and a can of Diet Coke.

Paul was a bit of a night owl; you could guarantee if you were in his company, you were in for a late night. I had never seen a guy do so much mizzing around as him. These were dodgy characters he was dealing with, and all was apparent as to the merchandise that was being transported. Bass—or space dust, or whatever you want to call it—was the main cargo. I could not stop laughing when every time we went out, he was saying, "Now we got to look mean, Max, we got to act hard—and by the way I've been putting in your morning coffee for the past week." I knew he hadn't, but it did get me thinking, didn't it? "I'd been under the weather a bit. I ain't kidding—I dropped one in your coke while you were eating your fish and chips."

My hands started to sweat, and the distant lights shone brighter than stars as we pulled in on a dirt track. Paul jumped out and opened the boot. I jumped out after him, bellowing, "You really did spike me." He ran into a field and disappeared into a thicket of bushes, and I could hear his clumsy feet cracking branches along the woodland side set in a backdrop of a dimmed summer sky. I sat waiting after shouting the occasional abuse after him. I wasn't pleased at what he'd been telling me, and things did start to fall into place.

Paul wandered back into the field at what he must have regarded as a safe distance, holding up a large bag. "Max, that car you just bought? I need a favour."

Well, that was it, and I snapped, lunging straight at him. I was on him, grabbing the bag off him, and asking, "What's all this, then?" He had big blocks of cannabis resin and weighed-out bags of white powder. I stood stunned, leering at the bag.

Paul just stood, looking at the floor and muttering, "I knew I shouldn't have told you. You're a cop, ain't you?"

I burst out laughing; he really did look white with fright. His mouth seemed all animated as he spoke. I was thinking this wasn't my usual self; the swine had spiked me, and I really was out my face. I could feel a big bad rock city coming on . . . Let me see, now, what day were we on? Tuesday?

"Take me back to the house, Paul, I've had enough for one night," I said, placing the bag back in his hands.

"Erm, we got to diesel up first. That's what I was going to do when you got that look on yer face and came after me."

"Let's get one thing straight, Paul. I ain't a cop, okay? And I ain't happy about the spiking situation, so can we leave it there? I got a good job now and I want to keep it."

Paul was frantic. "Do you see what I'm offering you? This is the life of Riley." He took the bag and pushed it in the already open boot.

"Hey, I don't want to get pulled with you, with all that in the boot," I said as he took out a large cylinder, unscrewing the hexagon lid after it were positioned on the roof.

Paul took a small length of hose and stuffed it into the cylinder and started sucking on the other end. 'Seven sovs for five gallons of heating oil—what do u think?"

"How much does the tank hold?"

Paul looked up and mumbled, "Just over five gallon." I was sure he got diesel in his mouth and was trying not to show it. "She'll do forty-five to the gallon, so work it out."

"Where are you getting the heating oil from?"

"I'll show you where it is next time we're out and about."

I woke the next morning and looked out the back window as I rose for work The alarm hadn't gone off yet, so I flicked it to the off position. It looked like it was going to be a fine day; there was that smell of carpet adhesive again as I made my way to the bathroom for a shit, shave, and shampoo. I trundled down the stairs and noticed the fires were left on in both rooms; the heat was stifling as I opened the curtains and opened the window. Paul wasn't far behind as I heard him close his room door and pass the landing to the bathroom.

"Right, I'll make the coffee," I shouted up.

I could hear the flush of the toilet as I looked up the stairwell. Paul had stuck his head around with that usual grin. "Yeah, no probs; you're not taking the pug?"

"Yep, and I want that shit shifting away from the house when I get back from work."

"So Nig, hang fire with that for a sec; let me think, don't go rushing in."

Donk had put his hand in his pocket and paid for the breakfasts. We were studying the plans for a proposed conservatory to be built in a small village somewhere up in Yorkshire. "Max, I want you and Nig to keep it clean, and watch where you do the cuts; there is plenty of dust sheets, so make sure you put them down."

"How long on this one, Donk?"

"Three days. It'll be eight o'clock finish again."

"Nig up for it?"

"Nig is happy at the overtime; his missus is five months knocked up like a gable end, so the money is welcome. Fifty-pound bonus, Max, if you build it same as the last one in three days."

Young Dink's big round face lit up whenever money was mentioned. "Hey, what's my bonus?" He was hovering around the counter, wanting more bread and butter.

"If you could lay bricks like these two can, we'd have a conversation, Dink, but for now shut it."

Young Dink came over to the table and sat in front of his breakfast, looking into it and rubbing his shaved head with his hand. "And it's no good turning up for work stoned, Dink. I can still tell, you know."

"Donk, look, the missus is giving me grief, you're giving me grief. You can bollocks; I ain't going this morning." Dink got up and stormed out the cabin, and I could hear the van door being slammed from where I was sat as the cabin was reduced to a quiet lull.

"Go and talk to him, Nig, we won't get that done in three days labouring by ourselves."

"Kev, why do you have to wind him up? It's your fault," Nig said as he rose from his chair and went after him. "I'm not giving in to him, Max."

Kev looked at me and laughed. "Where did you get the pug anyway, Max?"

"At auction, Bawtry. I won't say how much I paid for it, but it was a good deal. She started first crack this morning—plenty of poke, 1750 diesel. Eleven months MOT and plenty of ticket. Yours for 600 pounds—it even says 'DNK' on the plate."

"Hey, our Dink's looking for one; he's moaning about the Fiat I bought him."

Nig walked back in and picked up Dink's breakfast and disappeared again, and then he stepped back in moments later. "Right, I sorted it; we've got to give him a tenner each payday for the overtime. That's it, that's all he wants. It's fine by me."

"Ask him if he wants to buy a Peugeot."

"Don't sell it to him, Max. That Fiat was near enough brand-new when me dad got it for him. He's had it six months and look at it." I looked out the window at the shed on wheels and sighed.

Donk chirped up. "I've set another brickie on to deal with the out-of-town jobs. I want you up at my house. You'll be relieved to hear, Max: starting Monday, landscaping and walls all the way around the boundary; plenty for you to do. I'll still want you in the winter, if that's all right jobbing. Nine pounds an hour plus bonuses."

It was Friday, and I'd finished early. Donk was handing me my wages. Young Dink had been hounding me about selling him the Peugeot, and I'd agreed to a tidy sum of five hundred sovereigns minus the tenner overtime. That was a total of 840 pounds in one week for me.

"I'd better drop you at home, with all that cash on you, Max." Donk's Reactolite glasses had shaded because of the sunlight as I looked at his driving concentration in the Doncaster suburbs. I smiled and asked what time I was to be at his house Monday morning. "Eight o'clock, Max." We pulled onto the street where I lived. "We'll hang fire while you nip in and fetch Dink's log book. I disappeared into the house and fumbled with the documents on the mantel piece. I found the bit I needed and went out to the white transit, where Donk and crew were peacefully sitting.

Nig had gone in the back doors of the van and pulled out my tool bucket and spirit level; he took them over to the house, setting them aside the door. I opened the sliding door at the side, where young Dink laid on the dust sheets, grinning. "There you go, mate," I said." Your own plate; that's the spare keys. You have the other set already. Don't say I never did anything for you. Look after it, Dink." I shut the door.

Paul was pulling up just as they were moving away. I kept the door open to let out the heat. The fire was left on again as I waited for an explanation. Paul was grinning as he jumped out of his car. "It was just my way of getting at them, this whole society thing. I could see he'd been upset by his experiences in the jail. He was determined that the landlord should foot the bill. I scolded, "Hey, you just got to get on with it; don't hate for it. What if the whole place catches fire?" I was angry. I rushed upstairs and grabbed my portfolio and then rushed back down into the living room. I shook out the contents all over the floor. "You would be destroying the only bit of self-esteem I have left. This is all I have; think what you are doing." I sat down on the settee, frustrated at the thought of coming home to cinders. Paul put up his hands as though to praise God and went to speak, but he was frozen as he looked down at the collection of written works and at the pictures.

"But what are they?" he asked.

"Designs and poetry."

Paul bent down as if to gather up the work and selected a piece to study. "Hey, Max, these are good. I like this and this, and blimey, look at this." All of a sudden Paul seemed transfixed. "I'm going to write up the best music ever, and those are the some cover designs to go with the music. You see, I played in a band once. Perhaps one day, who knows?"

"Yeah, I see what you mean."

"Blimey, you really did these?" Paul helped me put the work back into the shabby folder.

"I'm trying to finish this one; can u see what it's trying to depict?"

"Not really, although it's a good likeness of the Predator, ha ha!"

"Don't laugh," I said, "this is serious and could very well happen."

Paul looked a little closer. "Right, I'll try and work it out."

"This may help." I reached down and took out the original piece, done in collage cuttings from magazines.

"So you have documented or predicted a warning?"

"Yes. The prediction *is* a warning. They are working to do this. One suspect has been traced to Leeds. I have new information that these are the targets. Operatives have gone to find where in Leeds they are; they've been tracked for some time now, they've also been operating from inside several prisons in the UK."

"How do you know this is going to happen?"

"I've studied at it. This is the final conclusion; this will happen if these terrorists are not found and stopped. Paul, I need your contacts. Do you trust me?"

"You really are mad, Max. This is genocide." Paul sat down, looking at the original and comparing to the drawing.

"Look, wake up to the world, Paul. Can you see now what it's all about?"

Paul put down the work and asked again, "How you know, though?"

"It's already been tried in the late eighties; although the plot was unsuccessful, they'd gone and unleashed the explosives in the basement."

"Sheek's, a van packed full of stuff. If they'd detonated that outside, it would have been similar to the Oklahoma bombing—total devastation," Paul mused.

"Right, well, just put this little lot away, and you're going to tell me about this bloody smell—a carpet glue, where's it coming from? Have you got some kind of project on the go?"

"Well, erm, hang on," Paul stammered. "I'll come clean. It's me solvent abuse—I sniff it."

I was taken back a bit and thought, "In his twenties and resorting to that? He's got access to all that dope, and he's sniffing a two-sov can of glue?" I said to Paul, "Right, at least now I know. Who do you work for?" Paul started laughing as he reached in his pocket and produced a well-rolled spliff and clicked his lighter to ignite it. "Hey, let me see the lighter a sec." Paul handed me a lighter shaped and looked like a cigarette. Immediately I had it in bits, turned the valve, and said, "Now try it."

He lit it after flicking down the lid and dropped it after it nearly took his eyebrows. "Don't be spiking me again, Paul—I ain't forgot, you know."

"How I ended up here is of no concern of yours, mate; don't you think it's time?"

Paul offered the half-smoked spliff. I knew he liked one for himself. "Better than that putty black you've been getting, Max." He never commented on the weed.

I took a few smokes; it reminded me of incense or joss sticks. "What's that you've laced in it?"

"Zero," Paul replied as I gave it him back, coughing.

"Right, I'm just up fer a shit, shave, and shampoo. We'll mizz out fer a pint and a game of pool. Do you know anywhere I can get all that and eat big? I'm starving."

We arrived at a pub well out of the way, the King Charles. "The grub here is ace," Paul commented as we pulled into the car park. I'd had a hard week and I thought I'd live a little, so we moseyed on over to the dining area and sat and fidgeted with a menu.

"No points for guessing what I'm having," I muttered as I made for the bar. Paul insisted on buying his own drinks, so I returned carrying a pint of Guinness. I sat down and re-examined the menu. "The fourteen-ounce steak with Diane sauce looks to fit the bill. I'm having that with all the trimmings." The waitress caught my eye and wandered over to take our orders.

After demolishing the steak and ordering up a sizable portion of cheesecake, I couldn't but help notice two broads—a brunette and a blonde, both looking over and smiling. I kicked Paul under the table and choked out, "One o'clock," over a mouthful of cheesecake.

Paul grinned and said, "The one on the right, she put me away for five years."

"Oh, she is attractive, though, don't you think? Come on, we'll have a laugh with them." I jumped over and asked if they'd like a game of pool. The blonde was quick off the mark and asked my name. "Max," I replied and held out my hand to greet her.

"Do you have change for the first game?" she asked. "You need to put your money on the table, you know; it's a fiver a game."

I laughed. "A couple of hustlers, Ha!"

Paul was waving me over. "What are you up to, Max? That brunette is a police constable. And would you like to start again and pay the bloody food bill?"

"Oh, I'd forgot, hang on." I pulled out my wedge and peeled off a couple of twenties. "That should take care of it. Right, come on. We'll stick them at pool, give you a chance to get your own back, hehe."

The girls were really good pool players, and I wished they had never mentioned a fiver a game; we got licked. Shirley, the blond, cracked jokes about how Paul came to be arrested, and I could see Paul wasn't taking the bait. "It's all right, Paul," I said. "I'll get a taxi if you want to head for home."

"No problem." Paul walked over and took his jacket. "I'll see you back at the house later, Max."

"Well, you can understand him being like that; it was you that busted him," I said, trying to defend Paul's integrity in his absence. "Is that right what you said? Fifty-eight kilos of dope in a warehouse? You actually caught him with that amount?"

"At the time it was big news around here," Shirley remarked.

The brunette wouldn't give her name, though I did keep probing her for her number. Every time I asked her, she smiled and said, "Like children, do you? I have two of them, you know."

After a brief conversation, I offered to buy the girls a drink each, Shirley offered to come to the bar to help with the order. "She really does like you. You should come here more often." I was amazed; I hadn't been with a woman for a few years, and I just clicked.

The night progressed on as I started on the shorts—Jack and Coke was going down well, so I ended up plastered. Shirley was kind enough to make sure the taxi home wasn't too painful, claiming she owed me for the drinks. She pecked me on the cheek at the same time, opening the door as she got out. I hadn't a clue where we were. The brunette, who had mostly remained quiet most of the night, was still in the front of the taxi as she directed the taxi to her home. She was tall, slim, and a total mystery. I wasn't quite sure what to say to her after she'd knocked me back a few times. Eventually the taxi arrived at her home: an open plan estate, with kids toys on the front garden.

I opened the taxi door and asked the driver to hang on a few minutes whilst I walked her to the front door. "I want to see you again," I said to her.

She put her finger on my lips and said, "Shh. I'll sort it." She opened her front door and disappeared into the house. I walked slowly over to the taxi and got in; the girls had left the driver with twenty quid, and he was asking where to next. I had to ring Paul for the address; I couldn't remember because I was too drunk.

On Saturday morning a thick head was the order of the morning, mixed with a cocktail of information that put Paul in the can, and he still hasn't learned his lesson. My head was swimming in it for him; I could see it was his own choice, so I decided not to interfere with his plans. Although it was a road to ruin, it wasn't for me to try and guide him clear of it, but the first thing he should have been concentrating on was not treading the same path that had put him in the can. It was always going to be a vicious circle of his tail catching him up, all the way through his life.

"What's happening today, Max, what you got planned?"

"I sold the Pug. Dink's on his way over to pick it up. Then I've got to run over to the city later."

Paul stopped me. "How much you get for it?"

"Five hundred bangers."

"You only gave 270 for it five days ago."

"Yeah, cool, isn't it?" I can feel a big bad Rock City night coming on. Want to go?"

"What's that?"

"Ooh, you ain't never been to Rock City? You got to go, it's a gas; you ain't lived until you've been. Three separate venues, a large main hall and two smaller venues, all in the same building. Rock till ya drop—I did my apprenticeship in there, mate, I ain't kidding. I met all kinds of people—Goths, punk, glam."

"So that's where you go at the weekend, is it, Max?"

"Yep. That's how it's going to be until I settle down."

Paul laughed as he headed for the front door with a spare battery he'd been charging in the back room. "Know what you mean, Max. Mortgage and kids and all that jive."

"Never mind that. Where are you off to this time in the morning?"

"Down south; I'll be back in the week."

After Paul had left, I thought, "He kept that quiet. And he can't have got rid of all that in one week, unless . . ." I remembered something. "He's fetching more and stashing it. "Well, well. I never I sussed it already; I will just wait until he comes back, and we'll see what's what. I'll just text Daz and let him know the script about the weekend."

I decided to go into Sunny Donny and to seek a few provisions; new clobber was needed, so I spent most of the morning scanning the shops and searching for the odd bargain. I lashed out on a pair of trainers and had to settle for a pair of tracksuit bottoms, all black. I couldn't find anywhere that sold Levis jeans and settled for lunch at McDonald's before heading back home, taking the XR3 through the car wash at the edge of town.

I got a text from Daz: "What's your ETA? I'll let Alex now you're on your way." It was all set, then; I just had to get there. I pulled up outside the house and gathered my new items and took them in. I ran upstairs, ditched everything I'd bought in my room, and went through into the bathroom to run the bath. I went back to the bedroom and ripped all the new tags from the bottoms and lay them on the bed. I picked out my best T-shirt and laid that out too, and then I went for a soak.

The sky was a cool pinkie colour when I came out of the house. I knew this was going to be a good night as jumped into my car and fidgeted in the glove box for the Saturday night rock tape. As I turned the ignition, the sound of Stun Lear filled the car, and I proceeded on the A1 M18 M1. This car could really move when it wanted to—wolf in sheep's clothing wasn't the comparison. A two-litre RSs Cosworth were the old XRr3 lump sat, with complete RS transmission and running gear. Many a cruise machine tried to match my superiority and got blown away. What a way to get to rock city.

I was at the rise to Annasley Park—and damn, blue lights. He must have tailed me off the motorway. I turned down the music, flicked out the spliff I'd half smoked, and downed the window with just enough time to clear the smell of the joint as I pulled in. I placed the spliff down my sock, and it must have been still partly lit as the sparks brushed off my jeans. I was trying to bite my lip and throw in a mint at the same time.

The patrol car pulled in behind, and a uniformed officer left the patrol car from the driver's side and walked over. I observed in the rear-view mirror. "Is this car yours, sir?" An officer who was 6'2" leered in at me.

"Of course, Officer."

"Can you give me the reg of the vehicle, sir?"

"Well, it's, erm . . ." I managed to fire off the first three letters as I pressed at my sock in an effort to douse the still smouldering spliff and stop the burning pain.

"Do you have documentation for this car, sir?"

"Yes, I have them here in my wallet," I replied, opening it as he helped himself to the contents. "It doesn't keep cash in it," I joked.

He took out my license and handed back the wallet, insurance, and the MOT. "Right, I'm going to ask you to step from your vehicle, sir, and go and sit with the officer in the patrol car. I will accompany you; step this way." I did as I was told. "You are not under arrest, but I must caution you if we find there has been an offence—oh, bollocks! It's me, Taylor. You remember me, don't you?" he said, tilting his hat back.

I was shocked. "What, Taylor? Yeah, I do. Christ the King School! Blimey, I ain't seen you since I left and moved to the local school."

"I just looked at your license there, and yeah, you're the guy we're looking for."

I went white, startled. "What, you got some bad news for me?" I braced myself. "Come on, Taylor, let me have it."

"Get in the back of the patrol car and sit." I jumped in, still bewildered.

The officer with Taylor spoke first. "I ain't even going to go into the speed you were doing fifteen miles back. I shouldn't be giving you this back." He waved my license in my face.

Taylor but in all serious—and I mean I had never seen him like this as a kid. "Look, who do you know in Chuckwalla that are police officers?"

"Right, what's this all about, Taylor? I'm kind of on a schedule."

"I'll give you a clue: Rubble."

"Right, now I'm with you; don't need to say anymore." Rubble is married to my half—sister.

"You've to go see him."

"What, that's it?" The other officer threw back my license and claimed everything to be in order. "Right then, Taylor. I'll be in Rock City later, if you want to pop down."

"Nah, the missus prefers something with a bit more class."

"What, who you married too? Do I know her? It weren't Sarah was it? We always suspected you and her."

Taylor laughed. "Your hair might be long, but you ain't changed a bit. Yes, it was her I married. Got two kids."

"Well, well. I knew you had it in you—a family man, eh?"

"Look, just cut the speed and get that bloody car changed; it's an instant pull."

"Yeah, right, Taylor. Thanks for the fright. See you around, kid." I jumped out of the patrol car. My heart jumped as they whacked the siren just as I was walking away, and they sped off. I made my way back to my car. Rubble, now that was an option. Now I knew the angels were watching; I was in deep shit. I had to report in and keep on it. No rest for the wicked.

I cracked her over and upped the music and hit the ton down Annesley Park as I relit the spliff. On the way into the old hometown, I managed a wee pose at the traffic lights. The town was alive with the buzz of traffic. The trees along the market had grown well since last time I'd last seen them, and the hanging baskets gave off the familiar welcoming scents. Despite some new ownership, the pubs still looked the same, with some of the local faces hid amongst the usual gatherings dotted outside the wine bar. Nothing had really changed—only the styles.

"Daz answered his intercom, "Hello? Ah, who is it? Is that you, Max?"

"Yep, it's me." The buzzer went, and I opened the door and ran up two flights of stairs.

Daz had his door already ajar as I walked in. "Hey, Max, long time no see."

"I was here last week; how was I to know you were away?"

"I wasn't—I was up the town and had my phone switched off. I musta texted you two or three times."

"I ended up down in Rock City on my tod until Alex turned up although, I had a decent night. There was a band on, an unusual name—Goldfrapp, a

Swedish band, I think." Daz was at the mirror with his afro comb fluffing up his hair.

"I heard. Alex told me everything you pulled—an actress you were seen snoggin' with it outside seen by Bev." We made our way out to the car.

"Hey, if you'd been where I'd been, you'd have lapped it up. Where is Alex? We meeting him?"

"We've got to go round for him at half past nine. Where did you get this from, Max? Auto trader?"

"Nah, it's a Bruce special, Daz."

Daz was all over it like a rash. "G Reg XR3—is this that Exercet you were on about?"

I popped the bonnet and lifted the lid. Daz's eyes seemed to kaleidoscope at the sight that lay before him. "Friggin' hell, Max, how do you stop it? It's been fitted with all the RS Cosworth running gear." Daz was soon under it tapping the sills. "What's the MOT on it, Max?"

"One and a half months," I replied.

"Get rid; it's a rot box underneath."

"It's got to be worth getting it seen to, Daz. Jump in; we'll pick up Alex, but you'll need to show me where he lives." I had turned down the stereo as King Cobra faded.

"Here he comes; have you seen the state of him?" Daz said as

Alex came plodding down the entry. Daz rolled the window down and insisted Alex wasn't getting in unless he took his Guns and Roses bandana off. Alex was pulling at the door.

"Right that'll do, stop teasing him, Daz. Let him in." Daz had that boisterous tone about him as he stepped out to let Alex in.

"Hey, Max, cool, you remembered the tape this time. Next track." Soon he and Daz were arguing over which music was going on, both of them grappling at the stereo all the way until we reached Rock City.

"Right, you two can catch a taxi home if there's any more of it," I scolded.

"It's him, Max, keeps trying to pull me bandana off."

"Look, Daz, leave his bandana." I leant up close to Daz while the music was still on. "Tide's coming in."

Daz fell out the car in hysterics as Alex flipped the seat forward and followed him out the car. They made for a nearby tree and leant on it, legs crossed arms folded. Soon Daz was chasing Alex around it, still trying to get his bandana off him. I had my stereo front in my hand and locked the car door, looking down at the queue outside the main doors. I figured we were better off at the Tap first.

"Mine's a Diet Coke, plenty ice."

"Ha ha, poor old Max got to drink that all night." Alex was having a playful pop at me.

"Oy you owe me a half a chicken, on nan bread with salad and mint sauce. I'll be reminding you."

Alex started scratching his head about last Sunday morning's events. "Where's Daz?"

"At the bar, I think." The Tap was mobbed; it was tight squeeze to our usual stance near the bell fruit machines.

"Still at the bar, eh? He wants to make haste—I'm gagging; look, I'm spitting dust." The whole place reeked of cigarette smoke, beer, petunia oil, and sweaty leather. Alex fit the bill perfect.

Daz appeared with his big hands around three lapping pints. Lager shandy, all right, Max?"

"Yeah a treat beats a Diet Coke."

"Man, give it here—I'm as dry as nun's crotch," Alex said.

Next I knew two soft lumps buffeted me forward while I was trying to take my first drink. How do you know her, Max?" Daz asked.

I turned around just as I viewed her ass and her black hair through the din. "Erm, years ago. Cop this a sec, Alex." He smiled and took my pint. "I'll be back in a sec." I pushed my way through until I caught up with her, resting my hand on her shoulder. "Yes, it's you—I'd know those swells anywhere. I ain't seen you in here before; who are you out with?"

She was a peach from Mansfield. Diana was her name. "I'm out with my two cousins, and yes they're female."

"Ha ham you ain't out of your depth with her maybe," I thought. I said to her, "Hey, you do look fab, by the way. I love the Goth look on you; it really suites you." Her hair was set high with purple and black streamers through it. Her face was pure white, and her brown eyes looked thick with mascara. Her lips where ebony, and she had on a tied-up-the-rear purple and black leather bask, and black jeans she must have put on with a shoe horn.

"Will I be seeing you later?" she asked.

"Hey, babe, it's me who wants the pictures, remember." I could see her smiling.

"You, erm, well, how can I say . . ." She stepped in a little closer. Then I could see who was stood behind her. Sheeks it was Caroline.

I grabbed Diane's wrist, and we somehow ended up at the side entrance. "This will do, right? I want to do you on canvas."

Diane burst out laughing. "For a second I thought you were serious," she remarked.

"Yes, yes I am." I want you to pose for me somewhere out of sight like you are tonight, dressed like this."

"Max I'm not working tonight, if you know what I mean." Her stiletto was grinding up my shin as she told me. We took a walk out the back entry.

Later on I met up with Daz, and he asked me, "Where you been?" "We're about ready to go. Here, drink that."

"Erm, a bit of business to sort out."

"You look like a big weight got lifted from yer mind, Max." Daz was wet through with sweat; it was pouring off him. "And yes, this is our second pint—and guess whose round it is in Rock City?"

After the long wait in the queue, I managed to collar Hobbit at the door. Old Hobbit stood with one pit boot resting on four slabs of Red Stripe. He and his crew must have worked that door since my apprenticeship here in the early eighties; it was his turn to guard the night's ration, for the after-party. I'd been to a few of those, let me tell you!

Hobbit was chugging a can of Red Bull as I leaned in over the desk. "Hobbit, old chap, what you running these days?"

"Hey, Max, what can I do for you?" he said, putting down his can. His head always looked freshly shaved, and Red Bull dribbled down his beard as he spoke, taking his rolling tin from his leather waistcoat and flicking off the lid.

"I need a slab," I told him.

"You need a what?"

"A slab."

"Plenty of them up there, Max." He pointed up the stairs and reached under the table to produced a slab of red stripe. "A tenner, Max."

"Right. Daz, cop that; we are going in first to the Rig or upstairs to the main arena."

Hobbit snatched the money. "Hey, Max, don't take that upstairs. Go in the Rig with it."

"Sure thing, Hobbit, we'll keep a low profile tonight. Okay, bro?" I said.

The three of us trundled through into the Rig. Alex was trying to break the plastic surrounding the cans of red stripe whilst Daz was walking with it under his arm. "Get off," Daz kept telling. "Alex, you're not having one; go see Hobbit for your own." Alex soon jump back when Daz made a grab for his bandana. "Aw, he's got his lip out again, Max. Look at him sulking." It was like watching a cross between the Freak Brothers and Laurel and Hardy never a dull moment.

The place was a hustle from bottom to top; if you like rock, this was the place it was at. When I said apprenticeship, I mean for the air guitar. Air guitar is expression release, a statement; it was cool, and above all it was fun. Although it can be dangerous and highly addictive—it's even better than the real thing, and I've tried both. Alex could be good with the lead breaks and tended to make it just right, which came as a result of years of practice. Daz would go more for the rhythm—it seemed to suit his big, bulky frame—and his facial expressions were second to none, full of concentration and timing. Me, I went more for the bass; to me it was the heart of the music, the beat, the source, the buzz. When you combined the three of us, presto and party time; you got the tunes, we got the talent.

Things were livening up, and we were in the thick of it. Diane had found a few of her friends and joined us, and they were happy to break cans with us. We were right near the back speakers, from which blasted an awesome saga of the history. Man, this place was legend—which brought me to the next part of the apprenticeship: sign reading. I got to be able to read the signs. A good place to start was to check out the regulars, distinguish the visitors, and get clued up from there. Take Daz: he had a regular women, and one never saw her here, but in the eighties you did. I saw him chat to loads of broads, but I never saw him chat them up, if you know what I mean. Alex had done the married bit and was currently going through divorce; he had kids, and I'd seen why he was going through divorce—it had all to do with reading the signs. I knew Diana was a visitor; she won't be here next week, so she would make the most of a good night, and I was happy to provide a little entertainment.

Other things to look out for in places like this were chapters (The Angels), who were usually okay once one got chatting, but beware—things could get out of hand. They were best avoided and left alone because they usually ran things anyway; I'd seen a few wish they hadn't crossed them. One guy had a sawn off up the chin over an incident; I never saw him in here after that night.

I'd cracked and was having a can of Red Stripe before they'd gone, offering the lasses another. Alex and Daz were up on the dance floor doing their thing while I was trying to mind read and read lips. "Just the one won't hurt," I said.

"Let's go upstairs; I want to find some people. I haven't seen them in here; they must be upstairs." Diana was pulling my arm, and I followed her through the leather and black up those famous stairs, the ones your feet tended to stick to. Diana stopped at the doors upstairs with her foot, holding it open.

"Cheers, doll," I said as I entered. I could see a band on stage, and the main dance floor was a mass of bodies, mainly Gothic and glam with a few diehard punks dotted here and there. "Who are you trying to find?"

She was looking at the stairs that led to the balcony. "I left them up here; come on up." We found a gap on the balcony and were leering down at the band. Her eyes scanned individuals around us. "Wait here," she said as she jumped out of view. Well, I hadn't a clue who the band was. It was mainly all distortion and feedback and a lot a dry ice under a mass of light coordination The band were clad in a pagan theme.

I could see Russell and Big Dave and a few others standing near the DJ box, hassling the DJ to play their requests; apparently the band was about to finish.

Diana pushed her way through and squeezed in at the side of me. "Ladies room," she whispered.

"Ah. I'm not sure who the band is. Found your friends, did you?"

"Yes, I spotted them in the corner. Come on, I'll introduce you this time." She moved too quick and I lost her. I ended up back down in the rig; I knew she would find me there.

Alex was rummaging at the last of the Red Stripe when Daz leaned over, pinning him down. "I've got it!" Daz held up Alex's bandana, all triumphant.

"I jumped in." Bloody hell, it's worse than I thought. Quick, give it back to him." I could tell they where pissed as me an Daz fell about laughing. Alex grabbed Daz's wrist and took the bandana back, and Alex headed for the carsey, bumping people. He was desperately trying to get the bandana back on his head. The two girls Diana had introduced were in hysterics.

I leaned over to Daz. "Russ and Dave are upstairs." Daz disappeared, and I was left chatting to Liz. Liz was the most attractive out of the three girls, and I could see she had dressed more or less to keep the guys off her.

She had the look of an Italian in her, that dark complexion in jeans. Liz was more of a rocker than she let on; her knowledge of the rock scene truly startled me. She'd told me she was twenty-three years old and that she was a part-time project manager within the local council; the rest of her time she spent as a student at the university, and she had come here for a change of scene. Diana had rang her at work, so she agreed to meet down here and was glad she came, although she preferred what she termed as soft rock. This girl truly did drop from the stars, and I couldn't pick fault with her at all.

Daz returned with Russ and Dave. "Any tinnies left? Aw, we ain't got to go to the bar, have we?"

"Should have been here earlier."

Alex stuck his head over my shoulder and said, "You get him from behind, and I'll kick him in the bollocks."

"Oy, I heard that," Daz said, and he was soon chasing Alex again; after seeing Daz take the empty glass with ice left in the bottom, I knew what he was up to. I soon heard "Ahh!" as Daz tipped it down Alex's back after he'd collared him at the speakers. We could distinctly hear it over the music.

Laughing, I turned to Liz and said, "Your friend's name, what's yer friend's name?"

"Oh, she's my older sister. Her name is Deborah, or Deb for short."

"She does look like you a bit, come to think of it—an older blonde version."

She gave me a cheeky giggle. "She's thirty with four kids—she's married."

I'd taken to a back seat in a corner just to the left of where we were all originally standing. Liz sat with me, chatting away about vegetarian diets and recipes. It didn't take long for Russ and Dave to hone in on Diana and Deborah, and I could see they were trying every trick in the book.

I turned to Liz and stopped her dead. "Hang on a sec, how are you getting home?"

Liz smiled. "We all came on a bus from Mansfield. We all met and came here with Diana."

"Is she going back with you two?"

"Why, yes, I think so."

"Right, next question. Have you got a fella?"

Liz put her hand to her mouth. "Well, sort of—it's not serious," she said quietly.

I seemed to hold her gaze as I took her hand and pulled her up. "Come on, this is soft rock." The main lights had come on, so it was the last song of the night.

We all ended up outside chatting and fooling around. The girls' bus had arrived, and we were just making sure they got safely on it. "Give me your number, then I'll buzz you," I said.

"Turn around, then." I did and felt a little pressure on my back. She had written on her cloak room ticket in eyebrow pencil. Liz pecked me on the cheek, gave Daz and Alex a big hug, and thanked us for the cans and a memorable evening.

Alex and Daz and I stood up near the car, talking to Russ and Dave. Russ was bragging about his new Ducati while Dave was showing us pictures of a smashed-up CBR 900. "Well, I don't know about you, Daz, but I would say that's definitely a write-off; that won't see the road again."

"Can't you get the bits, Max, to make it well again?"

"If you'd asked me two years ago, I might have been able to help you. I'm keeping my nose clean."

We ended up at a kebab house on the way home after entering Liz's number into my phone. Alex had enough cash on him to buy me back the same as I'd bought him the week before: half a chicken on a naan with the trimmings, which went down a treat after a night at the city. Daz had his wrapped while Alex stunk the car out with Donor.

"What's that you're doing, Max?"

"Just having a doodle, why?"

"I just wondered."

"Right, I'm off to bed. There's the cover; the ashtray's over there if you're skinning up."

Daz had just been to the phone box to talk to his missus, who lived up on the edge of town. He came back in the living room and sat down. I asked him "Hey, what happened to the chick from America? What's her name? Jo."

"I couldn't raise the cash to go back out," he said as he picked up the remote, flicking on the video. "Jeremy Mc Graph is on for the title," he said, and buzzing motocross bikes hitting air filled the screen. I put down my notes and lit a spliff. Daz grinned. "Anyway, I'm back with her now."

"I know; Alex told me last week."

"She's cooking breakfast for us, Max, so doesn't smoke too many of those. I told her ten o'clock. I don't know, Max."

"Yeah, I think they did hang around together."

Daz started laughing. "I know where this is leading. Your flat next door when it got burgled."

"Anyone said anything about that?" I snapped.

"The police will get to know before you, Max. It was me that phoned them, remember?"

"I know, and thank you for reporting it."

"I will let you know if I hear anything." Daz's eyes kept shifting to the left. "Have you seen who's in it?"

"No who?"

"A rough blonde smack head, so keep your voice down; she will be listening."

"Oh," I said as I relit the joint.

"Ha ha, I've heard many a story about you down there, Max. Who off?"

I handed my plate to his missus, thanking her for my breakfast. Then I remembered who went to the phone last night—Daz. "Thanks, doll, that was nice." I'd eaten all my scrambled egg.

"Daz butted in. "I think she's talking years ago, Max, at Rock City. Hang on, that's my phone. "He checked the text. "It's Alex. Can I ring him?"

Daz's missus was at the sink, and she yelled, "I don't know why you don't put credit on the damn thing."

"Oh, yeah, I suppose so." Daz lifted the phone and rang him. "Have you just got up? It's eleven o'clock. Eh, you're a dirty slob; we've found your half eaten kebab on Max's car back seat." It wasn't; it was just some bits of meat he'd dropped while he'd stuffed his face.

"Ask him if he wants to go for a run out," I prompted.

"Did you hear that?" Daz said into the phone. "Hang on, I'll tell him." He looked at me. "He says he's at work tonight, night shift. Says he's going to get his head back down. That's bollocks; I know he's meeting Bev at the Hole in the Wall." Daz started laughing again. "And don't deny it."

"I chirped up, "Hehe, I read his text messages whilst he was in getting the kebabs. Tell him."

"Are you lying, Alex? Alex says you're a cheeky monkey."

"Are you going to hurry up on that phone?" Daz' missus interrupted.

"Hang on, love, two secs."

I told Daz, "Tell him to keep that shut."

"Did you hear that? Alex says you're still a cheeky monkey."

The little one came running through after she slammed the back door. She was holding her knee, and Daz put the phone down. "What's up?" he asked as he lifted her onto his lap. She was burying her head deep into his chest, mumbling.

Her mum stood over the two of them, concerned. "Let's have a look." The little girl took her hand away to reveal a small graze on the side of her leg. "Aw, baby." She winked at Daz. "I'll get the med box outta the cupboard." The next I knew Daz was throwing her up and catching her in his arms. It wasn't long before she was giggling. "Now then, let's take a look." Daz passed her on to her mum. "How did you do this then?"

"I fell off my bike." The little girl still had her knuckles in her eyes. Daz was trying to sound sympathetic whilst her ma opened the first aid kit.

Later that day I was talking to Daz. We were on the M18. Daz had the window down while I cruised in the fast lane. He asked, "What made you move out here then, Max?"

"Change of scene." It was a scorcher of a day. I slowed down after I moved into the middle lane and then over for the A1.

I think Daz was impressed. "I don't know, Max, she runs okay, I'll give it that."

"Sometimes she won't turn over. Bruce said he'd fitted a starter, so it can't be that. The receipt is in the glove box, and the old one's still in the boot. I checked on the battery, and it works fine."

"Starter ring," Daz suggested.

"You're the second person that said that. Of course, the starter ring on the clutch housing."

Daz started laughing. "Ever tried doing one of them, Max?"

"Eh? Ah, it don't matter." A heat wave on the road distracted me.

"Oh, big bucks—that ain't no ordinary clutch, either," Daz insisted, nodding his head. "Get rid."

"But it's not MOT failure, is it?" I took my foot off the accelerator, and gradually the nose came back up.

Daz's hair looked like Medusa's. "Last time I went that fast, Max, I had a helmet on." He was trying to move the hair from his mouth; it had stuck all over his sweaty forehead, as he wound up the window. Mine was okay; I had mine through the back of my baseball cap, tied up.

It wasn't long before we were coming into Sunny Donny. "Hey, that's handy, Max, just off the Motorway. Hmm, and the town centre's just up there." He watched my eyes looking right, and we pulled in. "So this is where you've been hiding since you moved here. Get kettle on then, Max," he said just as I'd unlocked the door. "It's quite cosy. I was expecting something a bit more."

"Hey, I just lodge here. Still no sugar, is there, Daz?"

"I have it in coffee, Max. I'll make it; you go and get changed."

The cougar was busy for a Sunday afternoon. Daz sat with his arm over the back of the chair. "Set me up, Max. They're going out back; we're on." A couple of local bikers were putting their lighters and tins away in their cut-offs.

I sat fidgeting with my phone. Daz asked me, "Who are you texting?"

"Alex," I said as I stood up and moved over to the pool table.

Alex's text said, "If meeting her, I want in."

Daz was looking at each cue for the best tip, grabbing at the chalk. "You scruffy sly hound, you know if you get in first, she ain't going to find out about Diana."

I laughed. "I can't let her find out. Do you still see Rubble in the Cony Club?" I asked.

"You'll have to go in, Max. He still goes in there. Go see Big Tony; he'll be about somewhere."

Later I drove Daz back home. "Sure you'll be okay?" I asked.

Daz stood at the car window, leaning in and still grinning, The curtains were flicking outside his missus' house. My phone beeped. "Phone me in the week, Max," Daz said, and he turned and went in the house.

I sat and checked my phone. "The Priory, 9PM." Yes, it was her; I'd put the number under D. I'd tell Daz I'd see him later. Right now I had to call in and see my uncle.

Uncle Eric was in his usual place when I passed his window. I'd popped in at a Jacko's for carry-out.

"On the house," he said, handing me a half bottle of Teachers. "It's good to see you looking so well, Max." He shook my hand with a good grip. It was hard to imagine that some clown had robbed Old Jacko at gunpoint with a recommissioned pistol and made off with 150 in cash and a bag full of cigarettes. I wondered whether the armed blag was really worth it, considering the weapon would have likely harmed the user more than the person it was aimed at. That low life scum was still rotting in jail, eight years for armed blag. The police had caught the suspect, a teenaged male crack head who was known to us. After an anonymous tip-off, officers found the weapon hidden at his home address, along with an array of class A drugs.

Uncle Eric stood, and we made our way into the kitchen. "I couldn't really pass without seeing how you are, Uncle." Eric had spotted the whiskey as I placed it on the coffee table. "Coffee for me, please." A cup a coffee arrived with a good selection of biscuits, and I dived into them. Eric sat back down in his chair, picking up the remote and flicking through his new TV channels. He'd had cable installed and was obviously enjoying the options. "I need hold of our Pat," I said whilst sipping my coffee.

Eric was opening the half bottle and pouring himself a good measure into a tumbler, gulping at it. "You burned bridges," he said as he bent forward to place another log on the fire.

I knew I'd been outcast by previous events, and I took the foil off another of my favourite biscuits, chocolate mint. "I hear Celtic got beat by Motherwell."

He butted in, "And they won yesterday, 3-2. Last-minute goal." He reached for his book. "Ring him first." He gave me his book, opened at the right page, and I punched the mobile number into my phone.

"Pat, it's me, Max."

"Hey. I'm up the farm if you want to come up. I've took the dogs out; I'll wait."

"Okay. I'm at my uncle's; give me twenty minutes." I hung up and said to my uncle, "Eric, I got to scoot."

He was lighting his pipe as I rose to leave and gulped at the coffee. "Hey, and give your mum a phone," Eric said with a smile as he reached for the whisky.

A fine coat of dust lay over the surface of my car. I looked over at the stables, and visions of the horses came back. The stables where staked out with bales and looked unused, abandoned. Not how I remembered them. I walked through to Deadman's Wood and looked over to Checkpoint Charlie. "She's untouched," I thought. "It's all still there."

I spotted my bro's transit in the main car park on the way in. I knew he'd have made his way to the Dear Valley. I knew the route back, so I jumped the style. Too late—she'd seen me, and I couldn't jump back over.

The Range Rover pulled up. "I bloody well thought it was you!" Her voice was as pure as the Queen herself. I leant in among the dust. It'd been a hot day, and I offered her a chiggley.

"Spotted anything on the way up?" I asked. She tilted her glasses forward. "What happened to my dream?"

"Robert had it removed." I looked at the floor, gutted. The little white house had disappeared off the face of the earth. "Well, you should keep it in your trousers, shouldn't you." She pushed her glasses back.

"Eh?" I lifted my head. "How did he find out?" I jumped back as she hit the accelerator. Then I remembered the two had walked in on us. I was starting to cough from the dust.

"If you only bloody well knew what you did that night," she said, and tears rolled off her sun oil as she hit the throttle.

"It was just a—" Too late; she'd mizzed. I coughed and rubbed the dust from my eyes. I was just about to say it was just a one night stand at a party, in the little house that I'd wanted to buy and live out my days. This was going back to 1990.

If only I knew? Her voice haunted me all the way to the clearing. I could see Minx's little black head jumping up in the corn field to the left of me, and then Tammy shot across and back again, stopping dead and wagging her tail. She bolted towards me. No, it wasn't Tammy. Who was this little dog? I stopped and turned around. I knew my bro was close because I distinctly heard his whistle. Then he appeared, the two little dogs at the side of him. "Where have you parked?" he asked.

"Round near the stables. Good to see you, bro." The two little dogs were fussing around my feet. I bent down to let them sniff the back of my hand. "Hey, what's all this, then? Where's Tammy, still at home?"

"She was ran over by a train, killed. That's the pup of Minx. Didn't Ma tell you?"

"No, she never said. It's a bonny wee dog, though." I realized I must have seen Minx twice. "Did you keep any of the other pups?"

"Nah, sold 'em ages ago. They were queuing at the door for me."

"I ain't never seen a black and tan one." The little dog was sucking up to me.

"It happened not long after I visited you." Poor Tammy. Pat knew Tammy and I got on; he knew I'd be expecting to see her. "She's buried in the back garden. We're having a barbeque; Nicky will have it all ready by the time we get back to mine."

Later I sat with my bro and his missus, and they filled me in on all the local gossip. I checked my phone for the time: 7.30. Bro handed me a platter of Lincoln sausage and silverside steak with salad and a baked spud and grated cheese. It was gorgeous, but I couldn't eat it all; I knew I'd be downing another lot later. I made sure I'd at least eaten half of what was there. "I can't eat like him," I complained as Pat had finished his plate and put more on the barbeque.

"Smell it and weep," he said, dropping on another slab of silverside.

Nicky handed me a glass of Diet Coke with ice, and she asked, "So where are you off to tonight, then?"

"Thinking of going back to Sunny Donny. I've got work in the morning."

"Yeah, I meant to ask you if you are working Pat."

"I had a few weeks landscape gardening, got the sack, and dropped lucky with someone who advertised for a brickie. I'm doing okay."

"I could ask at Newark if you're stuck. Cabbies, mate." Pat was working for a haulage company, long distance. "And what do you mean lucky."

"Building conservatory basses, Pat. Sticking to what I know."

Bingo walked in through the back gate. Pat said, "Show it him, Max." I opened the wrap and laid it on the top of the wall.

Bingo took a taste. "Well, it ain't coke, that's fer sure. Ergh!" The aftertaste hit him. "Phew, where you had that, Max?"

"Ha ha, what do you think?"

"Strewth, gimme a drink." Nicky handed him a can of cheap lager.

"I need you to shift some," I said. "How much on the Oz?"

"I'll find you a price; give me your number."

Nicky had already placed her order and was already ringing around her pals when I left. Pat saw me to the door and said, "I'll sort you an ounce of skunk. You'll be all right with that, a hundred on the Oz. You can owe it me." He threw it on the seat.

"Hoo, plumb cake. Thanks, Pat."

"You can drop the cash off next time through."

Diana was flicking her brake lights at the main gate as I pulled alongside, turning my music down. "Did you book it?" I asked.

"See you down there." She sped off before she answered. The TR7 disappeared around the corner. I near enough smashed into the back of her as she braked to pull over. I swerved to miss her, hit the brakes, and slammed it into reverse, pulling in front of her as she stepped out of her car.

"You made it then," she said, taking her jacket and throwing it through my passenger window and into the back seat. She opened the door and slid in.

"I've hardly slept fer two nights running, so go easy, doll," I said.

"We ain't going in there, so you'd better spin round."

"What you got planned?"

"I want to go back into town; just drive."

Something had stressed her, I could tell. Something was wrong. Then I noticed she hadn't changed her clothes since last night. I put it to her. "Something wrong at home?"

"Stop the car," she insisted. We weren't far from the main exit. She placed her hands on her lap and turned to me as I pulled over.

"What's wrong, doll?"

"I haven't been home," she said, looking serious.

"But why?"

"I stayed with my two cousins. It's just that I haven't found time to go home." She giggled. "I want you to come home with me. Can we stop fer pizza or something on the way? Drop me back at the car."

"Don't mizz without me, then," I said as I went back to her car.

"No, leave yours here. Leave it at the front—it'll be okay."

I made sure I put the immobiliser on and took the weed from the glove box before locking up. "Hey, this is cool," I said, jumping in her car. The inside was heavily trimmed in black and grey plastic. She hit the accelerator. I wasn't expecting to see a girl like this living in a place like this. I was sure this was the ramper; the gauge was on the eighty mark, and she was giving the latest sales hype when she pulled up the drive after making the turn. Man, I thought I could drive. The crunch of the wheels made me ask if her folks were at home. I really was getting nervous.

"This was a last-minute decision, so thank yer lucky stairs I turned up at all. I don't live with my folks." She gave me that reassuring look, batting her eyelashes.

I thought to myself, "Right, play it cool, Max. Play it cool."

We'd settled for Chinese that she recommended, not far from the priory. I had at my feet the ingredients to make or break, because I ordered everything. For those of you who don't know where the ramper is, this was some house. The kitchen was huge and led through to a split level dining area set out with the biggest pine table I had ever seen, where I dropped the carry-out and begged her for plates.

"Right, Max. What's the surprise? It smells good." I opened the lids. "Mmm, that smells like roast duck in orange sauce, Peking style. What else did you get?" She found the king prawn balls, popping one in her mouth. "Oh look, spare ribs! Hoo, they're hot," she gasped. "Hey, and boiled rice. And look, fried Chinese mixed veggies with king prawns with ginger and lemon grass. Oh Max, you can go again. Hey, don't forget the sweet and sour." Before I knew it she was flying around the kitchen, opening cupboards and placing small dishes and bowls onto the table.

"You ain't got chop sticks as well?" I asked jokingly.

"You go through and make yourself at home."

It was a cool kitchen as I stepped through into the lounge. "Hey, how do I . . . Where's the . . ."

"It's here." She followed me through and switched on the light. With one foot still in her stiletto boot, she hopped through switching on the big screen TV. "What do u want on?" Diana asked. "Have a look through and choose something." She pointed to her video library.

"Well . . ." I probed whilst Diana sat for a minute, taking off her remaining boot.

"My housemate is away. We take it in turns with the house. I do work away a lot, you know, Max." Diana changed the subject as she got up and headed through to the kitchen. She walked back into the living room holding a bottle and trying to wind the cork screw in.

"Here, let me do that." I reached out to take the task from her.

She handed over the bottle of wine before she disappeared to bring through the crockery, eating utensils, and glasses. "Right, all set, we can eat now."

"I've chosen this." I picked out a video and she looked at it.

"Ah, this is one of my favourites—*Dances with Wolves*." She placed the video in the machine, reaching for the remote.

"I've only ever seen the second half," I explained.

She settled back on the settee and said, "You're in for a treat."

After the meal I laid back, stuffed. At the part where Two Socks got filled with lead, she moved closer, squeezing my arm.

"Fancy a bifter?" I asked.

She leaned back and laughed. "A what?" She looked confused.

"A reefer, a spliff."

"Go on, then, roll one." I produced the bag from inside my shirt. "Hey Max, sell me some of that."

"I'll do you half an ounce fer sixty bucks."

She got up and was soon back, counting out the cash from her bag.

"Max, I'll drop you at your car. Please get up." God she was up and showered, putting on her makeup. "Wake up, Max, I got to rush!" She was flying about like no one's business, and I reached for my jeans. "There's fresh coffee and toast in the kitchen."

"Thanks, doll." I was all horse. I grabbed my shoes and T-shirt and trotted through to the bathroom.

"And mind the seat," she shouted. I must have missed during the night. "There's a clean towel in the airing cupboard."

I washed and brushed up, and then I went on down and wandered into the kitchen. The hot coffee sat in the percolator, and I felt drawn to it. She was still upstairs, and I couldn't find the coffee cups. As I opened cupboards, she walked through, laughed, and said, "Try the one under the percolator."

"Oh. What time is it, anyway?"

"It's 5.30." I sat at the table filling a cup. Milk and sugar and hot toast and butter were already on the table. Well, I had thought it was hot, but the butter didn't melt onto the toast. "I did try and wake you earlier," she commented.

"Ergh, stewed coffee."

"It ain't. It's you—you're still stoned," she said, smiling. Then the nutty flavours kicked in as I rolled it around my mouth. "Do you have work today, Max?"

"Oh yeah, shit. Yeah, I have to be at work by eight. I got to nip home, change for work and grab my tools. I'll just make it. Hey, you look all business-like," I said as I studied her. She had on a smart pair of charcoal grey trousers and a white shirt.

"It's going to be a hot day, Max. I hope you brought your sun cream." Donk was up and about, getting things ready for marking the footings for the new run. "It's nine-inch blocks down there. I want it six feet high so they can't see over."

"Hang on, Donk, you never said anything about nine-inch blocks."

"I thought you knew, Max—didn't I say?"

"In a footing as well, are you trying to kill me?"

Nidge rolled up in a van and jumped out. "Hey Dad, Max."

"What do you reckon to Him, Nidge," Donk said. "He's moaning about the blocks."

"Tell him to stuff it, Max. He's been trying to get me to do it. He knows what's involved with that."

"Tenner an hour, Max."

"Phew, I don't know, Donk," I said.

"All right, Max, tenner an hour. Use the blocks that's there, and then we'll use four-inch double blocks with ties."

"Now you're talking. Tell you what—fetch me a load of four-inch blocks to start it, and I'll do it. I ain't busting my back in that footing."

"All right, Max, you'll have a day digging the first run out anyway. Here's where I want the soil put." Donk had line painted a section of ground in one corner.

"You'll still need a skip or two, Donk."

"Nah, this will take it."

"We'll see. We can't go higher than the DPC on next door's garage." I pointed it out.

"I never spotted it, Max. Damn."

"We'll still be able to put at least half there for today, I'd guess, but you still need a skip, Donk."

Nidge butted in. "He's tight fisted. Get on the phone and get Max his skip now—you've agreed to it; take Max's advice. I did tell you he was safe, Dad."

Dink pulled in and jumped out. "Hey, what time did I call this?" Donk said, fuming. "Our Nidge has been sat half an hour waiting on you."

Nidge was trying to twist Dinks ear. "Ha Ha, I bet he went to the cabin for his breakfast, and we weren't there. How's the Pug running, you little shit?"

"It's fine." Young Dink was winding up. "I'll smack you with the shovel!" He pulled it out of the sand.

"Hey, you two calm down," Donk said.

"I'll belt you with it," Nidge said. Dink held the shovel over his shoulder. Nig ran straight at him, knocking Dink in the sand.

"I'll take that," I said as I rushed over and took the shovel while the pair grappled around in the sand. They ended up throwing hands full of sand at each other.

Donk got the hosepipe on the pair of them just as I jumped out of the way. "I didn't lash out on sand for you two to throw it all over. Now pack it in." Donk had raised his tone.

"Talk about Cain and Abel, Donk, you reared a right pair there," I said as I stood keeping hold of the shovel.

"Right. At least you know what you're doing, Max. Let's go for breakfast."

Collie had turned up outside the house just as I came back from the corner shop. "Like trying to catch hold of smoke," Collie said from his car window. "I saw you go in the shop, so I hung on."

"Ah, Collie, just the man I want to see. Do you do welding?"

"I ain't got the welder anymore; I sold it. Why?"

"I need that," I said, pointing to the XR3.

"You best be taking it for pre MOT, Max."

"What about a starter ring, Collie, can you fix that?"

"Best weighing it in, Max, at the scrap yard. It's an expensive job to do that." Collie was stopping and starting the XR3 ignition. "It is a bit on the sticky side, isn't it? You've had yer running out of it. You ain't done bad for two hundred sovs; stick it through the block while you got MOT on it. I've got the stuff fer the rest of it, if you want to tart it up. Some boy racer will buy it.

"Paul wants it with a full MOT. He has what I need."

"What's that then, Max?"

"A big estate car, plenty of room for the cash jobs that I do. He wants 650 for it."

Collie stopped me. "The one on his ex wife's drive?"

"I don't know; he came here in it once when I first moved in."

"Yeah, it's worth more." Collie now knew which car I had in mind. "Granada estate diesel, fat as you like."

"That's the one, Collie."

"Hmm, you want that, do you? Leave it with me, Max—oh shit, I've locked the keys in, for fuck's sake."

I looked in the car Collie had turned up in, and right enough they were in the ignition, and the doors were locked as tried the handle. "Hang on." I nipped into the house and returned with my tools.

"We ain't got time for laying bricks, Max. Think I'm panicking here." I handed him the fat screwdriver. "Ah, Max, you know, don't you?"

I nodded. "Lift the door seal." Then I handed him my trusty saw. "The old American slide," I said with a grin.

Collie slipped the blade down, feeling for the bar that opened the door, and then *clunk*. "Phew, thank God for that." Collie was back in his car. "Follow me back to my house, Max. I've got something you might want, and I'll take another look at your car."

"Okay, hang on let me just lock up. I'll be right back." I took my tools back into the house and followed Collie to his yard.

Later on, Collie sat at his computer burning me of a CD with all the latest tunes on it. "You'll need this." Collie handed me a Sharp CD player. "Good quality; it will read a copy. I can fit it now for you, Max, fifty sovs." He reached under the coffee table and showed me the same player in the catalogue. "It's 170 sovs in there. Our Gurt sold her car, and I switched it fer a tape player; it's legit." Collie was under the dash playing with the wiring. He was also looking around the rest of the car for MOT failures. "Let's take it for a spin, Max."

Collie had finished showing me how the player worked. "Sheesh, it's a vast improvement," I said as Collie pulled out of the drive, slamming the brakes and whipping up the handbrake.

"Jump in, Max." We went for a spin through Bawtry and arrived back at Collie's without the tunes on. "That whirring in the back, Max, that's the wheel bearings; they'll pull it on that." As we pulled back on his drive, he jumped out and disappeared in his shed, coming out again with his trolley jack. He placed it under the car and elevated it. He was soon underneath, fidgeting and tapping. "Shit, the boot floor's rotten, and you need a new exhaust and mount—that's what the tapping is." He slid from underneath and pulled the keys from the ignition and moved around to the rear. "Help me out with all that junk, Max." Collie soon had the boot emptied and pulled the carpet up "You'll need that patched," he said as he removed the tyre from the tyre well. "Ah, there's the problem—a blocked drainage bung. I know a small garage that will sort it. I'll do the bearings for you; it's not as bad as I thought." Collie told me the number, and I entered it into my phone. I paid Collie his 50 sovs for the stereo after we had put all my spare bits back in the boot. "Six sovs a side, Max. Thirty sovs for fitting them. If you do one side, it's best to do the other as well." I agreed. "Saturday morning all right?"

"Ah, that's better," I said to myself as I slid deeper into the bath. After I had myself cleaned up I sat watching the TV, doodling a few sentences in my shorts. Paul was still away, and I sat drinking a few bottles of Bud as I checked my phone; no new messages. Time to phone Ma.

"How do you fancy a working holiday around November?" Ma asked.

"I'll think about it, Ma. I'll need to clear it first. What's it doing?"

"Helping a friend of mine erect a fence." Ma was full of loves and kisses when she rang off.

The next morning I arrived at work. A skip wagon had just pulled off the drive, and Donk was waiting on the street to sign for it. "We're just waiting on the ballast, Max. Nidge has gone for it. I want you to lay it while Dink gets the rest of that out; you'll need to mix it dry-ish. I want blocks on it tomorrow. We need that hedge out so I can stake the rest of the footing to the boundary. Nidge will pull it out with the transit."

Nidge came back with two coffees as I watered up the mixer and switched it off. I was stripped to my shorts and boots. "T-shirt on, Max, your back's red raw," Donk said, handing me back my tape measure and looking concerned.

Dink had brought a few foldaway chairs. "There's two more in the conservatory," he said, and he rushed back in the house for his coffee.

I came back with the Folding chairs, opening one up for Donk as he sat and raised his hands. "I think you're right, Max," he said, "there won't be enough."

"What you've done is right if it's going to be all nine-inch block or single skin."

"Yep, I'm with you. It's enough for a start, Max."

"What are we going to do about the finish? The four-inch blocks are a lot darker."

"Well have to render it, both sides."

I stopped him. "You'll need to put in expansion gaps every three metres. Fit mounts and Render each panel, and fill the gaps with the correct colour mastic. Each panel will need to be tied and expansion strips fitted between each panel."

"Write it all down, Max. You can go get what you need after dinner. Who are you phoning?"

"I'm trying to book me car in for pre-MOT. Hush a sec." When I'd got through to the garage, I asked, "Right, where are you?"

"Hexthorpe," the guy at the garage said after took the details of my car.

Donk handed me a pen to write out my list. "Hey, let me see that address again." I handed Donk the mats note book with the address for the garage scribbled down. "We do a lot of business with this lot. They service the firm's vehicles. Give me your phone a sec, Max." Donk went for a walk up the garden, looking at the next phase. When he came back, he said, "Forget about taking it Monday—we'll take it tonight."

"What, my car?"

"I told Bruce not to sell it you. I wanted you to buy the Renault."

The insurance on it, Donk—they wanted five hundred pounds Stirling. The XR3 cost me two hundred pounds sterling and two hundred to buy it."

Donk nodded. "It's a nice car, that Renault."

We waited to see the damage report on the car, kicking stones in the dusty car park. Donk went in to talk to the guy and came back out. "That's going to cost another two hundred, Max. I've had word with him. I looked at the list."

"How much if I get the bearings done?" Donk went in and came back out again. "It's 120; he wants it Monday morning." It was agreed.

"Come over to the house at 8.30." I put down my phone and headed into the house; there was no sign of Paul, and it was seven o'clock already as I ran up to get changed. I decided it was best to clog it up the back, up the A1, and head in to Mansfield through the back.

I arrived at 8.40 and crunched over the chuckies to her front door, clicking the door bell. The door came open, and she stood with her baggy house clothes on. "Fancy that," she said, "I was beginning to wonder."

"I ain't had time to put credit on, doll," I said, showing her my phone. "I never arrived home till seven." We walked into the hall and through to the kitchen.

"Overtime, Max?" she said as she grinned.

"Nah, doll, I'm trying to sort the car out expenses and all that."

She poured another glass of white wine whilst sliding onto the chair. A half smoked reefer was in the ashtray, and she took hold and lit it.

"Bring the car around the back, Max."

I did as she'd asked. It was the first time I really looked out the back door—mainly all woodland. She had the back door to the kitchen open as I was admiring the garden layout. "Sort of a maintenance free garden," I chuffed, standing in the kitchen doorway.

"Nothing to do with me." Diana took a bottle of Bacardi Breezer from the fridge and fidgeted in the draw next the sink with the bottle opener. "I just rent the place." She handed me the opened bottle. "That'll cool you down." She winked as she took her seat again. She was playing with her nails, filing them and painting them up, giggling about the weekend's events.

I sat opposite her, building a few spliffs. "Well, you know the one I prepared earlier," I joked. "Diana, I got to ask—what is you really do?" She smiled, putting her finger on her nose. "You'll tell me when you're ready. Come on through into the lounge—something on the TV I want to see."

"Hey, why ain't you been answering your phone?" Paul was muttering to someone else while I was trying to listen to his explanation. "And guess what I found in the bloody sugar caddy." Paul went quiet.

"Right, how much on the oz that's got to get shifted from the house, Paul?" I asked.

"Ninety, Max. There looks about two ounces there; that's 180 sterling. If you shift it, 150."

"When are you back?" I asked.

"Another week."

"Right, I'll have the money waiting."

Bingo text me back. My phone beeped just as I came down from the bathroom. What's going down, Max?"

I texted back, "Two hundred for two ounces. Can you collect?"

"I'm on my way. Buzz me your address."

At 10.00 I was on my forth bottle of Bud. There was a knock at the door. Bingo stood with Cyril, whom I knew to be Bingo's sidekick. I welcomed them in, and they sat and made themselves comfortable as I walked into the kitchen and came back to the living room with the sugar caddy. "One lump or two?" I joked. "It's in there; you'll have to fish it out."

Bingo sat easing the two packets out and threw them on a set of digis he'd pulled from his pocket. "Is it same stuff?" Bingo was smelling at one of the tight wraps. "They're both slightly over," he said, putting his digis away. We shared a spliff and did the deal, and everything was hunky-dory.

Saturday morning I unlocked the back door and removed the old wooden chair that sat there to release the bottom bolt. Paul had it well barricaded, I thought, and I entered into the morning sun. I was struggling to get a signal, so I'd stepped out the back door to see if was any better. "Collie what's the score. I'm coming over; we'll fix it on the street."

"I'm just in, getting the bearings. Be there around 10.30, Max."

Collie arrived around 11.15. "Try and help me open the back gate, Collie. I can't get it open, and they won't take the wheelie bin from the front of the house." The pair of us heaved and struggled, and eventually it shifted. "Hinges are rusted up." I remarked. "I'll fetch some oil," Collie said, he arrived back a couple of minutes later, drenching the hinges. He laughed at the wheelie bin, overloaded and surrounded by liners. "You'll need to put that out a few times Max."

"I ain't bothered; now the gates open." We spent the rest of the afternoon doing the repairs to the XR3.

"I've temporary re-mounted the exhaust, Max," he said as we jumped in to take her for a spin. "She's nice and smooth now, don't you think? Hang on there's my phone."

"What's your ETA?" Daz had texted.

"Hey, fancy a night at the city?" I asked Collie. He was another one who had never been.

"Nah, Max, our Girt won't go for it."

"Ah, well you don't know what you're missing." I helped Collie with his tools and paid him for his time. "Sure you won't stop for a Bud?"

"I'll take one with me. Thanks."

Neto was busy whilst I did the week's shopping. I'd spotted boxes of Bud on special offer and grabbed a couple, loading them into the car with the bags. "Hey, Bruce, how's things?" Bruce had pulled alongside.

"Hey, you've tided that up good; it looks well cleaned." He was laughing.

"Hey, quit the sales hype." I knew he was commenting on the thick layer of dust that lay over it. "Want to buy it back for three hundred? Just had the bearings in the back done. Drives like a dream."

"Ha ha, Max."

"What's eating you, Bruce?"

"We need a lodger; are you up for it? Three bedroom house."

"I don't know, I might."

"Well, you've got my number." He mizzed.

"Cop a load of these," I said as I placed a bag full of Bud Ice in Daz's hands when he answered his door. Kids had the main exit wedged open as they ran around playing tag. I ran straight upstairs.

Alex sat on Daz's throne, picking his nose. "Oy, get out of it," Daz said, Alex moving to the seatie. "They're in the fridge, Max. What time are we heading."

"He ain't going, Skint." I pulled out my wedge and ripped off a twenty and threw it at Alex.

"When's that till, Max?"

"When you next get paid, mate."

Alex leaned down to pick it up. "Daz, lend me your deodorant."

"You scruffy git, Alex, go get in the shower; we got time," Daz insisted.

When we got to Rock City, Bev saw me come in. we ended up in the women's toilet cubicle's. "Ah, yes, Max." I buttoned myself up and gave her the wrap. She left the cubical after I'd given her a few moments.

Alex clocked me, walking out. He was pushed up against me at the packed bar as I leaned over to him and winked. "Is that twenty spot enough?" Alex nodded,

The music was louder than I'd ever heard it. Alex was straight over to Daz, whispering something in his ear. The two of them stood with their mouths wide open.

Bev dragged at my arm, pulling me towards the dance floor as the intro for "Tarot Woman" played through the speakers. The dynamic duo where soon gathering around for the guitar to kick in. We head-banged through two of three classics. I had to stop because we were going ape. I turned to Liz, who stood with her back against the railing. I rushed over and stood smiling, waiting for my brain to settle. Her eyes were wider than ever. I said, "You'd better had not done the lot?"

Her face was beaming as the lights hit off her. "Aw, no." She was pure spangled as she draped her arms over my shoulders, as I grabbed for her waist. "My sister had the other half." She tightened her grip. Man I could feel the rushes through her body as I swept her over to the corner and sat the next tune out.

Her sister Deb arrived in front of us with the same wild, staring eyes. "Max!" She took three paces to the left, turned, took three paces back again, leaped over, and sat on the other side of me. I Jumped up and grabbed at the last of the cans that were near Daz's feet as Liz and Deb slid up to one another. I dodged between the reeling hair and swaying bodies that were freaking out.

Alex was on the floor after he'd seen a good opportunity for his famous sliding knee approach to a lead break. I'd placed my right hand on his head like I was healing his faith and said a few words to God as I looked to the heavens. Alex lurched up and disappeared through the swaying mass as I returned and jumped in next to Bev and Liz.

Deb was talking to Russ and Dave. "What's going on?" I said as I sat with my left arm around three cans, offering one each to the girls.

Daz's big round face appeared over the railing. "Ha ha ha, bag puss," Liz shouted at him. "It's my first one." She held up the can. Daz could see where the other two cans had gone as the girls sat cracking them. Deb sat back down. Well, that was it—I couldn't get a word in, edge wise. The three of them sat gassing most of the night.

"Friggin' hell. You heard them three. It's like watching them round a cauldron," Alex said as he stood in the middle of the floor, gorping over.

"What's up, Max?" Daz said. He was sweating hot bricks, and I could feel the heat off him as his Korus aftershave overpowered the hint of Chanel. "Still all right for a lift home?"

"Of course, Daz."

"I think Alex is going back to Bev's."

"Shit," I thought to myself.

"You look worried."

Daz, who was looking at Liz. "I got to make sure they get back okay." I pulled out my phone. "Hang on, Daz." I had a new text: "My house." I put away my phone. "I ain't staying tonight, Daz."

"That's a relief—you snore like a trooper." Daz grinned.

Russ and Dave were greeting anything female that came through the doors. I'd been discussing the old team tactics with the two of them in between their "Let's go home, darling" chat-up lines. Just as Russ latched onto Deb, who seemed to be enjoying his attention, I could see Daz up at the car signalling for the keys.

"Come here, Dave, I want you a sec. Are you in the car?"

"Eh, why, Max?"

Just then a pair of warm hands covered my eyes. I turned around to see it was Liz. "Don't go away, Dave," I said as I took Liz to the side and jumped up to sit on the wall. Liz came to rest in front of me as I pulled her in close. She was trembling. "You can either come with me or go with your sister; your choice," I told her.

She broke my gaze and kissed me. "Not talking, are we?"

"I can get you a lift with Dave and Russ." I took my mobile from my inside left pocket. "Do I get yer number now, then?"

"You already have it."

I put my hand to the side of my head as if to shoot myself. "You need to put it in there." I shook the phone in front of her. "The last number you gave doesn't ring out."

She took the phone and entered her name and number. Then she rang and produced her phone from her handbag. "I'll need to stay with my sister tonight," she said as she handed me back the phone.

I beckoned at Dave, who came over. "Can you take her and her sister back, Dave? They're from up your way. Hey, and behave yourself."

Dave laughed. "Sure, Max, I think those two have gelled anyway." Russ had his tongue right down Deb's mouth. I put one hand over my eyes and put my phone away.

"Phone me in the week, Max," Liz said. "I'll be waiting for you to ring me."

"If Russ's doing it, then I'm having ago." We nearly fell over the back of the wall as she broke the embrace.

"Phew, Max, I'm addicted," she said as she stepped back. "I hope you're a safe driver," she snapped at Dave.

Daz sat on the XR3 wing with his arms folded, and he looked pissed off. "Are we right or what?"

"We'll stop for a kebab," I said as the five of us walked up. Alex had gone with Bev. "She was wearing that bask," I said to Daz, letting him in the car.

Russ and Dave stood with the doors open to let the two sisters into the back. "That swine had me gripping permanent handprints into the dash last time I got in with him," Russ was toying with Deb as her head shot out of view.

Back at Diana's

"What did Liz tell you?" Diana asked me.

"Not much, doll." Diana pushed herself back into the settee, and I thought to myself, "Don't blow it now, Max, play it cool."

I woke freezing cold. Diana must have pulled at the sheets and was curled up with the majority, clutched in the ball of her stomach. She was still sleeping as I sneaked on my jeans. She must have heard me clattering around in the kitchen as she stepped through. This was a woman who looked beautiful any time of the day, and it was nine o'clock Sunday morning. She had tanned a good part of her weed and downed two bottles of wine by the time I got to her house, which must have been around 3.30. "Coffee, babe?"

"Please, Max. Remember where the cups are this time?"

"Fancy a slow walk out somewhere?"

Diana had changed out of her silk pyjamas and arrived back in the kitchen dressed fer a country walk. "This way leads into the back of the priory." She led the way through a narrow lane and onto a dirt track through the woods. It was still fresh, although the morning sun was already trying to heat up.

"You should get a dog," I said as I turned to Diana.

"It wouldn't be fair on it, Max, although I have thought about it."

"What do you mean it wouldn't be fair?"

"I wasn't planning on . . . Oh, Max, why did you have to bring that up?"

"You weren't planning on what?"

"Staying. I only rent, Max, can't you see."

"Well, try renting a dog."

Diana burst out laughing. "Come on, Max, through here." We stooped low under some small trees and came out at what looked to be a battlement that looked out across the largest of the lakes in the priory grounds. "Admiral Rodney had a fleet of model ships here once." Diana took in a deep breath.

"Makes a change from all that shit you smoked last night; you where proper licked, doll." I took hold of Diana's waist and pulled her towards me. "We'll call this our secret place. We can meet here if you like—only somewhere we know."

"Yes, if you like. Only somewhere we know. Take me down to the oriental gardens, Max." We sat in timber framed pagoda. Diana had been quiet on the walk down into the gardens. "It's so beautiful here, Max. Thank you." She snuggled up. I wasn't quite sure what I'd done as my head started spinning. She looked at the floor, and tears fell from her eyes. "I can never make you happy," she blurted out as she clumsily rose and walked over, staring into the massive leaves.

I got up and turned her around. "Hey, doll, come on and come here." I pulled her in tight to me, holding her hands. "What's brought this on?"

Diana took my hand and sat us back down in the pagoda. "I've had tests done," she said calmly as I looked into her eyes. "I can't have children."

"Aw, so that's what's eating you, doll? We'll have to rent one, then. If you do it right they'll pay you," I joked.

"Max." She put her head onto my shoulder.

"Can you eat that?" I said cynically as we both looked at a plant. "Looks like rhubarb." She elbowed me in the ribs. I could see she was smiling again.

That evening I ended up at Pat's, paid him his dollars, took another ounce, and arrived back into Sunny Donny late. I sat trying to work out why Alex would text me, "Submarine." He still wasn't answering when I rang him. What was he up to?

The next morning I sat at home with my usual morning coffee, when the front door came flying open. "Max!" Paul's eyes were like plates.

"You are absolutely cooked. Look at them eyes."

Paul threw his bag on the chair and walked over to the mirror. "Whoa, I see what you mean."

"Fresh stuff?"

"Ha Ha, how'd you guess?"

I put down my empty mug and got up. "Back in two secs." I ran upstairs to get my shit ready for work. I returned peeling off 150 from my wedge, handing it to Paul on the way out.

"It's safe, Max," he said as I left the house.

"Donk, I'm here outside the garage."

"Two minutes, Max. I'm just on my way down."

A short, stubby mechanic stood explaining about how he was going to tackle the welding whilst rubbing on his barrier cream. Nig and Donk pulled into the car park, kicking up dust. "Do you know we ain't had a bad day since you started, Max?" Donk said.

"Weather-wise, you mean?"

"Look at the tans we've got, eh?" Nig said. "The missus has invited you for tea tonight, Max. Cash job in for you."

"Sure, Nig, love to, mate."

"Friday, Max—your car won't be ready till then." Donk had just secured the chain, ready to pull out another piece of the remaining hedge with the transit. "Woo, that's another strip out. Get your string line out, Max, let's see how we're running." Nig backed in, ready to rip out more privet hedge as Donk secured the chain around another root. "Thick as your wrist, look at that."

A young teenager sat sunbathing over next doors. She seemed to be finding the entertainment amusing as she ran to and from her house with cold drinks.

"Right, ready for mixing this afternoon, Donk," I said. "We can use all that road stone The ground's a bit soft down that end."

The week had passed, Friday evening came, and I got my car back with a full MOT. Liz was waiting at the corner of the university as I tried to throw the A to Z in the glove box. Her hands swept under her ass as she walked over to the car and opened the door, stepping in. Her flared skirt revealed the best part of her legs. "You look stunning, angel. I thought we'd have a run out to Matlock bath."

"Where is that?"

"Derbyshire."

"I have to back by eleven."

"Oh, we'll easy make it."

"Is this your car, Max?"

"Yep every nut and bolt. Do you like it."

She shrugged. "I prefer bigger cars, but this will do; it's very quick." I licked it into third and let her feel its awesome power on the M1. She was chortling on about some new recipe she'd tried. Her window was down as she enjoyed the cool wind in her hair.

Matlock was packed with tourists and bikes, and when I say bikes, I mean bikes—every pedigree to hit God's highway was here. I walked arm in arm with Liz, checking out all the new models that were parked down the whole side of Matlock bath. We spent time looking in at the little souvenir shops.

"Do you have a bike, Max?"

"I used to have all kinds of bikes, doll. Oh, check that out, an old Arial Square Four." It sat proudly between two Honda CBR 900 blades. Soon Liz was all over it, pressing this and squeezing that. "No, don't." Too late—she was on it. I chuckled, knowing the owner wasn't far away.

"Vroom! Hey, Max, I like this." She swung her leg back over to step off it.

I moved over to catch her as she stumbled. "Got ya." I flicked her back upright and taking her arm. "Let's slip in here for a pint and a game of pool." "It's a bit remote, but you'll get bed and breakfast there." The barmaid handed me a pint of shandy lager and poured Liz a pint of lager. Liz had put down her bag and was looking over at the pool table. Two customers had grabbed their backpacks and got up to leave, and Liz sat down, looking at the pub's surroundings. I brought the drinks over to the table, putting them down and placing a beer mat in front of her as I rearranged the pints, accidentally taking a sip of her lager.

"Did you bring it, Max?"

"Eh, shh," I said as I sat down.

"Pass my bag up." I leant down, placing it on the table in front of her. "I'll stick us names down." Liz made for the ladies room to powder her nose.

"I bet she don't see it," I thought. The pub looked busy, and I scanned the room; I estimated it would be at least half an hour before we'd be picking a cue up. Liz returned as I was just returning conversation with a couple at the next table. "Crikey she's found it," I thought as looked in her eyes. She reached for her pint and downed at least half before sitting down. I sat with my jaw wide open, numb. "Did you, erm, take—did you find . . . ?"

She squeezed my arm tightly. "I've saved you half," she said, slipping the wrap back in my hand under the table.

Well, when in Rome. I got up and made a beeline for the toilet. I busted back out the door after snorting off the back of a cistern. Sheeks, I felt like I'd just burned out my left nostril. Now I really did fancy a game of pool as the place blew out with sudden expansion.

The night led into close, heated debates over position and stun, swerve, and screw back. Liz turned out to be star as she strutted around knocking them in. I sat fascinated as she nearly seven balled me on the first game. I was beaten and sat trying to smile. She was a natural damn hustler and whipped the next guy.

"Huh, Max, it's half past ten." "Cinder's going to turn back into a pumpkin." She thumped me in the arm as I was just about to take the last swallow of my drink. "Max, we really must go." We stepped out the front exit; the sky was sheen of blues, pinks, and purples, and large gaps had appeared where bikes had stood outside the pub. Liz slipped her arm into mine as we hurriedly walked back to the car. It had turned chilly and I'd taken off my denim and placed it around Liz's shoulders.

We ended up back at the car and jumped in. "Hang on, Max, it's no good. I'll need to phone my sister."

"We won't do it in fifteen minutes, doll. Can't she cover for you?"

"What you mean, Max?"

"Whoops, might have said too much," I thought. Liz flicked her silky black hair over her shoulder and gave me that look. I said, "I know a place that'll be open till midnight."

Her eyes widened. "And then what?"

"Well, it's on the way back."

She went quiet, looking at her lap. She took her phone from her bag and wrote a text.

"I love this place, Max," she said as she looked up into the quarry. The scene was quite; a few local farmers sat playing dominos. We moved down into an unoccupied split-level room. There was a slight flicker in the log burner that was set in the middle of the room. "You never cease to amaze me—just look at this place. It's rustic." She took a gulp of her lager and sat down. "How much?"

"Seventeen pounds per night, each," I replied.

"Are you trying to seduce me, Max?"

"The landlady will cook something for you, doll, if you're feeling peckish. I know I am." Liz reached over and took a menu from the other table. I threw the keys on the table. "I wouldn't mind getting absolutely plastered."

Liz picked up her phone out of her handbag. "Two secs, Max, I'm listening." After a pause, she said, "That's sorted, Max, if you want to go have a word at the bar."

I looked deep into her green eyes. "What, you really want to stay?"

She squeezed my knee. "Yes."

I was up like a jackrabbit and talking to the landlady, who reassured me of a room with a fantastic view. When I returned, I said, "By the way, I've ordered us a small feast. Technically they stopped serving food over an hour ago, but I told her we've missed our evening meal and we're starving. "The landlady came down, put a few more logs on the burner, and set out the table with cutlery and napkins.

"Try that," I said as I dropped two Jack and Cokes with ice and lemon.

"What did you order to eat, Max?"

"Well, I'm having top side of Hereford bull. Ouch!" She had kicked me under the table.

Garlic mushrooms stuffed with chopped onion and fresh sage arrived complete with a selection of dips. The landlady also returned with hot French bread and butter. Liz was soon getting stuck in. The landlady said, "That's the key to room five, just through there." She pointed through the bar.

"What do we call you?" I asked.

"Ethel," she replied she retired back to the bar.

The two of us sat in the car just as dawn was breaking. Pity we're going to miss breakfast," I said as I went to turn the ignition. *Grind, click.* "Oh, shit. Erm. Darling?"

"What, Max?"

"Right, hang on sec." I flipped the hood and got out. "It's no good, babe, you're going to have to give us a shove; the starter's stuck. I only got the car back from the MOT yesterday—it's not much."

She frowned. "Push?"

"Well, sort of shunt it." Liz jumped out, and I saw her appear at the rear-view mirror right as she thumped on the boot. I released the handbrake, rolled two yards, and slammed it into first, trying at the ignition again. She turned over and was up and running.

Liz jumped back in with a sigh of relief. "Thank God for that, Max."

"There must have been a frost in the night." I grinned and pulled away.

Later that day. "Daz, we got to do something about that starter ring—it's embarrassing me."

"Calm down, calm down. It's a big job, you know."

"That's the second time today."

Daz was counting his wages from the bus depot. "I can't just get on the tannoy and get Abe down here with the pull lifts. You know the whole engine and box has to come out. I told you to get rid, Max."

"I've just MOT'd it, Daz. I've got to do it if I'm going to keep it."

"It'll be quiet without Alex. He's out with Bev somewhere; says he might pop in later."

"When have I heard that before?"

Daz let one rip. "Ah, silent but deadly," he laughed as I wound down the window.

At Rock City. Daz was gutted. "What, no Hobbit?" I sighed. "Glad you brought yer wages."

I sniggered, walking in through to the kiosk. "Car's staying there, tonight, Daz. Sorry to say I'm getting hammered." The bar was packed, and the familiar city scents filled my nostrils as I checked out the chick beside me. "Cor, blimey, it's Debby Harry. Can I set you up something long and cool?" I asked.

"It's okay, honey, I got mine already," she replied. "Maybe later." She slicked her way out to the door.

Daz's neck was resting on my shoulder. "Put your tongue back in," I jested. I don't know what that cat suit's made out of, but I'm hooked—looks good enough to eat." We burst out laughing.

Five Jack and Cokes later, I'd gone to the bogs to have a little snifter and overheard a conversation.

"I've put the GHB in her drink twenty minutes ago." I had just as I came out the cubicle, and recognised the two males, who'd been hanging around the blonde I'd seen earlier at the bar.

I walked out. "Keep an eye on the blonde in the cat suit, Daz. I just heard something in the bogs from those two males that's been hanging around her." I walked over to where the rail was and stood and scanned the dance floor where I spotted her. The two males had come out the bogs and walked over to her and started dancing around her. Then her head suddenly whipped backwards as she hit the deck. "They've spiked her, Daz," I said, pointing as I beckoned him over. "That's her that was at the bar." Daz put his can on one of the upright wooden barrels used as tables. "I heard what got said—those two." I pointed to the two dropouts. They were round her like a fly round sugar most of the night, although you could tell she wasn't interested in their advances."

I stepped onto the dance floor to where she fell. "Right, that's enough," I demanded as they were pulling at her arms. Her head was reeling as her legs sprawled out. Out of the corner of my eye, I saw a straight left coming straight for me, and I flicked it down with an outside parry, giving a sharp push to his back of his shoulder and keeping him moving, bouncing his head off the railing. That was one down. I squared to face the other, who came at me as I caught him across the stop button with a strike from my elbow. I heard him slap off the floor after I stepped through, adding my full weight and landing a blow as blood splattered across his face. Suddenly I was being yanked backwards—well, sort of dragged—as I tried to reach behind for some sort of a grip, which was pointless as that powerful smell of Korus hit me.

I was pinned up against a wall with Russ, Daz, and Dave growling at me. "They GHB'd her," I kept saying.

"Calm down, calm down," they said as I kept trying to bust out of their grip. They'd pulled me away, around to the lasses toilets. I looked around the corner as the lights came on and bouncers fanned out onto the dance the floor.

"I'll settle this," Russ said, and he went rushing to talk to one of the bouncers.

"Shut the fuck up and stay here," Daz insisted to me.

I could see the two I'd been tussling with being escorted to the fire exit. "Ah, they'll get the bog run," I thought.

Russ came back. "You're lucky, Max. The bouncers think it was just them two at it." He laughed.

Dave swapped me his jacket and handed me a bungee. "Get your hair tied up." Daz let me go.

"Somehow I don't think they'll be waiting outside," Russ said, taking off his baseball cap and placing it on my head.

"Oh, I'll need my phone, Dave; it's inside left pocket. I need to make a call." I dialled 999 and asked for an ambulance, explaining a case of GHB spiking. I gave her description and where to find the victim. I saw the bouncers help her up and take her to the chill room. "We'll keep a lookout fer the paramedics; I just sent for them. Tell them where she is Daz. I'll go hide in the bogs till things cool."

Twenty minutes later Daz walked up to me. "Right, Max, you can come out—there's no one about. Oh, and the paramedics turned up and took her."

"I hope she'll be okay." I was naturally concerned.

Alex had turned up with Bev and her sister as they got wind, and Daz told Alex the latest. Tracy was flicking at her eyelashes in the mirror with her mascara when I walked out, slapping her ass and saying, "Hurry up, I'll wait in the hotel lobby."

Daz was waiting outside. Russ and Dave were at their usual stance, sniffing at every single female that came through the door and trying to catch their attention. "We'll drop you, Daz," Russ said as he and Dave gave up. "Coming, Max?"

"Erm, I've got something sorted. Thanks, lads, for tonight." I walked down as far as the next right. I swapped jackets back with Dave and wished the crew goodnight. I threw Russ his cap, releasing my hair from the bungee. Now this was what I called living. I was half cut and looked at the lights in those steps as I walked up the steps to the main doors.

It wasn't long before Alex and Bev were kicking up a din as they more or less fell in through the revolving doors. The lobby was busy with night club traffic. "Can I help?" a porter asked as he approached Alex. Tracy walked in behind and stopped dead and marvelled at the décor.

"I have a reservation," Bev said as she stepped forward. "Don't get too close—he will head butt you."

"Over to the desk then, please, madam," the porter replied.

Bev led the way over. "Yep, that's me." She gave the receptionist her details and turned and spied me whilst she stood at the counter. "And I hope it's the biggest, lushest, fattest room I ever seen. Hey, Max, you've got the same Landing neighbours everybody needs."

"Shut up, Bev be cool," I was thinking, shrugging back in the chair. Alex still hadn't clocked me; he was that inebriated. I pointed at him, sniggering. "Shh, don't say." I held my finger to my lips.

Bev took Alex under the arm to hold him up, walking him over and disappearing into the lift. I checked into our room five minutes later and sat waiting for Tracy to arrive. Twenty minutes later. "Ah, look at that for a view." I stood overlooking the city.

Tracy threw her jacket on the chair, moving straight through into the bathroom. "Max, Max!" She sounded ecstatic. "Look at this—it's big enough for two."

"I'll contact room service, send up some beverage. Are you hungry, doll?"

"Mmm, come here Max."

The next day Pat was out back washing the poop from his patio as the hose pipe wandered across my feet. "Bingo's been asking," he said as he flicked at the hose.

"I've been dissing, him, Pat."

"What you up to, anyway?"

"I need more weed."

"Don't keep dissing him, Max. Let him run for you."

"It's that sidekick of his I don't trust, Pat."

Pat was turning at the tap. "Look, I've just been stalling, that's all. If you see him, tell him the same time, same place." Pat came down the stairs as I sat patiently reminiscing.

"That's one I owe, and that's for one I'm taking." I peeled it off in twenties as we walked in the back door into his house.

Pat took from his pocket and placed a single 9mm round in front of the clock. "You know where it's buried," he said, throwing me a bag of green. My mind flashed back to those days, and my training we did in the killing house. And close quarter combat. I knew the round was from a series of magazines hidden, and the light brown berry that was buried with them.

I got up and knocked it over with my finger. "Put it back," I said as I made for the back door.

"Hey, Max, get back here."

I stopped and turned and faced my bro. "The correct authorities will deal with it," I said.

"I still think you're running blind," Pat replied.

"Look, bro, if I discover the location of the terrorists, I already know them to be linked with the same Al Qaida mob that was selling those killer pills, and that's been dealt with. If I find myself threatened and know them to be armed, then yes, I will be needing it—but not yet." I knew in my mind that something serious was about to happen regarding two large buildings. My mind wandered again. The only thing I could think of was the Trade Towers in New York, which looked similar to the plans found in the Renault 5 GT Turbo a few years ago. It was just a question of when and how and who, although it had been rumoured from contacts on the inside that they were going to fly commercial aircraft into them, which had been said in a conversation between two detained Asian bouncers who came from Bradford. Though hearsay, I found the source to be reliable, and I had already depicted as much in a drawing from a collage that I had pieced together from magazine cuttings early in 1999, from which I was still drawing the finished piece. I had also asked for the collage to be viewed online in an attempt to make America a little more aware regarding terrorism. "Look, just give Bingo the message," I said to Pat before I left.

I must have stood there two minutes before they realized I was there. I'd climbed up onto the garage and was staring in Noggin's window at his new address. Their faces fixed like quick drying cement as they sucked on what looked to be a large bubbly pipe. The table was littered with empty bags and half eaten carry-outs. Suddenly the place was in uproar as Jamie bolted for the door. I went to the edge of the roof and dropped onto the lawn just as I heard the back door click. I bolted up the path, knocking over the wheelie bin as I turned the corner. He sat straddled the fence as I got to him, grabbing his leg. "Max, let me go!" he screamed.

I reached up and took his hood with my other hand, pulling him down from the fence. "Gotcha." I dragged him onto the lawn and let him go. His mates were soon out the house with their tools and stopped. "What you going to do with that then, Noggin?" I stood waving my arms in a threatening fashion. They all froze. "Don't you move Jamie," I said as he tried to crab walk away. "I thought the better of you." Then I got to thinking who knew. "Who knew, Jamie?"

"Look, Max, I swear to you."

"So who else around here goes busting houses before they're brown" I would say I was very warm, wouldn't you, Jamie? It only takes one item to come back. If I find out any of it's been through your hands, I swear I'll see you down fer it. That was all my valuable possessions from my premises, and they even took my TV and found the keys fer my car after they busted in through the main door, loading up the car with all the loot and driving away. This happened Whilst I was out of town a few years ago—remember, Jamie?" He still denied all knowledge, and I pushed some more. "So why did you lick it when you saw me at the window?" Jamie still denied any involvement, and I thought to myself, "Right, calm down, let him go." As he got to his feet, he was still weary. I said, "I'll tan the living daylights out of you fer lying if I find you have. Then I'll run you in myself if I find you did that, Jamie. Now get out my sight." Jamie headed towards the front of the building and disappeared. "Right, Noggin, a word around the corner. Please tell me you weren't involved in that." Nogg shook his head. I didn't suspect Nogg and knew if he'd have gone fer the camera, he'd have told me so. "Right, back to business. How much are you paying on the ounce fer resin?"

"It's 320 on a nine, but there's a drought on."

"Frig, these boys need bringing up to date. I'll do you one for same price," I said as I held up three fingers. Nogg took down my mobile number. "It's Zero, Nogg."

"Yeah, I can shift it," he replied. "Buzz me Tuesday."

Chapter Six

"What was all that about, Nig?" "Dad's missus tanned all the downstairs windows down at the other house!" "What's he been up to?" I asked.

Dink walked over. "He's been poking that sixteen-year-old next door."

"He's been doing *what?*" I raised my voice whilst pulling my trowel from my bucket.

"They broke my sister's bed between them."

"It was his sister's house we were working on," I thought.

Dink was just setting down the barrow with the first mix and had returned to water up the mixer, getting ready for the next. "Well, I am truly shocked. Sod it—let's mizz for a breaky. Dad's got to hang around back at the house for the boarding-up service to arrive."

As I covered the barrow with my spot, I thought. I heard the story again in the cabin whilst having breakfast. Dink and Nig were having a volleyball of a conversation.

"Oh, she'll have him for half of everything."

"Yeah and that sixteen-year-old will get half of everything he's got left."

"Ha ha ha. He shouldn't have crossed onto forbidden pastures," I pitched in.

"My Dad's a fool, Max, this sounds dodgy," Dink said, and I remained silent. I had not seen Donk for a few days, so I decided to go and see him.

I pulled up at the house. Sure enough, the windows were all boarded up at the ground floor, including the front door—all double glazed units which are not cheap. "Nonce" was written in red spray paint on each board as I walked down the path. Donk was sitting at the kitchen table as I poked my head around the back door. "I've tried to ring you, Donk."

"Waste of time, ringing my mobile, Max. She smashed it all over the place." He reached in his pocket and pulled from his wallet the SIM card from his phone, throwing it on the table. Donk had all the signs of just crawling under a rock as he asked, "How's that wall coming on, Max?"

"Well, I laid another fifty blocks today. The side panels are nearly completed." I was trying to keep a straight face and tried to look sympathetic; Donk might have taken it the wrong way.

"Want a coffee, Max?"

"Sure. Mine's one sugar."

"She's through the front playing with the little one."

At that moment she came through, sounding like a herd of elephants as she burst in whilst looking frantic. She filled a child's mug with Vimto, diluting it under the cold tap, and she returned to the front room whilst saying, "Max do you want to take him to wherever it is you go and leave him there?"

Donk had taken his glasses off and replied, "Take no notice of her, Max." I knew Donk wasn't going to come up to the job until the wall was up at least six feet. "I want you here Friday, eight in the morning. You're coming to the auction; I'll still pay you for the day. Bit of a plumb cake." He winked. Then he said, "Shh," after his common-law wife walked back through to the front room. "Right, Max, so that's sixty bucks then. I'll put it on the slate."

At our secret place, Diana had pulled me into one of the turrets out of the rain. "We'll sit in the car awhile," she said as we ran back through the bushes with our jackets over her heads.

Diana was in hysterics by the time I got through offloading about Donk. "I'm just glad I got someone to talk to about it," I said as I put the seat back up. The rain battered off the car as I cleared away the condensation to look out.

Diana had drawn a spaceman from a well-known U2 album. "Are you serious about adopting, Max?"

I stared for a minute at the little face she drew in the helmet. "Yes I am. I've just seen everything in the future; it's going to be fine, doll, you'll see. I fancy hitting in on that Chinese takeaway again, on the way home." I cleared at the condensation again. "Hey, there's big puddles over there. We'd better mizz." I noticed a big patch of brown, muddy water around the car. *Click.* "Oh no, aw, come on." *Click.* "Oh, don't say the ignition won't turn over."

"Max, it's lashing down."

"Hang on." I ripped off my shoes and socks and rolled up my trousers. The water was five to six inches off the bottom of the door as I waded out. "All right, then." I walked around to the rear after instructing Diana to jump in the driver seat. "Right, try it." I could feel my feet slipping on the soggy grass as I pushed. *Vroom.* "Oh, thank Christ." Diana had it in gear just as I bumped it forward. Then I felt a sudden coldness as my vision was temporary blocked out. I was soaked right through; she'd hit the throttle, and the water had risen from off the back wheels. I stood ankle deep, looking sorry for myself as she came to a halt and stalled again.

She had the window down as her head came out. "It won't start—ohh." She put a hand over her mouth when she saw the sodden state I was in. She was trying not to laugh.

"Shit!" I stamped my foot forward, right on to a rough pebble, causing me to hold my foot in the pain as I fell forward and ended up laid face down in the middle of a large puddle. "Right, that's it!" I slapped my arms down to get up. She had her head in her lap by the time I walked, over resting my sodden arms calmly in the window opening.

"Max, I am so sorry—my foot slipped. I'm just glad we weren't sitting in that TR7 of yours."

I was chattering with the cold. "Right, Max, count to ten," I thought. Then I said to her, "Here is what we're going to do. You move back over; I'll rock the car forward, and then I'll try it." Diana was still in tears laughing as she slid over. I released the handbrake and went to the back of the car again, rocking it forward. She must have knocked it out of gear, I thought, as the car rolled forward easily now. I walked around to the door and noticed the car still moving, realizing the steepness of the gradient as I started to run and make a grab for the door pillar. I was soon running at a high pace to try and keep up, shouting, "Diana, handbrake!" My car pulled further away.

The back end swung around in a semicircle around a well-established oak tree. I came to halt, putting my hands to my eyes. Diana sat facing me on the passenger side, white as a sheet. Suddenly the cold didn't seem to matter anymore, and I'd just cleared the vision of the last car I smashed up a tree—an XR2 Bugaloo, which happened in a race with a Golf GTI.

Diana tried the ignition again, and the XR3 suddenly roared into life. I jumped in the driver seat.

Back at her pad, Diana reached over me. I woke in her bathrobe, and my arm was numb—the full weight of her head had just rolled off it. I rubbed to get some feeling back as the pins and needles tingled. It was 4.30. Hmm . . . I shook her. "I want to chat," I said.

She opened one eye and muttered, "It's not time yet."

"No, angel, I want to talk."

"What about, Max?" She turned to face me.

"Right. Tell me what you really do."

"I'm in sales." She smiled. "Now go back to sleep."

I was wondering if my watch had been turned on and that she might be a contact sent by 307 Battery—they knew for sure I was still active, although I hadn't directly told her about that. I thought it better not to. I also knew that when it was time for me to dry out from the drug abuse, she would be the one I could turn to for help to get me off this shit. I knew that her part in it was just the occasional spliff; I knew she did it just to be sociable—she never touched the hard stuff. I was beginning to wish I hadn't. My abuse with cocaine had started as something just to keep me going and awake, whilst I burnt the candle at both ends. I knew I had a drug problem, which was becoming abuse. At some stage soon, I needed to address the problem because I was becoming everything that I despised. The deeper the hole I dug, the harder it was to get out.

Back at the house, I was talking to Paul. "Right, one nine-bar, a zero, and drop me three in the caddy."

"That's 90 sovs on the ounce for the dust and 270 on the zero. We'll call it 540 for cash, Max."

This was my seventh week in the snow, and I was beginning to get cold feet. I had visions of being buried in an avalanche. Bingo was on time, leaving me with 360, which I added to the wedge. I had received a text message from Nogg: "Bert's meeting us at the lorry park, just off the A1." Bingo was kind enough to give me a lift. He was driving a Nissan as I briefed him on the rendezvous.

Paul was waiting around the back at the lorry. "Stop, out the way," I said as I walked over and got in. "Hang on, they're here." Burt had just pulled in.

"Remember this, Max?" Bingo was hinting at the car we were in. "It was one of my old Nissans—one I bought from a car auction and sold on to Bingo a few years back."

"Yeah, sure. I'm amazed you still have it."

"Here, Max. Who's that?" He was pointing at Paul as we arrived, turning a full circle in the lorry park.

"Oh, he's safe. Stop pointing at him—you'll spook him." Burt was frowning and grinding his teeth. Nogg was in the driving seat, staring out at Paul's boggy Fiesta. I jumped out of the Primera and walked over to Paul, who threw me the nine-bar as I jumped over to Nogg, who handed over the 320 pounds sterling. I threw the nine-bar to Bert, who checked the goods. "It's double zero," I said as I waited.

"Right, Max, it's all good." Burt looked pleased. "Let's all mizz."

Paul was smiling as I waved bye to Bingo and got in with Paul. "We'll sort the cash when we get back to the house."

The kettle screamed as I handed over the cash, all 540 of it. I could bend my wedge again. "Now then, down to business about this Granada. Straight swap with a full MOT, wasn't it?"

"Eh, yes, Max. I'll bring it over tomorrow."

"Can't we get it now?"

Paul hesitated. "Hang on, I got to make a call." After a brief conversation, he said, "Right, Max, let's go."

Twenty minutes later we arrived at Paul's ex missus'. "It's all right, Max, she knows we're taking it. That's the keys for it. Back it off the drive and hang on; I'll help you start it." We both walked over to the Granada. "That's the heater plugs there; wait for the light to go off. Right, now start it." She fired up first crack. "It's been standing two months, Max. Not bad, eh?"

I followed Paul back to the house. "I think you'd better sort the log book, Paul."

"Yeah, no probs."

"New car, Max?" Dink and Nig were admiring the size as I pulled it onto the drive.

"The brakes are still a bit rusty, but she runs okay. Sheeks," I said, checking my wad; I had 1570 in cash and was heading towards another three. I was thinking as I sat with the paper.

"Me dad's coming over," Nig said. "I've got the trestles in the van. We'd better get them set out and loaded up."

"Hang fire with that mix, Dink. I'll get that later," I said, putting down the morning paper. Forty blocks later, I took a ride over at Nig's house and started pointing his boundary wall.

"Here's 100 sterling, as agreed, Max."

That night I'd picked up Liz and took her to the abbey ten minutes later. "Yes, oh yes, yes!" Liz was going for it. I slumped back over the gear stick and found my way back over to my seat, gathering my breath.

I abruptly asked her, "Did he rape you? Your step father?"

Liz was arranging herself and putting up the seat. She took a breath and was quiet as I pulled up my jeans. "No. My mother overreacted," she said, putting her hands up to her eyes.

I suddenly thought of Diana as I lay back, adjusting the seat adjustment and sliding down the window before flicking out the ripped contraceptive. "You mean he did the time and he was innocent? Strewth." I reached over and held her for a while.

"I could do with a pint, Max."

We left the abbey and pulled into a local pub in Chuckwalla. The plough was its usual—it never changed a bit except the colour of the emulsion. We sat at a table in the back room, getting up in turn whilst playing pool. The two of us were also visiting the wall-mounted jukebox, putting on a good variety of tunes as I kept whispering, "Miss the next shot."

"I play to win," she shot back.

"Nah, you're not with it, babe. Just do it—I'll tell you why later."

Sam and Dave were good pool players, and they were studying form over a quiet pint over in the corner. "Want to have a game, chaps?" Liz cheekily asked the pair. "Me and Max will play you at doubles." They agreed as Sam set up the table.

"Best of three, losers pay Dave," I commented. I nudged Liz and winked. "No fancy stuff yet." Dave cracked them.

We lost the first two games on purpose, of course. "Now then, how about a small wager on the last game—forget the previous two games," I said, peeling off a twenty spot. "Winner takes all, one game." The pair stood and conferred, and after a few brief moments they said, "You've got yerself a game." Dave and Sam started to chuckle.

"Right—now play," I said to Liz. She had near on cleared the spots of the break as Sam downed three stripes, and I came to the table playing a snooker. Dave missed, hitting our remaining red spot and leaving Liz the pot and a shot on black. She slammed it home in the top corner bag. "Ha ha ha, hand over the money, guys." The pair of them stood looking at the floor. "That's a tenner for you and one for me," I said to Liz, who was buzzing.

She'd left them with five balls on the table after a spectacular sink on the black ball. "Come on, Liz, we'll get the nine o'clock special at the Gala; it's only a fiver in." I knew Dave would be after winning back his money.

"What's that, Max?"

"The bingo Gala; haven't you ever been?"

Nogg was where I thought I'd find him, on the bell fruit machines. It was still five minutes to the national, so I took the machine at the side of him. "Hey, Max, that last deal was okay. Happy, mate? I'll buzz you for another."

"Yeah, sure, Nogg, as much as you like handing him a ten-bag of green, bud—try that."

I returned to Liz with a pint of Diet Coke for me and a lager for her, We sat ready for the game to start, and Liz was trying her new dobber on an old ticket. "Why did you ask that earlier, Max?"

I slammed down the Dobber. "Do you know what they put him through?" Liz couldn't look me in the eyes; I could see she was missing her numbers. "Why didn't your Ma tell them the truth?"

"He used to batter her till she was crying." I stopped my game and grabbed her wrists, fixing her gaze once more as a full house was declared over the speakers and the numbers were checked. "He was never my real father," she replied.

"Yes, I do know him. Come on, I'm getting you out of here."

At the secret place, I was raging. "That poor girl's head is shot to pieces."

"It needed finding out, Max—you know the rules."

"And what about him? What they going to do about that? It took exactly two years working on him."

"He'd been taken down. He was a women beater, Max—over five separate incidents and three convictions before he met Liz's mum."

"Hup. How do you know all this?"

Diana broke away and stood staring out at the lake with her arms folded. "She is a dark horse," I thought as I leaned in beside her.

Finally she said, "Don't let it destroy what we have, Max. What if we were to contact her real father?"

"Oh, I don't know. I'd need to see how she felt about it. She's only nineteen."

Diana stopped me. "Look what's happened has happened.

"Can't you see she's growing up too quick? I need to finish it. I'll tell her I can't get hold of the snow anymore."

She butted in. "Well, she wanted it, Max. You never forced it on her. Come on home; you look tired."

At work. "You'll have that finished tonight?" Donk had turned up and stood looking up onto the scaffold.

"I might be short on blocks."

"You did say two weeks, Max. That's why I'm treating you Friday. Finished it a few day's early, eh?"

"Ah, that's if we fetch more blocks to finish it; I've just counted up, and we're at least twenty short."

"Nig, jump in the van and fetch Max his blocks. Dink, you get a mix on."

Later that night. "Seven sovs for that. Hey, I won't break it. Will it burn?" Paul insisted I put it in on a country lane. "We'll need a piece of hose." The two of us stood in the moonlight, dieseling up. "No stuff back at the house, I hope," I said as Paul stood spinning the hose to extract the remaining diesel before putting it in the boot of his car.

"You'll get three hundred miles outta that, Max. And no, I shifted the last of it somewhere safe. Still want the usual order this week? I'm off again next week for a few days. House is yours again."

Thursday. Paul had just gone out. I'd just taken my phone from the charger as Collie appeared at the door. "Ended up with it, I see," Collie said.

"Oh, the Granada is like driving a boat."

"What's Paul done with the XR3?"

"Sold it someone in town." I smiled.

"They've been back on the phone hassling him. He's mizzed out, the way he got 350 for it." Collie grinned.

"I thought five hundred was steep for the Granada."

"He wanted 6 and a half when I quizzed him over it"

"Now you know what he's like, Max."

"The XR3 stood me at 410 sterling, so I did all right out of it."

"Hey, what do you want for the mountain bike?" Collie asked. It was the one I used originally to get to work; I'd only used it for a few weeks until I bought the XR3. I'd completely forgotten about it, and it had been sitting in the back room for some time now. "I have something for you, Max, to ease the boredom."

I laughed. "I hardly get a minute, Collie. Here take a seat."

Collie was clutching a white carrier bag, sitting down emptying the contents. "PlayStation, Max. Straight swap."

"O.K deal, if you rig it up, and let me see it working." Collie started to uncoil the leads, wiring it to the TV and tuning into the correct channel.

"Hey, this is fun." I said. It took me a little time, but I was getting the hang of snowboarding in the game. Collie left with the bike, half stripping it to fit in his car.

Later I was in town and had called into my half—brother's shop to inquired about his well-being and to ask if his missus and kids were fine, not having seen them for time. I also asked if there were any new updates. "Max, we've lost 'em. We think they've been in Glasgow." Tony was rechecking his information. "One of the two you rumbled is still detained on a life sentence. But the other was released from jail and broke his parole. He has been tracked there."

"What do you mean, lost him? He must have got the fuck out. Probably used a false passport." I was left dismayed, knowing the remainder of the gang couldn't have seen me. "I left no trace; they're still in the UK somewhere, Tony, I can sense it. Damn." I stormed out the clothes shop, furious. "Yes, Glasgow, of course. He will have moved there, where he is not known."

"It's possible the old man knows," Tony said while I was on my way out.

"Right, I'm going to see Rubble; he wants to see me anyway." I knew by the term old man that Tony meant Griffon.

Rubble stood at his front gate, and I knew he and Tony had kept in touch with Griffon. I had the window down as I pulled up. "What's on your mind?" Rubble had asked.

"I need her pulled out, Rubble—Diana, I mean."

"How did you find her out?" he asked.

"I just had an inkling," I replied. "Even when she was at personal protection classes, I kind of knew she was something special. Although I haven't directly told her who I am."

"She's been briefed about you. She knows what you are about," Rubble prompted. "She's twenty-one pillar regiment and works for the CPS."

"Damn, crown prosecutor I knew she was. I just needed it confirmed. I'll need to go after them, and I'll need it cleared."

Rubble looked at floor. "It's going to take a month or two, Max; you know the score."

"I need it done sooner. What about the lead in Manchester?"

"Warm, Max. Some of his associates recently flew in from Amsterdam. They're at Leeds."

I knew then TR1A had kept Griffon informed, and that Griffon had made a decision to put the surveillance aircraft up. I also knew that TR1A. "I want them on twenty-four hours watch. What's the latest on their origin?"

"We're still checking it—looks like that passport you handed in five years ago is ringing true."

I knew it—my crew in the past had hit them then hard and fast. This all stemmed as the part of information passed to me from a stolen car, although at the time I was roasted by my superiors. "Well, I hope someone has notified the American authorities, because if they're going to try and pull that stunt off, they'll need told."

Rubble went quiet and then said, "You can't yet. You need hard proof and reliable sources so they know who to look out for."

"We'll start with that prick that just jumped parole." I left it at that. If only I had took those plans from the Renault GT 5 when I had the chance. I could still see the outline of the buildings in my mind.

Tracy sat on the park bench eating a chocolate bar, and she took off her earphones when I arrived. I could hear "Sweet Child of Mine" as she flicked the switch to turn off the walkman in her hand. "What you got planned, Max?" she asked, putting her belongings away. "I thought a walk into town get a bite to eat." She was dressed in her usual black and baggy college clothes, and the breeze was flicking at her hair as we walked along the boulevard.

"How's the acting coming along?" I asked.

"It's okay. Bev will be home, if you want to come back later."

"Fine; shall we pick up a video on the way? I have my card. I need to be back by eleven, to check something out." She was fine about it as we entered into the pizza shop, sitting down and looking at the menu.

"Hmm, this one looks tasty. By the way, I told my sister we didn't get up to nothing at the hotel."

"Hey, no wonder Alex was taking the piss. Look at what he's put," I said, showing her my text messages. One read, "Give 160 bucks for a few coats of looking at." She giggled and handed me the phone back. "So you want it kept stung?" I said.

"I have been seeing Rob for over six years now."

"I thought, *It doesn't matter,* as the girl came to take our order. I knew Rob would go off on one if he found out I'd taken his woman to the hotel.

Paul stormed into the house, slamming the door. "What's the matter—been busted?" I asked.

He knew I was only kidding as he went for a beer in the fridge. "No, Max, just family." I grabbed a beer while the fridge door was opened and clinked his bottle. We went into the living room, where I had the PlayStation set up. Paul reached down to switch it on. "Don't mind, do you, Max? Two players?"

I nodded and asked, "What's the problem?" as Paul picked up the joy pad.

"My brother's been arrested. He's in court tomorrow."

"Why, what's he been up to? Has he been caught twocking?"

"Nah, it's worse than that. He's only gone and blown up the local phone box."

I sprayed my beer as I choked out, "What?"

"They've striped out a load a fireworks from the cash and carry, and boom." Paul looked gutted. "Cops have got them. They're being charged under the prevention of terrorists acts. We're talking years."

It was Friday, and I sat in the cabin with Donk having my breakfast. "We've got to pick her up," Donk said suddenly.

"Who?" I asked as I gulped down my coffee.

Donk's face was beaming. "Me fancy bit. I'll just ring and tell her to bring that friend of hers."

"Erm, Donk, that's not a good idea."

"Why, Max? She's a little darling."

"Look, I have enough on my plate. What's this auction all about, anyway?"

"It's a plant sale, Max. I'm after a Bowser."

"Still getting that cheap diesel, Donk?"

Yep, and it's white. Pound a gallon."

"I ain't too keen on picking any of them young bitches up, Donk, but I'll still go to the auction."

Donk was soon on the phone to his fancy bit, arranging a meet. "Right, that's sorted, then. It' just her we're picking up."

"Got 180, any advance on 180 . . . Sold!" The auctioneer dropped his gavel, and Donk stepped over and took the docket to pay for his new Bowser.

The three of us went to the canteen and sat discussing what had just gone through the sale. She accidentally kicked my leg under the table as I tried to move my chair back, so Donk didn't notice. Eventually I retired to the toilet to take the heat off myself. I texted, "Ring me—urgent," and went back to where the two sat.

I rejoined the conversation just as we were about to leave, and then my phone buzzed. Thank god Diana returned the call. "Hi, darling," I said out loud, making sure the two overheard me. "What are you doing tonight, babe?"

"Are you okay, Max?"

"Yeah, honey. Can I call over later?"

"Sure, Max. I'm not at work tomorrow."

"Fine, 8.30 then. Bye, angel, see you then."

I could hear the young lassie say, "I thought he was . . . ?"

Donk sat laughing. "I thought he was. Hey, you kept that quiet, Max." He handed over my wages: 350 pounds sterling.

"The CPS are not very pleased." Diana sat in her usual place in the kitchen as I walked in the back door. Some files sat in front of her, and I knew the name on the front—also marked confidential. "I've brought them to let you see them, Max." She gathered them up and handed them to me. "They're not to leave this house."

"Hey, I thought you said you where in sales." I started to read the contents.

"I am," Diana remarked. "I'm selling you this story." The penny dropped.

We sat over a few bottles of wine going through them. "This is mainly all domestic abuse," Diana said, handing me the bombshell.

"Ah, yes, we knew about this. They took him out over it. How did you get your hands on these?"

Diana took back the files, saying nothing and switching on the TV. "Work it out, Max. You're an intelligent guy. We set it all up for you." I went quiet. "From start to finish—and it ain't over yet." Diana produced a mini tape recorder. "I planted this in your car; it's voice activated." Diana switched on the tape, which held the whole sex encounter with Liz and the rest of what was said on that evening in the car.

"I must be psychic; I did think on you when this was happening," I remarked.

She switched the tape off. "Yes, I know, Max." My mind flashed back, and I remembered I called in with more weed. "The CPS smell blood on the domestic abuse. On the other hand, they are not happy over the charges made by his wife over this other issue."

"He did time for it," I commented. "But you heard her say on the tape that he didn't do it."

"It's my job to sort this mess out," Diana snapped. "Do you consider him to be a danger to the public?"

"Erm." I stopped to think. "Well, he was involved in a counterfeit ring years ago—that was pretty extensive, babe. When they took action over these sex abuse charges, his own crew closed him down. Yes, I would say he was a big danger. He could easily set it up again; he's good at laundering the proceeds, and his crew will run for him, especially if he's found not to be not guilty on this."

"Can't you see what will happen?" Diana reached over and squeezed my arm to reassure me. "You'll be his blue-eyed boy, Max, if you start to put right the storey, having got Liz to eventually tell the truth. We can amend the conviction due to evidence you found out." Diana pointed to the tape recorder. "He will worship you; that's why we've gone to so much trouble."

"Ah, I see now, I see, yes. Take out the charge that took him down, I get the credit while you lot gather evidence on a bigger charge, counterfeiting.

But won't Liz be charged with perjury?" I was concerned. "Hmm, I'm not too sure I should get involved. He might smell a rat."

She got up and took my hand, leading me upstairs. "That's my decision," she said That look in her eyes told me everything I needed to know.

I never went back to Sunny Donny the next day. I spent most of the day in Chesterfield. Diana must have dragged me around every clothes shop before dinner, although I did like what she had bought. She sat going through all her latest buys, and she even had me trying out different items that caught her eye. "I've got to tidy you up a bit, Max." I think she was trying not to offend the rock scene on which I was so keen.

"Hey, the food here is good," I said as I got stuck into a seafood platter.

She was eating a very elaborate sandwich. "Now look, Max, I got to leave for a while."

I slammed down my knife and stared out the window. "How long are we talking"?

"Could be indefinite," she replied. "I've been briefed on a task ahead." She waited for my reaction.

I didn't like what was evolving. I could see she was upset as she was telling me. "But what do you mean, indefinite?"

"It's another assignment, Max."

"Shush, babe, you'll get your wish. That's all I can tell you."

Daz could see something was wrong as I walked out the bathroom. "I ain't bothered tonight, Daz. I need to go somewhere—I can't say."

"You've had that face on for over an hour now." Daz was looking engrossed as he sat watching a recording of motocross. I could see the advancing skin line as Alex stood at the mirror combing his hair, putting on his bandana, and getting set to catch the bus into town. "We will miss you tonight, Max."

I tried not to get into deep conversation with the pair. "Say hi to Hobbit and behave yourselves." I got up grabbed my bag and walked out the door.

I checked the fuel as I entered the car: there was half a tank. I looked at my phone; "Secret place" was the new text.

It was still light when I arrived. Daz had let me use his facilities to get changed and refreshed. I called in at my bro's on the way out of Chuckwalla. He was up the backdoor, and the barbeque was smoking away. "I'll take two on the green, Pat," I said as I sat down.

"Bloody heck, look at him dressed up like a dog's dinner. Meeting a wench, are we, Max?" Pat's missus never missed a trick. "Hmm, what's that you're wearing?"

"It's Issey Miyake. Cool, isn't it?"

"Hey check the new watch. That must have cost," he said as he studied the new Omega Sea master sent by 307 Battery. He was all over me picking and flicking. "I might even start owning up to you," he said jokingly.

"Ignore him, Max. Do you want something to eat?" his missus said.

"I've got to be somewhere in exactly twenty minutes, otherwise I'd love to, pet," I said, putting up my hands.

Diana's car was already parked as I arrived, and dusk was just settling in. I walked through the thicket as quietly as I could, careful not mark my new trousers and shirt. She stood in her usual place, looking out over the lake with the mini binoculars I'd lent to her. I stood a little while, admiring her before I let her know I was there. "You look fantastic." She had put on the white two-piece suit she'd bought earlier.

She turned and greeted me. "Tonight we go in, Max."

"What?" I was startled.

"The priory restaurant, honey. I booked it. Come on, walk me down." she smiled. Now this was dream come true—the restaurant was an exclusive restaurant I'd always wanted to try out in the priory grounds; the waiting list to eat there was massive.

"How did you manage to pull that off, Doll?" I had to ask.

She laughed and said, "I have ways and means," in her fake German accent. "Hey, I've heard they have lobster on the menu. Hmm, isn't seafood an aphrodisiac?"

"Is it? I'm not sure."

"Max, I can't wait to get you home. I want to make the most of tonight. Oh, by the way, we're going to a club in town." Then I noticed she had that distant look, although I knew what she was thinking. She was studying the geese and the swans in the smaller lake, and their reflections in the water as the sun disappeared over the tree tops.

"White and pure, just like you," I said, taking her hand. After a brief spell of silence, I asked, "When are you flying?"

She turned to me, looking around at individuals in the room. "Shh, not here, Max." She put down her other hand on top of mine as the lobster arrived. I was checking out the hall marks on the cutlery as I took charge of my meal.

When we finally made it back to her place, she told me, "I didn't know you dance like that; you sure made my night."

"I'm glad you drove tonight, doll. I'm not quite sure how many cocktails I had, but those Harvey Wallbangers did the trick."

She reached for the wine in the fridge, grabbing two glasses and leading the way up to her lair.

It was four thirty, and she stood staring out the window naked. I hadn't let her know I was awake until I said, "That's how I want it—how the light sits on you."

She turned and walked over to her wardrobe, opening the door and taking out her house coat and wrapping it around her whilst sitting beside me. "Yes, we'll do that someday, Max, but not now." She laid bed next to me.

"Ah, my paint pallet and easel aren't here anyway; remind me to bring them over." I squeezed into her. She felt cold to the touch. "How long have you been standing there? You're freezing—look, goose bumps like golf balls."

She cut me short. "I'm scared we won't, Max." She was crying. "It's Monday," she whispered.

By her sudden change in mood, I knew after Monday I wouldn't be seeing her again. My eyes filled up, and we lay on the bed just staring at each other. During that Sunday we never left the bedroom.

Things were looking a bit touch and go. Donk was in the kitchen arguing with his missus indoors, and his attention turned to me. "Max, you just go up and start the wall at the front; that'll keep you going for few days. Plasterers will be up there—they'll have made a start. Just keep your eye on 'em, Max. Make sure they wash that mixer out. Hey, and tell our Dink that he can get that car shifted off my drive and down to the scrap yard."

"What, the Pug?"

"He's smashed it up, pulled out on a lorries and put his missus in the hospital. They're on about charging our Dink with dangerous driving."

"So that's what you're arguing about, Donk." This I had to see, and I jumped into the Granada and made my way up to the job.

"Sheeks, you've made a right pigs tab of that." The whole of the driver's side was buckled into the roof.

Nig rolled up. "I told you not to sell it to him, Max."

I was still walking around the smashed Pug, scratching my head. "How come both sides are crunched up?" I asked Dink.

"The lorry pushed us across the road, and a bus got the other side."

"Just look at the state of it," I said as I pushed my hands into the creases in the metal.

"Don't talk to him, Max. He's nearly killed his missus. She's in intensive care with spinal injuries. You've gone too far this time," Nidge raged, pointing his finger at young Dink as Dink mizzed into the house.

I walked back to the job at hand at the front wall, taking my trowel from my tool bucket, throwing into the batten, taking up my building pins, and unwrapping the line. "What. you think he meant to do it." I set my level on the new layer of concrete in the footing.

"Max, you don't know how he is. I grew up with him, remember." I reached in my tool bucket for my tape measure to work out the three-metre panels. "All day I was telling young Dink to keep his distance with the odd."

"And did you try to kill her?" I hurled at Dink. Dink knew I was only kidding.

My phone beeped on the way home from work, and I looked at it whilst I sat at the traffic lights. "I'll be with you always." I knew she'd gone. A horn hooted behind me, and I guess this was the first time I admitted it to myself as I arrived back home and texted back, "I love you."

I went into the house. Paul wasn't around, and I went upstairs to sort a change of clothes and run my bath. I heard the phone beep again. It read, "Now you tell me, love D." Yes, yes!

I was jumping around bouncing off the chairs when Paul walked in. "Sounds like fun whatever it is, Max," he said as he went into the back room.

"It's all I wanted to know." I ran and kissed Paul on the forehead before running upstairs, remembering I had the bath running. "Erm, don't go away," I shouted down to Paul "We're on a mission."

Paul seemed to be a bit confused when I came back downstairs. "Mission, Max? What's this all about, then?"

"The difference between two years and five, Paul."

"Oh hey, what?" Paul went quiet and then got it. "I'll do it. When do we start?"

You're coming to Chuckwalla for a start, to introduce you, mate. Switch on a few lights." I knew for every one I gave him, I would get one of his contacts. Tit for tat; tactics always worked on the street. "First we need to turn yer brother anti-terrorist; maybe we can do something there. "Paul's eyes widened. "Eighteen months was the figure I had in mind, and then he becomes a scout. Of course, he will have a job to do on the inside."

Paul seemed to smile as though he knew this already. "We've been waiting for you to shine, Max." I was spinning out all of a sudden. "I checked you out, Max—turn left here." I left the road. "Right, pull in." Paul had his phone to bits in seconds, and his SIM card was in his mouth. "Did you time it, Max?"

"Yes, Paul. I can see what you're trying to do."

"Right, now you." It took me twice as long. "Something to practice, Max. I've been informed who the guy was that you gave the ninebar to." I went quiet. "Big man. He said there was no need to for him to buy from me." I was still quiet. "Connect, Max—you're the one. Commander One from Chuckwalla." This was my call sign from the Old Man Griffon. I knew Paul had gathered his information from the Gypsies; I'd seen his car parked near the caravans when I passed the site.

"So you've done your homework, Paul. That's why I picked you."

He stopped me. "Look, this is my decision. I am not saying that I'm 100 per cent, but I ain't got no option." I knew he'd been jolted with my drawings as he'd kept tags on my progress as I drew the work.

"Right, I'll take you to look and assess the situation. Listen in."

Nogg sat with two other hoodies arguing over the stereos that were piled on the coffee table, saying that they were nickered. "Look, this one's got knobs on. Where's Ant? I need some decent stuff. I can't sell this if I gave it away."

Paul sat, taking it all in. I was sorting Nogg a half ounce on the green. "Still getting it from the hall?" I said to Nogg. Paul sat quiet throughout our time in the deal.

Nogg chirped up, "Yeah, two for nineteen."

"Well that's sixty sterling on the half, Nogg. Surely you can work that out."

Paul prompted me to make it quick, and soon we were over to Daz's. Alex answered." He's over at his dad's; left half an hour ago.

"Hey, Max." Daz's father was washing down his car on the drive.

Daz was coming out the front with a soapy bucket. After throwing it on the car, he walked over whilst his dad took over. He crouched down at the window. "Russ went off with it," he said, looking at my reaction. I was just about to comment, but he continued. "And Dave got the other." He again waited for my reaction.

I laughed. "You're kidding me."

Daz keeping a straight face. "Well, you know them after-parties that Hobbit sometimes has."

"Ah, don't say anymore."

Too late—Paul heard him. "This ain't got nothing to do with you jumping on chairs shouting yes, does it, Max? And what was 'Ah yes, that's all I need to know' whilst you were reading your text messages?" Paul was laughing.

"What's he been doing?" Daz asked. He seemed curious as he leaned in closer.

Paul, sensing disaster, went quiet. I tried to play it down and said, "You're kidding me, I don't believe you."

"Ask Alex." Daz looked serious. "They've both found you out, Max: you're a dirty love rat, last time I heard."

I turned to Paul for backup. No sympathy. He said, 'You got to take the battering, Max."

It got worse. Dink said, Donk just informed me that this Friday was the last, and that he was only taking on cash Jobs. His missus collared me later that day while Donk was in the bank.

"What's he told you?" she asked.

"Well, he said he's only taking on cash jobs."

"He's a lying sick filthy. I've fucked him. I've told all the companies he contracts for what he's done with that dirty little slut. I'm having a field day with him, Max."

Ah, that's what happened. I had been told of how Donk's missus was out to ruin him. So that was how I was too soon be signing on. I had cause for concern.

Later at home, I was on the phone to Daz explaining that I was going to be laid off and had to sign on the rock and roll. He was on the other end trying to be sympathetic. "Right," he said, "I'm coming over." It was Saturday morning, and I wasn't too happy at the prospect of signing on.

Paul was in the other room listening in. "Well stone the crows," he commented. "You signing on the dole, Max?" He passed through and out the door.

"Right, that's it—I'm definitely coming over." Daz sat laughing. I could hear his missus in the background.

In town The Tap was brimming as usual; no signs of dismay. I looked into the masses, and Daz was bantering to Alex about some of Midge's memoirs. I'd butted in by saying, "I wished I could have stopped that." I wasn't around when Midge died, so I preferred them to change the subject. "Right, calm it down," I demanded.

Daz and Alex went quiet; they could see the tears in my eyes. I missed Midge and said, "Oh, and Bev's over there."

Alex was all of a sudden set in his usual pointer stance and looked over, focusing in on Bev. Alex was mesmerised as the starred and striped bask Bev was wearing sort of took him over. "Shut yer gob and get them in." Alex gave Daz his empty as Daz mizzed to the bar. I had turned and started laughing with a guy entered with another biker. They stood in their leathers with their helmets. I'd dealt them a bit of personal snow in the past and was inquiring about the after-party at Rock City. Alex soon shot away, moving over to where Bev stood.

"You'd better do one, Max," one of the bikers said as he spotted a uniform coming in the front exit.

"Hup. I'll catch you over at the rig." I had two wraps of snow hid on me, so I took a sharp exit out the back door and took to my heels, hoofing it.

Not far from Rock City, the two bikers had caught me up and seemed adamant. "Are you sure about this?" I asked.

"Yeah, Max. We were there at the party last week. Nothing happened." I passed the wrap to one of the bikers, who in turn checked and tasted the contents and then passed the cash as we drew near the car park.

"I'll seek a second opinion," I said as I approached the entrance. "Right Hobbit. What went off last week at the party?"

"I presume you mean the party." His eyes bulged as he raised his voice over the music. He leaned over and whispered, "Two young broads—the same two you been running with who locked themselves in a room all night. Ring any bells, Max?"

"Yeah, Hobbit that's the two I'm inquiring about."

"They left alone," he said as he snatched at the ten spot from my hand and passed me a rack of beer. I went on through and I entered into the Rig, noticing the place nearly empty and walking over to the bar. I winked at the barmaid to catch her attention, and she came over. I felt a bit naff ordering a Diet Coke whilst one foot stuck on top of twenty-four cans.

Alex and Daz soon rolled in, spotting the unopened slab near the heel of my foot. It wasn't too busy, and I had taken up a stance between the loudspeakers and the seating area in the corner. My mind was put to rest. The ace of spades had just kicked in; between the ordainment and the drumbeat, it blew my mind, and the bass eliminated the freedom of choice when I played air guitar, moving onto the dance floor.

Liz appeared, taking me by the arm further out to the dance floor. "Diana's in Brazil," she shouted in my ear. I spun with mixed feeling of relief. Although I knew she wasn't in Brazil, I'd checked my status and hers. Taking Liz off the dance floor again, I sat thinking to myself, but I was beginning to miss her already. "She's gone, Max. Wake up to it!" Liz was frantic. I knew Diana had been like an older sister with Liz. I was blown out and sat in at the side.

"Yes, I know she's gone."

Liz looked confused, although she knew more than she let on. "It's going for adoption, and I have a taker. I'm doing you a favour, Max. The words rang out and haunted me. Liz at least told me straight, knowing full well it was her only option. I knew in the next months there was going to be a shining light somewhere. "I'm also going back to my folks."

"When?" I said.

"Soon. Can you help me?"

"Anything, angel." I looked at where the cans were; Alex was making friends. I jumped back to life, bursting out onto the dance floor and over to the decks. "That's the one," I said as DJ Dave handed me a CD by Foreigner, and I selected a track from it, handing it back. There was an announcement as the manager came onto the microphone and the music was turned down. "Guess who got the DJ of the year? Rock City." We were all congratulating him as a flux of cans disappeared from the slab and the tune I requested pumped out. Alex flopped his famous air guitar stance, sliding on his knee. When two leather-clad strippers caught him under the arms pits and carried him off to the men's room, molesting him on the way there. And I meant really molesting him—one was feeling at his arse, and the other was trying to undo his shirt. Daz had to go over and explain a few things. I sat with Liz, laughing at the sight before us. I got up to help Daz peel poor old Alex away from them. sitting him down next to Liz upon return.

"Now don't move," I instructed Alex. Alex was still in shock, though obviously pissed out of his skull. Daz was soon over to DJ Dave just as Dave and Russ looked on from the rail, killing themselves laughing. Daz stood pointing the two out as they came out the bogs.

"Oh, nice work, Daz," Russ commented on his return as security were soon around the pair and moving towards the main door in due course.

Daz wandered back over, looking confused. Liz was trying to get Daz to sit down, noticing the sweat pouring of him.

Russ wandered over, squeezed in, and whispered, "I put them up to it; they're only larking around with him."

"What you mean?" I paused, pointing at the two strippers disappearing through the door.

"Well, someone said it was his birthday," replied Russ.

My sides where killing me. It came to tears of laughter as Alex was back on his feet, trying pull me up on the floor. "Argh," I groaned as I accompanied him. We did a good impression of Motley Crew, and Liz, Tracy, and Bev soon joined us, followed by Daz, Russ, and Dave.

The lights soon came on. "Those stars and stripes—that bask," we said in unison.

I'd stayed at Daz's all weekend. I got up Monday after a session in the plough that turned into a hangover. No work today. I'd been entering into a few doodles and fitted a few rhymes. "They're just rewrites," I commented, putting down my notes. Daz was cooking up a bacon and egg special; he didn't seem the slightest bit interested. The coffee was welcome. I got to scratch on.

"If you want to come along, I got to nip up to the snooker club first," Daz said as he handed me a breaky.

"Yeah, not looking forward to it." Daz was only a temp at the bus depot; he too was looking for work.

"Both on the rock and roll, eh?" I stood at the bar, chattering to one of the staff at the snooker club.

"Yeah. See what you can find out, Max." Daz was fitting new light bulbs to save Shirley from breaking out the steps. Shirley was explaining there had been another break-in, although nothing got took; they came in through there pointing to the fire exit. "It's about the third time it's been tried," Daz said.

"Didn't the CCTV catch them?" I asked.

An old guy stood listening and butted in. "I watched them from the window from across the road there. Some hoods stood throwing snowballs at it a few winters ago. They were in and out before the police arrived. They where well wrapped up."

"Hoodies," I remarked, correcting the old fella. "And they stood throwing snow balls at what?" I asked.

"The camera CCTV there at the side of the building," the old guy replied.

"Oh." I nodded and smiled at the cheeky misdemeanour.

"I think they disappeared in a nicked motor. I seen them screwdriver the door when the alarm spooked them. Don't know—it was dark, black, and fast."

"All sounds a bit," I said to Daz, laughing.

"Ignore 'em, Max. Chatterboxes," Daz said. "It'll be money for drugs they were after." Shirley muttered, "Bloody looters."

"Hey, this is as good as it gets," Daz said, commenting on the smoothness of the ride every time we hit a pot hole. "You did all right, Max. Plenty of room." We had just gone half way up the lane to the farm where my bro worked, and Daz was taking a piss.

I did miss the XR3's handling abilities. I was trying to kick up a little dust. "She's coming." I pulled over to let her by after a grab for the juice on the back seat.

Daz was grinning as the Range Rover passed. "You sly—"

I stopped him. "Hey, take a look at my dream."

Daz knew what stood there. "That wonderful bit of history, mate, and look what they did." "What you did in and around it, more like." Daz had one hand on the roof and the other on the dash as I hit the accelerator.

"Cat in the pigeons," my brother was shouting off the steps, from the upper hay loft.

Bro parked the Lorrie up there and helped around the farm. "Keep him out there, Daz." "Bro, I think you're relating to the session in the plough."

"Wait, I was just talking. You don't need to say out, Max," my bro butted in. "And there's always a fight breaks out. Twice the place got smashed up because of you!"

Daz was trying to back me up. "Look, Pat, it was cool."

I shouted, "Yeah, it was cool. It was bloody cool."

"All right, calm down."

"I bet it was Bill and Gaz, phoned and told I'd been in there having a quiet pint. What time do you finish work?"

"Early. Why?"

"I need some green."

"He's having to sign on," Daz butted in.

"What's happened—they catch you toking a spliff at work?" Pat started laughing.

"Nah, laid off. Anyway I'm having a small holiday."

That job up in Newark will be gone, if that's what you're up here to ask."

"No, Pat, I'll stick to what I do best. Will you be in around six when I bring Daz back?"

"Yeah, I'll be around. You can come out with the dogs. Don't keep me waiting."

"Right, bro. See you then."

Daz was playing pool with a couple of locals when I arrived back in the Leopard. "Any luck?" he asked.

"I have an interview tomorrow and some more numbers to check. And this lot." I threw the forms on the table as I sat down, producing a pen. We ended up back at the house playing the PlayStation.

"Hey, I've got something for you," Paul said, and he disappeared in the back room before coming back with an Adidas bag. "Cop a load of them," he said, unzipping it. "All top quality—thirty sovs each."

Daz examined the bag first, bringing out a top notch Phillips stereo. "Yep, I can get rid."

I put down the controller. "Crikey, there must be over a few grands' worth. Right, come on."

Nogg was just getting out of his work van as we pulled up. "Hey this is phat," Nogg said, looking at each item in the bag.

"I could see his interest." Fifty sterling each, and I'll leave 'em with you, Nogg."

He grabbed the bag and fired into his front door, dropping it inside and returning. "How much on the green?" he inquired.

Daz sat trying to reckon what the stereos were going to make. "It's 120 on the ounce. Can I drop one for you?"

Nogg stood thinking for a while. "I'll buzz you later, Max. Got to meet the missus. Drop me at mine; you're about ready for going up your bro's anyway."

"Not another country lane. What now?"

Paul was pulling in at the side of a workman's cabin. "Two secs," he said as he disappeared from the car. He came back with another guy who was in his late forties. "He's coming back to the house; his name is Tom." The fellow seemed okay as I let him in the car. "We more or less grew up with him, Max. He produces a bottle of strong cider." I learned that Tom was homeless and could see Paul was none too pleased at the situation. "Do you mind if we put him up for a bit, just till he gets sorted?"

"I suppose so, although you'll need to hide him when they come to check the house." We sat most of the night laughing and joking.

"When can you start, Max? Monday not too soon for you?"

"Yeah, sure." I was chuffed at the result.

"Oh, do you have a 714 certificate?"

"I have sc60."

"It's no good, Max. It's okay—I'll get one for you. Bring in a passport or your driving licence. I'll just show you how the pay structure works. It's 19 percent of the whole job, what they earned last week. I was looking at figures of between four hundred and five hundred sterling just for the bricky to build each shell. It's one and one, Max. I got a good lad to labour for you when you start."

"Thanks, Mr Jenkins."

"Be in the yard at eight sharp."

I'd been offered accommodation at another location whilst Paul tried to sort things with the association that owned the house, o give old Tom some accommodation. I'd decided to take Bruce up on his offer of sharing with them. This house belonged to Donk. "I want you in with them, Max; you need to keep in touch," he said as he signed off his phoned.

I got out the car and knocked on the front door. Bruce had two jobs: fitting windows during the day and flogging roses at night, and when he saw what job I had with Donk, things seemed to take a turn for good business. His mate hardly ever seemed to be about. "I'm just gonna take a look at what I'm gonna be living in," I said.

"I'll show you around," Bruce volunteered.

Out the back was a hound that looked as though he was sent from the devil himself. That was, until I heard its story. "This was an ex-RAF dog we're talking about here," Bruce finished explaining.

"Ex-RAF?" I replied.

"I couldn't believe they'd left this precious creature on a chain. He was running in his own doo. I wouldn't rest until I got control of things here." Paul looked disgusted when he saw what was at hand, giving me help to move things around and to get the yard cleaned. The back walls were topped in glass, and Max, the dog, was wild with hunger.

"That was his name," Donk explained as he walked into the back yard. He had came to see if I'd settled in. I had phoned Donk about the condition of the dog, explaining it was underweight; I was stepping in to help the dog. He warned me not go near it as he left the house.

The next morning I wrote a list of all Max's needs, making sure Jeyes Fluid was on the list. Now I could see a clever animal sitting there, although he was in a bit of a state as we looked through the back window.

Paul had turned up early to further help the garden get tidy and then mizzed out after he got too close to it. Let's say he had seen its teeth at very close range. The only thing stopping the dog from giving Paul serious stitches was his chain. "It's all yours, Max," Paul said as he made a rush for the door.

Max was a long-haired German shepherd. I fed him a mix of good quality meat and bone meal with other additives, and I spent the rest of the morning swilling out and disinfecting him until all was spotless. It was a hottish day, and he did like the hose pipe on him, though it was a shock at first. At first Old Max growled and snarled as I approached him and put my hand on top of his head. Then Max licked me as I slipped off his chain to let him run, knowing he'd roll in the Jeyes. I held the shovel, keeping my eyes on him at all times.

Donk recently had the yard concreted at the back, so the yard would be easy to clean up and keep clean. Bruce came through and commented, "That dog—don't let anyone near him. How did you do that?"

"His name is Max, and I noticed you show fear to him."

Bruce sat in the living room, waiting for the microwave to ping. "What do you know about dogs, Max?" he asked, walking into the kitchen to collect his chips.

"I've noticed you feeding at arm's length. I bought this," I said, showing Bruce a choker chain. "He's not to be kept on that." I pointed to the one in the yard. "Except when necessary."

Bruce closed the door to the microwave. "Well, I still ain't going out there." He retired to the living room.

That evening I took Max out for the first time. At first he was frisky through the excitement of leaving the back yard, and it took a couple of snaps on the chain before Max would respond. He really was an ex-RAF dog; I could tell his training had kicked in. He would sit, and he would come to heel, I noticed straight away. This dog had a handler who taught him everything. It was abuse that had made him like how he was found. Max would even walk at whatever pace I walked at. I never let him off the lead until I was sure. I tried him around the streets, where he would encounter other people, just to see how he responded. Sure enough he was a little edgy but on the whole well behaved. I now had new lodgings and a fearless dog.

Dave was up first next morning. As I came down the stairs he asked, "Cuppa, Max?" I took a cup from the draining board as I heard a knock at the door. Paul stood there, and I invited him in.

"Max I've had to give 'em the money back for that XR3.Can I leave it here? No room on the street."

There it sat, as I looked out the door smiling. "Can I use it?"

Paul threw me the keys to it. "Still insured for it, ain't you, Max?" I nodded. "Well, so long as you keep the petrol topped up, I don't mind." Paul came into the living room, and I introduced him to Dave, who was a powder freak and a plasterer, same as Bruce.

Paul looked out the back window. Max was all of a sudden there, looking at him. Paul laughed. "I was just about to say where's the damn dog." Max had him in a fixed glare. "Looks better already," he commented. Paul also noticed how clean the yard looked. "Hey, Dave, who did that to him?"

Dave walked through as all three of us stood staring at Max. "You mean the steel staples stitches on his eyebrow? Oh, someone tried to break in and threw a slate at him. It happened before we moved in; that's why they bought the dog in the first place—to protect the house. Max had his eyebrow held together with surgical staples. There was no need to let him get like that." He pointed to the yard.

"And look at his feet—who did that?" I butted in.

"He tried to escape. He jumped up some boards stacked at the back of the wall and ended up on the glass."

"Ooh." Both Paul and I were cringing.

"Donk found him and took him to the vet to get him stitched up."

"Why did RAF get rid of him?"

"They say he's a dog killer. He killed another dog in training. He just turned nasty."

"Nah, I don't believe that," Paul said. "He would have not been put in that situation; they're carefully selected as pups."

"Right, well, I'll see you later," Dave said, taking his sandwiches out the fridge as a car hooter outside sounded up. "That's him. Just going to work."

"It's half past eleven. I think Donk's been putting the fear of God into them over old Max," I said. Paul started laughing just as I went to open the back door.

"Hey, don't let him in here," Paul said, suddenly serious.

"No, I'm just going to feed him; back in a sec." I slipped out and took his bowl. Old Max fussed, the smell of Jeyes Fluid sweetening the smell of him. He soon jumped back down after I grabbed at his paws for a closer examination. He jumped down after I told him to. Paul stood at the window as if he stood watching gladiators about to do battle. I slipped back in the house, putting on the kettle. "I'll just give him this, and we'll mizz," I said, opening a big can of chum and lacing it in plenty of biscuits and hot water. "One big tin a day feeds him. Twice a day he'll get that until he puts the weight back on, and then I might give him some extra. Want a coffee while it's hot?"

"Erm, yeah, Max, no rush."

I slipped out, putting down his bowl and making Max sit before filling his other bowl with fresh water from the hose. I thought that it should have been common sense not leave anything near the walls as I nipped back into the house. We sat chatting while we drank our coffee and walked out the house.

"Max, I need to go to Sutton. I'll diesel the Granada up for you full tank."

"Deal," I said. "I'm not doing anything else." We jumped in the car.

Chapter Seven

Paul and I sat in the Granada. "Oh, my lucky day, the tank's nearly empty," I said. Paul was hinting he needed diesel too. "Come on, we'll nip up and see Donk. Tenner fer five gallons. And it's white; he'll only charge me a tenner to fill this. And you don't get it in your mouth—it's in a Bowser."

"I wondered where you was going for it, Max." He took the seat belt and clipped himself in.

"Hang on, I'll ring him." I took out my mobile and dialled Donk's number, getting the information. "We've gotta go up to the job; it's where we left it. I've to nip the tenner in on the way up."

"No probs, Max, I've got a fetch a couple of barrels."

I started laughing. "Donk will know—he ain't stupid. I'll pay him fer it." We stopped round at Paul's as he nipped in the house and then out to the boot of his car, throwing two barrels into the back of mine. He rubbed his hands and jumped back in as we made our way through town.

"Right, that's it, then. A full tank for Max and two five-gallon drums." Donk was happy with the thirty sovereigns Paul paid him. He went on to say, "That's all I'm bothered about, Max, so long as you see me about it first. I don't mind how much you have so long as you pay me for it."

"Don't tell him that, he'll be back for the Bowser," Paul said cheekily. Paul went in the house, and half an hour later he came out and got back in the car. "That's the last one; it's yours, Max." He threw me an ounce, and I slipped it into the glove box. Paul was counting a small wedge of twenties. "It's okay, I made on that one. Let's mizz."

We got to Sutton around dinner time. Paul had me wait for him for half an hour, and he came back smiling. I never asked what he was there for; he would have told me if he wanted me to know. I dropped Paul back at the house, giving him a hand out the boot with his diesel. I offered him the money for the ounce again. "Nah, it's a bonus, Max. You don't owe me nothing for that one." I went into the house with him.

Tom was looking a lot better; he was fresh shaven and had clean casuals, some of them mine that I'd left behind. I laughed and sat down. "How's things, Tom?" I asked. He was telling me of the procedures that were in motion so that he could become a proper tenant in the premises. "I have a few other items; if you want them, I'll bring them down." Tom thanked me for what we already did for him.

I went back to the house. Bruce was just in from work. "What time did Dave leave this morning, Max?"

"Half past eleven, why? He was muttering something about not getting picked up."

"I didn't hear you leave."

"That's because I never came in last night; I was around at hers."

Bruce had that surly look on his face and lowered his voice. "They've rang me at work to see what happened to him."

Just then the front door flew open. Dave walked in covered in plaster. "Get there all right, Dave?" Bruce asked.

Dave didn't look too pleased. "The car wouldn't start this morning, and I had no credit to phone, and the one down the street ain't working. Somebody had to come from the job to get me."

"At least it's half a shift," I commented.

"Aren't you working yet, Max?"

"I start this Monday. I timed it just right, getting a week off."

Bruce was looking out the back window. "Hey, has the vet been?"

"No, mate, I just tidied him up a bit."

"It's a good job. I don't need anything from out the back," he said, spotting Max off the chain. "I ain't going anywhere near that mad hound."

Bruce was taking his tea from the freezer. micro chips, and beefy pancakes were on his menu. Max the dog was up at the window watching us all in the kitchen. I slipped out to get his bowl. Max jumped up me and licked my face; he was getting exited and knew he was going to be fed. "Right, Bruce, how much do you pay for your dust?" I inquired as I stepped back in the back door.

"It's 120 on the ounce. Why, Max?"

I put down Max's bowl and went out the front door, stepped over to my car, opened the door, and took out the ounce I got from Paul from the glove box. "Smell that."

Bruce took a whiff. "Ah, that's fresh." He took a little dip. "Do me half of that for fifty, Max, and it's a deal." He soon got the money ready, putting back his wallet. I estimated two equal piles on the kitchen work top and invited him to pick a half measure. He soon had in a piece of cellophane ripped from a roll, sat on the breadbin, and put away in his pocket. Bruce then took his chips and his crispy pancake, placed them on a plate along with a can of lager from the fridge, and walked into the front room, where he sat and built a spliff of pure weed whilst his food cooled. He devoured his platter and then lit spliff and got smashed while he sat watching the news.

I stood and mixed up a large bowl of chum and biscuits and mixed it with hot water, taking it out to Max first and making him sit. I'd no sooner put his meal down, and Max was nosing his bowl to the side wall. I stood and watched him chow down every last morsel and returned to the house.

In the front room Dave passed me and went into the bathroom. I sat with Bruce and watched the end of the news. "Right, I'm taking Max out." I jumped up for his choker chain.

"You brave bastard," Bruce said whilst I was on the way out the back door.

I slipped the chain over Max's neck, led him to the back gate, and made him sit while I opened up the locks. Max would give a loud wine as the gate come open and I used a couple of sharp snaps to hold him back. He was getting stronger, I thought, as I walked him down past the train lines and around the block, settling him down in his kennel when we came back. At dusk he liked to lay on the fresh bit of carpet I put in his kennel for him. I smiled as he'd sleep with one paw over his eyes, rising to the occasional din outside.

The house was empty when I arrived back in. There was a knock at the door, and I walked to the front and opened it. It was Donk, and I invited him in. "Those two have gone out. Want a coffee?" I said as Donk sat down.

"Comfy, isn't it, Max? Better than that other house. The whole house has been refurbished right through." He got up, following me through to the kitchen. "Milk, two sugars, Max."

Max the dog soon had his head straight up at the window. Donk opened the door and went out to him, making a fuss; he then stepped back in after he smelt the Jeyes Fluid throughout the yard.

"I'm putting the kettle on. It's all right," I reassured him. "I'll put him on the chain when I'm at work and walk him at night."

"Who's bought all the new stuff for him, Max?" Donk was looking at his new bowl and his choke chain and a big batch a dog food. "How much did you spend on him?"

"Around sixty sterling," I said. "But it don't matter. I don't want—"

Donk stopped me. "Shh, right. I'll tell ya what I'm gonna do. A month's rent free—that's just between me and you. I want the dog kept like that. It's the best I've seen him."

I poured the water, added the milk, and stirred, giving Donk his coffee. "I've been giving him these in his food." I showed Donk the de-wormers.

Donk smiled. "It's one worry off me plate, Max. I just needed to know he's all right. Now, I've found a bit a work for you. A nice earner, Thursday and Friday."

"Yep, Donk, not a problem." I tried to sound eager.

"Be up at the house at 8.00 PM, Max. It's building another conservatory shell up in Leeds, o better bring yer tools."

"Erm. I start another job on Monday."

Donk stopped me. "Yes, I know, Max. I gave him a reference—I do know who it is. You'll be all right with them. They got plenty of work. I'll still want you the odd time though. Weekends, especially Saturdays and Sunday, so whatever you get offered, I'll better it." Donk put down his empty cup and left.

I'd woken in my sleep around 2.00 AM and checked my text messages. "Secret Place." Eh? I jumped up and looked out the window. Max was asleep, head half out the kennel and one paw over his eyes.

The night air was warm and quiet as I stepped out into the Granada. I parked it and made my way through to the battlements. All was silent—no Diana. I stood looking out across the moonlit lake as a shooting star caught my eye. I wrote something on my text, just something to remember, I thought. Damn, I'd got mixed up with her last text. I checked the date it was sent and then deleted it. Still no word from her. I stayed for a short while. I knew she was safe somehow. I returned to the car and drove past the ramper. Her house was in darkness and her car wasn't there.

Making for the motorway, I headed back to Sunny Donny. Paul's light was still on as I passed. I turned the block and called in. Tom and Paul sat watching TV and welcomed me in and offered me a coffee.

"Hey, who did these? These are good." There where black-and-white drawings on the mantelpiece of actors and celebrities. "Ain't that Spike Milligan?"

Paul started to chuckle. "It's just some I did a few years back, Max."

"Do some more, do loads of 'em, make them bigger—huge." Paul couldn't stop laughing. "I'll help you," I said. "Tom can be a roady; people will hire us. I'll do colour, you do black-and-white."

Tom came back in with the coffees. "All right them, ain't they, Max?"

I was still looking, amazed. "You really should take it further. You have a definite style."

"I might," Paul said. "Who knows, Max, who knows."

Before I knew it outside was light, and I looked out of the curtain. Tom had retired to his room, and Paul and I had been playing the PlayStation. I must have fallen asleep, because Paul woke me with a coffee. I checked my phone: 11.50, and nothing—no messages, no missed calls. Paul was clutching his UB40. "Coming, Max?" he asked as took hold of my legs, moving them off the settee to get me up and moving.

I muttered, "I gotta go check on Max, give him his dinner."

"We'll all go if you like." He left the room, and I heard him running upstairs. "Tom isn't stirring," he said as he came back down. The both of us left him asleep and went over to my place.

I slipped through to Max, giving him a few biscuits taking up his bowl. Dave must have gotten picked up this morning because he was already gone. I entered in the back door, flicking on the kettle. "You do the coffees; I'll fix this for Max," I said, opening up another tin and slipping a few tablets into the chunks. Paul reached and grabbed the bottle of milk whilst commenting Max would put weight on now whilst looking out at him patrolling the back walls. Every time someone passed in the back entry, he'd sound up then shut up, just to let folks know he was there. I slipped out again, making him sit. This time I put the bowl down and made him wait. Whilst I was filling up his water bowl, Max wouldn't eat all his food. He'd nose his bowl over to his kennel and save a bit. I noticed he put it in the shade. Even Paul saw him doing it. I mucked him out, dropping a bit of Jeyes Fluid and swilling out the yard. Both of us knew why he did that. Poor old Max wasn't used to large meals. "He'll learn to trust you, and soon enough he'll be eating large," Paul commented. The coffee was ready when I slipped back in.

Tracy spotted me as she came out the college. She was dressed in her usual black setup, complete with baseball cap and headphones. I sat on the Bonnet with my arms folded as she wandered through the traffic, smiling as I jumped up and embraced her. "Max, why didn't you call me?"

"Erm, I've been busy, babe. Come on, let's go for a drive, and we can catch up." I'd taken the XR3 and filled the tank.

"I have some marvellous news," she said, anxious to tell me. "I've been accepted at university."

"Oh yes, that's fantastic, we must celebrate. And I know where." I tried to sound jolly and happy for her.

"Max, you're crazy." She gave a look of reassurance as she sat back, and the Bonnet dipped and hugged the road along the M6. "How long before we get there now, Max?"

"Another hour, angel," I said as she turned the music back up.

She seemed to burst to life on the approach into Blackpool. "No, Max, I insist we go half." We'd found a bed and breakfast on the seafront an marvelled at the lights from the bed.

"No time to waste—come on, let's do the scene." Soon enough we were in and out of the arcades and the pubs along the promenade, eventually ending up on the north pier, where we bought candy lollipops and licked at them whilst watching the tide coming in. "Right then, I know this restaurant we can eat. You can tell me all about uni."

We left the pier and walked. I'd picked an Italian restaurant further in town. We'd already passed it earlier, and I'd noticed it looked quiet in all that candlelight. "Yes, we can accommodate a table for two," replied the waiter as we were led in over the terracotta and marble floor. The host sat us at a neatly laid out table and left us to study the menu. After pointing out the different wines to accompany the meal, he relit the centre piece.

"Mmm, I love the smell of candles," she said quietly. I couldn't quite put my finger on the new alertness in Tracy's face. It must have been her acceptance, I thought, although she did seem radiant. "Spicy garlic and herb minestrone soup followed with lasagne is beckoning me," she said, putting down the menu.

"I think I'll have the same," I said, agreeing with her choice. The waiter suggested an order of wine to accompany the meal, but Tracy said she didn't want any.

"Ah, Rossini—listen to the melody," I commented on the Italian music in the background. The soup arrived complete with a basket filled with hot garlic bread. She was content; I could see it mixed in with her newfound glow as she grabbed for the garlic bread.

I took up my spoon. "So where is this university?"

Tracy looked into my eyes and then said into her soup, "Australia."

"What? Say that again?"

"Australia."

"Australia?" I slammed down my spoon, getting up and moving the table.

"Max, I knew you'd be mad." I marched over to the window and looked out with my arms folded.

"Is everything all right, sir?" the waiter asked as he came over.

"It's okay, I'll be fine." I counted to ten and sat back down. Tracy started look concerned as the other people in the restaurant went quiet. I took up my spoon and fidgeted with the soup. "Right, Australia. Well, I am so happy for you."

Tracy started to smile. "It's my dream, Max," she said as the background music seemed to peak.

"I didn't mean to cause a scene," I said, clutching at her hand. "It's come as a shock, that's all. When are you going?"

"As soon as I have the fare, Max." She produced a letter from her inside pocket of her black denim. I read the contents as I tasted the soup. The soup was ace as I reached for the garlic bread, and the lasagne was second to none Tracy.

After the meal we walked up the promenade, taking in the sea breeze as we made our way back to the B and B. "I have something else to tell you—now will be a good time," Tracy said. We stopped walking and looked at the distant lights out at sea.

"What is it, angel?" I said, putting my arm around her waist and pulling her tight to keep warm.

"Do you love me, Max?"

"Why of course, babe, doesn't it show?"

"That's just it, Max—it shows, and I'm gonna . . ." She went quiet.

I turned her to me and stared into her face. "I love you." She took my hand and led me away back up the Promenade. We reached the hotel and trundled through the maze of stairs in the hotel, entering our room.

"Just hold me, Max," she said, pulling me onto her.

I woke still half dressed, and sweat was running off me. Tracy was rubbing her finger along the scar over my eyebrow. "You need to get off it." Tracy pulled at my arms to wake me further. "Max, you'll kill yourself if you carry on."

"Life is short, honey."

"Wanna know why I quit it, Max?" She left the bed and stood at the window.

"It's because you have your dream," I replied. "You needed to. I'm always in contact with it; I know I should cut down."

Tracy turned to me. "My dream, did you say, Max?" I went quiet, and she came back to the bed and knelt over me, taking my right hand. "Feel, Max. Feel what you did—can't you see?" She had my hand pressed into her stomach. The thought then hit me as I gulped. "I'm also giving life to dreams—there are two little dreams in there, Max." She rushed off the bed and showed me a picture that she pulled from her jacket—a funnelled scan. "Look, Max, look."

I was in deep shock. "Eh?" I looked at the picture. "Why, that's . . ."

She put her hand over my mouth. "It was me that sent it you—the text 'Submarine'. They're just over a month, Max. I've been assured it's gonna be twins."

I grabbed her off the bed, squeezing her and spinning her around. I was numb and felt elated. "But I can't go to Australia," I said after I calmed down.

"I'm not asking you to, Max."

"But hang on . . ." I reached into my jeans. "I want you to take this." I put the roll of money I had saved in her hand.

She opened it out and spread the notes over the sheets. "Max there must be—Oh, Max!" She grabbed me and cuddled.

I held her shoulders, staring into her eyes. "I want you to book the ticket and live your dream. You must take this—it's the least I can do, angel." She looked so happy. "This is how I want to remember you."

"Max I'll just take out the fare; take the rest back."

I put my hand over it. "It's dead money. I have a cash float in the bank. Loose change, babe. Here. I have a picture in my mind that is priceless."

On Wednesday morning we woke early and drove back to Mansfield. "Spend the day with me, Max. You're not at work."

"You can spend some of that dollar if you like. I wanna hand pick a new get-up for your flight out. And I don't want you skimping on the ticket; I'm sending you first class." We went around the shops and spent most of the afternoon at the travel agents. She had a first class ticket to Sidney, and she was alive.

"All this in a day," she said, looking at her bags in the back seat. We were parked at the top of the street. "You'll be at the airport, Max—I insist you see me away."

"I will be at work, angel; it's Friday morning," I said as I took her hands. "I can't be there. And I don't want you to tell who helped you."

"My lips are sealed, Max. So this is it, then." She opened the door and ran from the car. I undid my seat belt and bolted after her, catching her a yard from the gate. I turned her, and she was in a state as her tears smudged her mascara. "Max . . ." She buried her head into my chest.

"Shh, I'll see you again," I said, calming her. "Let's go back and get yer shopping. Come on, babe." I took her back to the car.

"I wanna get you a proper drink, Max." Bev said. She and Alex stood at the bar as I honed in on them.

"What's the occasion?" I asked.

"You know damn well, Max," Bev said firmly. "What will it be?"

"If I have one here, I can't have one in the city."

"Leave the car tonight; we'll sort everything," Alex butted in.

Daz appeared behind me, demanding the keys. I felt in my pocket and smiled at the three days' pay I'd received from Donk. It was a comfort somehow, knowing I wasn't going to spend a penny that night.

"They heard you pray for her," Bev whispered, and she disappeared into the din, leaving me and Alex and Daz to our own devices.

She'd left Alex clutching a small roll of money. "It's all gotta go tonight," Alex said.

I looked at it. "Hey, where did ya get that?" I asked.

"Bev said I'm to see you get a good night out and left me with this. Must be about fifty quid. I seen her draw it out of the hole in the wall."

Daz was suspicious. "Hey, are you sure?"

"Honest," Alex said, still clutching the small wad of notes.

I could hear the ping, the echo of a submarine in my head as the two of them stood in the middle of the Tap arguing. "Right, Alex, who has Bev come down with?" I butted in.

"Just me—she's off to meet some friends."

I stopped him. "You mean she ain't down with her sister, then? What, are you sure?"

"Max, she'll be lucky."

"Why?"

"Tracy phoned Bev from Sidney about two hours ago—something about her starting her degree."

"You've gone pale, Max, had a hard day's graft," Daz intervened.

I saw a gap in the corner and went to sit down. Daz and Alex followed. "Right, gimme a tenner outta that, Alex, and I'll get 'em in," Daz said.

"Better make mine a double Jack and Diet Coke, plenty ice," I said. "No, make that a triple."

Alex and Daz stood leering at me like a couple of key stoned cops with long hair. "I'll need more than a ten spot," Daz said, reaching out and swapping Alex a tenner for a twenty-pound note.

Later I was being dragged off the dance floor by Dave and Russ. "Come on, Max, that's enough," they said as they sat me down. The spew slashed through my fingers all over the pair of them. The rushed-down McDonald's became evident. I was looking around for something to jab in a wall to stop the room spinning.

I woke as Alex and Bev were pulling at my arms. "Let's get you cleaned up," Daz said, and as he pulled me up I noticed the brightness of the place.

"Argh." The lights were on, and security was looking at me, concerned.

"Hey, Max, come on. I ain't never seen him like this." The guards gave Daz and Alex a hand to carry me over as the familiar city aroma hit me like a dose of sniffing salts. Bev and Alex had the top half of me stripped as they took the night's remnants off in the sink. Then up it came again.

I woke next morning on the settee. Daz was just getting out the shower. "Argh, my head."

"Coffee's on, Max. Clean towel there when you're ready, and a clean T-shirt." He threw the two at me.

I looked at the clock as I rose: 8.30. Still holding my head, I moped to the bathroom and turned on the shower. I was still feeling groggy. I slipped off my jeans and underwear and showered, washing away the remnants of everything—the scents of a wild evening on the town. The flash backs took me back out the shower as I dried myself down.

I took my jeans, and Daz said, "Oh, what a state. Give 'em here. Try these instead—they're a pair of Alex's." Daz handed me a pair of black combat trousers.

"Eh, they'll do," I said, pulling them on." And don't wash my wages." He disappeared into the kitchen. The smell of eggs and bacon got the juices flowing back into the fur carpet that seemed to have lined my mouth. I realized I didn't have a toothbrush.

"What's that you've been trying to scrawl, Max? You left yer phone on the table."

"Hey, that's my diary," I said as I sat down, slipping on my T-shirt. "It needs a charge." I checked through the scroll. "Hup, I gotta get my car."

"You'll need a taxi down, Max. Get yer breakfast first." Daz stepped through with the coffee and my wages and a few other items from my pockets, adding my car keys. "Oh, and by the way, whatever that was you were in last night crashed." I'd heard this said before by other people. As he sat down the eggs and bacon, he said, "One of your nightmares again, Max."

I went quiet for a minute, trying to recollect, but I just couldn't. "Right, give me a taxi number," I mumbled as I got stuck in the food, taking a gulp at the coffee.

"I thought you was gonna shake yer head off last night." Daz smiled, and could see I'd been rubbing at my neck.

"It wasn't that bad, was it?" I asked.

"Let's just say you had a good night, Max. Here, ring that. I know you got some dosh."

"Hey, you can come with me," I replied whilst mopping up the remnants of the egg yolk with the last bit of bacon.

The taxi pulled away as I pulled out the small wedge and examined it. Daz commented, "That's gone down a bit." Damn, he had noticed.

"Erm, it's safe."

"Safe, is it?" He looked up.

"Right." I stepped towards the car. "I don't believe it—it's fired up first crack. The XR3 purred like a cat as Daz got into it. I cleared the screen with the wipers and noticed a piece of paper. I jumped out and collected it.

"What does it say?" Daz asked, looking curious.

"Nothing, just a ticket," I said, throwing it inside. "Right, up to mine, Sunny Donny; it's a new gaff." Daz sat all the way back, teasing me about my hangover as we entered the street. "Wait until you see this," I said as we entered the house.

The remnants of Bruce's party were all crashed everywhere. Bruce was just stirring as Daz waded through the empty beer cans and followed me through to the kitchen.

"What the—" Max was up at the window. I walked back in to the living room Two lasses around seventeen were draped all over each other, still asleep on the settee. Dave sat with a lass who was a bit bony in the other chair, and Bruce was curled up at the bottom of the two on the settee. Bruce rubbed his head, his eyes just flickering.

"Coffee, anyone?" I said. Daz was still in the kitchen, staring out at Max as I walked back in, closing the door. I checked the tins; someone had fed him last night. I slipped through the door and out into the back, retrieving his bowl and locking him on a short chain. I beckoned to Daz. "Just let him get used to you," I said as Daz appeared. Max started yapping at the end of the chain, up on his hind legs. I went behind him and stroked down his ears." Shush, Max, it's okay.

Daz would not come any closer. "Friggin' hell, Max frightened me to death. You coulda warned me."

Max dropped to his feet, reducing his bark to a whine. He sat still wagging his tail as one of the young lasses appeared. "Kettle's boiled," she mumbled. Max retreated into his kennel and laid down.

I took up his bowl as Daz was still shook up, looking at Max. "I see he's named after you," he said, following me into the kitchen. I was still grinning, looking through at everyone tidying up.

Donk soon arrived with Nig and Dink. "It's my landlord," Bruce said, rushing with a black bin liner as they all filled the front room. I took the coffee that Daz made and beckoned him out the back door. I could hear Donk shouting at Bruce. "And that music better not have been on all night. I don't want anymore complaints from the neighbours."

I was still trying to nurse a hangover as I took the shovel and cleared up Max's bit in the yard. I took up the hosepipe as Daz walked down the edge of the wall, looking up at the glass. "Shards; I bet they look pretty at night," he commented, looking again at Max.

Donk stepped out into the yard. "Hey, Max, that's you that brought it."

"What?" I said.

"Indian summer." Daz cracked out, laughing as I introduced Donk to Daz. "I'm telling ya, Max, since you turned up, there ain't been a bad day."

A couple of weeks went by after I started for Mr Jenkins. Runs out to the Dales were frequent, and I was beginning to settle in to a well-paid job. I had plenty of cash but no new information; they disappeared with no trace. I needed to backtrack to Chuckwalla just to check a few things.

I needed a plan. Bruce and I had our heads together. "I've got it—yep, it will work," Bruce said. "We need a driver, Max. You'll get fuel expenses and twenty-six pounds for about four hours of work."

I said, "Hey, what if we were to flog roses in Chuckwalla, to see if we can locate any dud notes?" Daz had left me with one, and I placed it on the table. "Hey, that's a mighty fine specimen. We can check all areas and compare on a graph the distribution tactics. It'll show, trust me, and we'll get to have a bit of fun on the way."

Bruce rubbed his hands together. "I like it, Max, I like it."

I came in from work shattered and sat down. Bruce was straight in with his usual chips steaming in front of me. He always offered, bless him. No matter how hungry I was, I always turned him down, knowing it was his tea. "It's on for tonight, Max. We pick her up at 9.00, and then we'll be out till whenever."

"We'll take the Granada," I commented.

Bruce nodded. "She'll clock down the mileage, Max—you'll be quids in. It's okay, Max, I already briefed her; she's experienced." Bruce and I had had our ups and downs, and I knew he was beginning to read me. "What's wrong, Max?"

"Nothing, it's the perfect plan; we'll find out."

"Nah, Max, what's wrong?" he asked as the women jumped in through the back door's.

"I don't want her using her real name," I said, looking at her name tag.

"It's been fixed," Bruce reminded me.

I headed on over towards Mansfield. She had two children to support, and she showed the photos. "It's okay, Max," Bruce said, "we'll be in Chuckwalla for the last half hour; she'll be in and out because these are all in a line. She only stays in busy pubs."

We timed it just right; her bucket was empty, minus one rose that she gave to me as she left the car. "Hey, ya did all right outta that, Max," Bruce said, laughing.

Two faked twenty-pound notes had been discovered in two different night clubs; I handed over the graph I had drawn up. "Right, she'll need to take those and hand them in," I said as I marked from which clubs they came. "Yes, that's two different locations."

Bruce nodded and got out the car. "I'll see you back at the house." He came back later with forty-six pounds sterling. "The hotels and clubs you took us in, Max. Nice one." He paid me my dues at two in the morning, and I made for my bed.

Beep, beep. I reached for my phone. It was 7.00, and I looked out the back; it was still dusk as I slipped on my work clothes and slipped them on, trundling downstairs to wash and brush up. I sat on the back step waiting for the kettle to boil. Old Max had his head up and alert, looking out from his kennel as I stepped out to take the morning air. I wandered over and took the chain off him to let him run while I returned into the house, making my sandwiches, preparing his breakfast, and downing a quick round of toast and coffee. Then I took up his choker chain and placed it around his neck before rallying him through the back gate and walking him down the back alleys.

This particular morning a youth I'd seen about the area walked past in a dark hooded top, and he held up his arms, trying to keep them away from the dog. Max had started yapping at him and near clean had him down by the throat just as I gained control, snatching him back from the youth. Max was still snarling and growling at him, and I had all on, holding him away from the point where there would have been no return. The youth ran away up another alley, and Max calmed down. "I can't let you have him; he'll get you put down," I said to him as he whined. stroked his ears and patted his side. "Walk on, Max," I commanded him, and sure enough he was right as rain all the way around the block. Other people passed him without any bother as I took him back and watered and fed him, putting him back on the chain. "I hate putting you on here," I said to him, stroking his ears.

Before I left for work, I stopped the car halfway down the street from the house where I knew this youth lived. There was no answer as I battered the door. I shouted in the letter box, "Anyone home?"

A woman in her fifties with rollers set in her hair and a pink house coat with slippers to match stood in full view when the latches came off and she opened the door. I inquired about the youth. "Oh, you mean my grandson. He doesn't live here."

"Well, the dog I look after seems to have some grievance with him. Can you give him the message that I would like apologise for not slipping the dog on him?"

"What do you mean?" She frowned looking startled.

"Look, missus," I said as I pointed into her house. "If I find that he was responsible for those stitches in Max's head, the dog I look after, then there will be more than me banging at yer door." I left it at that.

Later that morning I was on the phone to Donk. "I'm certain it's him, Donk. The dog wouldn't have done that to anyone else. Yep yep. I'll wait on then after work." I hung up.

The events that took place later that evening resulted in a baseball bat being used on the youth's right leg and ribs after the truth had been extracted from the youth; he was caught when we gave chase to him in the back alleyways. The youth was thin in build, white, and 5'10" with gaunt features. He had been threatened to within an inch of his life before he proceeded to tell us the damage to the dog's head occurred after he'd climbed onto the roof, removing slates to get into the property. He had thrown several removed slates at the dog in an attempt to shut the dog up and force him back into his kennel. I'd used the miniature recorder I'd taken from Diana. I played the recording back to the youth just before I set about him with the trusty bat. We left him rolling about, grunting and twitching in pain on the cobbles. I'd bent down, grabbing at the front of his top, and I reminded the youth if this matter went any further, the tape would go to the police.

The next morning at 6.30 I rose and looked out the back window. I smiled at Max, who was off his chain and scratching his ass up against the wall. It was a sight I'd only suspected, because an unusual amount of fur was being washed away with the hose pipe. He must have been on a moult. I reached for my clothes. Max had his usual walk, although slightly earlier than usual. One never know who one might bump into that time in the morning. I chuckled as I walked into the newsagents for the morning paper and a pint of milk. Max never bothered anyone as he sat outside whilst I went in to get served. He was steady all the way home, except for the odd cat who distracted him. At least my mind was at rest on the Max issue. An eye for an eye; that particular target had faded with the sun light.

I got to work. Mr Jenkins was doing all he could to keep up with other targets on the agenda. Occasionally an ex army would labour to me with no fuss or worry; if I turned my hand to it he was there. He knew the score and was fully briefed. This was a guy whose name I couldn't mention; official secrets acts would not permit me to. He could work silently, and I would communicate with him at work using field signals, although they were a little more advanced.

"We were at a blank, and they mizzed," he said in his message. "We never got close enough to put trackers on him; his women are secluded," he commented later in the van.

"Right, hold it there. You said women?" My ears pricked up.

"It's high-class clubs and casinos, where he meets them," he replied. Wanna porkpie?"

I smiled and took one from him. "Give me some details."

The ex army labourer had followed the targets to addresses where the two Asian males had used taxis for transport. "They haven't been seen for two weeks now. We've lost them."

Liz was pacing about like a banty hen as I slowly drove down her street. "And what time do ya call this?" she scolded as she entered the car. "I've been in and out of the house fer over half an hour."

"It's the bloody traffic in town, and I was held up on the motorway."

She picked up her bag and fidgeted. "Max I wanna play pool."

"Hey, I got an idea. Can you remember that stunt we pulled in the plough?"

Liz dropped her bag back into the footwell and started to grin. "Well the illuminations, are on in Matlock. Fancy a . . ." Her hand went straight over to my leg as she squeezed. "I just gotta text." She pulled out her phone.

I was already making for the M1.As sat playing with her phone and going through the glove box. She was talking about her favourite tunes and giving the latest on how she was going to go live with her ma down south. "Would you take me down, Max?"

"Erm, what, tonight?"

"No, but would you soon, though?"

"Anything, doll, but it's a bit soon.""Whatever do you mean?"

"Erm, drastic, all of a sudden."

Liz put down her phone. "I'll stay in touch, Max."

Now I knew she was serious. "Right, I think we'll go a different pub tonight, one further up."

The sky was set in peach and gold with hints of pinks, crowned with a mid blue. It was the backdrop as we entered the main drag into Matlock, and we were stunned by it. I had never seen a sunset like that, and I supposed I never would again.

Liz commented, "Sheesh, I'm thirsty." I found a space in front of the pub I wanted. I spotted someone that came out of the car park as I pulled in.

We entered into the bar, and the music was just so you could hear the conversation. The pool table was set to the right with a square of padded seats surrounding it. Liz was studying the setup and the layout of the table as she stepped over to me whilst I was just about to get served. "I see what you mean, Max. Yes, it will do. Mine's a vodka and Coke, plenty of lemon and ice."

"Sure, doll." I turned back to attract the attention of the barmaid. "Quick get that table," I said, Pointing, and Liz clicked her way over in her high heels, dropping her bag on the table top, taking off her jacket, and laying it on the shelf behind the seats. I could see the locals checking her ass in her French black trousers when she walked over—and even more so when she slipped off her jacket. The top she had on would have fooled the judge in a murder case.

I wandered back with her vodka and Coke and my usual shandy. All who were watching her stuck there necks back in. I slipped a coin on the pool table, giving the odd hello to faces I recognized. Liz was hitting it off with a bird at the side of her with similar interests, and I got chatting across the table to some mofo who was set at the table on the other side. Old Brit bikes was an issue with him, and I was picking his brains on old Arial Square Fours. A younger couple sat to the other side in summer casuals.

Our turn came for the pool table. I was having a bad game as I sat back down. I whispered to Liz, "The Seven Stars."

She slipped her arm around me after the black was sunk, resting her head on my shoulder. "Yes, Max, let's go. I'm hungry."

"You've time fer a few games yet, doll."

"You're on." Three games later, and she was still on.

"Right, my turn," I said as I put in my money, and it wasn't long before we were down to the black.

"Ha, yes, I win, Max," she said after she cleanly sunk the black. She had the respot position and two shots after I'd had my shot where the bloody white ball had ended up in the top left hand corner after a spectacular, "just belt it anywhere" shot.

"Oh, why did I have to hit it so hard?" I said after drinking the last of my shandy.

She was swilling the ice of her third vodka and Coke, clearly buzzing. "Hand it over," she said as she held out her hand.

I produced a tenner, holding it up in front of her. She swiped it from my fingers quicker than a polecat let loose in rabbit hole. "Easy come, easy go," I commented.

The stars had that tranquillity about them as we arrived at the Seven Stars Inn. We had driven through patchy mist on the way there. Just as Liz stepped out of the car, a tawny owl broke from the tree line and swept by her. Her face looked delighted at how it glided and swept down before her, its talons reaching out before changing direction. "Ooh, that was outta sight!" She marvelled at the night sky to where it rose and flew over a hedge. She started spinning around, looking up whilst walking through the car park to the main entrance.

"Hi, Ethel," I said as we approached the bar. I recommended the Irish coffee to Liz.

Ethel told us to take a seat, and Liz made a point of sitting where we'd sat before. Ethel came down soon after we were seated with two Irish coffees. "It has turned a bit towards Autumn," she commented, putting the coffees down at our table. "Will you be staying?"

Liz squeezed at my leg under the table. "Erm, yes, Ethel," I said.

"Same room then, Max. Will you require anything else from the menu?"

Liz squeezed me again. "Yes, Ethel."

"I'll give you a few minutes." She smiled, turning to put a few logs on an already well-lit fire before she disappeared through to the bar.

"What's that over there, Max?" Liz asked as she took up the menu.

"Looks like part of a yolk between oxen."

"Oh, Max, please let us get the stuffed mushrooms again."

"Sure, doll." I pointed out the garlic potato wedges to go with the dips. "Hey, and look at the cheeses." I pointed those out to her. "The soft Brie would be nice with the garlic bread."

Ethel came back down, and Liz was nudging me and pointing at the homemade apple pie and ice cream. "The works, then," Ethel said, smiling as she retired. The home cooking started to arrive on the table along with two more Irish coffees and the room keys. "Will that be all, Max?"

"Fer now," I reassured her as she rushed off to a group of what looked to be a walking party came in.

We sat and ate and compared and examined; we mixed and matched, and the flavours where mind blowing. Just then an older member of the group took his guitar from its case. I nudged Liz and said, "Shh, listen." A marvellous selection of chords filled the atmosphere as the man got up and retuned, taking a drink and nodding in our direction. Liz slipped her arm under my arm as she reached in to the feast. Then the clatter of spoons constantly tapped out a rhythm by one of the others sitting over in the corner. Liz sat observing how he moved them up his arm as the classical guitar kick in. A lassie who had taken of her Burghause was keeping time as her foot tapped out a beat, and then she sang in folk music. They played like that for three or four songs that where indeed folk and country and recognizable to sing along to—and we did.

The musicians welcomed a round of drinks of their choice after I'd offered. I went to the bar and told Ethel to stick it on my tab, and Ethel winked. "It's okay, Max, honest. I'll give them that on the house." She went to serve another customer.

I returned from the bar with two coffees. "No whiskey in that one," I said as I sat next to Liz. She could see me hinting at her in a nice way. The apple pie and ice cream was absolutely amazing. Liz was trying to keep the downstairs thing going. But I said, "Come on, doll, let's go through." She took a sip at her coffee. The cream was over her top lip, and she'd been licking it off since we came in. I chuckled.

The official last orders bell rang out at the bar. Liz started gathering things up like it was the whistle to go over the top, placing her items back in her bag as she drank the last of her coffee. "Right, I'm ready," she said, squeezing at my leg again. Ethel walked through and cleared the mass of dishes.

We walked up through the bar and through into the corridor and through to the door, I opened the lock, and both of us entered the room. "Ah, it's just how it was," I commented as Liz ran in and jumped on the bed. I went over to the window and looked out. A mist had gathered in the lower parts and looked like a scene from some astral plain; the tops of hills stuck out from the clouds of mist, and the sky was crystal clear. A new freshness was in the breeze, and as I opened up the Yorkshire light, laying my keys on the natural stone sill.

"Leave the curtains open, Max," Liz said as she came over to look out. "Wow, look—the starts are like diamonds. You can make out some of the major constellations, and there is Venus, and over to right that's the Big Bear."

I dipped my eyebrow and craned my neck to the side, trying to give the sky a serious look, and she kicked my shin and then jumped back onto the bed. I was left rubbing my leg as the black top she had on distracted me, and she noticed. She giggled as her arms opened wide to welcome me.

It was a job I'd been out to before—a conservatory that we'd already built and that I'd tested out. It was a traditional box pointing, the job required was finished, and the customer was happy with the effect. I never did see the customer because things were very much left to the assistance of a house cleaner, who would open up the property for us. I sat outside the job eating a pasty and supping away at my Diet Coke, feeling an easy day coming on. It was day rate as I studied the work sheet. I could cope with that, and I put down the phone; Mr Jenkins had just wanted to make sure I was at the job.

"Yes, ahh, hmm, yes—oh! Yes, you—oh!" And don't ever do that to me again, I swear! Down now, Diana." I returned back to the table and gathered up my jeans. Diana rolled off the table and onto the chair, exhausted, as we looked around at the mess we'd made. "I'll, erm—hang on, I'll give ya a hand."

"Max, we've wrecked the kitchen," Diana said, laughing. She bent down and stuck one of the cooking pans on her head. "Exterminate. Exterminate." I couldn't stop laughing as I went and sat in her lap.

"It's only broken crockery and a few corn flakes. Gotta brush." I sat squeezing into her breast.

"Mmm, Max."

"Don't worry, doll, I'll be booting the arse outta this job. What's the rest of the house like then?" What a surprise—she'd been here all the time. I managed to tear myself away from her and get some of the pointing up on this particular panel done. She spent most the day feeding me a variety of cold drinks. Diana had been telling me about Manchester and some of the fine places she'd visited, including the Hockney Gallery over at Saltford.

"I've been there," I said. "Joiner photographs. Hey, that's given me an idea. I'd better phone Donk, tell him I might be late home." Then I remembered the dog and changed my mind, explaining to Diana about him. "I gotta get back, angel. Is it okay if I come back? I'll need to go back to the house and walk him; the other two tenants I live with won't go near him."

She was sympathetic. "That poor dog," she said." Everybody's so frightened of him."

"Any more news on them dud notes, Bruce?"

"Yeah, Max. Three pubs in Mansfield this time."

"Nice work. Did ya mark them in for me? Can you see the spread yet on the graph?"

Bruce produced it as I pointed the out the areas where the phoney money had been located. He was looking and trying to make his tea at the same time. "Will you be out tonight with us tonight. Max?"

"Hey, yeah, that's a good idea. Some clubs in town I wanna check." I went into the living room as Dave walked in and sat down.

"House to you," Bruce commented. "I'm bringing her back, so don't be sat up all night."

Dave shouted back, "I'm going out."

"Right, I'm just taking Max out," I said, and I grabbed his lead. It was hard work holding him back as his strength built. "Easy, Max." We came back through the gate. "I'd better put you on tonight." I linked his chain on the longest setting. Then I took up the shovel and swilled down with the hose pipe.

Bruce was sitting in the front whilst Dave spent the last hour in the bathroom. "Any longer and I'm sending the dog in," I said as I banged on the bathroom door.

"Hang on, Max, nearly done," Dave replied.

"And I hope all the hot water ain't used up." Bruce was rising to bathroom door, listening at it. He stood with his plates and an empty mug just as I slipped out with Max's tea, taking the brush off the kennel roof to brush him while he ate his evening meal. "Bruce, is he out of that shower yet?"

"He's just bolted upstairs, Max."

"Right, that's my turn." I rushed to get a change of underwear and wash kit and towel. The bleeding water was freezing by the time I got in. "Ooo! It's a good job it's been a warm day," I shouted out, pulling back the shower curtain.

"Max, it's 8.30; you've got half an hour," Bruce yelled.

"Right, not a problem." I was upstairs deciding which shirt to wear, picking the white one.

"Hey who put Stakis on the list?" I said, looking at a root familiar to one I had already shown him a week or so ago.

"We have clearance, Max; they can't stop us entering now." We'd stopped at a late night store and got our munchies for the evening. I'd also bought a fun camera. Bruce's girlfriend was out tonight doing a good trade, selling a good deal of roses for charity. She had two notes in there, showing them to me as I marked on my A to Z.

"Christ they're passing them in Stakis," I said again as the flower girl came back out. "These are the same source. What do you know about gambling, Bruce? Well, if we do this now, we will get away with it. We can't leave it any longer.""Bruce looked confused. "Ha. Keep watching, Bruce, keep watching. There's the camera; I'll go in and put my arm around her, and you take the picture but make out you didn't get it, so take a few more. I wanna see what we get of who is in there. Then we'll change positions and take some of you. I need as many shots as we can muster up; we need to cover the whole place in every room."

After awhile we came out smiling. "Well, that was easy," I said.

Yes, her light was still on. It was three in the morning, and Diana had come to the window as I pulled up. I'd been keeping her up to date with Liz. "I think she misses you already," Diana said as she sat in her silk pyjamas, flicking through the TV channels. "She told me last night it's twins." She dropped the remote and turned to me and frowned. "Liz won't be able cope. She agreed to a taker."

"Yes, I know. Better let Liz decide nearer the time," I remarked. "You did say you would adopt."

Diana got up and sat next to me. "Shh, go to sleep, Max." She stroked my forehead. "I want you up early in the morning."

Mr Jenkins was on the phone the next morning. "Customer is happy, Max. Carry on with that; if you need to book in overtime, I'll cover it. I just landed two more contracts through that same job, so don't leave it because we need to go back. I want it left spotless."

I couldn't stop sniggering as I put down the phone. Diana had the coffees ready. "Have you been throwing out sweeteners to my boss?" I asked her.

"He is helping, Max, when all is said and done. Fancy kinky tonight?" She took the camera off the table.

"It's to take some photos of the new conservatory, although I do need a model." I winked at her. *Click.* I turned the camera and took a sneaky one.

"Hey, don't, babe. My hair's all over," she said, laughing as I reached for the door.

I prepared my first mix, careful to get the mortar colour just right for the next panel. "Ooo, Max, that's another good one." She sneaked up behind me and took a photo. I swiped the camera from her, grabbing her around the waist, sweeping her up, and taking her through into the new conservatory.

"Come on, then, let's do some pictures."

Soon Diana had her clothes off and was looking professional as she posed naturally on the new furniture. She ripped at the cellophane and wrapped it around her. "Yeah," I kept saying, "more." She was driving me crazy with it.

When I'd taken the last shot, she said, "You'd better finish what you started, Max. You can't leave me like this!" I put the camera down and took hold of her.

"Ever been to a casino?" I asked Diana after she had brought out some sandwiches and laid out a table on the lawn. I stopped work and joined her. "Mmm, these are ace," I said after the first mouthful of the BLT, tasting the fresh herbs and garlic in the mayonnaise.

"Casinos, Max? That ain't your style."

"That's why I'm asking, angel. You see that camera on there?" Diana looked and smiled. "It holds the key."

"Tell me more, Max." She dropped her shades over her eyes.

"It's what we took last night, at Stakis. Two notes that we recorded coming from there." I found myself telling her about the rose selling tactics. "It's live—they're at it."

Diana jumped up grabbing my wrists. "You mean . . . ?" She got up and picked up the camera.

"I want you to take it fer express processing."

It wasn't long before Diana was back out the house, changed and ready to go into town. She clicked her way over to her car, wearing a large-print, pastel-coloured summer dress, with her hair slicked back in a ponytail. "Are sure you'll be fine until I get home?" she asked.

"I'll have this side finished when you get back, doll."

"I'll bring something nice back for an evening meal," she said as she drove away.

Later I heard her car door slam as she came up the drive with shopping bags. I was just brushing down my handiwork as she arrived around the corner. I walked over to her and kissed her on the cheek, taking the bags from her as she fumbled in her handbag to put her car keys away. "My, you've been busy," she said.

I looked in the bags, setting them down on the kitchen table. "You did all this in one afternoon?" Diana had bought a long black evening dress, and I pulled its slinky material out its wrapping.

Diana smacked the back of my hand. "Dirty paws, Max." She grinned as I put the garment down, and she opened another bag and pulled out a white evening jacket. "This is for you." She held it up to me as she checked my size, and then she took another bag and showed me trousers and a shirt to match. After that she slapped a photo packet on the table as she sat down, taking of her stilettos and rubbing at her feet.

I went to the sink, flicking on the kettle and washing the dried sand and cement away from my hands. I was impressed she didn't miss a trick; as I poured the boiled water into the percolator, she had the photos spread. "This one here," she said, picking out one took in Stakis.

I walked over and looked at the ones I took of her. "Hey, these are better. I captured it—look."

She blushed; it was one with the cellophane wrapped around her. She grabbed it from my hand. "Be serious a sec, Max." She gathered up the photos, leaving the one taken in Stakis. You know who this is, don't you?" I nodded. "And him."

I nodded again and took from my pocket a hundred pounds in cash, showing it to her. "Now we know who is selling them. I already made a call."

She put down the photo. "Did they see you, Max?"

"I don't think they even suspected. Why?"

"What's this—to buy chips?" She was looking at the money. "These are real?"

"Of course they're real—I earned them." We laughed.

"What are you thinking, Max?"

"Well, those two work fer Liz's stepdad. I've got a plan," I said, staring straight into her eyes. "It's like I said, I made a call."

I'd been home and seen to Max, who'd really been shaping up. I was explaining it all to Bruce as I got into the Granada. "It will work." I had an hour and a half to get to Chuckwalla.

Jamie and Nogg stood where they said they'd be and jumped in the car. "Fiver each, Max. We gotta pick them up; they ain't here."

"You tell your folks about this, Jamie, and I'll kick you up like a chipmunk," I said.

Nogg cracked up laughing and finally asked, "Right, where are we heading?"

"Outskirts of Carlton," I said, and Nogg led the way. 'That's four hundred notes on the clean hundred." Nogg and Jamie disappeared, suspecting I was up to something.

The next evening Diana spent a lot of time getting us ready. She'd had me washed and groomed and looking like something out of a cartel. Diana appeared at the door with her hair tied up. Her dress was a smash hit from where I stood, and I could smell the Chanel perfume. "Any more film?" I asked. We stepped into the night air, and I noticed the leaves beginning to drop as the sweet smell of autumn mixed with her perfume.

"We'll park on the edge of town and take a taxi in to the city. We'll take my car," she said. We slid into her TR7 and did exactly that. On the way down, Diana had marked each of the four-hundred notes with an invisible marker. "Now it's all set." We changed them for chips on the way in, and the evening progressed. "Max, that's three times. How much are we up to?" she asked, having a ball. We'd came up trumps on the roulette wheel and moved on to the card table. "Yes! Max, we win again!" Diana had her hands on her cheeks as the card went in our favour. We were causing a stir with people congratulating us. "Right, let's get out of here," she whispered.

"Crikey, we made all that?" A total of 3500 lay in cash on her coffee table.

"I took five hundred away and said, "The rest is fer you and Liz," pushing the rest over to her side.

"I'm making the call, Max."

I stopped her. "No, it's too soon—trust me, there's more." Diana put down her phone. "If we keep it shut, that's our entrance in."

Diana squeezed my wrist. "It's too dodgy." She reached for her phone again.

"Okay, but it was your idea, remember?" I felt I had to remind her.

Diana put down her phone again. "Hmm." She put her head on my shoulder. "I really enjoyed tonight," she said as she topped off our glasses. "Got any weed, Max?"

"It's in the car." I rose to get it. I thought to myself, "Now that was some Friday night," as she led me upstairs for the first time.

I said, "We'll nip up the town first and call in the at the Moon. It's a bit early." Daz wasn't so sure, although when I said the round was on me, he was soon getting his jacket. "Car will be all right there," I said as we walked on up the town. People spilled out onto the front; the place was buzzing by the time we arrived. Liz's stepfather stood with the two bouncers looking over everyone. I caught his eye as Daz stood talking to Alex using my phone, and he beckoned me over.

"I just wanna shake your hand, Max. What will you have to drink?" Sheeks, he had a grip like a vice. "Where is it tonight, the City?"

"Sure is. Why, are you coming down?" The two bouncers started laughing.

He replied, "I hear you've been looking out for our Liz."

"I love her," I stated simply. The two bouncers cracked out again.

"Hey, give the man some respect," Liz's stepdad snapped, and the two gloaters shut up.

I stood straight-faced, staring them out before I spoke. "There's this fairy tale I gotta put right." I looked at Liz's stepdad.

"He doesn't pay for anything here," he instructed the two bouncers. "Make sure the bar staff knows."

I waved Daz over as Liz's stepdad disappeared into the pub. Daz and I stood at the bar as I saw one of the bouncers pulling in one of the barmaids. "Just ask fer me," she said as she came over. "Now, what are you having?"

"Sucking up to nonces now, are we, Max?" Daz said—quietly.

"That's just it, Daz, he ain't," Liz said.

"But I thought—"

"No, mate, he ain't." Liz stood the dock and lied.

I replied, "Where's my phone. Daz gave it back. "What did Alex say?"

"He's meeting us in the Tap and Tumbler, ten o'clock. Plenty of time, Max."

We caught the bus down and arrived in the Tap. Daz and I stood in our usual place near the bell fruit machines, as twenty coins dropped while I was playing the last of my change. "Your round again, Max," Daz said, taking the empty pint pots as Alex appeared.

He was rummaging in his jacket and produced a small boomerang. "Present from Bev," he said. I couldn't stop laughing. Alex said sharply, "I hear you've took to a big grizzly hound."

"Get one fer him," I said as I took the winnings out of the tray, counting ten coins into Daz's hand. "And get some crisps and nuts with the change. Hobbit can have the rest."

Liz had been on the dance floor most of the night. I was as drunk as a rat in a cider barrel by the time midnight came. I sat next to Diana, who had not long arrived. "I haven't told her yet," I said. Diana had on her Gothic look and was as beautiful as ever. So did Liz; they both looked wild in their costumes and painted white faces. "It'll be a surprise when she gets there."

Diana got up, remarking on how she had curbed her drinking, disappearing upstairs. Russ and Dave stood leaning on the railing talking to Daz and Alex, watching Bev and a few of her friends freaking out. Diana came back. "I'm taking you back tonight, Max," she said, looking at the state I was in. She bent down and reached out to help me up.

I had the full weight of Liz on my lap as we pulled up to where Diana was staying. Diana had already left the car as Liz got off my knee and dragged me out, helped by Diana. We were laughing and squealing as we fell about on the way over to her front door. Let's just say a few curtains were twitching.

These two where sober as we entered into the house, and Diana moved to take off the alarm as Liz helped me into the living room, dropping me on the settee. I could hear them in the kitchen laughing and joking as I spun off into oblivion.

On Sunday morning I woke up in between Diana and Liz. "What? Hey, did I . . . ?"

Diana had her eyes open first. She started to grin and half rose. "Shh, she's still asleep."

I looked at the time, 8.30, and then I realized I was naked. "How, when, who . . . ?" I was still confused.

Diana got out the bed and put on her house coat. I was scanning the room for my clothes. Oh, now I remembered. The flashback of two white faces and . . . Ohh. I heard Diana put on the shower in the bathroom. Liz turned and cuddled into the pillow as I slipped downstairs, finding my keys on the floor and loose change, picking up my jeans. The five-hundred-pound roll fell out. My head hurt as I bent down to pick it up. I slid on my pants and jeans and made fer the percolator.

Diana came through smelling like a spring breeze as she dried her hair. "Your turn, Max, when you're ready." She took over the coffee making process. "Oh, and Liz was sick all over your T-shirt. I had to put in the wash."

"Argh," was all I said as I wandered over and squeezed her waist on the way back through to the hall. The shower sobered me up, especially when Liz stuck her arm through the curtain and turned it on cold, smacking me on the ass and running off giggling. I woke up even more so when I switched the knob to red hot, trying to control it again.

On the way back down, Diana asked, "You're not working today, are you?" as the coffee aroma hit my nostrils, along with fresh toast. Diana sat at the table crunching away.

"Erm, just up till dinner, doll, then we'll go out somewhere fer lunch."

Diana slid a brown envelope across the table as I sat down. It had the firm's letterhead on the corner. "Mr Jenkins or someone from your firm called by with it. We must have just missed him last night."

I opened it. It was my wages, all 450 pounds sterling in cheque. "Hmm," I said as I crunched into a round of toast. "A week in hand as well—that's what I earned the first week."

"It was on the floor when we came in." Diana was still amused about last night, judging by her face.

Liz came into the kitchen and sat down. She was wearing a baggy white T-shirt and a pink towel wrapped around her head. Diana got up and poured her a coffee, laughing. "That was all over him, Liz. We'll need to go into town and by him one to wear."

I produced my roll from my pocket at her hint, peeling off a ton and laying it on the table in front a Liz. Liz was looking at my pay cheque, then the money. "Enough for a morning in town," I said as I smiled at the two of them, taking my coffee and entering the makings of a warm morning.

The day was a little cloudy but warm when the sun came out. I took my trowel from my tool bucket. There's a Sunday market I know . . ." I could hear the two of them in the kitchen as I studied my mix. I was well on my way to completing another perfect square when the two of them stepped out. Both had their hair ponytailed and were dolled to the nines.

"So this is what you do, Max." Liz was smiling just as I turned from the south panel. "We'll be back around 12.30.Is that okay, honey? There's fresh coffee in the kitchen if you want it." Diana unlocked her car, and the two of them slipped into it and drove off.

At a quarter to one, I had just brushed up when I heard the sound of two doors close in the drive. They were back, extracting shopping bags from the car and chatting about all the things they'd spotted on the market as they walked up into the house. "Hi, Max, had a good morning?" Diana winked, going into the kitchen door.

I followed them in and went to the sink.

"Stay there," Liz said, grinning. She was rooting in one of the bags from the market. "Yep, this will fit."

I looked at the T-shirt she had bought. It was a Miami Dolphins football shirt. "Yeah, I like it." I dried my hands and put it on.

Diana was back downstairs with a spliff. "Come on, Max, time to knock off. Hey, that looks fine on you." She passed the lit spliff to me.

Liz didn't smoke but didn't mind being around it. "Look at this," she said as she pulled out a pair of dungarees. "Ha ha ha, Andy Pandy, but in colour."

I took hold of them and held them up to Liz. Diana started to laugh. "Aw, they're cute—black, red, purple, and pink candy striped."

I covered my eyes as Liz stood clutching the bib under her chin, holding the rest on her hips. "Don't you like it, Max?"

"Yeah, doll—I'm just kidding." I still covered my eyes.

"Right, I know this place that serves up a good side of bull." There was a thump on my arm, and Liz frowned at me. "Hup, I forgot." I smiled at Liz. Diana was in the back flicking at her compact, trying not to laugh as I kept catching her eyes in the rear view. "I gotta call in and feed Max first, though; it's on the way."

My other two lodgers were out as we arrived outside the gaff. Diana seemed worried about the glass shards along the back wall, looking at Max. "Ooh, he's gorgeous, Max." The two stood looking as Max wagged his tail, quiet as a mouse.

"It's always with the females," I thought. Then I warned them, "Don't stroke him." But Diana was straight over to him, grasping his ears and cuddling him. I was left scratching my head. "Well, I never." Max was loving the attention. Liz also wandered over, stroking him.

I grabbed the shovel in case he got frisky, making an excuse to clean up his crap. I was jealous—he'd nicked my women. They'd have him tied up in ribbons and allsorts; he'd end up soft. I was beginning to wonder if I'd done the right thing, introducing them. "Right, ladies, ain't we got a dinner to get to?"

"Let's take him in the car, Max." Liz wouldn't let go of him.

"Well, I don't know."

"Oh, go on," she insisted. "You have a screen in the back."

"We'll try it, but any bother from him, and we come straight back with him."

To start with, Max wouldn't shut up; he'd yap at things that caught his eye—other dogs mainly. On the motorway he did settle down. Liz asked where I had in mind to go.

"Woolerton Park is the best place fer him. Then we'll get a bite to eat." Liz and Diana each took turns at holding him as we walked around the big lake. I sat with a bottle of water, pouring it into my hand while Max was licking at it. Max settled down as we pulled away. "He ain't asleep; he's just having a snooze. We'll walk him again later," I said.

"Where are we anyway?" Diana asked as the two of them looked out into the trees.

"The lodge. They do good food here."

"Hey, Max, this is fab," they said as we walked in through the gothic styled architecture. They marvelled at the heraldry and suits of armour, and we walked through to the dining area.

"I'm having the scampi chips and garlic bread, and all the trimmings," I said, putting down the menu. Both Diana and Liz settled for baked spuds, with green salad and mixed herbs and cream cheese laced with fresh pineapple, and a variety of dips that came with hot sliced pita bread. When it arrived it resulted in a series of hand slapping as I reached over to pick at their meals, and there were regular attacks on my tartar sauce too, in stereo. I had to make a peace offering because it was getting out of hand.

"I'll swap some garlic bread fer some of the pita and dip."

Liz couldn't stop laughing. "Now you're talking, Max."

Diana started moving the bowls up a bit closer. "Nah, garlic bread first." I slid that a bit closer as a heated exchange took place, resulting in one of us knocking over Liz's drink. "Whoops, waiter's on his way over—we'd better cool it." All three of us were reaching for the napkins, mopping it up. I was glad I had slid the garlic bread back—it would have been soaked through.

Diana ordered Liz another drink, and she looked at me with that "I'm about to crack" grin as her hand went up to her mouth. The waiter returned with another tall Coke for Liz. Diana turned away, looking out the window, and Liz sat with her hand up to her mouth with her eyes shut, chuckling away. I saw my chance and added all the pita bread and dips back down the table as Diana turned around. Liz dropped her hands and held her mouth open. "Hey, that's—" she started, and another free-for-all took place. Diana grabbed my half eaten basket of scampi and chips. I slid the dips back up the table.

"Aw, now come on." I stood up.

"Hmm, lovely, Max," she said as she popped one in her mouth. Diana was soon taking a drink, and I was sure I saw a puff of steam come out the side of her mouth when she bit into it, putting the basket back down. I grabbed back the basket. "That's bloody hot," she mumbled out. Liz was doubled over, laughing.

"Why do you think I ain't eaten them yet?" Are you okay?" I was making another grab for the dips, but she got me on the wrist this time as the flash of the spoon went past my eyes.

"Shh, people are looking at us," Diana said.

"Sod 'em," I said, rubbing my wrist. Liz was still laughing as Diana retrieved the dips. I gave up, concentrating on my scampi and chips, and what was left of the tartar sauce. "Right, I'd better check on Max."

The odd firework cracked over head, and I handed over the five-hundred roll to Nogg as we sat outside a Georgian type house in the posh end of Carlton. Nogg was soon back with a large brown envelope. I looked at him, amazed, and said, "Maybe a postcard from Costa Dorada or something," as he jumped in the passenger side.

"Eh, the thought crossed me mind," Nogg answered. We both burst out laughing as I pulled away.

Two thousand in counterfeit dollars lay on the coffee table. Diana was pacing about the place with the odd bouts of "Are you sure you weren't followed?" and "Hey, these are near enough perfect."

"Best get yer marker pen, doll. We'll try a different casino tonight and then a another one tomorrow night—or maybe even London."

"You are crazy if you think we'll get away with that." But she soon had on her coat as I gathered up the counterfeits.

Again we left the car at the edge a town and took a taxi. We couldn't believe it when they cashed for chips again, and we calmly walked through to games room.

"That's the last hundred on black. Fingers crossed, doll." We covered our eyes, listening for the ball to come to a rest.

"Black."

The bank paid as a pile of chips were pushed our way. "Right, honey, pick a number, and I'll pick the colour," she said.

I placed half the chips on red. We crossed our fingers as the ball went in to play. "Ha ha! We win again! That must be over six grand."

"Let's cash in," Diana said, tugging at me as I checked my watch. It was 12.40, and I could see she was anxious to leave. We sat in the reception area waiting on the taxi, which arrived to our relief.

"How many more days can you stretch the work at my house, Max?"

"A couple, doll. No rush, if you know what I mean."

A total of 6890 pounds sterling now lay on the coffee table. "Hey, that would buy me a descent Harley, doll. But I know you need it fer Liz." I took back another 500 sterling and slid the rest over the table. "Hmm, give me another 500, make it a thousand." Diana grinned and slid 500 off the top of the pile, handing it to me.

This time Nogg invited me in to the house. An arse wipe opened the door, inviting us through to the study. We sat while two of Liz's stepdad's associates put more in a loose term. "Still selling the green stuff, Max?" the one on the left asked.

"Why, want some?" I joked. "Do ya an ounce freeze packed and sealed fresh fer 120."

"Ha nice sales patter," he laughed. "Let him have it." His sidekick threw a package on the table.

"I make that four thousand," I said as I handed over the grand cash. "Are they as good as the last?"

"Maybe better."

Nogg butted in. "Come on, we got to pick our Gurt up on the way back. Best not to disappoint her. Don't mind me asking, Max, but that's six grand's worth you've had in two days. What you doing with it—wallpapering yer house with the stuff? Ha ha ha, that would be an idea."

Now four thousand in marked counterfeits laid on Diana's coffee table, and rolled a spliff, marvelling between the TV and the pile of cash. "Another casino," she said as she eased back with that look in her eye.

"What time is Liz due back?" I asked.

"She won't be here till tomorrow." She handed me the reefer.

"Wanna beer?" I asked as I got up to ransack the fridge of the alcohol that sat chilled and inviting. I thumbed about in the drawer for a bottle opener, remembering not to use my back teeth because they were starting to ache. "Night in then, doll; early start in the morning. I wonder if Max the dog's okay—I ain't been over to Donny's fer a few days. Fancy a ride out?"

Diana could see I wasn't going to settle until I checked on him. "I'll take you over in the TR, give you a rest".

At 8.30PM we arrived at the house. We walked in, and Bruce and Dave had their usual Bud cans and were watching TV. "Some mail there fer you, Max, looks official. It's on the window ledge," Bruce said whilst he turned his attentions back to the TV. I made a swipe for it and went back through the back, with Diana following. The backyard became flood lit as I stepped out. Max appeared from his kennel, and I was amazed—the yard was spotless, and I noticed freshly opened tins of dog food in the trash. Even his water bowl had been topped off. Max was brushing himself on me and whining.

"Shall we take him a walk, doll? Do you mind?"

"No, I don't mind." Diana took his lead from of the top of the kennel, handing it to me.

Later as we walked, I said, "Here, you have him a little while he ain't pulling so much." We stopped for a moment on the railway bridge as a train passed under. Max by now was walking at a steady pace and looked at ease. "I'll go in and get us a carry-out," I suggested as we came to the Chinese restaurant.

After taking Max back to the house, we ventured into the kitchen and placed the carry-out on the breakfast bar. Diana was looking through the cupboards for the plates, and I shouted to the gang, "Anyone hungry?"

"Yes, mate," came Bruce's reply.

"I'll take what comes," Dave chirped up.

Diana got the cartons out and pondered at what I bought. "King prawn with ginger, mixed veggies, boiled rice, bag of chips, and a large BBQ sauce.

Hmm, I like." She soon got the grub sorted onto plates. The smell of a spliff hit me as I took Dave's and Bruce's plates through. I returned with the half smoked reefer as Diana and I sat in the kitchen planning the next move.

"You're wanted on the phone, Max."

I rubbed at my eyes, disorientated. Was she kidding me or what? I looked at my watch: 8.00AM. Blimey, I had slept in. "Erm, who's that."

"You ain't been in to the yard fer two days, Max. And hey, has yer revenue card come through yet?"

"Everything's on the job, Mr Jenkins."

"When you gonna get that finished?"

"Couple of days, boss. A day to clean the job down."

"So we can say Friday then?"

"Yep, fine, sure will." I sniggered as I put the phone down. "He knows damn well it's only a pointing job." Diana slid toast and coffee over the table.

A few hours passed, and I'd just about got over two square metres done. "Doll, just what I need, more coffee," I remarked as she brought out coffee and biscuits.

"Very cleanly done," she commented, rewrapping herself with a scarf as the wind blew about her. I took the plate and coffee from her, and we sat down on an old garden bench, admiring the work.

"Be better when it's dry, of course." She jabbed me in the ribs causing me to spill my coffee over myself. I reached into my jacket and pulled out the mail I had retrieved from the house. She snatched it from me and ran up the garden with it. "Oh, doll, come on. I just wanna see what it is," I said as I made after her.

"Says Inland Revenue on the back," she teased.

"Hey," I said. "That's my—that's what Mr Jenkins was asking if I had yet!"

"You'd better open it, then," she said as she handed it back. I opened the letter, and sure enough, it was my 714 tax certificate. "What's all this, then?" she asked.

"It means I can subcontract, doll. You know, be paid the full amount fer the price of each job at hand, instead of 25 per cent removed from the price. So my next pay cheque will be 25 per cent better off. Let's see, that's nine per hour on a forty-eight-hour week, plus bonus, and one and day at double time should easily clear the five-hundred mark this week."

"Ha, you even got room service," she said with a smile.

That night at the casino, I said, "Bloody hell, it's brook bond." One of Liz's stepdad's cronies I'd seen earlier passed by as we made a break for the roulette wheel, Diana's favourite. "They're doing their dirty washing in the same place as us tonight. Hmm, that's the one in the photograph, isn't it, doll?" She squeezed my arm to acknowledge.

Diana wandered over to the foyer, and I sensed she was just about to call it in on her mobile phone. "An hour from now, this place will be crawling with cops," she whispered. I took the hint and remembered red, any number, placing all the chips over it. "Oh man, what?" she said in shock at my bet. The wheel slowed down and the room conversation dropped to a lull as I looked to see the results—red. A cheer went up. My number had come in.

"Right, let's mizz and cash in," I whispered to Diana as we raked up the chips.

"Sheeks, I never meant you to put the whole lot on, Max," she joked because she could see I'd panicked at the wheel. We stood at the cashier window. "Man, there's thrice as many chips as last time." Diana took out her phone. "Hello, can we have a taxi?" Diana turned to give the pick-up and drop-off details as the casher handed over the cash.

Back at Diana's place we had over twenty-four grand in cash on the coffee table. "Well, that's Liz's and your mortgage deposits settled, then. Better run the light over some of those bucks, doll. It will be interesting to see if we have any back."

Diana's was tuning in the radio. "Shh, the news is due on."

The report came over. "Yep, I heard it all right, angel." Two arrests made and ten grand in counterfeits retrieved from the casino, and twenty grand found with printing equipment from another suspect's address. I was spinning out, thinking at least six thousand of that was my doing at the casino.

Diana lay on the settee running an ultraviolet light over the night's proceeds. Already a small pile appeared to the right of the ones she was stacking as clean. "We got the six grand in counterfeit back amongst the winnings," Diana said, and she smiled. "We musta been sussed."

More than likely they hadn't noticed and paid us back, not knowing. I sat still trying to work it out. "So the ten grand the feds retrieved come from . . . Then that's . . ."

"Remember the one in the photo?" She handed me a cooked breakfast.

"Oh, right," I replied and smiled. "I should be nearly finished booting the pants outta this job soon, doll."

"It's been nice dealing with you, Max."

"Any coffee, doll? Hey, fancy doing any wallpapering later?"